# Woodspring

**Also by Elizabeth Buchan**

*The New Mrs Clifton*
*I Can't Begin to Tell You*
*Daughters*
*Separate Beds*
*The Second Wife*
*That Certain Age*
*The Good Wife*
*Revenge of the Middle-Aged Woman*
*Secrets of the Heart*
*Perfect Love*
*Beatrix Potter: The Story of the Creator of Peter Rabbit*
*Against Her Nature*
*Consider the Lily*
*Light of the Moon*
*Daughters of the Storm*
*The Museum of Broken Promises*
*Two Women in Rome*
*Bonjour, Sophie*

# Woodspring

Elizabeth Buchan

CORVUS

Published in hardback in Great Britain in 2026 by Corvus, an imprint of Atlantic Books Ltd



10 9 8 7 6 5 4 3 2 1

A CIP catalogue record for this book is available from the British Library.

Hardback ISBN: 978 1 83895 531 1
Trade Paperback ISBN: 978 1 83895 532 8
E-book ISBN: 978 1 83895 533 5

Printed and bound by CPI (UK) Ltd, Croydon CR0 4YY

Corvus
An imprint of Atlantic Books Ltd
Ormond House
26–27 Boswell Street
London
WC1N 3JZ

www.atlantic-books.co.uk

*Product safety EU representative: Authorised Rep Compliance Ltd., Ground Floor, 71 Lower Baggot Street, Dublin, D02 P593, Ireland. www.arccompliance.com*

MIX
Paper | Supporting responsible forestry
FSC
www.fsc.org
FSC® C013604

*For Belle*

*To live is so startling it leaves little time for anything else*

*Emily Dickinson*

# PROLOGUE

It was the place they all knew best – the elegant, light-filled rooms in the house, plus its niches and nooks in which they took refuge, the wood which sheltered the wildlife, the fields over which they walked.

Whatever happened at Woodspring, and whether they lived there or not, the *notion* of it remained constant.

# HARRY
# 1940

# CHAPTER ONE

The girl – no, more than a girl – opposite him in the railway carriage wore an unflattering hat and kept her gaze trained on the London cityscape as the train drew out of King's Cross. Sensibly, given the fug in the compartment, she had discarded her felted brown overcoat. Underneath, she wore a tweed costume which had been taken in to make it a better fit, an effort which had failed. But her shoes were of good quality and highly polished.

She looked determined, decided Harry Dane. Determination he knew about and recognised at a thousand paces. His wife, Lucy (his pretty, restless, fond-of-money Lucy) was gifted with it in abundance.

He transferred his attention to the London suburbs through which they were rolling. Rain slashed across the window, which did not add to the allure of what he was seeing. Back at Woodspring, the family home, spring would be advanced – new leaves here, the flash of a nesting bird there. The land would be stirring, absorbed by itself.

A handsome Regency house in Berkshire was not a bad lot in life to inherit. No matter he sometimes thought of it with exasperated love, usually after the second gin.

While he lived, his father tended to be both sharp and importunate on the inheritance issue. 'It'll be up to you, Harry.'

Five years younger, his brother Robert was happy about that. *You'll have to be serious which means I can be a wastrel, Harry.*

Robert had been gifted swagger and charm in bucketfuls, and Harry loved him.

His father's dicky heart gave out when Harry was in his early twenties. So… no roistering around the world for him. No exploring nirvana or exotic sex, nor – he had toyed with the idea – drugs to alter his state of being. *Tales from the East.* Instead, Harry found himself contemplating house repairs and theories on the state of the soil beneficial to his land.

Dreams vanished. That was their nature and demanded as decent a burial as his parent. The East might be closed to Harry but, undeterred, he kept a close eye on Germany, signed up into the Glosters and was commissioned in early '38 before Hitler really got going. His duty, he explained to his aghast mother. (Robert followed suit later. 'What's a chap to do but to copy a hero brother? It's the Glosters for me too.')

By then, Harry had met and married Lucy, six months after which Nell was born in September 1939. Life intensified. Being married. Training. Keeping an eye on the worsening situation in Europe. This was not to underestimate the shuttle diplomacy he was forced to conduct between his wife and his mother.

Before Harry left for his unit, he ordered extra chicory and sainfoin to be mixed in with the sowing of the clovers and yellow burnet in the North Field. The South Field would be government was not known for flinging the boat out), but even they exuded an elegance. Oh yes, wonderful elegance. Europe was so much better at that sort of thing. He had developed an instant taste for propping up gleaming bars, downing shots and observing huddles of journalists. Meetings, however, were conducted in discreet venues and he relished the conversations that took place in pavement cafés and bars. Their flavour was stimulating, their content sparky. If the outlook hadn't been potentially so disastrous, it would have been the best of times.

Every snippet of information conveyed back was subjected to analysis – and there were plenty from Estonia, Latvia, Lithuania and Romania. Not to mention Poland. 'Hitler,' Harry reported of the German Chancellor, 'believes in the Darwinian struggle for existence.' Life did not, could not, exist without conflict. 'He's instructing Goebbels to use incendiary propaganda as we saw in Austria and the Sudetenland to lay the ground for further military operations.'

Events eventually overtook Harry and the team. The Third Reich blitzkrieged into Poland, the plans hatched with the authorities for Polish resistance were abandoned and he and the others hightailed home just days after Britain declared war on Germany on 3 September.

'Can't you at least hint at what you're up to?' asked Lucy on his return. 'It's so trying, all this secrecy.'

They had been in the sitting room of the rented Mayfair flat. His work hours in London made it impossible to commute to Woodspring – trains to Hungerford were unreliable. Plus, Lucy flatly refused to live with his mother. Before he left, his mother had given him the phone number of her London friend, Marcia. 'She would rent you rooms in her house. Now that she's widowed.'

'And Lucy and Nell?'

His mother looked at him. 'It would be income for her.'

'Where is it?'

'Battersea. Don't worry. I'm told it's a respectable area.'

But Lucy wasn't having that either and the flat in Mayfair had to be found. The arrangement was that the week was spent in the flat, weekends at Woodspring, and the nanny that Lucy insisted they employ would travel with them. This was to make a fist of being a family.

Lucy was quite calm, as she tended to be. (She was a disciple of the legendary Diane de Poitiers who refused to laugh or cry because to do so gave you wrinkles.) She sighed and reached for a cigarette which she lit with a snap. 'So *what* are you doing, Harry?'

Underneath Lucy's so-far unwrinkled exterior, Harry sensed anger.

*... Assembling training manuals on demolition, partisan combat and handling explosives. Arranging for them to be translated into several languages, printed on edible rice paper and distributed to a secret network of guerrilla fighters. All of which seemed extraordinary to be doing from a small smoke-wreathed office with a clanking lift directly outside the door...*

'Paperwork. You know the sort of thing. Bumf.'

Lucy balanced her cigarette, red-ringed with lipstick, in the ashtray and took up her knitting. A shapeless something.

'Really?' Lucy was sceptical.

'The Guerrilla's Creed', as Gubbins would have it, was being created from scratch. It hinged on small groups harassing superior forces. These specialised units would surprise and run. Butcher and bolt. Their mantra: never, ever indulge in prolonged engagement. Picking the right men to lead – left-field thinkers as well as warriors – was crucial.

The Allies will need to invent, said Gubbins, many times. Therefore, training on his special units would commence forthwith and Harry was part of this process.

Lucy retrieved a dropped stitch. 'You're not a natural for the army, Harry. I would have thought the RAF would have been your bag.' She shuddered slightly.

'I'm twenty-nine, Lucy. Old. The RAF needs the young bloods.'

Lucy affected not to hear. 'You don't like military convention. Nor military manners, drills… all that.'

True. Plus, he considered the rigid gap between the men and the officers was non-productive.

'I'm touched you think about me at all.'

Lucy opened her eyes wide. 'Don't be absurd. You're my husband. Why wouldn't I? The question is: do you ever think of me?'

Harry wasn't going to lie. 'I've no time to think of anything much.'

He made them both a gin, slopping an extra slug into his. As usual, Lucy said, 'God, a gin does perk one up.'

Afterwards they repaired into the tiny dining room where Emily, the maid, served them supper of Brown Windsor soup and beef stew. They discussed events in general and studiously avoided reference to Harry's work. Lucy surprised him by admitting that she had sympathy for pacificists, adding, 'But, perhaps, that's because I'm terrified by war.'

‘That’s honest of you,’ he said, admiring it.

It was after eleven o’clock when they retired to the bedroom. Lucy sat down at the dressing table, brushed her hair and dabbed perfume at the base of her throat and Harry realised that she wanted to make love.

He chucked his tie onto the chair. And why not? Lucy had her needs and, in marrying her, he had promised to observe them. She rose to her feet and pressed herself against him. ‘I’ve missed you,’ she said. ‘I feel you are a long, long way away. Doing things I’ve no idea about.’

‘Sorry about that.’ He shifted out of her grasp. ‘Does it make it any better that this conversation is probably going on in many homes?’

Lucy settled herself in bed and drew up her nightdress.

Harry had always admired her figure. Like many women, she had got thinner recently, but it suited her. Her skin was appealingly pearly and she looked pretty and very feminine – the things which had attracted him in the first place. Their love affair had been fun until Lucy got pregnant.

With a grin, he cast aside his shirt, stepped out of his trousers and joined her in the bed.

The lovemaking was pleasant and happy enough and, afterwards, Lucy pulled her nightdress down over her legs, turned on her side away from Harry and said sleepily, ‘That was nice. You haven’t lost your touch.’

He was not sure what she meant, only that it annoyed him.

Soft and defenceless, Lucy slumbered beside him, her breath barely audible. Harry remained sleepless, thinking of the disaster that was coming.

War.

At two o'clock, he gave up pretence of sleep and padded down the corridor to the sitting room, lit a cigarette and smoked in the dark.

'There you are…' Lucy appeared and switched on the table lamp, which removed the comfort of the dark. 'I'm not going to ask what's the matter because you won't tell me.' She jerked her dressing-gown sash tight around her small waist. 'Whatever you're doing, it's wretched.' She reached for the cigarette box. 'Why can't we just live a normal life? It's bad enough we don't have much money. No money at all, in fact, compared with… well… others, and this flat is ghastly.' The match striking against the box sounded abnormally loud. 'Is it going to get really bad?'

No point avoiding it. 'Yes.'

Her intake of breath was uneven. 'Oh.'

An idea that had been roiling around his mind for some time firmed up. 'Lucy, what would you say if I sent you both to the States while it lasts?'

'Oh Lord, if the sacred Woodspring isn't safe enough, it means you think we're going to be invaded.' She took a drag on her cigarette and sent him a long, considering look. 'But, but… hold on… am I right in thinking you'd *like* to send us away?' She uttered a small, wounded sound and tapped ash into the onyx ashtray. 'You've grown tired of us.' Under the quilted dressing gown, her shoulders rose in a shrug. 'I suppose it happens in a marriage.'

'Unfair, Lucy.'

'Well,' she said with a glassy look. 'You didn't really wish to marry me in the first place.'

True – but not to be uttered aloud.

He pointed out, 'You don't want to live at Woodspring and I'm thinking of your safety.'

'You hadn't thought how ashamed I might feel leaving the country in its time of need?'

'Go and live with your parents in Norwich, then. Or your sister in York.'

'Heavens no. Never that. Is it easy to get to the States?'

He detected a hint of excitement. A willingness to part company.

Later, when they were back under the slippery pink silk eiderdown which Lucy so prized, she said into the dark, 'You think we should go?' Harry didn't answer. 'I'll telephone my Aunt Millie in Concord. She said in her last letter how lonely she was. We could perch there for the duration.' Another silence. 'Your mother will be pleased.'

Having settled matters, Lucy fell asleep. There was no such beneficence for Harry, who remained awake. Feeling utterly separate was familiar, and tonight it was more marked than ever.

The alacrity with which Lucy set about putting arrangements in train amused Harry, even while it sent a chill through him. Within days a passage had been booked for mid-February. Lucy veered between rigid practicality and flippancy – 'Let's hope there're no icebergs.' The flat was turned upside down, new suitcases bought, clothes packed.

The parting was worse than he had anticipated. He gathered Nell to him, both agonised and delighted by the sensation of her fragile frame against his and by the musky scent of baby skin and hair. Then, kissing her in a carefully casual way, he handed her back to Lucy in first class on the train for Southampton. Above their daughter's head, he and Lucy exchanged fraught glances; *do we wish to change our minds?*

Lucy said, 'Don't do anything silly while I'm away.'

'I'll send for you the minute it's all over.'

She looked at him. 'Will you? I wonder.'

'Unfair, Lucy.'

'Harry…' Lucy looked as though she was going to say something weighty, perhaps significant.

But she didn't.

For a second or two, the compartment was awash with the disappointments of their marriage – neither willing to acknowledge them.

Lucy shifted her grip on her daughter. 'Nell, we're going to have an awfully big adventure.'

That afternoon, Harry went to see Gubbins in his office.

'I want to go and check over the course in Inverailort, sir. See what I can learn.'

Gubbins did not look up from the papers he was signing. 'With a view to volunteering.'

It wasn't a question.

Harry reflected for a second. Lucy and Nell's departure had emphasised he was not especially happy. That was irrelevant but even so… 'I would like to do my bit.'

Gubbins continued to write. 'I wondered when you would get round to it.'

'You don't object, sir? I need to be active.'

'You don't think I would be sitting here if I was in a position to get my arse off this chair, do you?'

Harry smiled. 'Thank you, sir.'

'It won't be easy,' said Gubbins. 'You'll be joining a lot of younger chaps who are already A1 fit. They might not like you swaggering up from London.' He smiled grimly. 'The *soft* arse from HQ.'

'Sir.'

But Gubbins wasn't done. 'Volunteering for this kind of fighting, a man can sometimes feel that he's clearing out his life and taking a vow. A lot of them training won't come back from where they're sent, and they know it. Be careful of that fatalism. It can sap a man. Concentrate on becoming fit, fitter and more expert than you'll ever be again. Sharpen your brain. That's your weapon. That's all you need do.'

The girl in the hat was dozing and the book on her lap was in danger. He reached over and retrieved it.

Her eyelids snapped open. 'Thank you.'

She wasn't grateful but annoyed, which amused him. When he was thinking or dreaming, he hated interruptions.

At Glasgow, Harry changed trains. He had taken the precaution of booking a first-class ticket and, passing the third class stuffed to the gunwales with uniforms, boots and bodies, was glad he had done so.

Very soon the countryside changed and assumed the spongy green and brown of the Highlands. At Crianlarich station, a scrum from all the carriages descended on the platform café and demanded cups of tea, Harry among them.

The train climbed steadily as they continued northwards, and the scenery became wilder. They rolled through Tyndrum and Bridge of Orchy and across Rannoch Moor.

My God, the moor was bleak. So bleak. Intimations of what was to come. Then it was on to Fort William, with Ben Nevis looming in the distance. Then on to the viaduct at Glenfinnan, the place, so he read, where Bonnie Prince Charlie had raised his standard in the rebellion of 1745.

Finally, Lochailort was reached.

Alighting from the train, Harry was struck by the silence. He looked about. A dozen or so other men had also disembarked and, to his surprise, so had the girl with the terrible hat. She was carrying a rucksack. The porter heaved a heavy-looking suitcase onto the platform and she tipped him.

A sergeant major waited, all spit and polish. He issued commands and marched the men away, leaving Harry to wait for his scheduled transport. It had been held up and so – apparently – had the girl's. Harry broke the silence by asking her where she was going.

'Murray Cottage. Near the Lochailort Inn. I'm here to care for Mrs Turner. Perhaps my message didn't get through.' Under the hat brim, she looked tired and unhappy. 'I'm Faith Yorke.'

'Clive,' said Harry. 'Clive Brown.'

Eventually, his car turned up. Harry had a word with the driver and turned to Faith. 'I can give you a lift. Apparently, it's not so far out of our way. We can telephone at the Lochailort Inn.'

It turned out Faith Yorke had not been expected to take up her post that day. 'There's been a mix-up,' she said on her return to the car. 'They thought it was tomorrow.' She gestured to the view out of the window. 'A bonus. I'll have a day before the job starts.'

'It's an isolated place,' he commented.

'I'm used to it. I was living with my grandmother up a mountain in Switzerland until recently. But she… died and I had to find a way of keeping myself.' She added, 'I have a knack with elderly ladies.'

He was struck by her… was it humour?… or wryness? Very soon, the driver drew up in front of the cottage and carried her case to the front door. Faith Yorke got out and said, 'Thank you for taking me out of your way. Goodbye.'

Harry settled back onto the car's upholstery and lit a cigarette.

# CHAPTER TWO

Harry had briefed himself on where he was going pretty thoroughly.

Much of Scotland north-west of the Great Glen, and swathes of Inverness, Ross, Cromarty and Sutherland had been designated a Protected Area by the Home Secretary and permits were required to enter the area.

A clever, informed choice of terrain from which to develop this new art of war. The tough terrain and jagged coastline was perfect for learning fieldcraft, survival and use of the boats. A sparse population made secrecy easier to maintain, the training with live ammunition safer, plus the railway provided the transport link.

The staff car deposited him at a Gothic-looking grey house settled damply under the hillside, behind which rose the hills of Seann Cruach and An Stac. (He had studied the map.) He had also learnt that its owner had been turned out of her home without so much as by-your-leave by the MI (R) requisitioning team. It was war. *It was war*, and it was a fair bet that none of his fellow officers billeted in the uncomfortable rooms gave this eviction a second thought.

'Ach, you're at the big house,' commented an elderly

drinker at the Lochailort pub where Harry fetched up the following evening.

Harry took a mouthful of whisky. 'Couldn't say.'

The old man levelled a hard gaze on Harry. 'No need for that. We've been keeping secrets since the Bonnie Prince raised the standard.'

'Never underestimate the Highlander,' said Peter Dunant who had come along with Harry.

Peter was tall, fair and clever and Harry had taken to him on meeting him that morning. He raised his glass. 'Good advice.'

Secrecy was the order of the day. Many of the students at the big house had no idea of who was the guiding hand behind the set-up and were told to shut up if they enquired.

'Ours is not to reason why,' said Peter, who had abandoned teaching at a well-known boys' school when war looked likely. 'An easy decision,' he said. 'I seized the day.' An eyebrow flicked up. 'From one cohort of insane males to another.'

Officers were accommodated in the main house. Non-commissioned officers were billeted nearby. Other trainees were in tents and huts. The area behind the house bristled with a fiendish obstacle course and shooting ranges. The defile between Seann Cruach and Tom Odhar hill acquired the nickname of 'Sniper Alley' and huts colonised the islets in the river which meant wading through the water and wet clothes.

The *pièce de résistance* was 'Mystery House', a derelict building in which replicas of the enemy sprang up and presented moving targets to test reflex shooting.

The weeks went by demanding much of him.

Most days, new instructors arrived, plus ghillies, mules

and ponies and, with them, the multiplication of courses and tests.

Getting fit. My God, it was hard and painful.

Harry's flesh was being stripped down to the bone. Every day, a fresh physical challenge was thrown at him.

Seventy-two hours up a mountain and down. No sleep.

Fifty-mile hike carrying explosive in sodden clothes.

Blisters. Fucking blisters. Aches and stiffness. All that.

'You know what…?' said Peter. 'I'm beginning to think RTU a heavenly option. The rest would be silence.'

Return to Unit: considered a fate worse than death.

Peter had a fund of quotations from English literature ('And why not? It's my livelihood'), which he did not hesitate to unleash. Surprisingly strong and resilient, he was unlikely to be RTU-ed. Whereas a couple of the others had been and took it badly.

Peter was surprised to discover that Harry was married. 'Do you think about your wife and child?'

'No,' admitted Harry. 'It's a dereliction but I don't. It's a relief not to worry about them.'

Today, they were sent out on an exercise issued with little warning – which was its point.

His kitbag turning heavier by the second, he sweated up the initial slope of the hill behind the house which led to the even steeper An Stac.

'You poor buggers,' the sergeant issuing the orders did not distinguish between the officers and the men, 'are to sweat it to the top, do an about-turn, keep well hidden, descend the mountain, cross the railway line running into South Morar and make for Arisaig. Got it?'

It was one of those hot days which the Highlands could spring out of nowhere and, mercifully, the sun kept the midges at bay. Harry's heart thumped and he was doused in sweat.

*Keep out of sight.*

Harry dropped down and dug his fingers into the heathery turf. Out of the corner of his eye, he saw Peter wriggle out of his line of vision. Allowing himself a couple of minutes to get his breath, he then hauled himself into a crouching position.

They were being tracked by the ghillies. As cunning as devils, they were. Correction: the ghillies could outwit any devil. Periodically, shots rang out as they closed in on their prey and ran the men to earth.

It was stop-go progress, and the sun was losing warmth by the time he had made it to the coast. The sea was calm. The tide was out, revealing rock pools which jolted memories of salty, grubby childhood holidays torturing garnet-coloured sea anemones with a stick.

The pickup boat to transport his group over to Skye, where the exercise would continue, was not yet due and he settled himself to wait in a cleft a little way back from the cove. He could smell the sea, taste brine. Not unpleasant. The breeze felt good on his heated body. He knew, though, to take care not to cool down too much. He was tempted to shuck off his boots but to be caught without them on was a cardinal sin.

His adrenaline was dropping and with it came a warning flush of exhaustion. He dug into his pocket for a peppermint, an aid not permitted but he didn't care. The sugar hit his system with a satisfying thud.

The tide was now on the turn, swishing up the beach and around the outcrop of black rocks. The sun was still shining and Rum and Eigg were traced on the horizon.

Picture-postcard stuff.

This was the remaking of what he was. An experience to reshape him. There was a chance, a sizeable one, he wouldn't survive what was to come. Therefore, every sensation, every texture, every whisper of feeling was to be acknowledged. If he couldn't do anything about dying, that much he could do about living.

A rowing boat was making slow progress into the cove and ran up the sand. The oars were shipped. An androgynous figure stood up, dropped the anchor and jumped out. A minute or so later, whoever it might be was foraging among the rocks.

He cursed. To move was to risk being spotted. He looked at his watch and ran over the calculations. He had half an hour's grace.

The sun had dipped and shone directly onto him. His lids closed.

When next he opened them, a face hung over his.

His focus sharpened, torpor vanished and he sat up. It was the girl from the train, this time wearing trousers that were too big for her, plimsolls and a black beret crammed over her hair.

'Do you always wear clothes that don't fit?' he asked.

'Needs must.'

The training clicked in. Observation and assessment. Fine-featured. Long eyelashes and plenty of them. Lovely skin. Green eyes with a touch of hazel. Not beautiful but interesting.

'You must shift.' She was polite but firm. 'You're sitting on the samphire. One of the better patches.'

'A please would help.'

A slight movement of her lips. 'Please.'

Harry's bag held the fuses for the night operation on Skye. 'If you turn your back for five minutes, I'll disappear.'

'Ah,' she said – and he pictured the speculations sifting behind the green eyes. She pointed to his cumbersome army-issue boots. 'You're one of them.'

'I shouldn't be talking to you.'

'Then you shouldn't fall asleep in samphire patches. There's a war on and it's needed.'

Who could argue with that?

'How come you know the area so well?' he found himself asking.

'I used to come here with my grandmother for holidays. She was friends with my now employer, Mrs Turner, and I was allowed to run wild. Wonderful, wonderful freedom which I made the most of. Rock samphire, not the marsh samphire, likes salty creeks and coves and I thought I'd harvest it.' Somehow, she was sitting down beside him. 'You look done in.' She searched in her bag. 'Here.' She proffered raisins on her palm. 'These always help.'

'Thank you.'

She watched him eat before turning her attention to the now setting sun. 'You don't have to worry. I won't say anything.'

He thought of the fuses, plus the revolver with the live ammunition, stowed with them. 'I've no option but to trust you.'

'You could kill me. I'm a fluent German speaker. And French for that matter. I could be the enemy.'

He glanced at her sharply. 'Killing you would spoil the samphire.'

They stared across the glittering water, Harry repeatedly scanning the horizon. 'Not joking about the secrecy,' he said.

Clearly offended, she said, 'I said you could trust me.' Then she softened. 'You and your lot are off to Skye tonight, aren't you?'

*For God's sake*, he thought. *The whole bloody local population knows what we're up to.*

A strained silence fell between them. A bird skimmed the mirror-bright water. Behind them, a peewit sounded, the notes slicing through the warm air.

He checked the time.

'I've been watching some of you,' she said. 'I know we're to turn a blind eye and ask no questions. But it's hard not to notice.' She glanced down at her stained hands. 'Do you mind the hard physical attrition? Do you really have to march fifty miles non-stop? It all seems ridiculous. Absurd. Men shouting at each other.'

'It is,' he said. She had put a finger on the farcical element of combat that had been nagging him too.

She looked at him. 'But it has to be done.'

He couldn't stop himself. He reached over and touched a stained finger. The contact reinforced the ridiculous notion that he knew this woman. 'Put it this way, there's no quarter given.'

She glanced at Harry. 'Sorry. I shouldn't be questioning you. But how do you keep going? Is it faith? Or a technique?'

He had been mulling over those questions. He and the men were being taught to excise anything fatty or inessential in mind or body. If you like, it was a purging process. 'Vocational,' he ventured.

'Is it like being admitted to a holy order? You know, pain and deprivation with a promise of resolution and paradise at the end? The way poor people have been kept in submission for centuries?'

'If you mean the idea of the endgame when enduring the extremes, then yes. It induces acute yearning for warmth, dry clothes, food and the delights of bed.'

He hadn't intended to be so frank. She raised a hand and her sleeve fell back. Shockingly, a substantial knotted scar ran up the underside of her wrist.

She clocked his gaze. 'From childhood. I fell out of a tree.'

He must be going mad for he wanted nothing so much as to trace the scar to its source. He knew about scars. How their terrain felt under a fingertip. How they could ache.

He laughed. 'I'll match you. I once had a fish hook stuck in my foot.'

She pulled down her sleeve. 'I must go. If you *are* going to Skye you'd do much better with a rucksack and rubber boots.'

'Personal experience?'

'I've lived in Switzerland. My mother was Swiss. She died when I was young, but I spent a lot of time with my grandmother and I looked after her until she died. The Swiss know about mountains and equipment. And climbing.' Faith was matter-of-fact. 'They have to think hard about those things to survive.' There was a hint of nostalgia.

'Rucksacks are invaluable for walking and climbing.' She gave hers a nudge with her foot. 'It's my companion. I can hide my life in it.'

Harry found himself clocking the oddest thoughts. It was true that, if war slowed some things down, it also speeded up others. In his past, falling for someone took weeks. This had taken a couple of meetings.

She adjusted the straps. 'Do you think we can win? Living in Europe made me see how small England is, despite the Empire.'

It was an unusual attitude. By and large, the English were quick to assert their superiority. 'When the Americans are persuaded to come in, then yes. If they ever are persuaded. The talk is that Hitler doesn't let his generals do their job. Or listen to them. That will probably do for him.'

She turned away and he was presented with her profile. Fine and delicate. To his consternation, the sight awoke a tenderness which he had no business to feel. 'What made you take the job here?' he asked.

She stared at him. As if the question was completely idiotic. 'To earn a living. Women do, you know. Luckily, my step-mother is much younger than my father which leaves me free to acquire skills and qualifications.' Her voice dipped. 'That was the plan at least but the war will get in the way. I did think of offering myself as a wife to a tea-planter out in Malaya or somewhere.' She turned her head and smiled. 'But I'm not interested in being married.'

Harry had a vision of Faith being bedded by a tea-planter with a drink problem presiding over a gin-lashed existence. 'Bad idea. Very bad idea.'

Above them, a seabird called. Harry stared at Faith and, driven by an impulse to which he could not easily put a name, leant over and kissed her.

Her lips were salty. The seabird screamed and they drew apart. 'I'm sorry,' he said insincerely.

'I'm not,' she said. 'That I'm not interested in being married doesn't mean to say I object to being kissed.'

He kissed her again, this time tasting tea and a suggestion of cold cream.

'I'm sorry I took you by surprise,' she said.

'That was also bad. Very.'

'The talk is of real bullets being used.'

Harry said nothing.

'I try to imagine what it will be like for you all, fighting and killing. The physical horror of it.'

He thought of the thuggery and killing methods in which he was being instructed. Shooting from the hip without hitting toecaps. Using a pistol muzzle to jab a man in the genitals, the butt for the back of the neck. Who knew if these would work for real? At the least, they offered the reassurance of learnt techniques.

She looked up at him. 'Your name isn't Clive, is it?'

'No.'

Faith moved away. 'Take care of yourself.'

'Enjoy the samphire.'

He was pretty sure she watched him until he had loped out of sight.

What was he doing?

One answer was that he had been lured into a honeypot trap. It happened, was happening no doubt, all over the place, and the enchantment of the moment turned sour.

In this war there would be no safe assumptions.

He hadn't heard from Lucy before he came north since her telegram announcing safe arrival. Communication across the Atlantic took several weeks and Lucy was not much of a letter-writer.

Did he wish to hear from her? In his dark moments, he admitted that he didn't mind. Other times, conscious that his connection to her was withering, he craved news of Nell. Finally, at the end of May, a letter had arrived. Searching for privacy, he went outside and sat down facing the loch.

The envelope was air-force blue and almost weightless – airmail was still sufficiently a novelty for him to note it – and his commando knife intended to slit throats did double duty as a paper knife. Inside, a couple of pages of thin writing paper were folded around a photograph.

Nell. A black-and-white toddler sat on a rug on the veranda of Aunt Millie's house waving at the camera. Waving at him? Harry inspected it obsessively and was gratified to see that she looked sturdier than the last time he had seen her.

Lucy's words sprang out at him from the insubstantial paper.

*We got here without incident (apparently liners are much faster than the U-boats so nobody worried much) and we have settled in brilliantly. Aunt Millie's community is delightful and so interesting and lively...*

Reading between the lines: Lucy was telling him she was glad not to be at Woodspring.

*The big plus is that we can get eggs and milk. Nell is getting plenty of fresh air and Martha, the maid in the kitchen, has taken to her in a big way. My aunt found a trove of old materials in the attic, and I've made a pair of quilts to donate to the poor which means I can hold my head up as I have done something. Don't worry about Nell. She is getting the best in every way possible. She is sitting up and wanting to walk. We are very comfortable and I'm sorry to be so unfeeling but the food here is wonderful.*

He read the letter twice. Stared at the loch. It was unlike Lucy to be so cosily domestic. He smoothed out the paper. Harry had a suspicion she was leading up to telling him something.

He had to wait for the second letter.

*Harry... about the future. It's been difficult to write this, but I must nerve myself to have it out with you.*

*I like America. It's freer and faster. I think it suits me. Americans don't carry around so much baggage. It's not who your family are but what you're going to do.*

Harry thought: I'm right.

*Harry, be truthful. You wouldn't have married me if Nell hadn't been on the way... and we've been separate in many ways before I left. I never knew what you were thinking. I didn't understand what made you tick. You weren't interested in the things I liked.*

*I have met someone else and it's serious. Actually, the speed of it has bowled me over. He's American. His name is Benedict Treadgold Junior (he will lose the junior bit when his father dies and he inherits the mail-order business, which is huge), and we just clicked right from the moment we met. Will it hurt to say that I have never felt like this before? Is this a shock? It is to me but I think this is deep and true in a way that... well, you will know what I mean. Nell is safe and well. You can trust me as her mother to ensure she gets the best of everything.*

*Benedict will ask me to marry him, and I am hoping we can arrange the divorce quickly and without fuss. Nobody will know about it much over here. Not like a divorce back home.*

*Lucy*

*PS. I think... I suspect... my decision will be a relief for you.*

*PPS. I will be well looked after as his business is a very good one.*

The speed of Lucy's cutting free winded Harry. It took him several days to ring his mother and brother to tell them the news.

'Rough comfort, bro, but may be for the best,' said Robert.

'Bugger off, Rob. You never liked her.'

'Beside the point, old boy. She was your wife, but I wondered...'

'What?'

'Well... it was a question of needs must. Not the best basis for marital bliss?'

# CHAPTER THREE

Lochailort Inn was enjoying a thriving trade. Its owner, a Miss McCrae, claimed kinship to the King of the Fairies and was fond of reminding her clientele of the area's Jacobite past. An unbeatable combination.

If Miss McCrae had worried that her takings might dip after the area was declared restricted, she needn't have bothered. A stream of Admiralty and War Office personnel, wives and friends of the staff officers headed for it like thirsty lemmings.

Peter and Harry pushed into the crowded back room which smelt of tobacco and the peat which Harry associated with Scotland. It wasn't luxurious but no one cared. It was clean and, for those who had been suffering on the hillsides for the past twenty hours, paradise.

Fatigue colonised every nook and cranny of his body and, my God, he ached. Gubbins had been right. Harry's fitness was of the lower order, and he was being outdone by the irritatingly cocky men in their early twenties.

Using underhand tactics, and abandoning Peter at the bar, he managed to secure a space on a bench and sank down to nurse a more than welcome beer.

The death of his short marriage still shocked him.

*Needs must.* Yes, they had married because Nell was on the way. He remembered the night fuelled with champagne and lobster and Lucy saying, 'I shouldn't be doing this but it's very nice.'

He remembered, too, his recoil when she relayed the news of the pregnancy. 'Are you going to let me down, Harry?'

Yes, that moment when he was confronted by a fragile-looking Lucy with terror in her eyes, and picked his way through obligation, his real wishes, and his ignorance of marriage.

Years of conditioning – how to behave honourably – channelled his reply. 'No, I won't let you down, Lucy.'

Even so.

Mea culpa. Enjoying himself being shady in Europe, he *had* neglected to concentrate on building a partnership. Lucy decided wifedom was irksome and gave the thumbs-down to a country existence at Woodspring. True intimacy eluded them. He trusted Mr Mail Order would supply the lack.

The man in a lovat-green tweed suit next to him said, 'You look dead on your feet but I'll thank you not to spill your beer over me.'

Harry nodded. 'Warning noted.' He dragged his gaze from the floor and looked up and fatigue and regret vanished. Faith Yorke was at the bar with an older man who was plunged into a lengthy altercation with the barmaid over the change for sherry and whisky.

The exchange bought colour to Faith's cheeks. She turned away, caught Harry's gaze and shrugged. He made his way over to her, aware he was traversing territory far more problematic than any mountain he was ordered up, even with a murderous ghillie on his tail.

At his approach, she smiled, and he thought that he had never seen such a beautiful mouth. 'Your lot have been busy.'

'No comment.'

'It's odd you're all here, I don't think Hitler will bother bombing the Highlands.'

'Depends…' He paused… if, by any chance, there was an intelligence leak about their activities the Nazis could certainly drop a payload of ordnance. 'They might just for fun.' Discretion meant he could go no further than that. 'Another sherry? Or something else?'

'What I wouldn't give for a glass of good wine.'

'I could introduce you to a good whisky. Not a bad alternative.'

'Perhaps. But I miss the wine. Like drinking gold.'

The altercation at the bar had wound to a close and Faith's companion joined them. He was, at a guess, twice her age, grizzled and well pickled in tobacco. Faith introduced him as John Gilray, Mrs Turner's driver, and the three of them made stilted conversation until Gilray, who was casting covetous eyes at a group of Highlanders in the corner, said, 'If you don't mind, Miss Yorke.' He sidled away.

Faith accepted the second glass of sherry. 'Do you know what's happening in London? Mrs Turner regards the news as something expressly invented to make her life uncomfortable, and she won't listen to it.'

'Perhaps she's wise.'

Faith rolled her glass between her fingers. 'I'd like to see some action… be in on it.' Up went an eyebrow. Ironic and self-deprecating. 'Why, you might ask, particularly as I have no idea what action is like. But I'm single and should be helping the country.'

'One of the services? I'm told the navy has a brilliant hat.'

Faith laughed. 'Nothing like a good hat. But I would be serious.'

He was checked. Of course she would be, and she was right to make the point. Harry spotted a piano in the corner. 'Would you like some music?'

He was absurdly pleased by the spark in the green eyes after he launched into a ragtime riff. A few bars in, and the hum in the room subsided to a mutter. Harry followed this with a spirited version of Beethoven's 'Ode to Joy' from his Ninth because… because most of them would be aching one way or another. For the death of peace. For the waste of life. For the waste of everything this war would be.

He finished with a tribute, playing 'The Flowers of Scotland' with a yearning and sweetness. The bar fell silent.

While he was playing, Faith took herself off to sit in the far corner. Did the choice of music offend her? A lad in a kilt now offered to take over at the piano and Harry went across to her.

At his approach, she turned a face so filled with misery that he was taken aback. He sat down and took her hands in his. 'Tell me.'

It was a command.

'Life,' she replied. 'Music does that to me.'

'Well, that would make accompanying you to a concert a bit tricky then.'

'A concert?' She was startled. 'Here? I don't think it's possible.'

'Should be though. Music is food for the soul.'

'Isn't it so.'

There was an awkward pause – as if the intimacy, gossamer thin though it was, had been too much. She broke it. 'Do you have family up here?'

'Can't say. Ask me when it's all over.'

Faith spread out her fingers and he noted how delicate they were. 'How long, O Lord, how long will it be?' Harry was silent. 'Well, we'll just have to keep listening to music and making jokes.'

Faith looked at Harry as if she was analysing him right down to the last fibre. He found himself saying, 'The war mustn't kill the capacity to feel and to take time to feel.'

He had never said anything of that kind to Lucy. It was as if he was speaking in a foreign language, one that contained the colours and the seduction of the illusory travels in the East.

'I haven't loved many people,' she said, her distress now put aside. 'My universe has been small. Which is nothing to boast about, of course.' She got to her feet. 'I must go. Mrs Turner disapproves of late hours.'

'Will you come again?'

'Can't say. Transport. Mrs Turner's mood for the day.'

'Don't you find it intolerable?'

'Yes,' she said simply. 'But that is how it is.'

He accompanied her to the door and the Highland air washed over them. Imprinted into the dusk were the shapes of the hills and ridges. Faith breathed in audibly. 'I fell in love with Switzerland and its beauty. But it's beautiful here too.' She searched for the word she wanted. 'Elemental.'

He understood.

*

In early July, training was stepped up.

For this exercise, he and Peter had been cast as escaped prisoners of war. Loaded into a lorry, they had been dumped twenty miles from base with orders they must remain together whatever happened. The remainder of the students had been divided into squads tasked to prevent them returning.

'Gentlemen, there might be a fight,' said the instructor.

Hours later, as rain lashed down, he and Peter wriggled as they had been taught along a steep railway embankment to find the optimum place to cross. Behind them, their pursuers were gaining. The odds of remaining undetected? Pretty low. If they stood upright, they would be silhouetted against the skyline. If they remained prone, rate of progress dropped to a crawl.

They were spent, right down to their sodden boots. Plus, soaked and fed up.

Harry dropped his head down onto his arms and inhaled wet, peaty earth.

Their pursuers closed in.

'Freeze,' he hissed at Peter. 'Think nothing. Become nothing. If one of us is caught, he must not look at the other. Or even think of him.'

'What are you talking about?'

'Bushcraft,' replied Harry. 'Learnt it from an old Africa hand.'

'Have you been at the brandy, old cock?'

They were on them. Harry lay flat and motionless and willed himself to sink into the ground. His hands were cut but he dug them into the turf.

He was nothing. He must think nothing. Not of Lucy. Nor his daughter. Certainly not of… Faith.

Peter chose otherwise. He hauled himself up into a crouch, a stark target. Unsurprisingly, he was captured only six feet or so from where Harry lay.

'You bugger,' he said later in the uncomfortable Nissen hut which served as a dormitory. 'I don't know how you did that.'

Harry laughed. 'Nor do I. It was a technique taught by this chap who had lived in Kenya. In the bush, or on the savannah, the trick of vanishing can save your life. Apparently, all the rangers practise it.'

It was typical of Peter that he got it. 'I'm going to make a point of studying that one. Could add considerably to the *joie de vivre*.'

As Peter had more than one woman on the go, it might indeed.

Later in the week, Harry wangled a few hours off. Commandeering a staff car, much to the annoyance of the sergeant, he drove down to the bay below Murray Cottage.

The chance that he might be spied from the cottage was fifty-fifty, odds worth taking.

The road needed repair. Jolting along it brought home the difficulties of getting anywhere in terrain such as this before the machines arrived to flatten obstacles and carve out roads from the greens, the duns, the purples and yellows.

Parked up, he leant against the bonnet of the car and lit a cigarette. The weather had turned fine and hot. Within minutes, he felt his cheeks begin to burn. The almost calm sea glittered. Further out, the islands were wreathed in haze. It was incredibly beautiful. Those shimmering colours and shapes hailed from another dimension – or so it appeared to Harry in his quasi-exhausted, almost feverish state.

Gunfire crackled in the distance. Time almost up, he ground his cigarette out with his boot, got back into the car and turned the key in the ignition.

Nothing. He tried again. Silence, except for an engine cough. He got out, hauled up the bonnet and stuck his head under it.

Footsteps approached behind him. 'Dirty plugs?' said Faith.

He kept his gaze on the car's innards. 'I'm glad you've come.'

'So am I.'

He emerged from the bowels of the engine. 'Probably flooded. Nothing to be done for the moment.'

She was in an unflattering, shapeless frock, bare-legged with plimsolls. The material was too heavy for the weather, and a sheen of sweat beaded her upper lip. He handed her a cigarette and they smoked companionably.

'Jacobite country,' he said, after a moment. 'Bonnie Prince Charlie landed at Arisaig before making his way to Glenfinnan to raise the standard. He left from around here too. After Culloden. Beaten.'

Faith inhaled audibly. 'Always war.' Harry didn't reply. 'I wonder,' she said, 'if the land, any land, remembers what has happened to it? The fighting and the bloodshed and the competing interests. Do those Jacobite battles bed into the rocks and heather up here? I sometimes try and listen,' she continued, 'when I'm most alone.' She finished her cigarette. 'Sounds ridiculous.' She shot him a look. 'The point is that the land here has not been changed that much. Not like other places. London, say. Humans have been forced to work with it as it is. It hasn't been violated in the same way.'

'That's very wise of you.'

She giggled and the mood changed in an instant. 'I am so.'

Harry pointed to the path leading down to the beach and they descended, slithering down the steeper bits. One part was treacherous, and he turned back to help her but she shook her head, negotiating it with the skill of a seasoned walker.

The beach was littered with driftwood, seaweed and a segment of orange peel. Harry scuffed it with a foot. 'Who knows when we'll see oranges again.'

'Don't.' Faith sounded anguished. 'It's going to be as awful as the last one, isn't it?'

'Probably.'

She drove a hand into her pocket. 'And for nothing too.'

'Not so.' Harry captured her free hand. 'The last war was awful. The waste. The stupidity. But this time round, it's evil. Hitler wants to conquer us physically and he wants to control our minds and morality as well. That's what we'll be fighting. To stop it happening.'

She glanced down at her hand in his. Slowly, her fingers curled within his grasp. A gesture of agreement and acknowledgement.

He leant over and kissed her. It was a tentative kiss, one of exploration and of questioning.

She stepped back. The sun caught her hair, and he captured briefly a lock of it between his fingers.

'Harry, are you married?'

'Yes.'

'Is she good and kind and lovely?'

'All those things.'

'And you love her?'

'It looks like Lucy and I are divorcing.'

'Have you been married long?'

'No.'

'Children?'

'Nell. She's still a baby. Nearly one.' He paused before saying something he never normally did. 'She was on the way when we got married.'

Faith looked past his shoulder to the Skye hills and her cheeks were flushed. 'Then you must consider her.'

She bent down and picked up a piece of driftwood and he was made aware of how slender she was under the lumpy dress. The wood was smooth, bleached almost white and its curve fitted the palm of her hand. 'I wish I had been born in the future. In my dreams I'm doing all sorts of things which women don't normally do. I hate waking up.'

'What would be the main difference?'

'Education. Although I'm sure I could do something about that. And I will. But earning money, proper money, to make a good life.'

He was stirred by her predicament. 'After the war you could train… as a teacher? Work in an office?'

She dropped the driftwood, which fell with barely a sound onto the sand. 'I'm thinking of bigger things than being buried in filing.' Her eyes burnt into him. 'You wouldn't understand.'

That caught him on the raw. 'I can try.'

'You won't succeed,' a smile flickered but she was serious, 'because it will never happen to you.' She placed a hand on his chest. 'You'll never be at a disadvantage because of your sex.' The smile turned into a tease. 'Only your brain.'

He covered her hand with his. 'Unfair.'

'Very.'

Watching her flushed cheeks, he felt for the first time that it was true: things must change. The old assumptions must adapt.

'Will the war last long? People are going to suffer and will have to make sacrifices, and everything will have to be on hold. It's horrible to contemplate but I'm twenty-seven and I can't help wondering if by the time it's over it'll be too late for me.'

He was caught by her ambition. 'Maybe but maybe not.'

Their hands fell away.

'Please don't worry that you'll humiliate me by answering no, but,' her hands clenched, 'I think… I may be wrong… I think you would like an affair?'

The sun seemed very bright. The salt in the air very marked.

Because the implications were so enormous, he took a moment to answer. 'Yes.'

# CHAPTER FOUR

At Inverailort the men were deep into the specialised arts of ungentlemanly warfare.

Their instructors' names were Fairburn and Sykes, and Harry still hadn't worked out which one was which. They were balding, fresh-faced, courteous and quite possibly over seventy.

The classroom was bare, except for a sofa and a mattress. One of the duo lay down on it. 'Gentlemen,' he said softly. 'If you are ever so unfortunate to wake up at night to find a man strangling you then I recommend...'

His words died a choking death as his companion dived across the room and grabbed him hard by the throat.

The men shifted uneasily.

They needn't have worried. The body on the mattress arched upwards so strongly that he threw his attacker across the room (who performed a somersault and landed on his feet).

He addressed the audience. 'So you see, gentlemen, few situations are impossible to counter.'

Not quite true, concluded Harry, but the belief was a useful one with which to go into a fight.

Scepticism aside, he was becoming expert in disparate things. In the craft of sniping, in dodging snipers, in the pitfalls of forged identity cards and passes and in the art of survival on minimal food. He knew now how to deploy plastic explosive for crude explosions as well as for a precise cutting job. Add expertise on operating foreign weaponry, on how to improvise a weapon and how to use the knuckle-duster and the hunting knife. Plus, when all else had failed, the art of killing with no weapons.

In this theatre of war, there was no place for subtleties and anguishes of conscience. That luxury was for peace. Here, now, there was only the imperative to subdue and to kill. And yet, and yet, as he trained with the weapon of the day, he was locked into the trap of thinking most of the time of Faith and of how violently he desired her.

Next up. The 'Three-Day Venture', a test designed to simulate a real guerilla operation.

Where?

Lochailort, Morar and the railway, possibly ranging up Lochaber and across to Achnacarry; the details were secret.

'It will call on every bloody thing we've taught you,' said the instructor. 'Just so you know.'

During the '45 Jacobite uprising, a Captain Blood had led daring raids on the English and their arsenals. So… the instructor enjoyed his little joke… the operation was dubbed the 'Captain Blood Attack'.

Although he would never bound up the hills with ease of a man born and bred in the terrain, Harry was as fit as he ever would be and had absorbed the lessons of survival. First rule: brains, wits, cunning and resolution must never plummet into their boots. Or their stomachs.

'Listen up, you poor bloody buggers,' said the sergeant issuing the rations and a lesson on nutrition. 'You have oatmeal, army biscuit, sugar, salt, some bully beef and dried fruit. And ten cigarettes. My advice to you is, don't waste 'em.'

This diet had been worked out by a surgeon commander who had been on an Antarctic expedition. 'He needn't have bothered,' said Peter, only half joking. The odds were low that the men would embark on any future 'butcher and bolt' operation with a three-course meal tucked inside them but, as the instructor pointed out, 'You should know what's good for you in the unlikely event you can lay hands on it.'

With the mission statement came the rucksacks, based on the Norwegians' Bergen. Large one for marching orders. Small one for battle. (Faith would approve.)

Binoculars. Compass. Map case. Holster. Ammo pouch.

Before they left, Harry managed to track down a phone in an office and asked to be put through to Murray Cottage. Faith answered.

'It's your friend from the beach,' he said.

She would be aware that the operator at the exchange would be listening in. 'How nice.'

'Just to say, I dropped my glasses there and will be going back on Saturday to look for them.'

He replaced the receiver.

He should be analysing the fighting being tested on the topography. Its limits and efficacy. He should be thinking about the character of the land and its demands made on the men moving across it.

He should be thinking strategy, tactics, endurance.

Not of faith.

His fascination with Faith was not to do with her looks. Or her directness – *are we going to have an affair?* Nor the fact that she was different to most of the women he had encountered. With other women he had been snared by a white shoulder or a fragile wrist. An unspoken invitation. Not this time.

Did rebellion often fuel her thoughts, he asked himself? Aware that, occasionally, *he* fought against the expectations for men – to be the hero, the defender, the leader, he reckoned that a woman at a greater disadvantage might feel the same.

On Day One, the instructions were to cover ten miles in two hours, heading towards Achnacarry.

The going was rough, the ground boggy and treacherous with hidden dips. Progress was easier inside the tree cover but when Harry, Peter and Dave, the third man in their group, emerged from the trees it was to face a steep, rock-strewn incline dotted with dense clumps of gorse and heather. As they picked their way up the evilly slippery paths, the pace slowed right down. On cue, at the top, rain swept down.

As it was doing now. It dripped down Harry's back and into his boots and he remembered Faith's advice about rubber shoes and vowed to search some out.

Up ahead, Peter caught his foot in a hole, went crashing down and failed to get up. Harry hunkered down beside him.

'My ankle.' Peter was grey-white. 'Give me a minute.'

'You carry on,' Harry told Dave. 'I'll catch you up.'

He extracted a pressure bandage from his first-aid pack and valuable minutes ticked by as he eased Peter's foot out of his boot and wrapped up the ankle. Peter cursed with pain as they inserted the foot back into the damp boot.

'Go,' he managed, grey and sweating. 'No argument.'

The instructions were that if any man was down, he was to be left.

Harry consulted his map. 'There's a road to the south. If I find a telephone box, I'll give them your coordinates.'

'Sod off,' said Peter. 'Make sure you organise a decent funeral.'

Harry left him. On he went, thighs groaning and chest pumping. The rain had brought out the midges, which dived in happily for the kill.

He took a reading from the compass and turned east. Out there, the others would be doing the same. He scanned the road which ran across his path for a telephone box.

*No exposure.* Otherwise, he could expect close fire from guns and rifles. Not funny – and disastrous if it went wrong. Last week, a chap had lost an eye, and another had been shot in the leg.

When he sighted a telephone box, he risked it to phone HQ to report Peter's plight. Later, much later, hidden in some trees, he pulled branches over himself and slept for three hours.

He awoke disorientated. Peered up at the sky through the branches. Dawn was a way off and the silence was profound. He was cold, damp, aching, aware that his life was in danger of becoming a mess, and filled with longing. When his mind cleared, he fuelled up with nuts and raisins, relaced his boots and set off.

His (limping) late-evening arrival at Achnacarry House, the turreted ancestral home of the Camerons of Lochiel, coincided with a couple of the others from the unit. After a rigorous debriefing and a meal with some remarkably fine whisky, they were ordered to rest up.

Camp beds had been erected in Nissen huts in front of the main house, airless and impregnated with the stale sweat of males tested to their physical limits. He stretched out under a threadbare blanket. The exhausted warrior. The blood vessels through which the adrenaline had surged seemingly slack and useless.

Sleep eluded him.

He thought about Lucy.

She was not to blame for finding Mr Mail Order. He and she had married for the best of reasons, and the worst of reasons. It could have worked but it hadn't. That was that.

One positive was that Lucy's defection had nipped in the bud an exhausting struggle to make a go of it. For that he should be, and was, grateful.

He thought of Nell, the daughter he would lose. Not in the biological sense, of course, but she had been ushered through the door marked 'United States'.

He pictured her being cradled by a smartly dressed Lucy on the deck of the liner. (Lucy liked her furs and wore them whenever possible.) Nell would not have understood about partings, and the reasons for them. All she would know later was that her father was absent in her life.

At last, he slept.

On return to Inverailort House, he booked an overseas telephone call to coincide with lunchtime in the US. It was answered by Aunt Millie who uttered a little scream of excitement.

Lucy came to the phone. 'I wondered when you would call. You must have got my letter.'

'It's not easy to keep in touch, Lucy.'

'It's a little bit juvenile, all this secrecy, don't you think? Provision should be made to make phone calls.'

In that moment, he knew for absolute sure that Lucy was right to call time on their marriage. 'This man you've met… we have Nell to think about… is he to be trusted?'

'As trustworthy as you, you mean?' the reply flashed back. 'I wouldn't be doing this unless I meant it and I take offence at your suggestion that I haven't considered Nell.' She softened. 'I'm sorry, Harry. I never intended it to be this way but it's best to be honest. I've contacted the solicitor and he's agreed to make the legal arrangements for the separation providing you give the say-so, which I am hoping you will.'

'How's Nell?'

'Walking. I promise to teach her to say "Daddy" when the time comes. I *think* she misses you a bit.' There was the smallest of pauses. 'I will miss you too, Harry.'

A little of the affection that had been there in the early days surfaced. 'I hope all goes well, Lucy.'

'New world, Harry. It's very exhilarating.' She caught her breath in a way unfamiliar to Harry. 'Your mother wrote to tell me that I've been wicked and faithless.' Another breath. 'Well, I have been but tell me, Harry, am I not owed a life too?'

'You are.'

'I'm sorry. Harry. It just didn't suit me. I really don't want to spend years and years opening the village fete, judging the marrow competition and freezing to death in that house.'

He thought of the Dane forebears who had lived in Woodspring since it was built. Buffeted through the generations, as far as he could deduce from the records, by the need for money. The endless conniving to keep it afloat and within the family. And, always, the unchallenged assumption of its occupants that those who lived outside its purlieus were there to serve them.

'I understand.'

'You were always fair,' she said.

The pips went. 'Please kiss Nell and tell her that Daddy is thinking about her.'

Time. The operator cut them off.

Stiff and sore from Operation Captain Blood, he waited under the cover of trees for Faith on the Saturday afternoon.

He watched her emerge from the cottage and negotiate the path down. She didn't spot him at first, leaving him at liberty to observe the way she walked, the line of her neck, the colour of her hair. He waved and she halted for a long moment before approaching him.

He smiled. 'You look as though I'm going to slaughter you.'

'Can you blame me? That's what you're trained to do.'

'We make exceptions.'

She grinned. 'I can think of a few I wouldn't mind you slaughtering.'

'Where's the strong independent female?'

'I mean… *I* wouldn't mind slaughtering.'

He took her hand and drew her back under the tree cover

and placed his hands lightly on her shoulders. 'It's very good to see you.'

Under the tree canopy, the smell of dry undergrowth was strong, mixed with a hint of salt from the sea. Stillness and light filtered through the branches. He wanted very much to know what Faith was thinking, to understand what had brought her to this point.

'What is it?' she asked.

'I'm curious about you. That's all.' He picked up his rucksack. Packed into it was a rug, a half-bottle of whisky and a couple of cheese sandwiches which he had managed to wheedle out of the catering unit. 'We've chosen a good day.'

Faith followed behind him as Harry led the way through the trees parallel to the sea. The cottage now out of sight, they reached a strip of turf and a trio of ruined crofts overlooking the bay. Harry nudged stones out of the way and shook out the rug.

'I knew very little about the Highlands before I came here,' he said. He glanced at Faith. 'It's been a revelation.'

They settled themselves on the rug outside the least damaged croft which still had remnants of its roof.

He passed over the tumbler with the whisky. 'I expect these were lived in by the crofters before they were driven out in the Clearances.'

'My grandmother talked about them when she brought me here. As a neutral Swiss she took an interest in persecution.' Faith squinted at the whisky. 'It's not much use now for them but I sometimes think how it must have been. No home. Nowhere to go. Probably no possessions or money.' The whisky had gone to work. 'An outrage. And please don't tell me the past is different.'

'No right-thinking person would dare to do so.'

'I must know a lot of wrong thinkers then.' She was very wry. 'Philosophers and the political pundits think we're progressing into a better and more civilised state, but,' she became more passionate, 'I don't believe them, Harry. We're appalling as a race.'

Harry recollected the two elderly instructors and their arts of ungentlemanly killing. *Go for the genitals. Stick your fingers in their eyes.*

He thought for a moment. 'Perhaps the idea of constant progression is the problem. It's a good one to believe in but things seldom go in a straight line.'

She turned her head and smiled at him, 'Very wise,' and a hand grabbed his heart and squeezed it.

'About what you asked me last time we met.'

She swallowed and looked away. 'About… having an affair? I *was* out of order.'

Her sudden diffidence was at odds with the confident physicality that he had come to expect from her – the climbing, the boating, the samphire-picking.

'I wouldn't have asked but for the war. Knowing we might not survive has an effect.' Before Harry could reply, she continued, 'You gave me some encouragement and I knew you would not laugh or make a crude joke.'

He rolled his glass between his fingers. 'Sex is serious, of course, but it's also funny, sad too. Unpredictable. All that.'

'But do you think it's important…?'

The questions were a form of seduction in themselves. Debating them in this way was new to Harry. That, too, held power over him.

'Yes and no,' he replied. 'But you'll get all shades of opinion on the subject.' He looked up. 'Is that to dent too many romantic notions?'

A smile flickered. 'We all know that there's often a gap between expectation and what actually happens.' She turned her head away. 'You see, there was someone in Switzerland. But it turned out he just wanted to take advantage. Which he did.'

A dart of jealousy struck through Harry. Unreasonable and unexpected. And yet, knowing this about her was to draw him in tighter.

'I'm sorry.'

The *shush, shush* of the sea broke the silence which fell between them. Gulls and curlews poked about in the turf on the edge of the shoreline.

Faith twisted her hands into the folds of her skirt. 'I was hoping I appeared a seasoned woman of the world. The sort who turns up in silver lamé, address book stuffed with notable people.'

'Not necessary.' He thought of Lucy. 'The point is we're talking honestly and trying to decide what *is* important about a subject that isn't often aired.'

'I like that too. I don't have anyone to confide in. Certainly not about something like this.'

He reached over and touched her arm. 'No one?'

'No siblings or cousins. Just my parents who were only children too. Only children seem to attract only children.'

'I have a brother, so I've disproved your theory.'

She digested the implication.

'If we have an affair,' he said, 'I will take very good care of you. I will try to make it a good experience, one you will treasure and remember.'

The thought of her remembering, of him being in a past, was surprisingly painful.

'You're very sweet, Harry.'

'But you – we – must care. Life is tenuous.'

Her eyes flew to his.

Groaning as his overworked muscles protested, he got to his feet and pulled her upright. Then he drew her into the ruined cottage, bent over and kissed her.

The mouth under his was willing. He drew back and looked into Faith's eyes. She nodded and he unbuttoned her dress and she helped him ease it off her. He took off his own clothes. Glancing up, he saw Faith had wrapped her arms around herself. She looked defenceless but not without determination and… some poise.

'Has anyone… did the man who took advantage… tell you you're beautiful, Faith?'

'No.'

'Then I'm telling you.'

She gave a small sigh. 'Thank you.'

When they lay down, he traced the long line of haunch and the curve of her thin waist. 'You must tell me if you want me to stop.'

It wasn't very successful, as it turned out. Faith was apprehensive. When he asked if he *should* stop, she squeezed her eyes shut. 'No.'

To his surprise, he felt an impatience that he didn't know her well yet and could not reach her in an important way. He set about making it as easy and pleasurable as he could for her, who, even if she had some experience, was still uneasy and unsure.

They lay side by side and the sun slotting through the empty doorway warmed their exposed bodies.

'Thank you,' she said, with a degree of formality that both amused and touched him.

'You make it sound as if I was conferring a favour. I wasn't. We are both here because we wish to be.'

'I was thanking you for laying the ghost of a bad experience.'

'I hate him, whoever he was.'

Faith murmured something which he didn't catch. He reached for her hand, which felt very slender in his. 'I hope, I think, you agree sex should be pleasurable and both sexes should enjoy it. It's not a crime and it certainly should not be off-limits in the ridiculous way we've been made to think about it in the past.' He thought of what lay ahead. 'Maybe the war will change that.'

Her hand curled within his.

He wanted to tell her that the good in this encounter, and there was a very great deal, was partly due to her initial directness because it had opened up the conversation, dug the channels through which emotion would flow.

Faith sat up. 'I must go.'

'I wish you didn't have to.'

They reached for their clothes and soon they were fully dressed, which made Harry feel stupidly formal. He gathered up the whisky and the glasses and stowed them with the rug in the rucksack.

Faith was trembling and, again, his heart contracted with tenderness. 'Aftershock,' she confessed. 'Being reborn…'

She stopped. He shook his head. 'You're lovely, Harry.'

Harry let the rucksack drop, reached over and pulled her to him, enjoying the feel of her body against his.

The return took longer. They did not speak much. Faith walked behind Harry who led the way back up to the path and the trees. They came to the parting of the ways.

'I don't know when it'll be possible to see you again. But I'll try my best.'

Faith said, 'Please take care.'

Still shaken, Harry faced in the direction of Inverailort. Then he turned back to Faith. 'You do know it was the beginning?'

He was sure. He had never been so sure.

# CHAPTER FIVE

Hitler ordered a total blockade of the United Kingdom which, despite the convoys achieving miracles, meant shortages. The Battle of Britain raged, and pilots, still with baby down on their cheeks, lost their lives in droves.

The training intensified. If Harry imagined he had already been through the mill physically, he had to think again. Bones, flesh, mind, were battered. Tested. Tested again. And again.

How to develop the mental capacity to deal with what lay ahead? The injunction to be 'good for anyone in any way, men', was thrown at them in lectures, which wasn't that helpful. He found better inspiration in a different coinage: speed, silence and sinister efficiency.

He yearned to know how Faith was. If she was miserable. Or reasonably content? And, yes, Lucy and Nell were on his mind, demanding careful consideration.

'What's up with you?' asked Peter. 'You look as though you have a permanently wet arse.'

This was a condition that most of the recruits suffered from most of the time.

Harry said, 'We need to get hellishly drunk.'

'I agree.'

An end-of-summer, end-of-term feeling permeated the camp.

He and Peter pinched a jeep and took off for Lochailort Inn. Peter's ankle had healed and he drove fast but competently, leaving Harry at liberty to observe the scenery, a succession of greys, greens and brown. Living with every sense on high alert was tiring but it had its upsides because he now noticed many more things.

'When it's over what do we do with our expertise in sniping, shooting, stalking and demolition?' He asked the question but didn't expect much of an answer.

Peter shrugged.

'Do you think you can return to teaching after this?'

Peter stared at the road. 'No idea. But killing another human being will change me.'

'Still willing?'

Peter's answer came eventually. 'Yes. And you are too.'

There was no need for further discussion. This was where they were.

'We'll keep in touch, Peter. When it's over.'

'Never crossed my mind we wouldn't.'

Whatever else happened – love, death, injury – that was good to know.

Harry ended up somewhat drunk in a corner. Peter seriously so. Too drunk to trot out any Shakespeare quotations. 'We need action,' he said, peering into his glass. 'We've had enough. But the word is that we are on the move.'

Harry echoed. 'On the move.'

Several of them were slated to be shipped off to battle areas. Some to be infiltrated behind the lines where the odds of staying alive nose-dived.

'Peter, we're on the move.'

'Just told you that, old boy,' said Peter. He stabbed a finger down on the table. 'We're on the move.'

For which they had been trained… and for which the men, some mad, some bad, some stupid, some brilliant, yearned. Now it was happening and Harry thought, *bugger it*.

The bar was crowded. This evening, a red-haired youth was at the piano, belting out songs, and Harry joined in, giving his tenor voice an airing. Peter swigged whisky and settled further back into his corner. 'You've got a great voice,' he said. 'Why aren't you at La Scala?'

'My family consider opera singers are the works of the devil.'

'Fools.'

'Give me the car for an hour or so, Peter, will you?'

Peter enlarged one eye and closed the other. 'You can have it all night as far as I'm concerned.'

Twenty minutes or so later, Harry drew up outside Murray Cottage and knocked on the door. At this time of the year, it was still light until late but dusk was beginning to swathe the cottage in gloom. He knocked again.

The door opened. Faith stood in the doorway with an interior light shining on her hair and he thought his drunken heart would burst.

'Harry…'

'Yes. I'm sorry I didn't warn you. Do you mind?'

She glanced over her shoulder and shut the door behind her. 'No. No.' She leant back against it. 'Is something wrong?'

He moved towards her. 'I wanted to remind myself of something.'

‘What could that be?’ she murmured.

He ran a finger over her cheek and traced the line of her jaw. ‘That.’ He touched her throat. ‘And that.’

She quivered at his touch. ‘Harry, I’m glad you’re here. I wanted to ask you something. It’s so hard to talk, there’s so little time, so I’ll be direct. I wouldn’t want to take it… us… further if you were messing around.’ She glanced down at her hands. ‘Please be honest.’

For a second, he was filled with terror that he had muddled sex with feeling. ‘Why do you think I’m here? Drunk and out of bounds?’

‘God knows.’ She bit a lip. ‘I’ve been thinking about you.’

In turn, Harry thought of her slender body and her willingness to take a risk. ‘If *I’m* honest, I didn’t expect how it would be.’

There was a hint of a tease. ‘And that was?’

He shoved his hands into his pockets. ‘Special.’

‘What I did… we did…’ she said. A flush mounted in her cheeks. ‘I’m ignoring the temptation to put myself down. It’s hard to escape a certain upbringing. Those are the bad moments. Being made to feel that I’m the fallen woman is the result of social pressure.’ She hesitated. ‘It’s better to acknowledge one’s… desires and to be one’s own person?’

‘Yes.’ In his drunken haze he especially admired the clear thinking. ‘With a bit of luck, this upheaval will change all that.’

She scanned his face. ‘The war is so big. So violent. And God knows what will happen. It might beat us.’

‘It won’t beat us,’ he said. ‘A warrior speaks.’

‘I like the “us”.’

'So do I.'

Again, a tremor ran through her. 'Will you get into trouble for being here?'

The drink had got in the way of logic and coherence. 'I want to know about you. Your past. Your family. Who you are. But there isn't time and there won't be time. So… I came here on the off-chance we could snatch a few minutes.' He grinned. 'Send me food parcels if I'm court-martialled for escaping.'

'You're risking the courts martial to see me?' She leant back against the doorpost. 'Very romantic. I'll rescue you.'

'Can't wait to be rescued.'

They exchanged glances, containing questions. She was laughing but there was no time for answers.

Footsteps sounded behind the closed door and a voice called out, 'Faith.'

She said hastily, 'I hope I made you happy… you know…'

'You did,' he said.

'It's important to me. Especially now.' She thought for a second. 'We need pleasure. I don't mean in a frivolous way but in a deep way.' She added, 'I've been puzzling it out.'

Harry was stung by the sadness underlying the observation. 'Does that mean you haven't had much in your life?'

She gestured at Harry. 'As I get older, I'm better at… er… shall we say… discovering delights. Then there's sun on your back and a good cup of coffee.' She grinned. 'Actually, that's not a given over here. Not in Britain.'

Again the call: 'Faith? Where are you?'

'Mrs Turner obviously wants me.'

He caught her hand. 'I'll try and get over again. Soon.'

'I must be careful. Mrs Turner doesn't like me to socialise.'

He lost patience. 'That's ridiculous.' He pulled her close. 'Ridiculous. We should plan your escape.'

She disentangled herself. 'Now that is ridiculous.' She vanished inside before he could answer.

He had been issued with the heavy Colt .45 instead of the Webley revolver and it chafed his thigh. It was the trade-off. Soreness in return for the comfort of knowing that, if his hand fell to his side, it would rest on a pistol butt.

It was late evening and they were conducting what underground intel said was the penultimate exercise. It probably wasn't. Almost certainly wasn't. Being suspended in the liminal territory between the real and not real was part of the process. What they did know was that the men were fed up with the promise of action which, for all the talk flying around, had not materialised.

A light rain was falling. The 'enemy' had been dumped behind him and his brief was to shake them off. Harry slipped around the dark side of the rock abutting the road and, from there, followed the stone wall running up the steep hill, a route impeded by bog patches and rocks. It was now so dark that it was difficult to spot the boulders strewing the pathway until he was smack up against them. Five hundred feet or so up he stopped for breath. A stick would have helped but was forbidden as an unnecessary accessory. A torch was also forbidden, which meant, if he didn't want a broken leg, he had to go slow.

What a bloody, useless, futile business this was. Was violence truly a condition of existence? Were the men, was he, like Hitler: cut from the same cloth only disguising it better? Whatever, it was a bloody cock-up and a waste of sweet, sweet life.

The flash of rebellion vanished as quickly as it had arrived. Probably a consequence of his unsettling feelings for Faith, a state of mind no professional would permit.

Put one foot in front of the other. *Go... on...*

He was also discovering something with which he must deal, especially when it was for real, not just a torturous exercise. It was disconcerting to be on one's own without backup.

Twenty minutes later, he emerged onto thickly tussocked ground, interspersed with patches of heather. He was approximately 2,000 feet up, his night vision had adjusted and, up here, it was easier to anticipate the hazards.

Up ahead, a shape moved. He dropped to his knees and flattened himself on the turf. Water seeped through his battledress and, hoping for a drier patch, he moved to the right. A wind was getting up which made his wet clothes feel unpleasantly cold. The shape ahead had disappeared and he pulled his compass out of his pocket and took his bearings.

Keeping the wind on his left cheek, he began his descent down the other side of the mountain and made good progress until another bout of rain eliminated the wind, which forced him to consult the compass – it was always a mistake to stop as fatigue tended to kick in. Turning a degree east, he missed his footing, a ferocious pain shot through his leg and he went crashing down and hit his head.

He must have blacked out. For how long, he had no idea. While in that state, he saw Faith very clearly, hovering above him. He looked up at her and managed to say: 'you're very beautiful'. She smiled down at him and his heart lifted in a way that was quite new.

Harry came to. He was soaking wet and shuddering with cold. Pulling himself upright, he examined his leg. As far as he could tell, nothing was broken but it was possible he had chipped the bone. The effort to move was beyond him.

*For Christ's sake*, he thought. *What had all that training been for?*

He felt around for the compass but failed to locate it. The sky was lightening, and he reckoned it must be close to four o'clock. If he did not check in with HQ within three hours, a search party would be sent out.

The cold intensified and an icy river flowed deep and treacherous through him. Shuddering with what felt like the onset of fever, he tried to resummon Faith but failed. Incautiously, he turned over and lumbered up on all fours, his injured leg stretched out. Taking a deep breath, he tried to hoist himself upright. A flash shot through his head.

Back on his stomach, pain-racked and sodden, he explored the limits of his endurance. Endurance he had been taught was as much to do with the mind as the body. The situation required an act of will. A resolve to duke it out with injury and immobility.

He lapsed into semi-consciousness. This time, he dreamt he was behind enemy lines on the run. Fear, he found, had a taste, the fear he and the others had worked hard to master. It sat on his tongue as he fled in the dream like the hunted deer he undoubtedly was, the lessons of stealth and guile in which he had been tutored shed like its spoor.

When he woke, he was being carried down the mountain in a makeshift stretcher by a posse organised by Sergeant Troy who was in charge of picking up the wounded from the exercise. 'Won't be long, sir,' he said, 'and we'll have you sorted out. Took us a while to find you.'

Harry rolled his head to one side and was sick.

'It can take you like that, sir,' said Troy, not unsympathetically.

Back at base, the doctor said, 'Nasty blow to the head, Captain Dane, and the leg needs a bit of attention. Complete bed rest for three days. No argument.'

Trapped on an uncomfortable bed while head and leg healed, Harry thought about Woodspring. The house, serene and a little dilapidated. His ailing mother, retreated inside. The land, forty acres or so which he strove to nourish with good practice. The farmer who grazed his cattle on them. The men from the village who worked in the gardens. And so on.

Always a presence in Harry's life, he took it for granted. It had been built, and run, in a certain way. Would that way, would those assumptions survive? Who knew. Here, in this place, with the guns of war (so to speak) sounding and thundering, did he mind?

While Harry recuperated the weather turned ferocious.

'The worse it is, the better for us,' he remarked to Peter who had come to see him.

Peter passed over the whisky he had smuggled in. 'You still in la-la land on the drugs?'

'In bad weather,' said Harry, 'the average soldier takes shelter. The commando can take advantage of that and achieve the objective quicker.'

'Good God,' said Peter. 'You are off your rocker.'

'True though.'

'I'll remind you next time we're out there in the pissing rain facing the enemy.' He leant over Harry. 'The grapevine is humming. The London Chiefs of Staff want to bring the Commandos under their wing, but Gubbins is having none of it. No one will lay hands on his baby. The orders are to train harder.'

Still the men waited.

Harry was operational reasonably quickly but he had shed some of his peak fitness.

'Bad luck, sir,' said Sergeant Troy. 'I'm sending you on additional marches. You'll be tougher than a nut by the finish.'

'Enjoying my mortification, sergeant?' asked Harry as he limped back from one of them.

The other man grinned. 'I am that, sir.'

They understood each other perfectly.

The last operation had been nightmarish. Ninety miles in rotten conditions. Still, he managed the first three days in record time, his leg and head held out and he got back to Inverailort with a day to spare.

He and the men handled explosives – which entailed blowing up several good trees and large tracts of mountainside – and practised using larger landing craft.

Unlike the smaller versions these were buggers to land, which meant, when the ramps went down, the men were often out of their depth and weapons inundated unless they held them above their heads. A couple of the troops nearly drowned, and Harry swallowed a quantity of seawater which left his throat like sandpaper.

At the first opportunity, he phoned Murray Cottage.

At the agreed time, he waited on the curve of the road by the loch. Rain lashed down. It would be uncomfortable for Faith and he wondered if she would duck out. He underestimated her. A figure with a rucksack came into view and his heart performed that peculiar double somersault.

She was wearing a substantial waterproof and a pair of men's trousers held up by a belt ratcheted tight. A fisherman's hat was crammed down on her head. She looked terrible and, yet, wonderful – which was the paradox of Faith.

Stepping forward, he misjudged her pace and they found themselves positioned awkwardly against each other. For a moment, sensing that whatever happened next would seal the future for him, Harry hesitated. Faith raised a rain-slicked face to his and he found himself kissing her with the abandon of a teenager. With no restraint. No finesse. Just desperate longing.

After a startled second, Faith responded.

He brushed his lips over her cheek. Only a little while ago – the married staff officer in London – he would never have imagined that he could feel as he did now, standing in the pouring rain with a creature of light in his arms.

'I only have half an hour,' said Faith. 'Mrs Turner is ill.'

The rain made it impossible to hold a conversation. Harry took her hand and they walked back in the direction of Murray Cottage. When it came into sight, they took shelter under the trees.

'Do you have enough dry clothes?' Harry asked. Stupidly, he could think of no other question.

Her thumb pressed into his palm. 'I'm not in the workhouse.'

'Even so.'

'Working for Mrs Turner is no better or worse than what I was doing before. If I was being treated badly, I wouldn't stay.'

'Promise me you'll try and get something else… better. What you've always wanted.'

'That means you're going away.'

He shrugged.

She gazed over the loch. 'Looking after Mrs Turner may be boring and yes, yes, I'm sometimes miserable, but I'm warm and have regular meals.'

'But it's not food for the soul. Not for the ambitious Faith.'

'No.' She shook water from her sleeve. 'But that's what many women had to face after the Great War. They were left with nothing, except to cast themselves on the mercy of relatives. I'm not like that, I promise. I will do something.'

The intimacy of the admission made him catch his breath and he thought, *I've never been so happy.* And… *Remember this moment.* Summoning his wits, he said, 'I've been thinking. You have languages. Use them. Go and work in an international organisation. They need you.'

'Hadn't thought of that.' Faith tried to wipe her face but, given the rain, a useless gesture. 'It's a good idea.' She turned to face him. 'I have to go.'

He hated the thought of her going back to the cottage. 'The word at the camp is there's a hotel in Fort William. They don't ask questions. Would you like me to book a night there? Warm, well, warmish, but private.'

'Ah.' Faith was amused. 'The men have sorted out their arrangements. Good for them.'

'It sounds calculating. But it isn't.'

She touched his cheek. 'No. Desperate times.'

'Will you come?'

She sounded preoccupied. 'Mrs Turner needs day and night nursing and I'm arranging it. I could make the end of the week. I think.'

'I'll blag a vehicle on the Friday. Hike to the Lochailort road. I'll be here at five.'

He watched her figure dissolve into the wall of water. Only then did he turn and retrace his steps.

# CHAPTER SIX

It was a fine, coolish early evening and Harry picked Faith up without incident. They did not talk much on the drive. Faith did not seem inclined, and Harry was concentrating on the road. Anyway, being together was the point. Language, he realised, existed and worked beyond the vocalised.

They drove into the outskirts of Fort William and parked in front of a large, grey-stone house with a sizeable garden. The owner, tall and dapper in a tartan waistcoat and tweed jacket, proffered the book to sign and did not ask awkward questions, which was something they had discussed.

'I don't want you demonised or the subject of gossip,' he had said.

She replied, 'I'm doing this of my own free will.'

The room was cold, which was not unexpected. The wallpaper and dark paint were dire but the bed looked comfortable and was made up with thick blankets and good-quality cotton sheets.

Harry lit the gas fire, drew the curtains and shut out the falling Highland night. He rummaged in his bag and produced a bottle of claret. 'You'll never know what it cost me to get hold of this.'

Faith sat on the edge of the bed, her expression unreadable. 'You're not regretting anything?' he asked.

'Never,' she replied. 'I'm just preparing myself to remember everything. I want to be able to remember exactly, and precisely, and I'm worried my feelings will get in the way.'

He sat down beside her and held her close. 'And how do you want to remember it?'

'You must know.'

'This has never happened to me before,' he said.

She chuckled. 'Comparisons are odious.'

'I was stating a fact.'

He wanted to add all manner of things which he had never in his life imagined uttering. That he would give up everything. That he would die for her. That without her his life would be wanting.

Hunger drove them out to find something to eat and they managed to track down cold game pie and a beer at a nearby pub. Faith sat up on the high stool and devoured hers.

She had tucked her feet under the stool, the sensible lace-up shoes encasing them giving no indication of their elegance and beauty.

The pie pastry resembled sawdust, but the meat was moist and pleasantly gamey. Harry couldn't manage his and put down his knife and fork.

Faith eyed him over her glass. 'Not hungry?'

He thought how odd it was that love, so full of gluttonies, took away the appetite. He reached over and took her hands. 'Why do I think I know you so well?'

'Because…' Faith's eyes sparkled. 'I don't know but let's enjoy it.'

He thought for a moment. 'I don't know where we go from here.'

'That's easy. You go to war.' The sparkle died. 'Pray God… pray God… it'll be fine. I'll return to Mrs Turner's. Which I suspect won't be for long. She's very ill. Poor thing. It's horrible for her. And Harry, you have a daughter to think about. Before anything… or anyone… else.'

'True. But I have to think about you, too.'

'You don't *have* to, Harry. I'll find something. I promise.'

He brought up the subject which had been troubling him. 'When I suggested you might be a filing clerk or something, I wasn't thinking. Of course you can do other things. Women should. I'm sorry for being so… old-fashioned.'

She acknowledged the – sort of – apology with a grin. 'You're not as bad as Switzerland where women still don't have the vote.' A teasing note crept into her voice. 'You've made up for it. A bit, I'd say.'

'I sincerely hope so.'

'You pointed out that I have languages and could use them.'

The fire in the grate glowed. Glasses clinked. Someone laughed.

He had the odd notion that he was sealed off from their surroundings. That he was existing on a different plane.

They walked back to the hotel through the dark, with only the blacked-out shapes of buildings and the pavement beneath their feet for guidance.

In the hotel room, the bedspread had been turned down. Harry turned off the main light and switched on the bedside lamp, which made things look better.

Faith stripped off her gloves and Harry flung his jacket onto a chair. On the way back to the hotel, he'd had a troubling thought. Knowing what she did about the covert operations at Lochailort and with her languages, Faith might consider volunteering for secret work.

'When you leave Mrs Turner, if you do, you won't do anything dangerous? Please.'

She looked down at her hands. 'Harry…'

'I know I don't own you. I know, I know.'

She had made no move to take off her coat and he eased it off her shoulders. 'You mean the sort of work with the life expectancy of a butterfly?' She meant his, and him.

He thought for a moment. 'Listen, I don't want to encourage this because London will be dangerous. That's why Lucy and Nell went to the US. But if you do fetch up in London, you're to ring Marcia Jossell, a friend of my mother's. She's widowed and rents out rooms in her house in… Battersea, I think. I've never been there, but my mother has talked about her. Go there. Please. I'll get the number to you. I'll find you there.'

He bent over and kissed her, enjoying a faint aroma of wood smoke and cold. After a few seconds, her arms snaked up around him and he lifted her up and carried her to the bed.

When he fumbled with his belt, Faith took over. The buckle was rusty from seawater, and she had to work hard to loosen it.

Everything was right.

Yet, he found it wasn't enough. He wanted Faith so badly that what he was doing was no longer sufficient in the profoundest sense. It did not come close – he could no more fuse her spirit with his than stop this war.

Halfway through, he looked down at her. She lay beneath him with her head turned just a little and glanced up at him through half-closed lids. She was flushed and her eyes were wet.

He took a long time over what came next. For one thing, the privacy was intoxicating and precious. For another, he wanted to imprint on his memory the exact feel of her skin, the shape of her face, the way her hand fell onto the bed in the aftermath when she was at peace.

They never did get to drink the claret.

In the morning, they breakfasted in a gloomy room overlooking the garden. There was one other couple; she in a twinset and pearls, he in a brown tweed suit that had seen better days.

Harry gave a polite 'good morning' as they made for the table by the big window. This was a mistake: the draught coming from it was savage. A light rain drifted over the laurel hedge and dampened the autumnal trees.

'What *was* your story to get the night off?' he asked.

They were both a little tongue-tied by what had transpired between them, leaving them exhausted by their feelings and their implications.

'An old friend in Fort William has asked me to stay.'

He stared at the dregs of tea in his cup. 'You've no one to look after you and I can't dictate but I don't want to go into battle knowing you're not safe.'

She toyed with her bowl of porridge. 'That's so sweet, Harry, to be so concerned. It makes me feel… cherished.'

When he dropped her off in the car, she leant over and kissed him on the cheek. It was a light, unmemorable kiss and he turned away. Perhaps thinking better of it, she put her hand under his chin and made him look at her. Then she kissed him for a second time – and that was memorable.

For their swansong… yes, it was happening… the briefing was ultra-detailed.

Operation Malt Whisky. A pre-dawn raid.

A-section will land from the sea, they were instructed, and will face live ammunition (deployed by those murderously inclined ghillies). B-section would defend the coastline. The orders were to secure the beach and establish a beachhead, preparatory to a raid into the interior.

'You could get yourselves killed,' said the instructor. 'But this is the moment to operate under real-life conditions. What more can you want? Profit from it.'

'What did I say about abandoning one set of insane males for another?' muttered Peter.

Picking the men, Sergeant Troy among them, had not been difficult. After all the training, even those with minor wounds and scratches were up to snuff. Harry was in command and Peter was his number two.

A couple of hours before it began, 'the enemy' climbed into the waiting lorries and were driven off through the night to do their bit. They had no idea where they were going. Nor when they would be called on.

A wind got up as A-section filed down to the quay. The sea writhed around the wooden piles, much as Harry's thoughts were doing. Surprise was crucial, said Gubbins. *Never tie yourself to any single spot. Begin every move by planning a line of retreat. Study the land. Know every road. Every path. Every hollow. Do not hesitate to kill the enemy agent or informer.*

*Above all, provide leadership. Never instruct any man to do anything you would not do yourself.*

Ten minutes to launching. Landing crafts 1 and 2 would lead the assault. Landing crafts 3 and 4 would provide covering fire and backup.

At this moment coded signals were being sent to points down the coast warning them of possible disturbance. The police were on hand to damp down any alarm in the civilian population.

Five minutes to go. Harry inspected the men and the kit – weapons, first-aid packs, including morphine ampoules (to be handed back smartish on return). 'Listen up,' he said. 'A bird tells me that, in a day or two, this will definitely be for real.'

There was a muted cheer.

'So let's make this one go like clockwork. We've learnt the stuff. We know what we're doing. It's second nature. And don't let yourselves down.'

The last sentence had not hit the spot. He could tell. Maybe the men had trained so hard they were past such sentiments. He noted his shortfall.

The landing craft were brought up alongside and the men embarked. Armaments were handed down and stowed, including the Bangalore torpedo, an iron pipe into which explosives were tightly packed, designed to breach wire defences.

The craft bucked and swayed in the swell.

It was time to go. Harry raised a hand, dropped it and the operation was under way.

They nosed their way north to Glenuig Bay and round the point. Out at sea the swell was trickier to navigate. Without warning, the wind dropped. Not good. Engine noise travelled over the water. Harry ordered them to be cut and the men to row.

As he calculated, the oars dipping in and out of the water rendered their progress almost silent.

He scanned the terrain. A faint light to the east outlined the dummy defences which had been put in place and the pillboxes at each end of the beach, manned by soldiers with Bren guns.

The run-in began.

Inch by watery inch they crept over the water. Harry smelt the salt and ozone, felt his toes cramp in his boots, the prickle of adrenaline as the shore came closer.

The absurdity of what they were doing struck him hard. Then it didn't. It was necessary. The risk of death was sky-high when they went into battle for real and the men knew it. Here they would learn how to dodge it for as long as possible. And to achieve their objectives.

Faith had said, *Philosophers and the political pundits think we're progressing into a better and more civilised state, but I don't believe them, Harry. We're appalling as a race.*

Spot on, Faith.

The shore took shape and his vision sharpened. The beach was not large and couldn't offer much in the way of cover. A stretch of wire prevented access at the obvious landing point and painted canvas dummies crouched beside it.

He ordered them to row to the less obvious place to land, which would give them a few seconds to disembark before the onslaught.

Too late.

An 'enemy' voice issued surprisingly clearly over the water. 'Let 'em have it, sir.'

They had been spotted – and the shoreline erupted. Bren guns spat out ammunition. Tracer bullets whined over the landing craft. Mortars smacked into the water. Very lights and parachute flares lit up the scene with a strange and repulsive light.

Landing crafts 1 and 2 hit the southern end of the beach and shuddered to a halt. Landing crafts 3 and 4 came in behind them.

Harry was the first to jump overboard. Water swirled into his boots. Bullets whistled around him. Knife in hand, he headed up the beach with Peter behind him and forged a path to the pillbox.

Its defender was manning his Bren gun with vigour and bullets pounded into the sand. His aim was so close that a bullet singed Harry's cheek.

Fear, bowel-churning and shaming, crawled through him, followed by a surprising reaction: outrage. Using the trees as cover, he and Sergeant Troy sneaked up on the pillbox from behind and circled around it.

It happened too fast to take evasive action. The snout of a gun poked from a slit. Its operator fired. With a groan, Sergeant Troy fell to his knees and clutched his abdomen, before pitching forward.

There was no lull in the bullets. Harry crouched down, secured a dummy grenade and lobbed it through the gun slit.

Pre-arranged and agreed, the grenade signalled that the raiding party had taken its objective.

'Sir…' Corporal Bates crouched beside Sergeant Troy's unconscious figure. 'He's wounded.'

Harry felt for Troy's pulse. It was weak and sporadic. He looked for the wound. A bullet had smashed into the groin. He swung his rucksack off his shoulders and extracted the first-aid kit. Thank whatever gods there were Troy was still out cold as Harry slapped on a pressure bandage and jabbed him with morphine.

'Radio the medics.'

'Radio's buggered, sir,' said Bates.

Harry bit back the obscenities. 'Organise a stretcher and get him to the nearest house. And telephone. There's an ambulance on standby.'

The 'defenders' had withdrawn into the tree cover and had legged it up the hill, which would give them an advantage. The 'invaders' followed them into the trees and, bending double, began the slog through greasy mud up the slope.

The men behind Harry grunted and swore under their breath. The smoke was acrid and foul. He and the men reached the top, where the plan was to blow up the 'defenders' and to prise them off the ridge.

B-section behind them gave covering fire and sent tracers over their heads. Everyone lay flat as the demolition boys wriggled forward to lay fuses and hightailed it back. One of them threw himself down beside Harry. His blackened face broke into a grin. 'This will be fun.' Before he finished speaking an explosion shook the ground and a layer of earth shot skywards and returned in a blinding hail of dust and stones.

Objective achieved.

Harry raised his hand to signal the retreat. The men zig-zagged down the rise, the 'defenders' regrouped and resumed fire, and the noise was ferocious. Harry threw himself into a landing craft, pushed it out into the water and steadied it.

'Row until we get the engines going.'

They rowed like the possessed. The mortar bombs plunged into the water left and right, shudderingly close. As they approached the open water, Harry's adrenaline drained and exhaustion settled over him.

The day had dawned when, the engines coaxed into life, they made full speed.

Harry made for the crofter cottage. With autumn in sight, the temperature was dropping, the air sharp and salty.

He had no idea if Faith would come but he hoped she would spot the Land Rover and they could grab a few minutes.

Loping down the path above the bay, he paused. Perhaps it was his heart beating with extra intensity which sucked in available oxygen… perhaps… but he sensed that he was crossing a boundary that had been in sight for some time now.

Strange how meeting – knowing – Faith had altered his vision. That sea-change. The earth appeared to exude colour and scent. Unleash a wildness of sensation. Each tuft of heather burnt into his vision, moss on walls created wild extravaganzas, the stones littering the peaty paths were as smooth and white as eggs.

The wind gathered force and the sea, on other occasions so joyous and sparkling, looked grey and troubled when Faith appeared. Slight and windblown, with mud splattering her chin. He wiped it away with a hand that wasn't quite steady and pulled her close.

'Are you all right?' She was anxious. 'That last exercise… it's being talked about all over. A man was badly injured?'

He allowed himself to say, 'It wasn't absolutely straightforward.'

'Can you tell me?'

'No.'

'I can't stay. Mrs Turner died last night.'

'I'm sorry.' He offered his hip flask to Faith. She took a mouthful, closed her eyes and swallowed. 'Lovely. All peaty and fiery.' She added, 'Mrs Turner was a very nice woman and I'm sorry.'

'How old?'

'Eighty-five.'

He nodded but thought: *she's free.*

Faith didn't look at him. 'What you've been doing is make-believe,' she said eventually, 'but the injury to that man won't be.'

Harry was silent.

'I can't help feeling we're make-believe as well, Harry. Two people thrown together because a big spoon stirred the pot. It makes for unreal decisions.'

'Not true, darling Faith.' He lingered over the endearment he hadn't used before. 'You know that.' She shook her head. 'You do, you do.'

She was the first to blink. 'I do.'

'But…' He thought of what he had to say and how he would give anything not to say it. 'I'm leaving tomorrow.'

'Then it is goodbye.'

'Not goodbye, merely a space.'

'All right.' She rested her head on his shoulder. 'If you are going, I need to know what you might be facing.'

'Can't do that.'

The silence, broken only by the birds and the sea, acted like the best and most sympathetic of companions.

He slipped his arm around her shoulders and, for a minute or two, they talked over what was happening on the Continent.

'It's easier for us over here,' she said. 'Things are happening. Terrible things, but we're not occupied. We can enjoy so much still. Wildflowers are the more beautiful precisely because the threats of pain and death *are* over there.' She smiled and turned her face. 'I have faith in wildflowers, Harry. So must you.'

'If our air force isn't up to it, Hitler could invade.'

They were silent.

Faith asked for more whisky. The hand that accepted it shook slightly. 'You have a daughter. After it's over, you will want to be with her.'

Fear took a grip. '*You* won't do anything rash, Faith?' he said hoarsely. 'Promise. Keep out of the war.'

She frowned. 'You, of all people, asking me that?'

'I am.'

She sent him a crooked smile. To his horror, Harry felt his eyes mist over. Faith leant over and placed her thumb lightly over one of his eyes. 'What is it? Fear? Us?'

Her thumb was the lightest of touches. 'Both.'

She removed her thumb. 'It's unwise to say "us".'

'Are you regretting "us"?'

Faith touched the signet ring on his little finger. It was an extraordinarily intimate moment, different from the others they had shared. 'I don't know anything about you, Harry. Yet I feel I do. I feel I know about you as a little boy, at school. Your life afterwards. But I don't. Of course I don't.'

The admission was awkward and stumbling and touched him deeply. He took Faith's face in his hands and kissed her. She tasted of whisky and sea salt.

He caught his breath. 'Don't cry.'

She closed her eyes properly. 'Don't talk.'

Again he kissed her and felt that he was dissolving to nothing.

A while later, Faith said that she must go.

He glanced at the sea, where white breakers were now rolling over the surface. 'Wind's getting stronger.'

She ran her fingers through her hair. Astonished by every aspect of her, he watched.

'No regrets?'

'No.' She looked up at him. 'And yes.'

'Why?'

'Saying goodbye will be hard.'

She was standing well back from him, outlined against the ruin of the croft. It must have been a trick of the light but he had an impression he was looking at a photograph, two-dimensional and a little faded.

Harry took her hand. 'I would like to make promises of all sorts. But I won't.'

'No,' she said. 'No.'

It was easier not to draw out these moments. Without a backward glance, Faith walked away.

He watched her figure retreating back up the path and vanishing into the trees. The anguish which sat in the pit of his stomach felt like a stone.

## CHAPTER SEVEN

### April, 1941

Harry had been sleeping. Or thrashing about in what passed for sleep these days, which tended to be patches of oblivion interleaved with unsettling dreams that prodded him back into wakefulness. So it went on.

On leave after a major operation in Norway, he was technically idle until later in the month when he would report to HQ. He had reckoned without Peter who said, 'Forget lounging about, old boy, I need you.' Peter had been seconded to London with a cohort of men from Inverailort with a brief to teach house-to-house street fighting in the bombed-out areas. He had bribed Harry with free passes to the Hundred Club and the Bagatelle. 'You can't refuse those,' he grinned. '*Compañero.*'

Their billet was a run-down hotel off the King's Road and, after a lightning visit to Woodspring to check on, and to soothe, his ailing mother (whose normally immaculate nails were bitten to the quick), he had arrived late the previous evening.

The hotel room was typically high-ceilinged with a rattling window and gritty sheets. He was hungry but breakfast wasn't served until 7 a.m. and there was no point in getting up.

He shut his eyes. *Sleep will you, dammit.* Instead, he thought of his mother's stoicism. He thought about his effort to cultivate herbs in the North Field which, on inspection, looked like nothing much and was probably a wasted experiment. He thought about the house, which needed attention he couldn't give. He thought about Lucy and Nell, who were growing less substantial in his mind. He relived the large-scale commando raid on the Norwegian Loften Islands. Operation Claymore, which had earned him promotion. *A brilliant success, lads.* Fish-oil factories, oil dumps and ships destroyed. Germans captured. Their code books captured.

Full marks to the hunter-killers.

His thoughts were increasingly channelled into unfamiliar byways.

'Men,' he had observed to Faith, 'are locked into a myth.'

She understood.

There were no weak links in the male armour, ran this (very successful) myth. Only warriors. No downy softness beating under the breastplate. No question of refusing to take up arms. No question of not giving your life for your country.

'Some men refuse to fight,' she pointed out. 'That takes courage. They're tough.'

Myths could be reshaped and turned inside out. By something as simple as his longing for a woman he didn't really know, and his duty to protect a child. *I love a woman and a child: therefore I don't want to die.*

Sometimes he said Faith's name out aloud to reassure himself that she had been real. How had she done it? So coolly flattening his defences and becoming as necessary as anything in his life. Before leaving Inverailort, he had bribed the replacement for Sergeant Troy (whose war was over) to drive over to the cottage and post through the letter box a frantically scrawled note with a PO box number and Marcia Jossell's telephone number.

At 6 a.m., Harry was driven with Peter and the men over Battersea Bridge and a sluggish river. Along with coal dust and a hint of gas, he could smell rain in the offing. The muscle in his leg ached, a legacy from Inverailort.

Grit was everywhere. Coating buildings, soft underfoot. Having been bombed incessantly since the previous September, London exemplified a geography of destruction. The bombs were bad enough but, when turning for home, the German pilots had a nasty habit of letting loose a final payload without bothering about targets, intensifying the destruction and homelessness. What was left was rubble, mountains of brick, stone and burnt wood.

And the dissonance. Minds fracturing. Lives fractured. Hearts pulverised.

Six commando recruits had been assembled and tasked to double in and out of empty, crumbling buildings – *get the feel.* For the finale, Peter planned a special test of nerve, running a wooden plank up on the third floor between two ruined houses with a nasty drop below.

'Over we go,' said Harry.

One of the men turned a fetching shade of ashen. 'I'll wait until there's enough bodies to cushion my fall.'

Harry went first. Honour bound. He balanced on the plank, refused to look down, took a breath and went for it.

Afterwards, the men were loaded into a waiting truck and hauled off to the railway sheds at Clapham Junction, to be paraded in front of an engine with a gleaming brass trim.

The jokes about model railways and Hornby engines came thick and fast. The driver was wary that his freshly prinked machine would be sullied by a band of boy-men, if good-natured about it. That evaporated when the corporal asked, 'How do we blow this baby up, sir?'

Working out how to do so took time. At the finish Harry declined Peter's offer of a lift back into the centre of town. He was meeting Robert who was with the Glosters but, after Harry phoned the mess, had managed to wangle a pass up to London for the evening.

Hungry and thirsty, he stopped at a café overlooking the river which served a passable cup of tea and a rock cake that tasted of soda.

He observed the river through the window. Where, for the thousandth time of asking, was Faith? Had she contacted Marcia Jossell? Would she be living with her? Was she… the question burnt him… still alive? In the pre-war days no one asked if the young and middle-aged were still alive. Now they did.

*Faith.*

Over a second cup of tea, he reread a letter from Lucy, now the most fervent of Americans. There were references to white picket fences and Thanksgiving and doughnuts.

Marshalled along by American dollars, their divorce was almost through: 'So good of you, Harry, not to put up silly obstacles. So much cleaner.' Lucy could afford to be conciliatory and cheerful. The financial arrangements of the divorce were generous, plus she was going to marry a rich man. She wrote that Nell was well and loved the teddy bear they had brought from England. ‘Everything’s worked out well, don’t you think, Harry?’

Robert was waiting in the bar of the hotel off Piccadilly when Harry arrived. He was in high spirits. ‘Congratulations on being promoted, *Major* Dane. For some reason the powers-that-be must rate you.’ He squinted at Harry. ‘The haircut suits you.’

‘The moustache doesn’t suit you. Get rid of it.’

They grinned at each other.

‘How was Mother?’

‘Not herself, but uncomplaining as usual. Her heart’s playing up. You must go and see her.’

‘Wilko,’ said Robert. ‘It won’t be for a bit.’ He paused. ‘I find it hard mixing home with… everything else. Woodspring doesn’t seem important.’

Harry understood.

‘You don’t know what number Marcia Jossell’s house is in Battersea Church Close, do you?’

Robert shuddered theatrically. ‘Sixty, I think. Way back, I endured a hideous afternoon tea there and had to be calmed down by Mother on the swings in the park.’

‘I’ll try and look her up,’ said Harry. ‘Mother would like to know.’

‘Glad you phoned, bro,’ said Robert. ‘Shame you couldn’t give me a contact number for *you*, which means, I think, that you’re doing something hush-hush.’

‘Can’t say.’

They were dining on a limp piece of fish. (At Harry’s expense. Robert excelled in the role of the cash-strapped brother.)

'*Harry*… I'm not a fool. A call-out to the regiments for volunteers to a special brigade? Does that ring a little bell?'

'No.'

'I'm putting myself forward.'

'I wish you wouldn't.'

'So you can get all the kudos?'

'I'm thinking of Mother,' said Harry. 'Plus, if I'm killed it will give me pleasure looking down and watching you run Woodspring…'

The brothers exchanged a look.

'It's war. Whatever we do is going to be dangerous.' Robert polished off the fish skin. 'I don't see why you should have all the fun.' He leant over the table. 'I'm sorry about your marriage. What went wrong?'

'I don't run a mega-dollar mail-order business,' said Harry. Then regretted the mean spirit. 'Lucy did try but she never wanted the life that I offered.'

'And Nell?'

'And Nell,' Harry repeated with real anguish. 'At least she's well and looked-after and in no danger here.'

'No need to get upset. She's safe.' Rob smiled at Harry. 'I'll say this once, I don't want you to think that I'm fond of you or anything, but I feel for you. I really do.' He leant back on the chair. 'Shove over the cigarettes, there's a good man.'

'Major Dane… Major Dane…' The hotel manager was shaking him.

Harry had only just fallen into a deep sleep. 'What… *what?*'

'Urgent telephone.'

'Harry,' said Peter down the line. 'The ARP lot can't cope with the bombing. It's bad and they want our help. A truck's coming for you.'

Harry stumbled back to his room to dress. Legs into trousers which wrapped themselves around his ankles. Hands into shirtsleeves. A fumble with the belt clip. Vision clouded.

If the Air Raid Precaution wardens couldn't cope, it must be an inferno.

The truck was waiting, engine idling. Harry hauled himself in and joined four other men slumped into the back. It was difficult to make out their faces, but their breath was drink- and sleep-laden.

They drove towards Battersea Bridge hearing the roar of plane engines, followed by the rattle of ack-ack.

*This is what people must feel hell is like*, thought Harry. Noise, dirt, being in the dark.

Over the bridge, they turned right into Battersea Church Road and then, inevitably it seemed, right again into Battersea Church Close.

For God's sake.

The driver halted and the men dropped silently onto the tarmac. Two had ordinary ropes wrapped around their waists, two had the commando toggle ropes.

The bomb had wreaked havoc on the houses at the end of the Victorian terrace and the ARP wardens were pulling aside rubble.

The men broke into a run. Within seconds, they were digging alongside the wardens. Every so often a hand was raised. Everything halted and they listened.

Nothing.

A body was brought out from the house next but one to the end of the row. A young woman with blonde hair minus her arms. Harry looked away.

A void opened under the house.

He edged towards it. 'Hello…' His shout was muffled by fetid air released by the bomb. He shone his torch around the hole. A snaky slither of earth caused the ARP warden to cry out, 'Sir, keep back.'

He and the team moved on to the house at the end of the terrace. The back of it had been blown off and the front door had been blown out.

They stood. *Listening.*

The listeners heard the cry. Then a second, filled with pain and fear. The warden pointed up to the first storey.

'You'll need the ropes to get up there,' said the ARP guy. 'The stairs have gone.'

One of the team, a Sergeant Trelawney, rattled the drainpipe to test and shimmied up it. Harry followed, secured the rope to the junction of the pipe as a safety measure, reached the window and swung his leg over. The door to the room had been blown off its hinges and pitch-forked at an angle into the room. Harry's torch revealed a couple of chairs, a single bed and a chest of drawers almost smashed into matchsticks.

'A body, sir,' said Sergeant Trelawney, his torch traced the outline of an elderly lady with her head half obliterated.

He turned away.

The training kicked in.

'Leave her for the moment.'

They fanned out into a corridor heaped with fallen plaster and laths, accompanied by the creaks and groans of the house as it rocked on its foundations.

The door to the adjoining room was wedged shut. A cry issued from behind it. They shouldered the door, which yielded, and squeezed into the room.

Thickly shrouded by dust and plaster, a woman lay face down on the floor, pinned by the legs under a bedstead. Arm flung out like a rag doll's and motionless. Her nightdress was in shreds, the colour of her hair obliterated by dust.

'Dead? Alive?'

Trelawney felt for a pulse at the neck. 'Alive.'

It took several minutes to shift the plaster and to ease the bedstead away from her legs, which looked badly injured.

'We'll have to splint her,' said Harry.

While Trelawney searched the room for pieces of wood, Harry began the slow process of rolling her onto her back. The movement made her surface, unfocussed and grey of skin. Gasping with pain, she closed her eyes. 'Don't touch me.'

'I'll be as gentle as possible.'

At the sound of his voice her eyes opened.

It was Faith – and the inevitability of it hit him like a hammer.

'Harry?' Her mouth barely moved. 'Am I dead?'

'No,' he said, choking in the plaster-laden air. 'You're bloody living so don't do anything stupid like dying on me.'

'How did you know I was here?'

'I was going to ring to find out if you were.'

Her eyes moved from left to right, taking in the damage.

'Why are you here?'

'To rescue you.' He touched her cheek. 'It's my fault you're in this mess.'

Tears traced runnels down her dust-caked cheeks. 'It hurts. It hurts.'

'I know, darling Faith. I know.' Tenderly, gently, he wiped the dust from her eyes and mouth. 'Listen to me. Sergeant Trelawney and I are going to splint your legs and get you to the medics. The stairs have gone so we'll let you down out of the window. It's going to be difficult and you must be brave. But I know you are.'

Incredibly, she managed a half-smile. 'I wrote you a letter…' Her voice trailed away.

He leant over and kissed her. 'Shush.'

'Please…' There was a long pause. 'Can I ask?'

'Anything.'

'I think I've wet myself. Please don't let anyone see.'

He ripped off his battledress jacket and covered her bottom half. 'I promise.'

She fell silent. Outside the ARP wardens were shouting instructions to get out of the house.

Trelawney hovered with two batten-shaped pieces of wood. They moved Faith's legs into position, splinted them and bound them up with the toggle ropes. She screamed once, then bit down hard on her bottom lip.

Harry made sure that he tied the sleeves of his jacket around her waist.

Faith relapsed into unconsciousness, which made it easier. They carried her into the front room and lowered her out of the window down to the ambulance waiting below.

Trelawney and he slotted the bed in the room under the windowsill, wrapped a rope around one of its legs and followed.

'You go first, sir,' said Trelawney, who had observed the interactions between Harry and Faith.

He was down the rope within seconds. 'Which hospital?' he asked the stretcher-bearers as they loaded her into the ambulance.

Faith was again conscious. Harry retrieved his jacket and covered her with a blanket. 'They didn't see.'

'Stupid to mind.' Her face was creased with pain.

'I'll come and see you,' he said. 'I know where you're going. Do you want me to contact your father?'

'He died.'

'I'm sorry.'

'Harry.' Her lips moved. 'Wrong moment, but I never told you that I loved you.'

He bit back his anguish. 'And they say timing is everything.'

'Sir, out please.'

The ambulance needed to depart. He bent over and brushed his lips across her cheek. 'I love you, Faith.'

The remainder of the night was taken up with the rescue of the body – which was almost certainly Marcia Jossell – and the stabilisation of the house and the rest of the close. Harry and the team worked themselves to a standstill, dealing with the anguish and suffering. There were the screams of the burnt and injured. The weeping of the bereaved. The disgusting smell of sewage and fat from damaged drains – and the danger from escaping gas which threatened those who toiled in the ruins.

When dawn broke, he and the exhausted men took stock. At the end of the street where they were working someone had lit a brazier. A couple of women were boiling kettles.

As dishevelled and dusty as they were, the women managed to hand out mugs of tea. If they had lost their homes, they hadn't lost their humour. 'Here…' One of them thrust a mug at Harry. 'I'm looking for a new husband. Fancy it?'

He swallowed a heavenly mouthful. 'If I were free – ' the tea slid down his throat, scraped by dust and gas – 'you'd be my first choice.'

The men were dispatched back to their billets with orders to rest up for the day and Harry took himself back to his hotel to wash and shave. Feeling marginally more human in a fresh shirt, he hailed a taxi.

At the hospital, it took persuasion before the ward sister allowed him in. He was not kin, he was told. 'But she doesn't have any.' He exerted every iota of charm. It was not visiting hours. 'I know, I know, Sister, but I may be called on at any minute. I know you'll understand.'

The ward smelt of disinfectant with a faint undertone of blood. It was noisy with the cries and groans of the injured, for the intake from the night's bombing had been heavy. He dreaded what he would find. How injured was she? How would she heal? *Could* she heal?

The numbers were so great that Faith's bed was pushed right up against the wall. She had been propped up and a cradle placed over her legs.

She looked broken and very ill.

'Hello, darling.'

Incredibly, she managed a smile. 'I knew you'd come.'

'They'll try and chuck me out in a minute. But I'm not going to let them.' He laid the back of his hand against her cheek and she nuzzled against it.

'The pain?'

Her reply was slow. 'Morphine. The cure for the condition of life. But it makes me stupid. And thirsty.'

He made to pour out water for her from the jug but it was empty. 'I'll go and fill it.'

'Don't be long,' she managed between cracked lips.

When he returned, Faith had fallen into a twitchy doze. Using the ruthless tactics that were now second nature, Harry pinched a chair and placed it by her bed.

If he had any truck with God, he might be calling on him to come to Faith's aid. But he didn't have any truck with God and he couldn't call on him. Furthermore, a glass jar had been lowered over him, cutting off every consideration except for the girl who lay in the bed beside the chair.

Faith shifted and cried out. Harry took her hand, and she quietened. A little later Faith opened her eyes. 'Harry, have I lost my legs?'

He felt an irrational rage. 'Haven't they talked to you?'

'They're busy. Very…' She was barely audible. 'There're so many… Anyway, I'd prefer it was you to tell me the bad news.'

He held on to her hand for a few more seconds before pulling back the blanket and sheet draped over the cradle.

She was still in a hospital gown, which had rucked up over her thighs. From the knees down both legs were swathed in heavily bloodstained bandages.

'You have your legs.' The rush of relief almost prevented his saying the words. 'But it's bad.'

She inhaled sharply. 'They feel… odd.' She struggled to continue. 'But perhaps it will be all right.' She turned her head away. 'I don't want you to see me diminished.'

'Diminished?' he said angrily. 'Diminished?'

When she fell into a doze, Harry continued to sit beside her and dozed himself. When he woke, he went in search of the ward sister, who he discovered in the sluice. She was standing quite still, head bowed, holding on to the edge of the basin. Her cap had lost much of its starch and her apron was stained. At Harry's entrance, she turned and frowned. 'What are you doing in here? You are supposed to have left.'

'Sister, I know you've had a hell of night,' he said. 'Would you like me to organise tea and sandwiches?'

He watched her hover between yes and no, her cheeks hollowed out with fatigue. Then she said, 'That's very kind and it's not often we get an offer like that. But the hospital will organise something.'

'When do you go off duty?' he found himself asking. 'You work inhuman hours.'

Under the blast of his charm, she thawed. 'It's not normally this bad.'

'I can always get my men to do some fetching and carrying. Let me know if you change your mind. Meanwhile, and I know I'm asking a lot of you, may I use your telephone?' He gestured to his uniform. 'I have to report in.'

'Just this once.'

It wasn't easy, far from it, but he negotiated time off from Peter's operations until the following day, took a taxi to Selfridges, co-opted an assistant and instructed her to put together a parcel of necessities. Once she knew why, Miss

Denton rose to the challenge. 'It's terrifying,' she said more than once, assembling nightdresses, talcum powder, a hairbrush, a toothbrush and a face flannel and packing them up in brown paper and string. 'If I could get my hands on Hitler.'

On his return to the hospital, Harry was met by the ward sister at the entrance to the ward.

'You can't see her,' she said.

'For heaven's sake.' Irritation with the rules made him sound more belligerent than he intended. 'She needs someone.'

'All my patients do.'

He found himself begging, something he did not often do. 'Please.'

'There's a crisis and the doctors are with her.'

'Bad?'

'We're not sure.' She rationed her words and pity stirred for her exhaustion.

'Can I see her afterwards?' He shifted the parcel from under one arm to the other. 'It will help her and I'll take her off your hands as soon as you will let me.'

The pale face under the cap softened. 'I can't promise, but if you wait over there.' At the door to the ward, she turned back. 'There's so many of you, you know, and I can't bend the rules for everyone.'

'Sister, is she going to lose her legs?'

She gave him a look which reflected rage and impotence. 'It's possible.'

He waited on a hard bench, in the grip of a fear that was nothing like the apprehension he had felt on the Norwegian raid.

He thought of the bandages wrapped around Faith's legs. That was war and it was a war which had to be fought. *That* was realpolitik. Only now he realised that her suffering could erode his resolve and his capacities.

He wished Robert was with him. His brother would make a joke. Light a cigarette. Fix him with a gaze which would tell Harry that he understood better than he ever let on.

The porters came and went, bearing stretchers. Nurses hurried in and out of the ward with stained aprons. The clatter of bedpans in the sluice and the hum from the sterilisers was constant.

When, finally, he was granted permission by Sister Drake (they were now on naming terms) to see Faith, he was exhausted by emotion.

At his approach, Faith opened her eyes and her hand edged over the sheet. He picked it up and kissed it. It had been dyed by iodine and smelt of hospital. 'I've told the redoubtable Sister Drake that I will take charge of you once you're out of here.'

She breathed a sigh of relief.

'But it might take a bit of time. You mustn't get an infection.' He rubbed his thumb over her stained hand. 'What were you doing in London?'

'Mrs Turner's son got me a job. Invoice clerk in a firm exporting to French Canada…' She struggled to speak. 'Awful.' Her breathing was slow. 'I used my… French.'

'Don't worry. You won't be going back to it.'

'Harry, it's my job.'

She seemed to fall asleep. In the next bed, an old lady shouted out at regular intervals. Faith stirred and opened her eyes, and he felt his heart go into free fall. 'Hello, Harry.'

They exchanged a long look – and he could truthfully say that he had never felt happier or more precarious.

'Will you promise me something, Harry?'

'Yes.'

'If they think I'm going to die, you'll tell me.'

He frowned.

'You would tell me, Harry, wouldn't you? I need to know, to count every breath. To think about what everything has meant. To say goodbye to you properly.'

She was becoming agitated. 'I promise. But you're not going to die and when you're out of here, we'll be together. I'll find somewhere. I'll have to come and go but the main thing is you'll be the base. When you're healed, I'll take you to live at Woodspring. Away from the bombing.'

He could see Faith there – walking with him through the wood, up to the field that had been sown with the sainfoin and burnet and down to the dip where the bourn rose in the winter. He could see her in the drawing room, in the bedroom, mounting the stairs to the floor where the nurseries had always been.

Woodspring would suit her.

At this moment, it seemed the only sane place in the world.

'Harry… I'm going to be sick.'

He snatched up the enamel bowl on the bedside table and held it for her. She retched up liquid and bile. 'Sorry… sorry. I can't bear you to see me like this.'

'I don't mind.' He wiped her face. 'I don't.'

It was true.

# CHAPTER EIGHT

It was difficult to find anywhere to live. London under the Blitz – a new term used by the journos – was battered. One minute you had somewhere to live. Next you didn't.

He had let the flat in Mayfair go and it took him a hard search before he located a ground-floor furnished flat in a terrace between Victoria Station and the river. A section of the terrace had been damaged but most of the houses were still habitable.

The front door to the house was intact and opened into a well-proportioned hallway. Flat Number 1 had two large sash windows, a cornice miraculously still in place and beautiful weathered floorboards. There was a tiny kitchen, a bathroom with a gas heater and bedroom that could accommodate a double bed.

He put down six months' rent, trousered gratefully by the landlord, and made enquiries about help in the flat. Verity from next door offered her services and undertook to cook and clean while Faith was bed-bound. Next, he opened a bank account in Faith's name and deposited a sum which would see her through for six months if he was injured, captured or killed.

The relief was immense. Wherever he fetched up, and the orders might arrive any minute, Faith would have a roof over her head and funds on which to draw.

He returned to Selfridges and threw himself on the mercies of the redoubtable Miss Denton who had set about stockpiling sheets, blankets, towels, crockery and a kettle. Bearing them back to the flat, he thought about Lucy and her unhappiness at Woodspring. 'Coffee is always on the hob and Nell *loves* a soda,' wrote Lucy in her latest letter. 'I'm told rationing has begun in England which must be very trying. I have to stop Nell eating too much chocolate. It isn't good for her…'

Their exchanges were glacially polite. He wondered… and he didn't care for the thought… whether if he and Lucy had felt more for each other the mechanics of their separation and divorce would be less civilised.

Still ill, still weak, still compromised, Faith was discharged from hospital because there simply wasn't the capacity to keep her. Harry gave a final once-over of the flat. Verity had kept her word. Dust was at a minimum, the windows washed, the bed made up, the bread wrapped in a tea towel and a pint of milk stood in a bowl of water.

'One step,' he coaxed later as she made painful progress from the taxi to the front door. 'Two steps.'

'You sound like the nursery rhyme.'

'Yup, I'm the big, bad wolf. Three steps.'

She clung onto the rail and sweat beaded her upper lip.

'I'm going to carry you.' He gathered up the alarmingly light and frail Faith… as if… as if… he was carrying his bride across the threshold. She smelt of hospitals and ill health but he didn't care. Kicking open the door of Number 1, he edged inside, down the passage and laid her on the bed.

Faith took off her hat and chucked it down beside her. Her gaze travelled around the room. 'You arranged all this. For me?'

'Of course.' He knelt in front of the gas fire and felt for his matches. Giving off immediate warmth, it popped companionably. Harry came and sat on the bed. 'Am I hurting your legs?'

'If I'm honest, I can't tell. They hurt whatever happens and I'm black and blue from the injections.'

'Let's get your coat off.' He unbuttoned it and eased it off her shoulders. 'A cup of tea, I think.'

'I'd rather a whisky.'

'You're to drink as much fluid as possible, so tea it is. Doctor's orders.'

'So this is my future,' she said, with such tenderness that Harry almost could not bear it. 'Being bullied.'

In bed that night, he asked her if she was coping with the memory of being bombed. 'Were you frightened you wouldn't be rescued?'

Painfully, awkwardly, she shifted closer so that they were touching. 'I wasn't thinking logically. I knew I was there and injured but I convinced myself I was someone else.'

Harry lay very still.

'It's funny. Living in London you go over the possibilities. You prepare yourself. I vowed that if I was bombed and conscious I would not cry or panic. When it happened, I didn't panic. I just thought: the worst has happened, and I might die but it didn't matter because…'

Harry had an appalling vision of Faith trapped in the rubble, trying to be rational.

'... we'd had had each other for a while. Lying there, I went over you and me. That helped. Not entirely. But a lot.'

The urge to wrap her in his arms was almost overpowering. 'I wish we could make love,' he said.

Her fingers slid down his torso. 'My hands aren't damaged,' she said.

She was uncertain and weak, and Harry was a touch embarrassed, but they managed.

Afterwards, he got out of bed to wash, returning chilly and goose-fleshed, and got back into bed.

Faith stared up at the ceiling. 'Harry, I hate being like this. Useless and reliant on you. I was going to be so independent.'

He slid his arm under her and cupped his fingers around the curve of her shoulder. It was a touch he had missed badly. 'Does that hurt?'

'No.'

With his free hand, he took one of hers and held it over his heart. 'Do you trust me?'

She turned her head. 'Do you need to ask?'

'You must let me take care of you. As you would me, I think.'

Faith gave a little sigh. 'Dear God, I do love you, Harry.' Her fingers tightened. 'You've no idea how much.'

He felt the happiness that only she had brought him gather at the back of his mind – and an immense drowsiness. Cradling Faith, he went to sleep.

The following morning, Faith insisted on getting up. 'It's not good to lie in bed.' A vein running down her hand was startlingly blue against her white skin and she looked exhausted and apprehensive. But when Harry leant over to help her up, a familiar humour lit up in her eyes. 'Bet they didn't teach you this on the course.'

'You shut up,' he said tenderly. 'Concentrate.'

By the time she was fully dressed, Faith was white and sweaty. With her clinging on to his arm, they shuffled down the passage into the room where he had set up a table and chair.

He placed a cup of tea on the table. 'I insist you have a spoonful of sugar.'

'Sugar! The stuff of the gods.' She laced her fingers around the cup and bent over it – searching out the sugar gold in the liquid. For a second, she looked frighteningly older, and doubt placed a hand on the nape of Harry's neck and squeezed. What had he undertaken?

Faith was wounded.

Faith was possibly crippled.

What would her trauma have done to her?

She took a mouthful of the tea and her eyes beamed amusement over the rim of the cup. Suddenly, she was familiar again. 'I hadn't thought much about it, but I suppose my things were destroyed by the bomb?'

A stew of plaster, lath, pulverised furniture, rags, broken hairbrushes, a wash bag…

'Pretty much. Were all your possessions there?'

'Most of them.' She appeared stricken at the thought. Then not. 'Didn't have many. Clothes, photographs, a plate belonging to my grandmother. I was fond of them and would never have got rid of them but they're only *things*. I know that now.'

'Not even the photographs?'

'A couple of my parents. Separate ones. One of my grandmother. I'll remember what they looked like while I can and when I can't it'll be time to let go.' She looked up at Harry. 'My father died not long after Mrs Turner.'

He laid a hand on her shoulder.

Caring for someone so weak was a new experience. Changing dressings, administering her painkillers. Harry had had no idea of the tedium involved, the patience required and of how, with the best will in the world, frustration erupted. But at night as they shared the bed, he would hold her gently and feel her breath in the hollow of his shoulder.

They had a couple of weeks. Mostly, Harry only left the flat for provisions and some fresh air. Once, he experimented by commandeering a taxi to take Faith out for a meal at a nearby café. This proved tricky as she was still pretty much immobile. She was also inclined to nausea.

'Talk to me,' she begged him when she was at her worst. 'Anything. Everything about you and it might stop me feeling sick.'

Talking about himself never came easily. 'That's the first time I've been invited to act as an anti-emetic.'

Faith pressed a knuckle to her mouth. 'Always a first time.'

They exchanged a look. Already, there were memories.

'I love the colour green,' he said. 'That's something about me.'

'Emerald? Moss? Hunting green?'

Tempted to say, 'the colour of your eyes,' but, because it was sentimental, Harry hesitated. 'Dark green generally. It reminds of the woods near Woodspring.'

Later, when they were in bed, she asked, 'Favourite piece of music?'

'Schubert's string quartet. I took Lucy to a concert the night she told me she was pregnant…' He hadn't meant to refer to Lucy. 'That's when we decided to get married.' He squinted down at Faith. 'I often think I got married because I almost cried while listening to it.'

She murmured: 'That's not the reason. You know so.' She closed her eyes. 'Did you like school?'

'I'd be lying if I said nothing was good. But it was a brutal place and you had to become brutal to get through. But I grew to love… well, grew very fond… of my friends and they me. The bonds between survivors are tough ones.'

'Manly sports?'

'It was a boys' school…'

It didn't take much to transport him back to the rugby scrum. Scott and Wharton, the two props beside him, with the rest of them writhing like a crab whose legs were out of control. He could remember the bruises, heads cracking, limbs being grabbed in grips like steel traps. One bruise had been up by his scrotum. God knows how it had got there. The jeers when one of them missed a pass.

The cold. The streaming, bloody noses. Endless services in the chapel, the drone of the sermons, the eternal search for somewhere private… to lick wounds. To think.

'You were never alone,' he said. 'Or rarely. It was as if the school had set out to invade and conquer both the boy and the man-to-be.'

Faith gave a short laugh. 'Like Hitler.'

'Like the wretched Hitler.' One by one, he kissed her fingertips. 'All that does stick in the memory.'

They were silent.

The sash window in the bedroom had warped and it was difficult to close it entirely. A car in the street ground its gears and seemed to be almost in the room.

'Do you want to know about me?' Faith was sleepy.

'Not at all…' He was teasing but felt a stab of guilt that he hadn't interrogated her.

'If you do, you'll have to wait. I can only say that being born a female is profoundly tiresome and wasteful. If I had my way, I'd abolish the sexes.'

He laid a hand on her breast. 'God forbid.'

'Time's up, old boy,' he was informed on reporting in for duty. 'Back north for a training push. Things are hotting up for the unit. Can't say where and can't say when.'

He had been expecting the order but the news winded him and he returned to the flat to tell Faith. What colour she had left her face, but she took it calmly.

'It was only a matter of time. We knew that.'

He turned to look out of the window. 'You don't have to be stoic.'

'We both do.'

Harry thought of what the following weeks might hold. Fear. Danger. Much danger. Physical hardship. Mental hardship. Being placed in a position where he must take difficult decisions, no doubt split-second ones, plus living with the consequences.

'How has Hitler managed to do all this?' Faith was asking.

He thought. 'Right-wing dictators tend to invoke fear of "others" to justify their actions. That's how he's done it.'

'Poor us then.'

Faith had been resting in the chair and he took hold of her hands. 'The decree absolute is not through yet, but nearly.' He gripped her tightly. 'Marry me, Faith, when it is. Please.'

She swallowed.

'When the war is over, we can live at Woodspring. There's a chair in the drawing room overlooking the garden which is waiting for you.'

'Help me get up, Harry.'

He slotted his hands under her armpits and pulled her upright. She steadied herself by leaning against him. She looked calm enough but there was turmoil behind the green eyes. 'Because we are having… this… you don't have to marry me.'

'You are being deliberately obtuse,' he said, kissing her.

'Let's think about it when the decree is through.'

He made his preparations and left nothing to chance. He gave a phone number to Verity and money to pay for it with instructions to phone if she was the slightest bit worried. He bought a cheap camera and film and made Verity take a photograph. Faith insisted on putting on a dress which Miss Denton had provided and stood beside him.

Harry packed the camera up in his kit.

The night before he went north, Harry managed to get a bottle of good claret and bore it back to the flat. Faith was in the kitchen wrestling with potatoes and a very small piece of pork. That morning, she had insisted on going shopping. She needed to do so, she said, to begin building up her strength.

He gave her the wine. 'This time we will drink it.'

'Excellent plan.'

'Did you manage the steps?'

'Verity helped me.'

'How did it feel?'

Potato in hand, she leant against the sink. 'Peculiar. As if they had been replaced by different legs and they didn't belong to me.'

'But they're working?'

'Jury's out until I've practised a bit more.'

He thought of Faith climbing the Swiss mountains and rowing her boat on the lake and felt bitterly angry. To mask it, he lit a cigarette. 'Let's not wait. Let's start the wine now.'

After two glasses each of the divine claret, Harry scooped up Faith and bore her off into the bedroom.

'You'll have to help me.' She was struggling with her skirt.

Harry removed it and chucked it over the chair and applied himself to the buttons of her blouse. This took time but finally they were skin-to-skin.

Faith smelt of soap and warm skin. 'Don't spare me, Harry. This has got to last.'

He understood.

Even so, he went very carefully. After a while, Faith pulled him closer. 'Harry.'

Towards the end, he realised she was crying and he was too.

# CHAPTER NINE

The Mountain Warfare course to which Harry had been assigned was at Braemar in the Cairngorms, not Inverailort.

The first day was spent replenishing their stores in the town before the troop spilt and fanned out to separate hill-camp bases from where they would tackle the highest peaks.

Day Two. Harry was loaded up like a Sherpa. Tent, provisions, weapons. To practise maintaining balance with the load, he kept his hands in his pockets as the instructors had taught. 'The stones and rocks are not your friends, gentlemen. Nor are the bogs and the peat. They will hate you.'

*Keep your balance, gentlemen.*

The ascent began. The climb was measured at approximately 1,000 feet an hour. Ten minutes after the start, the men stopped, adjusted their sweat-rags and windcheaters and discarded their sweaters. Each time they rested the sweaters went back on. The trick was not to sweat but not to get chilled either. It took management.

It was important not to lose energy, and permission had been given to eat on the marches. In Harry's pockets there were cheese, biscuits, black chocolate and dried fruit.

On one stop, Harry dropped down onto a convenient rock and ate his chocolate. Peter was beside him and he felt the warmth of the other man's now solidly muscled body.

'Any regrets volunteering for this?' he asked him.

Peter chewed a date. 'No, because I wasn't going to spend my time taking orders from idiots in the other services.'

'They're not all idiots.'

'True. But it cheers me up to think they are.'

Harry laughed and it struck him he hadn't laughed for some time.

Peter was concerned. 'You're worried, old boy. I can tell. The girl in London.'

It was a relief to confess. 'Yes.' He looked away from Peter. 'I did what I could to help her, but it probably wasn't enough.'

'Never is,' said Peter.

Peter told his stories of London conquests – the blonde Marty, the sweet Elaine. Tales of kisses and hotel rooms rolling over Harry. Until he realised that Peter was being a friend and diverting him.

'Which one do you favour?'

'All of them,' said Peter.

The chocolate was bitter-sweet and coated the roof of his mouth, which was great. He looked at the white-capped peak that they were due to climb. Snow and ice filled the upper crevasses and the gullies.

Somewhere among that lot were camouflaged sharp-shooters with rifles and telescopic sights, ready to open fire as the men made the ascent. Once at the summit, they were to descend without being shot up – clinging to a (misguided?)

faith that base camp had managed to bag a hare or guddle trout for the evening meal.

Peter nudged him. 'With me?'

Not to put too fine a point on it, the remainder of the ascent was bloody awful. But he, Pete and Sergeant Trelawney made good time without being felled, although a couple of shots whistled close to them. Three thousand feet up, the troop found themselves positioned on top of a scree slope.

'Right, you timewasters,' said the instructor with an unholy satisfaction, 'you're going down that and if you didn't listen to my instructions on how to tackle scree that's your misfortune.'

Hovering on that crest, Harry was poleaxed by fear. Intense and shaming.

'Who was the bloke who flew too close to the sun?' he asked Peter.

'Icarus.'

'That's us.'

'Take your time, Major Dane.' The instructor was at full throttle. 'Why not have a tea party while you're at it? It'll be fun. You can have the entire Reich on top of you. Are you going to fuck off or not... sir?' He was enjoying himself.

Harry had no intention of being told twice. Summoning his energy, he turned to the left and ran with his arms thrown out. Then turned to the right.

It was exhilarating and mad. And dangerous.

Dislodged stones cascaded down the slope towards the men below, one of whom swore as a large one smacked into his ankle. Considering the hours it had taken to ascend the mountain, it seemed only a matter of minutes to get down. He and the men arrived at the bottom, blown and played-out, craving nothing more than to chow down on a meal and to sleep.

The troop tackled the stew – rabbit, and tough – and their instructor hunkered down with them. 'You must learn the ropes,' he said. 'Keep a constant eye on the weather. Mountains are different terrain to anything else you've tackled. They change in the blink of an eye. Check once, check twice, check ten times your clothes, equipment, food, dry twigs and matches. You may have to die fighting, but give yourselves a chance to live while you can.'

Fatigue had chewed Harry up. Yet he was sleepless. As dawn fingered the sky, he thought of Nell. He thought of Lucy. Driven by her strong instinct for survival. With Lucy married to Mr Mail Order, Nell would almost certainly make her life in the States. Did he mind? No. He had never been the Englishman who considered that life elsewhere was intolerable. Plus, if he didn't survive, she would be tucked up in another country with another identity.

Above all, he thought about Faith. Materialising as she often did. Clearly etched. Had he absorbed everything that made her Faith? Body, eyelashes, skin… her will?

*Faith darling, I am aching, damp and exhausted but the thought of you makes those considerations drop away. I'm writing to you in my head because there's nothing else to hand, plus the censor won't get his hands on the letter.*

*I've been rethinking what courage is. I'll be facing the bullets at some point and I hope I'll live up to what is expected. But the other sort of courage is to give you my love, all of it, and promise to keep it whole and living.*

*I wonder if you will accept my promise. What about Lucy, you might argue, and the promise you gave her? Yes, I married Lucy and, because of Nell, I am connected to her for the rest of my life.*

*You must not mind me saying being married was not all bad. But I confess to ignorance. I had no idea of true scorching feeling, the emotion that really does change the inner world. The arrival of certainties that transform the spirit.*

The sun came up and spread rose and opaline colours over the sky, and Faith vanished.

The camp was packed up and they returned to base for the debriefing and a wash and a shave. They had half an hour to doze on the straw mattresses on the put-up beds in the officers' hut before being roused for the next exercise.

'On yer feet…'

He was nursing a cup of coffee when the sergeant tapped him on the shoulder. 'Message from London sent over from base.'

The message was from Verity. The flat in Victoria had been bombed and Faith had again been injured and admitted to hospital. He needed to get in touch.

Harry placed a call with the hospital and waited an agonising ten minutes to get through. A staff nurse came to the phone. Septicaemia had set in, she said, and could Major Dane come down to be with his wife as the situation was grave?

He sat in the train grinding slowly, oh-so slowly, back to London, swigging whisky from his flask. Approaching the outskirts of the city, he worked out why he found the staff nurse's wording odd.

She had referred to Faith as his wife.

*

This time, they had put Faith in a smaller, mercifully more peaceful, ward.

Under a clinically tucked-in sheet, she lay motionless and did not stir when he called her name.

The report on her injuries was bad. Ruptured spleen, broken ribs, severe lacerations on the recently healed legs. Sister Drake, who had appeared briefly, did not hide her concern. 'She's in a serious condition.'

Mounting vigil at the bedside, Harry listened to Faith's faint breaths which barely moved her chest. He took up her white, frail hand in his. Every so often, he checked her pulse.

Where had she gone? What was she dreaming? Perhaps she was in the boat rowing around the point? Perhaps he was with her and they were lying together, her breath falling on his bare shoulder, a foot anchored around his leg?

With Faith so silent and wounded, he should, by every measure, feel very alone. But it wasn't so, partly because the habit of Faith living in his thoughts was so strong. Longing for her touch, he leant over and brushed the hair back from her forehead and she murmured.

Love was annealing. It softened and tempered. Negated anguish and disappointment. Suggested possibilities. Gloriously so.

A nurse moved between the beds, taking temperatures and giving injections. She was small and thin and the trolley was too heavy for her. Syringes rattled softly in the enamel kidney bowls and the trolley wheels hissed over the linoleum floor. Light filtered through windows that needed a clean. A couple of the patients sat in their chairs, clearly traumatised.

Again he touched her cheek. Faith opened her eyes and looked up at Harry. She had read his thoughts. 'I was dreaming that we were in the rowing boat on the lake. You were at the oars and the wind was against us. I worried you were getting blisters.'

Her speech was drowsy, faint.

'And?'

'It took all your strength.'

'Where were we going?'

'I don't know. We were just together.'

The question of where they were going was obviously distressing her. 'It doesn't matter where we were,' Harry said quickly. 'We were probably in Arisaig, and samphire is everywhere.'

'No, it isn't. That's the point.'

'All right. We're in Switzerland on the lake there. It's snowy and there's ice in the water. No, it's spring and we're walking up the mountain to see the wildflowers and I have a stick. Why do I have a stick? I'm supposed to be fit.'

'No idea.' She gave the ghost of a chuckle. 'I often wonder about your fitness.'

'We both have on proper walking boots and, once up in the Alpine meadows, the air is like wine.' Faith fell silent and her face creased in pain. 'Have you had pain relief?'

'I wouldn't mind some more.'

Sister Drake had gone off duty. Harry found the staff nurse, who was not as sympathetic as Sister Drake, and explained that Faith needed help. 'My wife… my wife is not someone to make a fuss. Would it be possible?'

'We have to wait for a doctor before I can give her anything.'

'Where is he?'

The staff nurse was tired and looked at Harry with disdain. 'Do you know how many patients are requiring attention?'

He got the point and returned to Faith. 'Where does it hurt most?' he asked her.

She opened her eyes wide and he read acceptance in their depths, which frightened him. 'My ribs. It's hard to breathe.'

'Shall I sing you the rib song?'

'Idiot.'

He had made her smile, which was worth a king's ransom.

'Think of the future.'

'With a bit of luck the war won't beat us after all.'

'Like I promised, I'm going to take you to Woodspring.'

'Tell me…' Her voice was faint.

Again, he described the house: his study overlooking the ha-ha, the blue bedroom where they would sleep, the wood which could be seen from the drawing room. The nurseries at the top of the house.

Time telescoped. Emotion made him light-headed, as if an anchor had been cast aside.

He felt her fingers twitch.

Harry sat on with his hand cradled against Faith's cheek while she dozed. The staff nurse came and ordered him to go. 'You can come back in the evening,' she said.

He eased his hand free, stood over the bed and said softly, 'I'll be back.'

'Harry…'

The staff nurse was pulling him away.

'Harry, I do love you.'

The figure of the staff nurse between him and Faith prevented him from replying.

But he carried her words down the ward and out into a shattered London, and walked along the river which was grey with silt from the bombing. It was a still day and the whiff of burnt rubber and gas hung in the air.

Turning up into the Strand, he went into a Lyons' Corner House and ordered tea and a sandwich. Lacklustre was too kind a description for the sandwich, but the tea was welcome.

He imagined a future with no violence and killing. A generous, unafraid existence, encompassing spirit and body. He and Faith must, *would*, live with respect for the gift of their lives, for animals, for the land, for the house and its land.

At the appointed time, he returned to the hospital and was met by the staff nurse at the ward entrance. She stood in front of him, starched and straight. 'I'm sorry, Major Dane.'

'What do you mean?'

She led him into small room off the main ward and made him take one of the two comfortless chairs in there.

She sat facing him. 'Mrs Dane has died.' The words hit him like giant stones. 'As you know, she was seriously weakened by her previous injuries.' The face in front of him seemed frozen. 'She wasn't strong enough.'

He needed time to make sense of it and dropped his head into his hands. 'I should have been here with her.' He raised his head. 'Did you know she was dying?'

There was a silence.

'*Did you know?*'

'The doctors had been concerned.'

'And you made me leave her.' It was a fact. Harry stared at the staff nurse and vented an icy rage. 'Don't you understand that no one should die alone?' She reared back in her seat. 'They should go loved and held and… my wife… was alone.'

She got to her feet. 'I'll ask one of the nurses to bring you a cup of tea. We find it helps.'

There was no denting the implacability of the staff nurse, who had to face similar situations five times? ten times? a day. How else would she survive?

As he drank the tea, the iciness dissolved, submerged under his now white-hot shock and misery. Death, he had told Faith… when they had been together, alive and happy… death was something he considered most days. Who in his position did not?

'Harry, darling, you're not to,' she said. 'Keep it at a distance. Like I will. Must do.'

Up till now, he had regarded the prospect with distaste and impatience. For Faith's sake, death was not for him.

Now, he wasn't sure.

They took him in to see Faith, washed and prepared for the obsequies. He bent over and kissed her for a final time.

The war had beaten them both. Bigger, harder and crueller.

'I'll take you to Woodspring as I promised you,' he told her. 'There's a place by the wall under an oak tree. You'll like it there.'

There was a lot of administration to be seen to and questions to be answered. When it transpired Harry was not her husband or next of kin there was a song and dance about releasing her body which, while the bombs fell, continued into the night. But a new batch of wounded were arriving, the staff and administration were preoccupied, and he was given permission to arrange transport and burial. He was also given Faith's death certificate.

On the way back to the flat, he convinced himself that Faith was not dead. Could not be dead. She was still with him. He could hear her pace beside him down the street. Feel her breath on his cheek. Hear her voice in his ear.

*Harry.*

NELL

1975

# CHAPTER TEN

Nell Dane had no idea that she would inherit Woodspring.

Constructed as she wished, with no ties to clutter it, her life was smooth and orchestrated. 'Nell?' her mother, Lucy, tended to answer those who questioned her about her daughter. 'Nell? She's a bird who likes to fly alone. A professional woman. Done very well. Works for the Red Cross in Geneva. Went to university there too. Has a beautiful flat with a view of the lake.' A pause usually followed. 'Of course, her stepfather would love to have her here in Baton Rouge in his firm.'

Lucy's description was fine. Just fine. Nell could live with it, even if sharper listeners could pick out that Lucy disapproved. She understood why her mother wanted her grounded back in the States and employed in her stepfather's petrochemical business.

'You could make serious money,' said Lucy. 'Take it from your stepfather.'

Having made his first fortune in mail order, Nell's stepfather had moved on to richer pickings. Naturally, her mother had had no objection.

'America was good to us,' said her mother. 'It took us in when your father sent us away. So very convenient for him.'

'It wasn't convenience. It was the war,' said Nell. 'He wanted us safe. You were happy to go and I didn't have any say in the matter.'

'If you say so,' said Lucy.

No petrochemicals and exorbitant salary for Nell.

No.

*No.*

Early on, Nell decided that her work must be with displaced and traumatised people. It was an obligation. Her *moral* obligation. Given that she wasn't easy company, and a lone wolf by nature, the question was how she was going to bring these objectives into play. After leaving the University of Geneva, where she had chosen to study rather than in the US, Nell solved these considerations, rather brilliantly she thought, by working for the Red Cross in the Geneva office.

'Being solitary, or thinking you are, can be the emotional refuge of a child from a broken home,' said Thelma, Nell's then therapist in Geneva. 'Given your father neglected you.' Thelma was American, studying behavioural therapy in Europe, and happy to sharpen her professional claws on Nell.

Having a therapist was still wild… even in the States. Socially dangerous. *The stigma, you know.* The growing schools of gestalt therapy, family therapy, group therapy jostled for attention, claiming to be mainstream… Nell didn't want any of those. She just wanted to talk out her feelings.

'My father didn't exactly neglect me…'

'Would you prefer to say he was absent from your childhood? How old were you when he died?'

'Eleven or so.'

'Why do you think you decided not to accept your stepfather's offer?' asked Thelma at another session.

'My stepfather is ruthless, the business doesn't care how it treats the environment or people. And…'

'*And?*'

'That's it.'

'I don't think so,' said Thelma.

Nell encountered Thelma's professional gaze, didn't like what she inferred from it and signed off the sessions. However, if Thelma had ranged around Nell's mind with a scraper which was, at times, excruciating, she had learnt one thing from the process.

*Know thyself.*

Yes, fun could be poked, or criticism levelled, at the way she salved a social conscience and would defend it robustly. Yes, Nell took the point that it was no hardship to work in a regulated office with congenial colleagues and a machine that dispensed proper coffee.

No… no. It wasn't like dealing with the nightmarish and traumatising realities of working in the field.

What was the alternative, she would reply. Sweetly and calmly. To do nothing?

That voice was often the most insistent, the most determined of questioners. *What could she do – this solitary child who had grown into a solitary woman? And how, being solitary, would she do it?*

The answer was to organise, coordinate and strategise from the desk. She liked the comfort of her desk, and the figures and text on which she could focus and forget her context and from where she came. *Chacun à son... well, whatever you were.*

She had obeyed Thelma's injunction.

She strove to know herself.

Currently, she was creating a memorandum of understanding between the Red Cross and outside agencies. Tough and complicated work, it siphoned up her expertise and patience and required minute attention to detail. Dry, dry stuff. Yet, on its provisions, wrangled out of many meetings, rested the broken lives of the dispossessed... the cries and sorrows arising from wars and famines and the crimes of dictators.

In the evenings, she returned to her flat with its picture-book plate-glass windows, ate dinner overlooking the view and slept the sleep of one who had successfully corralled inconvenient emotions with the routines of an ordered life and did not wish to change any one part of her careful construct.

Thus, when the call from the solicitor, a Mr Fraser Allen, came through to the house in Baton Rouge, Louisiana, where she was visiting her mother – and avoiding her stepfather – to inform Nell that she was now Woodspring's owner, she was curt to the point of rudeness.

Fraser Allen would have needed to have possessed the hide of an ancient rhinoceros not to have clocked the message that the information he was relaying to his new client was unwelcome.

'Mr Allen, explain to me. My father died in 1950. It's now 1975. Who's been living there?'

'Your Uncle Robert.'

'Uncle Robert? I knew I had an uncle somewhere, but I didn't know anything about him.'

Mr Allen was as taken aback as she was. 'He was your father's younger brother. Like your father, he suffered in the war and kept himself to himself. He died a few weeks ago. Your father did not wish for you to be burdened by the house until you were older. He instructed my father, who was handling his affairs at the time, that he wanted you to be free for as long as possible. An agreement was reached that your Uncle Robert would occupy it until you had turned forty. He assumed that your uncle would live until that date.'

'How… perverse not to tell me.'

At his end of the transatlantic call, Fraser Allen clicked his tongue. 'It was done for the best reasons, Miss Dane. Woodspring is quite a responsibility.'

Nell sought out her mother who had retreated to her bedroom. 'Why have you never told me that I would inherit? Why did you never say there was a house? And why didn't you tell me more about Uncle Robert?'

Lucy's recent facelift had been painful, recovery was stop-go, and she was irritable because she was terrified it hadn't worked.

'Good Lord, Woodspring. I had almost forgotten about it. When we were married, your father wanted me to live there. I never liked it.'

'But not to tell me anything about it.'

'I didn't know what your father was planning.' She shrugged. 'No need to look like that, Nell. Why would I say anything? There was plenty for you here.'

Because of the stitches her face moved in a disconcerting manner.

'And the mystery uncle?'

'I know as little as you.' Lucy was dismissive. 'But he wasn't right in the head. Went doolally. Nobody wanted to talk about it.'

*The stigma, you know.*

'And you never gave me any sort of heads-up?' She paused. To be scrupulously fair, she had never thought much about her shadowy family history.

'I didn't think it was that important.'

At this stage of the healing process it was difficult for any emotion to register on Lucy's features and Nell couldn't work out what was passing through her mother's mind.

'At least, I could have visited my uncle.'

The stitches did, it transpired, permit Lucy to move her head fractionally. 'Told you, he wasn't right in the head,' she said.

'But not even to warn me that I might inherit.'

Lucy said through stiff lips, 'I imagined a cousin or somebody might have got it. Or it might have been sold. I hated the place.'

'You deliberately kept quiet. You thought if you said nothing it would all go away.'

'Well, it did.'

Nell perched on a pink bedroom chair and tallied up the many bottles on the dressing table, which was decorated with swags and bows in matching pink. Thelma had suggested that the dislike Nell so often felt for her mother should be acknowledged and then she must move on. Lucy was Lucy and that was that.

OK, Thelma.

'I'm off back to Geneva,' she said. 'I could take a trip to the UK and go and see it. Perhaps sell it.'

'So you're still persisting with this… career?'

'In case you hadn't noticed, it's my chosen work.'

'Your stepfather won't hold open the job in the firm for ever.'

As always, at the mention of Benedict, a shadow fell over Nell.

'I'm not going to work in his firm.'

Lucy took up a sparring position at her side of the ring.

'You ought to get married.'

'I don't wish to marry.'

'But you must want children. You're reaching the dangerous age.'

Nell raised an eyebrow. 'I don't want children.'

'How can you be so… hard?'

Nell bit her lip. 'If you saw the things that we deal with at work, you would have reservations about bringing children into the world.'

What she could have said was: *In my experience, families don't work that well.*

Which she also should have discussed with Thelma, but it was a painful area.

'You don't *see* things. You're stuck behind a desk all the time.' Lucy turned away. 'How did I produce such an… unnatural… daughter?'

She was posturing. And a touch hypocritical, for someone who had made a point of having no further children after Nell. ('Too exhausting and ageing, darling.')

'Nell…?'

'Don't pretend, Mother.'

Nell retreated, leaving Lucy to dab at her weeping scars.

She called Fraser Allen and informed him she had complicated work commitments, but that she would fly over from Geneva at the first opportunity. She also asked how easy it would it be to sell the house. Mr Allen did not reply directly but said he would work around her schedule, adding she would need stout shoes to walk over the land.

'It's that big?' Nell was startled. 'What are the running costs?'

'Substantial, I'm afraid, but your late father set up a fund to help with them.'

*Woodspring.*

Nell recollected a photograph of the house sent over by her father which she had kept in her treasure box before both were lost in the move to Baton Rouge. A Regency building with a bow window and a front lawn stretching across to a wood in the distance. As with many things at that time, it hadn't meant much. Or anything.

She had seen her father once, only once, in New York. The year before he died. She had been ten and thrilled to the bottom of her little soul. This was the stuff of the stories she loved. A grand reunion, instant happiness and – secretly, secretly hoping – a joyous future as father and daughter.

There had been a grand fuss with all the arrangements. Where to stay? How to get there? Her father was seriously enfeebled from war wounds, said Lucy, and required full-time medical care. Was there a doctor? Which hotel? Could her stepfather arrange transport from the docks?

Her father was nothing like her imaginings. He was gaunt, had trouble eating and couldn't walk far. He asked stupid questions such as, 'Did she enjoy school?' and it was clear he knew nothing about her life in Baton Rouge.

Towards the end of the visit, he said: 'I'm sorry we don't know each other very well.'

He had given her a doll which sat on her lap. It had eyes of startling blue and a frilly dress. While he talked, she kept her gaze focussed on it. 'It's my fault, Nell. I hope you will forgive me.' He added. 'Events weren't in our favour.'

Looking back, Nell realised he had done his best, but he was in pain, fatigued from being in an unfamiliar setting and unused to children.

Nell confessed to Thelma, 'I ought to have loved him. I ought to have missed him.'

'That's a lot of "oughts",' said Thelma.

Nell associated those stiff and repressive 'oughts' with the idea of having children. Which was way, way different from the gloriously committed, rueful, yearning, unfathomable (to her) responses that the friends who had taken the plunge had to parenthood.

Lucy rarely mentioned her ex-husband except to say he had cut a dashing figure in uniform and played the piano. Now, on the eve of her departure back to Geneva, Nell pressed her one more time for details.

Lucy looked up from the article she was reading in the *Reader's Digest*. 'You know the main stuff. He was something of a war hero. Did something secret, I never quite knew what. But very Boy's Own. Wounded in Normandy after the invasion and retired to Woodspring. He never married again.

Odd, that, because he was good-looking and Woodspring is supposedly very desirable. He was ailing, of course. Maybe nobody wished to take him on.'

'Don't you find it strange?'

'What?'

'You were married to my father. You must have known most things about him once. Then you didn't. Isn't that peculiar?'

Lucy used her finger to mark her place. 'Not *so* strange,' she said. 'Best to shut it off. You can't be doing with guilt. Or feeling that you might be punished. You know… what's it called? Nemesis.'

Nell laughed. 'What *are* you talking about?'

'What the Greeks went on about. I saw an article about it.'

In late May, after returning to Geneva and arranging a four-month leave of absence from her job, Nell arrived in London, took the train to Hungerford and then a taxi.

From the back seat, Nell observed an English landscape and pulled the belt of her trench coat tighter. The heat and humidity in Baton Rouge would be building. In Geneva the summer was dancing in, fresh and exhilarating. Here, apparently, it was chill and gloom.

Ahead were problems and decisions.

'You'll need to be back here smartish,' said Gabriel, her boss. 'We're not a charity.'

'Yes, we are,' said Nell. 'That's precisely what we are. But I take your point.'

Ingratitude was a waste of time. Yet and yet, her father had strung this stone around her neck.

The taxi stopped to allow a tractor to cross the road. The temptation to scamper back to what George, her ex-lover, dubbed her 'solipsistic existence' was overwhelming. 'You mean – ' she had deflected the accusation – 'that the self is all that can be known to exist. And that is true.' George said that she knew exactly what he meant and she could call it what she liked but it didn't alter the facts, To counter the memory, she wound down the window and inhaled damp air.

Woodspring lay five or so miles north of Hungerford in the village of Yew Green. The taxi drove down the main street, passed the church shaded appropriately by yews, turned right and headed up a drive flanked by fields.

Fraser Allen, the solicitor, waited to greet her on the front steps. Medium height. A reliable-looking face. Well-worn suit. She liked him on sight.

'Welcome,' he said and helped her out of the taxi. 'Welcome to Woodspring.'

She looked around. What she saw was strange but not unpleasant. The trees in the drive were dressed in newborn green but, as she has been warned by colleagues, no sun shone in benighted Albion. Lichen had written hieroglyphics over a grey-stone wall. Weeds poked through the gravel and the paintwork on the windows needed attention.

The front door was open.

'If I'm honest, Mr Allen, I haven't absorbed the idea of Woodspring yet.' She gestured around. 'Does all this land belong to the house too?'

'I'm afraid so.' Mr Allen ushered Nell through the entrance. 'Not that I'm in a position to know – ' he was very dry – 'but I imagine being told you've inherited a substantial property which you had no idea about does shake one up. Your father knew he wouldn't make old bones and thought carefully about his arrangements. He didn't know your uncle would deteriorate over the years, nor that his unexpected death would alter the timetable.'

She shivered. In this place, her father's place, she felt she had taken a step towards him. And yet, not.

They progressed into a hall.

She took in the details. Flagged floor, a fireplace, a couple of chairs, black-and-white hunting prints. It smelt unlived-in – and despairing. 'Would my uncle have appreciated being evicted by forty-year-old me?'

Fraser Allen said, 'The terms of your father's will were explained to your uncle many times and, it was felt, he agreed to them. Although we couldn't be sure. According to my father, Major Dane felt that his generation had had their youth stolen by the war. He didn't wish that for you.'

'I had no idea,' she murmured, shocked by the sadness which lay behind the planning. 'I know next to nothing about him.'

Fraser Allen glanced at the file he was carrying. 'I inherited your family's interests from my father. I do remember my father telling me that Major Dane regretted that you and he did not have more contact.'

'Then he should have done something about it.' Nell was tart. She paused. 'Sorry, shouldn't have said that.'

Fraser Allen was decidedly cool. 'Your father had to battle with extreme ill health and you were still very young.'

He suggested Nell inspect the house and she followed him down the passage to the drawing room which had the bow window she thought she remembered from the photograph and a fireplace with a marble surround. A small study leading off it had a bowl of lavender on the shelf. The dining room had a dinner service displayed on a walnut sideboard. The curtains and upholstery on the sofas and chairs were modern, colourful and looked expensive. And newish. Evidently, Uncle Robert had not held himself back from the endowment fund.

'If my uncle was impaired who took charge of the house?'

'I did. My wife, Ada, kept an eye on the curtains and furnishings.'

'How did the house function… meals and laundry…?'

'The Frys. Pamela and Tommy. They were employed by your uncle. She runs the house, he organises the upkeep of the grounds. They live in the stable block.' He paused. 'I know they're hoping you will keep them on.' Another pause. 'When we knew you were coming, Mrs Fry set to work to ready the house for your arrival.'

Nell judged Woodspring was approximately the same size as the house in Baton Rouge where Lucy employed (or to be more precise, bullied) a cook, a maid and a gardener.

'I'm thinking of selling Woodspring,' said Nell.

He raised an eyebrow. 'Yes, you have indicated this might be an option.'

'My life's not here.'

'No,' he agreed. 'Why don't I show you the bedrooms?' As they went upstairs, he said, 'I always think it's an advantage that the family never added on to the original house. It means it isn't so large and the original architecture is preserved. Easier to look after.'

'Mr Allen, are you trying to influence me?'

'How could I possibly do that, Miss Dane?'

There were several bedrooms on the first floor. Generously proportioned and, such was the positioning of the house, light and airy. The nursery floor above had smaller rooms and barred windows.

She imagined her father and uncle looking out of them.

'Some of the windows need repair.' Mr Allen poked at a sill. 'I didn't like to authorise it until you arrived.'

'But I'll be selling,' said Nell.

A fleck of paint fell to the floor.

'Of course,' said Mr Allen.

They went back down the stairs. At the foot stood a woman in a sensible pleated skirt and beige cardigan.

'This is Mrs Fry,' said Mr Allen.

Nell held out her hand. 'I gather from Mr Allen that you're the guardian angel here.'

Mrs Fry's demeanour suggested that she was far, far more than that. 'That's very kind.' She pointed down the corridor. 'I'll show you the kitchen.'

The kitchen was well appointed, with a sweep of marble surfaces, a butler's sink, taps with nozzles and a battery of saucepans and casseroles. A tray set with cups and saucers was positioned on the scrubbed table.

'Why don't we have tea here?' Nell had taken to the kitchen.

'I usually serve it in the drawing room,' said Mrs Fry.

'Ah,' said Nell. 'Of course.'

Drinking tea was oh-so normal. Thank God for that. Two days ago she had been at the headquarters in Geneva at work on a demanding memorandum. Today, she faced a solicitor across a tea tray laid by a housekeeper in a house of which she was now apparently the chatelaine.

Mr Allen positioned himself on the sofa. From which vantage point, he went through a list of practical details. Provision in the will. Building insurance. Contents insurance…

Her normally sharp, sceptical brain turned to mush, each item on the list seemingly exerting a force pressing her into service.

Mr Allen seemed to understand her confusion and made his goodbyes. He would return in the morning, he said, to show Nell over the grounds.

Nell carried the tray back to Mrs Fry in the kitchen.

'My husband and I are very sorry about your uncle.' Mrs Fry brushed imaginary crumbs off the table surface. Hers was a country burr, pleasant but cool and detached. 'But he didn't suffer any more than he usually did. It was all so quick.'

'More than he usually did?'

Real regret crept into her voice. 'Captain Robert was more or less a recluse. Like your father, his war wounds changed his life. He was shot in the shoulder and sustained a bad head injury which impaired him.'

'I never met him,' said Nell, conscious of her American inflection. 'Which I'm sorry about.' She was too. 'Did you know my father?'

'No.'

'You've been running Woodspring for some time. '

'Nearly twenty years.' The other woman nodded. 'It's a good house to work in. But it needs more people in it.'

A reproof that the Dane brothers had failed in their duty to people Woodspring? It was, Nell supposed, an old story. The sap in families ran dry. The energy dwindled, trickled and vanished.

Mrs Fry placed a piece of paper in front of Nell. 'The timetable for the day,' she said.

Nell glanced at it. 'Goodness.'

'It was necessary to have a timetable with Captain Robert. Supper is served at seven. Then I leave you in peace.'

There was obviously no negotiation to be had.

'Great,' said Nell, her American twang sounding extra, extra marked. 'But in future you don't need to stay to serve supper.'

The bedroom prepared for her overlooked the garden and had thick velvet curtains. Apparently, it had been her father's bedroom. The furnishings were simple. A bed, a chest, a chair. But everything was of good quality, as was the pearl-grey carpet and the single painting of a boating scene on a lake she recognised as Lake Geneva.

She contemplated it.

The water, the mountains, the colours… all familiar to Nell. What was unsettling was to find a reminder of them at Woodspring.

# CHAPTER ELEVEN

She slept well, awoke next morning and wondered where on earth she was.

In the kitchen, she discovered Mrs Fry had laid out toast and scrambled eggs. 'This is ridiculous,' she said. 'I can make my own breakfast.'

Mrs Fry placed the coffee pot on the table. 'It's how Captain Dane liked it to be,' she said. 'Let me know if you have different requirements.'

Nell said, 'Mrs Fry, I'm not sure how long I'll be here, and you mustn't worry about coming in early.'

'It's part of my routine.' The other woman sent Nell a look as much as to say, *Please don't undermine my job.*

*Fair enough*, thought Nell.

She smiled at Mrs Fry.

Mrs Fry's tight lips relaxed a trifle and it struck Nell that they were both women who now found themselves in a tricky position.

As promised, Fraser Allen turned up on the dot of eleven. 'I'm glad I warned you about stout shoes. It rained in the night.'

It was also chilly, and Nell was glad of her coat. 'Is it always this cold in May?'

He led her around the back of the house, bypassing the stable yard. 'There's thirty acres or so of land that comes with the house,' he said. 'Most of it lies beyond the small wood you can see over there.' He pointed to trees enclosed behind a dry-stone wall.

He led Nell over a field towards them. 'We're now in what's always been known as the South Field. The North Field abuts it up there.' He pointed to a hedgerow which marked the boundary.

Nell shaded her eyes and gazed dutifully.

'When your father and uncle were alive, the North Field was let to Bob Merchant, a local farmer, to graze his cattle. Apparently, your father had strong ideas about the health of the soil and had it planted up with wildflowers and legumes.'

'Wildflowers and what?'

'Legumes. They fix nitrogen into the soil which makes better grazing. I think that experiment was halted when your uncle was in charge.'

'Was my uncle very bad?'

'He got worse as the years went on and his grasp on land management slipped away. He did try but he grew increasingly unable to make decisions. Anyway, Bob Merchant's now sold up. Couldn't make a living.'

'It's ridiculous that I have all this.'

'Yes, it's an unequal world,' said Fraser Allen, with the wry note she was learning to recognise.

Fraser Allen probably ran up against those inequalities every day of the week – a reminder that it wasn't only Nell shuffling around the hard facts and hard decisions.

They returned to the house via a cobbled stable block. 'The

original stables,' said Mr Allen. 'The Frys occupy that part over there.' He gestured to a door which had a planted-up stone trough beside it and windows above the door with red curtains. 'I'll introduce Tommy.' He knocked on the door.

Tommy Fry was shorter than his wife and wore a tweed cloth cap which appeared welded to his skull. He explained that he maintained the garden and the outbuildings and would show Nell his plans for both.

He expounded at length. There were bits she understood. There were things she did not. Every so often, she caught Fraser Allen's eye.

'The Frys have their separate fiefdoms,' she observed to Fraser Allen as they returned to the house. 'I wonder if they ever fight over them.'

'I doubt it,' he replied. 'They're a good team and looked after your uncle very well.'

Again, she detected reproof. 'I didn't mean to imply anything untoward.'

'You should know that the Frys have been very loyal. They were tireless in making things easier for your uncle.'

*Oh Lord*, thought Nell. I'm handling things wrong.

She didn't like the idea that she – the professional negotiator – had been maladroit. It jangled.

Later, she and Mr Allen sat in the study overlooking the front garden and combed over the paperwork. Legal documents, bank accounts, schedules of upkeep and papers connected to the house reaching back to the 1800s.

Nell studied the current bank statements for the house. 'There are a lot of outgoings. Is the fund set up by my father sufficient, do you think?'

'Probably not,' replied Fraser Allen. 'Tricky.'

'Then the finances will have to be rethought,' she said. 'Whatever happens.'

The ensuing silence was broken by Fraser Allen. 'These are the contracts for the Frys' employment. After your uncle died, they were anxious about their position and asked to have them drawn up.' He passed a typed sheet over the desk to Nell. 'Naturally, we couldn't expedite it until you have signed it.'

'I can't sign until I've decided what is to happen,' she said, 'but of course they must stay here until I do.'

'There's a lot of information, Miss Dane,' he said. 'You'll want to take your time to go through it.'

'Call me Nell.'

He thawed a little. 'If you wish.'

He packed up his briefcase. 'I don't wish to presume but if you would like to meet my wife, Ada, she would gladly give you some advice about the area.'

The area? Ah, the area. Nell had not really focussed on where she was and where the house fitted in. The best she knew was that the nearest railway station was Hungerford.

'Can I buy a cup of coffee in the village?'

That amused Fraser Allen. 'No.'

'Then, how do I get to Hungerford? Are there taxi services?'

He had thought of that one. 'We must arrange for you to obtain a driving licence and then you can use your uncle's car. He didn't drive it but Jim from the village would chauffeur him around. It's in good condition.'

From thereon in, Nell knew she would be observed. Closely and no doubt with comment.

Fair enough. She had flown in from a foreign lair.

A stranger who wouldn't know how to fit in… she could hear the cut and thrust of the gossip. An outlier who would assess her inheritance with alien eyes and, quite possibly, dispose of it without a qualm.

It didn't take long to work out this was horse country. A smooth slope in the distance behind the house led up to a downland. At certain times of the day, horses and riders were silhouetted against the sky. She enjoyed picturing their glossy flanks, the rise and fall of the canter, the mud splatter and the moment they wheeled for home, knowing the nosebag awaited at their stables.

'Oh yes, the horses,' said Ada Allen. 'They keep the area going, but they're concentrated mostly up in the Lambourn area.'

She was dressed conventionally enough, but with her long blonde hair and very pale lipstick, Ada exuded subversion. They met by the canal in Hungerford and repaired to a window seat in the Currant Bun, overlooking the water. 'Red warning: it's not Fortnum's,' said Ada, intent on making it clear she was familiar with much smarter venues than a tea-shop in a country town.

She ordered tea and polenta cake which, she confided, had scandalised Hungerford with its foreignness. 'One of the waitresses is Italian and it caused an awful fuss with some who said they didn't want that sort of thing here. But we've got used to it.' She pointed to the menu, which now proclaimed in a bold duo-language approach, *Italian patisserie.*

If Fraser Allen fondly imagined that his wife would be a source of advice, he was wrong.

Ada said, 'Let's not talk about Woodspring. You don't want to know all that.'

'No?' said Nell.

'No,' said Ada, and launched into descriptions of dashes up to London to shop and attend matinees, managing to cloak them in a strong suggestion of the clandestine. Double the fun. 'It's what keeps me going. I live for my trips. They're the most thrilling part of my life.' She added, 'They're building a new venue for the National Theatre on the South Bank, you know. It'll be glorious.'

This was a woman whose emotional life was not located in Hungerford. 'Does Mr Allen... Fraser... ever go with you?'

'Fraser is a very nice husband...' Ada assumed the expression of someone who had found life a little disappointing but was marching bravely on. 'He and I are great friends and understand one another. Life here is... a bit... tedious unless one has something to look forward to. I often think I should throw myself into drugs and sex parties, but then I reckon they could be a bit tedious too.' She looked out to the canal and the barges anchored up by the bridge. 'Fraser is married to his work. I get my kicks from the theatre. It's a balance. If I can escape and have a wicked time in London, then I can put up with making scones for the elderly and helping at the church.' There was a long pause. 'As bargains go, it's not that bad.'

'I don't know much about life in England,' said Nell.

Ada ordered a second pot of tea. 'I don't expect you'll be staying long. I wouldn't. I mean, you have your work in Geneva.' Longing swept over her features. 'Sun. Snow. The lakes. Handbags and lovely food.' She added wistfully, 'The *men*!'

Nell laughed. 'The men are just like here, I expect.'

'Yes, but they're beautifully dressed.' Having settled the argument, Ada continued, 'I do feel for you. Uprooted and all that.'

'It's difficult to know what to do.' Nell dropped her guard.

Ada leant forward and said very seriously, 'Be warned, life here is dull. Unless you like horses. Or tramping about in the rain.'

Get to know Woodspring, Nell instructed herself. Dig into it. Find the past lying underneath. Find its future.

The initial impression of emptiness and abandonment having receded, Nell found herself responding to Woodspring's elegance and to what she intuited was the conviviality of its Regency origins.

It was not the sprawling pile of her imagination and, now she could see it for herself, not as expansive as the house in Baton Rouge. Better still, on inspection, it had been well maintained and was many coats of paint away from the groaning, decaying mansion of the gothic novel and her imagining.

Taking notes, she made several tours of the rooms. Drawing room: bow-windowed with alcoves. Study: book-lined. The landing: hung with hunting prints. The light, spacious downstairs rooms all had excellent bones. There were one or two antique pieces of furniture, period chinoiserie wallpaper, and a French clock. A jarring note was the umbrella stand in the hall which was a hollowed-out elephant's foot. That would go. Absolutely it would go.

The main bedrooms were spacious and, like the one she was occupying, had washbasins. Her uncle's room had a single bed stripped of its bedding and minimal furniture. On the bedside table was a tray with a dusty glass and medicine bottles.

She hovered. Could she catch something of him? Or just an intimation of suffering?

She backed out and closed the door.

Above the nursery floor a flight of stairs led to an attic. This appeared to span the width of the house and had a couple of skylights. Planks had been laid across the joists to make it safe to cross. Boxes were stacked at one end, a couple of old-fashioned steamer trunks among them.

It was very still. Silent. Cold.

She stepped cautiously over a scattering of mouse droppings and ducked the spiderwebs spun silkily between the rafters. Generations of rats, squirrels and mice must have made free with this shadowy place.

Might she discover traces here of the family of which she knew little? The scraps of minds and bodies which she could pull to the surface and examine. The broken toys, old clothes, trash and treasure. Embers from a past generation which could fan into life.

She halted.

'Good God,' she said aloud.

Underneath the second skylight, the floor had been swept clean and an extensive model railway colonised the floor space. An elaborate one, lovingly constructed. The track ran through textbook snow-capped mountains. Between pine trees, one of which had lost a branch. Past a lake painted an unnatural blue. A red-roofed village with a sharp-steepled church.

In the first moment of encounter, the fusion point between imagination and child's fantasy, she was transported back to Switzerland. Where she had been – was and would be – content and purposeful. She was breathing in astringent air. Pebbles shifted in the stream racing down the mountain. Pines trees dipped in truncated curtsies. The real railway line below glinted in the sun.

Its replica seemed to be in good order, if dusty. The rails were in good repair. The paint on the model station was relatively unweathered. The artificial trees fluffed out. An engine waited on the siding, carriages in the station and a brightly painted station master on the platform.

She crouched down beside it and stared at the mountains, water, trees until her vision funnelled down to a pinprick on which she focussed hard. It was a trick she had perfected in childhood. When she was eight… nine… ten? Mostly, when she needed to escape.

A child had loved this. Would have scurried down the highways and byways of make-believe. The child, she realised, that she had never been.

The old sadnesses welled. Ones she had anticipated and calculated that adulthood, and a good job, would send packing.

Abandoning the attic, she ran downstairs, grabbed her coat and scooped up the Woodspring deeds.

These were well-thumbed and splodged – so suggestive of past handling by bluff men with spatulate fingers who smoked and drank and swore great oaths to protect the territory drawn onto them.

Guided by their thumbprints, some heavy, one bloodstained, it took a good hour to tramp over the fields. In the short time she had been here, the temperature had risen a few degrees but rain still came and went, slicking her hair and skin with moisture.

Rabbits had scattered spoor. A blackbird sounded. She looked around to see if she could spot his perch. Blackbirds sang at the beginning of the nesting season, didn't they? Or did they? Her knowledge of natural history wasn't great.

The route back took her through the wood which could be seen from the house. Treading over the woodland floor – Tommy Fry had explained it was called 'the duff', which intrigued her – she noticed the leaf mould, the splintered twigs and the secret niches where fungi grew. No doubt in the tree canopy birds claimed sovereignty, yielding only when dark fell and bats took over.

A stone wall marked the perimeter of the wood which faced the house. A wrought-iron gate was set into it. Turning to shut it, she noticed an engraved stone tablet set into the wall, its inscription obscured by lichen. Hauling a tissue out of her pocket, she scrubbed at it.

*Faith* emerged. Then, *Yorke*. Faith Yorke? *1915–1941. Victim of the bombing.*

The dank, wet soil smell intensified.

She stared at it. The words and dates spelt out a past shedding of blood. It was that old paradox. Death nourished life, which demanded memories in order to live. So who was Faith and why was she here?

The rain lashed down and she ran back to the house. Mrs

Fry met her in the hallway. 'If you give me your wet things,' she said, 'I'll deal with them. I've left coffee in a thermos in the study.'

'Mrs Fry, you're a powerhouse.'

Her reward was the suggestion of a smile, and she padded on stockinged feet into the study and over to the window.

Her sense of unreality deepened. Here she was. The woman from Geneva, looking across the neglected formal garden to a wood with a curious memorial. Meanwhile, rain hissed on the panes.

*Faith Yorke?*

She padded back into the kitchen and tackled Mrs Fry who professed to be at a loss. 'Something to do with your father?'

Most lives remain hidden, or elements of them. That Nell knew to be true. Her father's life most of all.

If she was honest, she hid a lot of hers too.

'Shall I bring you more coffee?' asked Mrs Fry.

It was a ploy to evict her from the kitchen. Nell laughed. 'I'm going.'

Better to focus on the present. She returned to the study to wrangle with the questions to be asked and the decisions to be taken.

She reminded herself that she was good at dealing with the present. Practised at executive behaviour. A certain crispness was necessary, added to an ability to put down a marker without ducking and weaving.

Did she like this house, this very English place?

Would she, could she, take on its welfare with all the subsequent upheaval? Or not?

The walnut desk was handsome. So was the chair, which might have been her father's. The notion wasn't particularly comforting. Books roosted peacefully on a shelf. Those were probably her father's choices too. The room's arrangements disinterred his mindset – the reach of it – which she had never had the opportunity to explore.

She thought back to her teenage years and the conversations held with her mother which – Lucy had ensured – had been few and far between.

'Your father would have visited more often, or had you over, but he was ill,' said Lucy in response to the young Nell repeatedly asking why, *why*, her Daddy had never made the effort to see her. 'He made it to New York, remember?'

Lucy tended to clothe explanation in emollient terms. 'There was a war. Things were appalling and he was badly wounded. Took him a long time to get over it.' Her gaze drifted into the distance. 'What am I saying? His wounds killed him in the end.'

'If you didn't want him over here, or to see him, I could have gone to the UK on my own,' Nell pointed out when she was older.

'Don't be ridiculous. You were a child.'

Occasionally, the older Nell let fly. 'I hate him.'

Lucy never really minded if Harry was under attack. 'Nell, you must remember your father did what he thought right. He sent you over here with me for safety.'

'But you often say he couldn't wait to get rid of us.'

A child, and a teenager, are mostly incapable of being rational. That Nell now knew. What use are logic and common sense when dream worlds and piercing emotions dominate head and heart? Plus, a teenager is a hot hormonal muddle. *Her father had sent her and her mother away because he didn't want them.*

By the time Nell worked out that this was not true, Harry was dead.

# CHAPTER TWELVE

Making breakfast in the kitchen, Nell burnt the toast just as Mrs Fry arrived. She dropped it into the bin and threw open the window.

'I found a model railway in the attic…' said Nell, acknowledging the silent verdict on her cooking abilities. 'It's lovely. Did it belong to my uncle?'

Mrs Fry searched in the cupboard under the sink and held up a bottle of Air Wick. 'Yes. Captain Robert spent a lot of time up there with it. It soothed him and kept him happy for hours.'

Nell smiled. 'I sense you were fond of my uncle.'

'Captain Robert was a sweet man,' said Mrs Fry, sadness evident. 'What happened to him was so unfair.'

Nell spent the morning combing through the house's documents. She made lists. 'Money', 'Repairs', 'Outlay'.

She telephoned Fraser Allen. 'Sorry to be a pest.' At his end, Fraser Allen demurred at such an idea. 'A silly thing… but does the model railway in the attic belong to my uncle?'

'No idea. Is there a problem?'

'No.'

'Do you have any idea of how to find out who Faith Yorke was? There's a memorial to her at the entrance to the wood.'

'I'll get back to you on that.'

'Finally,' she turned brisk, 'we agree Woodspring is probably going to need more money to run and maintain it. Whoever is here. Does it have any rent coming in?'

'No.'

'So, could I get a mortgage?'

There was a long pause. 'As of this time, women are not allowed to hold mortgages.'

'How medieval.'

'Ah.' Fraser Allen sounded cautiously optimistic. 'We could work around the problem, perhaps.'

'Back to square one, then, and to think outside the box. Would the land beyond the wood be sellable? To a local farmer? Perhaps to build houses? I've been looking at some figures. I believe the UK has an acute housing shortage.'

'The UK's unemployment figures are also rising, which depresses the economy, and housebuilding might be on hold.' He was clearly a little shocked. 'But anything is possible.'

'We should explore that possibility.'

'I must advise you that if you are going to sell the house, it would be best to leave the estate intact. I must also warn you that it's listed.'

'Listed?'

'Grade ll. Which means the house must not be altered or demolished. Otherwise, you could be prosecuted.'

He rang back a couple of hours later. 'Faith Yorke was a friend of your father's…'

'Friend?'

'I wouldn't like to speculate, Miss Dane.'

'Nell, for goodness' sake.'

'I wouldn't like to speculate... er, Nell.'

His tone was that of a man who had been dragged by the seat of his pants into the second half of the twentieth century. 'She was killed during the Blitz and your father brought her ashes back here.'

'He must have loved her,' she said.

'He stipulated to your uncle that her memorial remain where it was and should be maintained and repaired as necessary.'

'So he did love her.'

'I can't comment.'

Out of the corner of her eye, Nell caught a movement. A ripple of leaves in the bushes flanking the front steps. A shape emerged.

A small boy. With damp, tousled hair, in a pair of trousers that were too big and a green sweater with patches that had seen better days. Wellington boots. He was angel-fair but with dark eyes. There was desolation there, she saw... no, sensed or understood... in a flash.

He looked towards the study. Irresolute, it seemed. A child's calculations churning through his mind?

He swivelled, headed towards the back of the house and vanished like... like, she supposed, fair angels must.

An unhappy child, and she had encountered some, she had been one, always drove a stake into Nell's heart. There it would inconveniently remain, refracting echoes of bewilderment, of grief, of frustration.

'Mr Allen… Fraser… do the Frys have children?'

'No.'

'There's a child here.'

'Possibly belongs to someone come to see Mrs Fry?'

'He didn't look as though he belongs to anyone.'

Fraser Allen almost lost patience. 'I'm sure there's an explanation.'

'Could it be the model railway?'

'Or he's on the scrounge from Mrs Fry.'

Nell attempted to return to her paperwork. Unusually for her, she couldn't reprise efficiently what she had already blocked out. Dilapidations here, boundaries there, income here, outgoings there. Her concentration having been stolen, she abandoned the papers. Feet clicking on the treads, she climbed the stairs to the attic.

Close to the top, she heard a scuffle. An animal? The attic door was open… and she knew that, on leaving it previously, she had closed it.

Stepping inside, she sensed that the air in the attic was charged differently.

'Hello,' she said. 'Is there anyone here?'

In the silence, she heard a faint indrawn breath. Fragile and tremulous.

'Who is it?'

She walked across the planks towards the model railway – and there he was. A small boy. Five years old? Younger? Surely not? Wearing a patched jumper, sitting cross-legged, clutching the Hornby engine.

He looked up at Nell with dark, haunted eyes which seemed to her to convey a great deal of sadness. Nell understood. She had experienced the same, lived it and eaten of its fruit.

She hunkered down beside him. 'It's OK, little one. Who are you?'

He was silent.

'What's your name?'

In asking the question, she had raised her hand. The effect was startling. He reared back. 'Don't hit me, miss.' The request issued from dry, sore-looking lips.

'Why would I do that?' She spotted a bruise on his arm. 'Did you fall down?'

He whispered, 'Mr Robert said I could come.'

'Where's your mum or dad?'

He shook his head. 'This is a big engine.'

She eased herself down beside him. 'Isn't it. Can I have a look?'

He thought about it before handing it over. 'He's called Thomas.'

'Thought he might be. Thomas the Tank Engine.' She held the engine carefully. 'Does Thomas belong to you?'

'He's my friend.'

The fair hair was tangled and in need of a wash. In fact, all of him needed a bath.

Time and energy had been spent by Nell working around complications in her life and work. Alarm bells now sounded: a small, unwashed, possibly badly treated little boy suggested just such a complication.

'What's your name?'

The question bothered him. 'Aunt Molly calls me Joey but Uncle Jim calls me a pest.'

‘I’ll call you Joey. It’s a nice name.’ She gave him back Thomas. ‘Are you hungry?’

Joey cradled Thomas as if his life depended on it. Perhaps it did?

‘Stay there,’ she said. ‘I’ll be back in a minute.’

Down in the kitchen, Mrs Fry was nowhere to be seen. Nell searched in the cupboard for the biscuit tin, poured out a glass of milk and took them upstairs.

Joey was sitting where she had left him, still cradling Thomas, but tear streaks now staining his cheeks.

‘Why are you sad, Joey?’ She handed him a biscuit.

‘Because Thomas is sad.’

‘Oh dear. I’m sorry about that.’ She handed Joey a second biscuit and the milk. They vanished within seconds. ‘Why is Thomas sad?’

‘No one likes Thomas.’

‘You like him.’

The little face cleared for a moment. ‘Yes.’

‘Do you often come up here to see Thomas?’

Joey nodded. ‘I like Thomas.’ He got to his feet. ‘I’m going now.’

Before Nell could stop him, he vanished. She heard him clattering down the stairs. Then, silence.

Into the silence slid a disorientation which she could not explain. Then she understood. She should not have taken Joey so literally. What he was telling her was that no one liked *him*.

*

Mrs Fry was scrubbing the kitchen table. She eyed up the tray with the milk-stained glass and the biscuit tin which Nell was returning to the kitchen.

'Mrs Fry, who is Joey?'

She frowned. 'Has he been in the house again? The little devil. He was told never to come back after your uncle died.'

'But who is he?'

Mrs Fry wasn't in a hurry to answer.

'Joey lives in the village. A lovely little boy.' She inspected the scrubbing brush. 'Molly Baker's nephew. His mother, Molly's sister, was killed when he was very small. And it's no point asking who the father is. Bess... the mother... always said she didn't know either.' She wiped down the patch she had scrubbed. 'Or wasn't telling.' Her voice sounded husky. 'We have our views, of course. But gossip can be harmful. After Bess died, Molly persuaded her husband to take Joey on.' She dropped the brush into the bucket. 'I don't think anyone's happy in that set-up.'

'Is he properly looked after? I wouldn't have thought his aunt would allow a boy of his age to roam around.'

'He's quite safe round here. It's not the big city. Everyone knows Joey. He isn't the first and he won't be the last to drift around the village.'

'Gave me a bit of a shock.'

'I'm sorry about that. It won't happen again.'

'I didn't mean that, Mrs Fry. I don't mind him in the house. I was concerned that he seems so... lost.'

'Your uncle took a shine to him. Right from the word go. Bess used to help with the Captain and she brought the baby with her. Because of his… experiences in the war, your uncle was quite childlike and they got on. The model railway belonged to your father originally, I think.' She picked up the glass. 'Would you like me to have a word with Molly? Stop him coming?'

*Not to fret over a child.* Yes.

*A small, sad boy clutching an engine.* No.

'No need, Mrs Fry.'

'If you would pardon me asking, Miss Dane…'

'Nell…'

This instruction for informality had to be absorbed and her name was pronounced awkwardly. 'Indulge me,' said Nell. 'It's an American thing. I'll call you Pamela.'

'If you'll pardon me asking, will you be coming to live at Woodspring?'

Nell glanced at her feet. She was wearing leather half-boots and immaculately tailored trousers. They exuded expense and Geneva and were laughably unsuitable for the mud and damp of Woodspring.

'Probably not,' she said. 'But Pamela, I'll make sure you and your husband are not out of a job.'

Late that evening, she rang her mother in Baton Rouge.

'How's the face?' It was always wise to kick off with the question her mother would consider the most important.

'I'll never trust that surgeon again,' Lucy replied in anguished tones.

'Jeez,' said Nell. 'What's gone wrong?'

There was a long pause. 'The local paper, you know, the *Baton Picayune,* ran a piece on me. They wanted to write up my charity work and my association with the Society for the Preservation of Historic Houses.' Another pause. 'The reporter wrote… she wrote that I looked as fresh and glowing as if I had been standing in a wind tunnel.'

'Ah.' Understanding dawned. The surgeon had overdone it.

'Everyone knew what that meant. It was rude. Cruel.'

'But are *you* happy with the results?' She could hear Lucy moving restlessly around and pictured her pacing the room with the receiver tucked into her shoulder.

'No use crying over spilt milk. At least I've lost the spare chin.'

Nell smiled. That was Lucy's genius – an unparalleled ability to ignore the uncomfortable.

It occurred to Lucy to ask after Nell. 'What's going on with you? When are you coming back? *Have* you thought about your stepfather's offer? He tells me it's your last chance. He won't put himself out again.'

'I won't be taking it up. I'll write and explain that I'm not interested in the job. Or the business. He knows that.'

'You were plenty interested in the comfortable childhood it gave you.' Lucy was sharp.

'Was I? Yes, I suppose I'm guilty of that.'

'Many would give their eyeteeth to have had your advantages. Think again, Nell. You'd have a good life.'

'Never,' she said.

'You're so rude about your stepfather who only has your welfare at heart.'

'Right,' said Nell. 'Right.'

'I don't like that tone,' said Lucy.

There was a scramble to get the conversation back on course.

Nell went first. 'Mother, I wanted to ask you something. Did you know a Faith Yorke?'

There was a silence.

'She died in the war and Father buried her at Woodspring. There's a memorial up to her by the wood.'

'The wood? Oh yes, the wood. I remember. Dimly.'

'Her name is on it. Killed in the Blitz.'

Lucy's sigh was prolonged. 'So he did find someone else. Your father never mentioned it.' There was a hint of rasp in her tone. 'I shouldn't be surprised.'

'If he brought her back here, he must have felt deeply.' Nell glanced at the papers on the desk in front of her. 'He didn't marry her, did he?'

'Not as far as I'm aware. But once I left it was difficult. Communications were terrible. Later, we were only in touch over practical matters. Schools. Things like that. Nothing much else. And not often.' There was a marked pause. 'He never said he'd bury me at Woodspring.'

'Mother, you're the one who wanted to marry someone else, plus you hated Woodspring. Anyway, you were tucked up in the US.'

'There are many ways of leaving,' snapped Lucy. 'Bear that in mind. He was a great romantic, always yearning after something or other. He never got over the war putting paid to his travels. He told me once, we were arguing, that I was the sort of woman who gave the Empire its tricky reputation and it was a good thing it would be gone one day.'

Nell repressed a giggle. Good on her father. Not for the first time since she had fledged from the angry teenager, she said, 'I wish I'd known him.'

Not for the first time, Lucy took this as criticism. 'You can be very critical… cruel…'

Thelma had described the loss/departure of a parent as a primal rejection. A child, she said, needs to work hard to get over it. An adult even more so.

You had to hand it to Thelma. She was fluent in psychodrama. The language she used to brilliant effect, plus she had a point.

Nell altered tack. Sort of. 'I'd have liked to have seen Woodspring when people were living in it. Not empty like now. It should have a family here. Children and comings and goings.'

Too late, Nell had squeezed a trigger and Lucy was off. She homed in on the well-worn catechism. 'Have you met anyone yet?'

It ran in a particular order and Nell knew it off pat.

*The biological clock is ticking.*

*You must marry a reliable man.*

*What happened to you and that nice George?*

This was rich. Lucy didn't hold with 'nice' – *nice does not the harvest bring in* being one of her sayings. Those who worked for her in the antebellum mansion were well acquainted with the colour of her flag. Lucy might be fair in her dealings, but she was not nice.

The call wound to a close in the customary manner, Lucy being desirous of more information about her daughter's love life, Nell withholding it.

'Will you ring your stepfather about your decision?'

'No. You tell him. He won't be surprised. As I said, I'll write a letter later.'

Lucy sighed. 'I never know what's with you two.'

Nell put down the phone. Shook off the unease. Shook off the thoughts of her stepfather.

But George?

They met on the plane to Geneva. He was *en train* to chat up the private clients for his bank. She was on her way to take up her job with the Red Cross. They drank gin, ate the free peanuts, and made a date to see each other in the city.

Why on earth did he need to chat up private clients, Nell wanted to know. Surely, she argued, they don't need their hands holding? They have money and you are making more of it for them. That should do.

George had the fair hair and the blue eyes of a marauding Viking. The blue intensified as he explained that private clients had big egos that required massaging. Otherwise they took themselves off elsewhere. Also, he said, private clients could lie about their circumstances, and it was as well to keep an eye on them.

'You mean if you take them out to an expensive restaurant you might spot they're criminals?'

He shrugged. 'Mock away.'

They enjoyed their affair. George came and went from London and they saw each other as much as possible. He was worldly and kind. He showered her with good things: gold chains, meals, a ski trip, all generously bestowed, and gave her comfort and fun.

During the time she was with him, she lived a strange, unreal existence. She felt exposed, stripped down to a person that she didn't recognise. George set her ablaze but, terrifyingly, she burnt out. She hated her burnt-outness. It left her vulnerable.

'I love you,' said George early in the affair. 'Madly.'

She didn't reply and, in doing so, opened a wound that festered, although she didn't realise it at the time.

'Have you thought about us?' he asked a few months later.

'I think about you a lot. You're a wonderful person.'

'No, about *us*.'

'Not really.'

Two years later, he said, 'Nell, I need to know where we are going. Are we going to get married? I would like to… and I need a steer.'

They were wrapped up together in the bed in her apartment. When she didn't answer, he got up out of bed and began to dress.

'You're leaving?' Nell was startled.

Fully dressed (in the style that favoured Europe rather than London, including a linen shirt that matched his eyes and very expensive shoes), he walked over to the bed. 'Enough…' He spoke in a precise manner which told Nell that he had been rehearsing this scene. 'I'm getting out. I love you and I want to marry you, but you don't.'

She pulled herself upright on the pillows. 'Can't we stay as we are? We have a good time. It works well.'

'You've no idea, have you?' George said in the same measured fashion.

'I've no idea what you're talking about, if that's what you mean.'

'That's it. You don't. You can't imagine what it's like to love someone and to not have it reciprocated.' He smiled grimly. 'It hurts.'

'I do love you.'

He touched her chin with a none-too gentle finger. 'Don't patronise. I used to think I could crack that strange heart of yours and all that was needed was patience.' He straightened up. 'Bad market play on my part.'

'Don't say that.'

'It's true.'

It was. Despite Thelma, Nell was still in the process of digging through the layers down to the sediment of her own nature. What she now knew was that the prospect of being close, cigarette-paper close, to someone panicked her.

Tears arrived, which made it worse.

He slung his sweater – cashmere, very expensive – over his shoulders. 'Nell?'

Why was she made like this? Was it that a component in her demanded to be sad? A need to be pulled apart by someone, fibre by fibre?

A tear trickled onto her chin and she wiped it away. Intrusively and inappropriately, it crossed her mind that the scene resembled a painting she was fond of in Geneva's national museum. A demanding man, a woman, an open door. The paint strokes indicating finality.

Her equilibrium, such as it was, performed a deep dive but she said nothing and did nothing. Even when she heard the door to the apartment slam shut.

She never heard from George again. Once she thought she glimpsed him at the airport and her heart was squeezed into a vice. Then she spotted that he was with another woman who resembled Nell a little. They were laughing.

# CHAPTER THIRTEEN

Who was Faith Yorke? So far, Nell had made no progress in answering the question.

She got in touch with Ada Allen and suggested lunch in Hungerford. Ada was keen but declared that restaurants in the area were dire and why didn't Nell come to Allen Towers (as she put it). 'Just soup and some fruit,' she said. 'Informal.'

She was greeted by Ada who was wearing flared trousers with platform shoes. 'Fraser says I have to be careful how I dress in town, but I thought you'd appreciate it... Do you like the shoes?' Nell was ushered into a dining room where dishes were spread in profusion over the sideboard and the napkins folded into swans.

'Prawn cocktail? Or melon?'

The melon was cut into cubes and threaded onto a stick. The prawn cocktail was presented in a wine glass. Prawns were arranged around the rim with a slice of lemon cut into a butterfly shape.

Touched that Ada had gone to so much trouble, Nell spooned up the prawn cocktail, gagged, and said how delicious it was.

'Mixing in the salad cream was a little tricky.' Ada inspected her portion. 'It's so hard to keep up,' she said. '*Good Housekeeping* is full of recipes from the Continent. But you try getting hold of olive oil. The only reliable shop is Boots who stock it for ear complaints. Of course, in London it's different.'

Nell thought with erotic longing of the garlic, the glossy sauces, the pastas and ragouts across the Channel, and felt so guilty for doing so that she accepted a large helping of sherry trifle.

'Are you settling in?' Ada poured out coffee from a silver pot into minute cups. 'It must be so different.'

'In a way. It's all been a bit of a shock. I didn't know until my uncle died that Woodspring would be mine.'

'Honestly?' Ada shot a sideways look at her guest. The solicitor's wife treading warily before voicing her opinion. Then, dropping her guard, 'I did think it all a bit odd. It was so sweet your father wanted you to be independent as long as possible. But a risk. Yes? You might have been settled elsewhere with a family and it would have been impossible for you to take on Woodspring.' She smiled cheerily. 'It's so lucky that you're unencumbered.' She backtracked. 'Sorry, sorry, did that sound rude? As if you were on the shelf. It's none of my business. About your private life, I mean. Do you… have you…' She picked an abandoned cherry out of the remnants of the trifle. 'I think I sloshed in too much sherry.' Then, somewhat unconvincingly, 'Oh well, best not to be too nosy.' She dabbed at her mouth with her napkin.

'You mean do I have a lover?' Nell was wry and, to her surprise, a touch rueful.

'Gosh…' Ada leapt to her feet. 'I didn't mean…'

Of course Ada would want to know if Nell had a lover, if Woodspring would have a custodian and if the house would survive in its present form. If it had been the other way around Nell would have speculated as fiercely.

'Are you asking if I'm staying or planning to sugar off to my old life?'

'Sorry.' Ada plumped back down onto her chair. 'Curiosity killed the cat and all that. Fraser says it will get me into trouble. *Has* got me into trouble, but I say what is life but to ask questions? You're not angry, I hope.'

'No.'

'Sex is such a fascinating subject but when I was growing up you were never allowed to mention it,' said Ada. 'Blank sheet. With unspeakable consequences if you erred.'

Nell surveyed the room. Ada's warmth and charm was written all over the ruffled pink curtains and the cluster of china cats on the mantelpiece. 'Ada, do you know who Faith Yorke was?'

'Ah…' Various expressions danced over Ada's face, chief among them unashamed delight at mining a subject that might contain gold. 'Well…' She stopped herself. 'You should ask Fraser. He's been digging around. I mean, going through the papers.' She shot a look at Nell. 'He'll give you the *official* version.'

'I rather wanted the unofficial one.'

'Oh, good.' Ada settled in. 'Have you ever seen Terence Rattigan's *The Deep Blue Sea*?'

Nell laughed. 'No. Should I have done?'

'Well,' said Ada, 'it's all about the illogicality of passion and the scandal it causes.' The pale-pink mouth morphed into the tragic. 'It's very sad. Very true.'

'And Faith Yorke? Was she my father's illogical passion?'

Ada looked embarrassed and checked herself. 'Lordy, lord… I hope I'm not overstepping the mark, and don't tell Fraser we had this conversation, but when did your parents divorce?'

'1942, I think. No. Yes, they must have done. My mother married my stepfather in the autumn of 1942. If you're worried about hurting my feelings, don't be.'

'Are you sure? After all, it's in the past. Long gone.' Ada didn't wait for the answer. 'Apparently your father met Faith when he was posted to Scotland and they fell in love. They were going to get married, I think. But Faith was killed in the Blitz. Your father was so devastated that he insisted on bringing her ashes back to Woodspring. You can read it in the files.'

Nell contemplated her empty coffee cup. Of course she knew that her parents had gone their separate ways, but the facts behind the facts of a long-ago happening had an extraordinary capacity to sting.

'He must have loved her very much.'

'Do you mind she's at Woodspring?'

She took her time to answer. 'I think I might.' Ada's pencilled eyebrows climbed upwards at this wanton rejection of a grand love, and Nell reconsidered. 'Perhaps I don't.'

Ada was relieved. 'I hope I haven't made you angry?'

'Heavens, no.'

'It must have been fun going to live in America. Hamburgers and sodas and all that. And your stepfather was running a big business. What was he like? Huge cigars and a gold watch-chain? Or a lean and hungry Robert Redford?'

Nell didn't answer.

*

She booked a meeting with Fraser Allen in his office.

'Ada warned me you might wish to see me.' Polite. Professional. A hint of steel. 'She was worried she had said too much.'

'That's very sweet of her.'

'Prudent, I'd say.' He smiled affectionately. 'She made me promise I wouldn't drive her out of the house as a loose-tongued woman.'

'Then you're honour bound.'

Nell sat with her hands clasped in her lap. 'Tell me about Faith Yorke. If you can.'

He pushed a file across the desk. 'After your phone call, I did a search in the office archive and found this. It had been put on the wrong shelf. I think it'll provide some answers. There is a death certificate for Faith Yorke, which is fortuitous. A great many records were lost during the war.'

Again, that sting of long-ago facts. 'It would have been odd if my father hadn't found someone else.'

'Clearly, your father was conscientious and arranged his affairs carefully. It's evident from his papers that his primary aim was to make sure you were provided for.'

'I wonder why my uncle never made contact?'

'Your uncle's mind deteriorated after your father's death. It was a slow process but inexorable. I don't think he knew who you were. By the end, he was a recluse. It was,' Fraser Allen permitted himself lawyerly regret, 'such a waste. People said that before the war he was… quite something… handsome, brave.'

'Pamela Fry said something similar.'

'He followed in your father's footsteps. His war record is impressive.'

'My poor grandmother,' said Nell. 'What sadness for her. What she must have gone through. Both sons badly wounded.'

Fraser Allen approved Nell's distress. 'Mrs Dane died in 1943. Mercifully, she never knew what happened to the Captain and the Major.'

They exchanged a look.

The war still remained on the horizon. Not yet out of sight.

He broke the silence. 'While you're here, there are things that need deciding. Are you willing to tackle them now?'

'Admin?'

'Shall we say essential matters.'

The business was dispatched. Nell, who was still getting used to her uncle's car, drove gingerly back to Woodspring, made a cup of tea and retired to the study.

The file handed over by Fraser Allen contained a stack of papers. Plus a black-and-white photograph and the death certificate.

*Faith Mary Yorke...*

Her death was recorded in June 1941.

A note in what she presumed was her father's handwriting stated she had been born in July 1915, the daughter of Ginevra and Paul.

Nell bent over the photograph.

It showed a couple in a room with a large window. She wore a floral dress which was too big for her. He was tall and appeared healthy and fit. His arm was slung around her shoulders, and they were looking at each other. The space between them seemed charged, irradiated with desire, their heartbeats matching. Together, they exuded a deep, contained happiness.

Generally, Nell never felt the need to step into other lives. Her own took sufficient energy to work it out. Gazing at Faith and her father who were both frozen into the past and yet seemingly alive, she would have given much to join them in the photograph.

To say, 'I'm your daughter. Tell me about what you shared with this woman. Teach me about desire and a raging heart that I may use the lessons in my life.'

How did you know that someone was right? How did you prepare the seedbed in which one could grow happiness? That elusive state. That white-hot experience?

She closed the file.

Grabbing her jacket, she headed for the wood. The plaque, of course, was still on the wall. Stark but eloquent. Acknowledging grief and finality but also, embodied in its terseness, the suggestion of an earthly Elysium.

There were questions that required answers.

What of her wish, her need, to return to her old life? The one she was trying to make better.

*To increase Red Cross influence on the European Commission's policy, legislation and practice so as to improve the humanitarian situation of the most vulnerable.*

George said… he said… that it was all very well, but Nell never actually got her hands dirty. It was all paperwork and looking out of the office window at a glorious view. *Have you sat in a grilling sun and dealt with a queue of desperate people?* Nell's defence was that, if an organisation was to function, someone had to be in the office. Clever planning and analysis were the key to successful aid.

This and that. And so on.

George would listen with that sceptical expression of his…

A cry came from the direction of the wood.

An animal?

Then a second cry, frightened and distressed.

Without hesitation, Nell ran towards it.

A few yards inside the trees, a small figure had collapsed beside the path.

Nell quickened her pace. 'I'm coming.'

A wan face, a mess of tears and dirt and tangled hair. It was Joey.

'Have you hurt yourself?' She knelt on the path, stones biting her knees, and took his hand. 'Let me look.'

Nose and eyes streaming, Joey flinched and reared back. A movement Nell recognised from previously, a reflex learnt from fear and distrust.

'Joey, I'm not going to hurt you.'

*I'm not going to hurt you.*

Familiar words etched in memory. The difference being that she meant them.

*I must punish you, Nell. It's for your own good.*

Joey was trembling. 'Did you fall?' He pointed to his leg. Nell rolled up his trousers to reveal a serious-looking bruise and a swollen ankle. No socks. 'OK,' she said. 'You're coming with me. I'm going to take you back to the house.'

He was resistant to being lifted and he wasn't as light as he looked but she managed to gather him up and held him against her chest. After that initial resistance, his head fell against her shoulder.

It was as if he had folded into her, was being absorbed into her blood and bone. *Help me.* Nell cradled his head and inhaled the smell of unwashed, untended child.

An unwanted one?

Her back and arms protesting, she was in danger of dropping him more than once and was forced to go carefully.

One step. Two steps.

This… this… was what it was to be burdened by a child. To stoop under the weight of a small body. To be at the mercy of the milky, clumsy, demanding and unreasonable. To be possessed by a spirit, by a life, that required finessing into sanity and wholeness.

Joey's breath was in her ear. He whimpered in distress and pain and the sounds grated like chalk being dragged down a blackboard.

'Joey, I'll make it better.'

Nell checked herself. Promises should never be made unless they were to be kept.

Yet, lumbering with Joey across the lawn and up the steps, she realised there was nothing so urgent, *so right*, as to comfort and heal a child.

Pamela met them in the hall. 'I saw you coming.' She peered at Nell's burden. 'Joey. I should have known.'

'He needs help,' said Nell.

They carried Joey upstairs to Nell's bedroom and laid him on her bed.

'Save us, he needs a bath.' Pamela wrinkled her nose. 'He's filthy.'

'He might have been there all night if I hadn't heard him,' said Nell.

Joey shivered and trembled. Nell sat down beside him. 'Let him be for the moment,' she said. 'But the doctor should take a look at him.' She looked up.

'I'll phone Dr King,' said Pamela.

Joey lay quiet as Nell stripped his scrawny body down to a ragged pair of underpants, revealing bruises and marks on his back, and wrapped a blanket around him. 'You're safe,' she told him. 'Safe.'

Joey's eyelids shuttered down. The urge to catch him up and hold him tight was so strong, so imperative, that Nell was forced to catch her breath.

She focussed on the swagged curtains at the window. Always, always, the first precept of working in her field was to deploy logic and never to be overcome by distress. *That* was what she was good at.

Dr King arrived a couple of hours later in a pale-green Ford Cortina. 'Not again,' he said, surveying the swaddled, drowsy Joey. 'What have you done this time?' He bent over him. 'You going to let me have a look, young man?'

Dr King didn't think Joey's ankle was broken but very badly sprained. He strapped it up and made him swallow a junior aspirin.

The bruising and scars?

'Those worry me,' said Dr King. 'He's often bruised. But he won't say anything if he's asked. Too frightened. Too young to understand.'

'He's getting beaten or injured at home?' Nell said, the bleakness of the thought catching her by the throat. 'Are you sure nobody knows who his father is? Who could help?'

Dr King and Pamela, who had come up with a glass of milk, exchanged a glance.

Dr King cleaned his glasses with his handkerchief. He ignored the last remark. 'It sometimes happens with unwanted children. Joey's mother died in an accident and her sister, Molly, bullied her husband into taking Joey on. It was not an auspicious situation.' He replaced his glasses. 'Joey isn't the only one. There are several children in the area who are badly treated.'

'Around here?' She should have known that even in a gently rolling, tamed setting there would be suffering.

'Even here. Nice village. Nice town five miles away. Schools and doctor's surgeries. Churches. All you could want.'

She wanted to back away from this problem and to leave it at that but Joey's wan little face on the pillow anchored her to the spot. 'What can we do?'

Dr King was packing up his bag. 'Keep an eye on him? Molly has a new baby and it's not easy.'

It was agreed Nell would keep Joey at Woodspring for a couple of days. Dr King would drive to Molly and Jim Baker's cottage, inform them of the situation and return with clean clothes.

Later, Dr King dropped in the clothes for Joey. 'Molly and Jim weren't pleased but when I mentioned the bruising, they went quiet. If you could look after Joey for a little, let him sleep and eat, it will help a lot.'

Nell and Pamela Fry went to work. They made up a bed in the room her uncle used to sleep in and ran a bath.

The bath was fought against – but necessary. Within seconds of lowering him in, the water was a murky grey. When the women lifted Joey out, he dragged himself into the bedroom and hid under the bed.

Nell went down on her knees. 'Joey,' she said, 'if you come out, you can have a piece of chocolate.'

'Big piece,' he said.

Pamela said, 'Don't be cheeky.'

Eventually Joey's wet, slippery, shivering little body eased out of hiding.

Nell wrapped him a towel and sat him on her knee.

How to soothe a child's fear? She cast back to the things which had helped her so long ago.

'Goodness,' she said, wrapping her arms around Joey. 'I have a parcel on my knee. I wonder who it's from? Where do parcels come from, Joey?' She felt him slump against her and relax. 'I think the postman might have brought him. Don't you?'

Mrs Fry came up with Joey's clothes, hot milk, a cheese sandwich and the chocolate. They dressed him in pyjamas, the crotch of which had a rough darn which must have rubbed his little thighs, and propped him up in the bed. Nell fed him the sandwich and made him drink the milk.

As white as the linen pillowcase he rested on, he slipped into sleep. Nell sat beside him.

'You think you know about suffering children,' George once flung at her, towards the end. 'But all you know about is lists.'

What do you do with a child? How does a child think? What does a child crave?

Asleep, Joey became beautiful. The bewildered features were chiselled into pure lines, the eyelashes feathered his cheeks, the newly washed hair fell back from an untouched forehead.

A curious response to the sight crept through Nell. A witch's brew of sadness and burning outrage for every bruise on Joey's flesh. A desire to defend him so intense that it took her breath away.

So intense and, yes, so piercing and sharp that it shocked her.

# CHAPTER FOURTEEN

Joey remained in bed for two days with not much improvement. He ate what was given to him and slept but never spoke unless pressed. And never smiled.

Pamela and Nell conferred. 'He's a very frightened little boy,' said Pamela. 'Shocking.'

They had met in the kitchen. Pamela was agitated enough to abandon her customary hovering and to sit down at the kitchen table, where she folded and refolded a dishcloth into a square. 'It's worrying what you don't see under your nose. No one says anything, of course.'

Could the bruising be the result of an accident? *Children had accidents.* Or was Joey ill? *Wasn't there some fearsome disease that made one bruise?*

At the idea, both women looked down at the tabletop.

The conversation went back and forth. Underlying it were the unspoken fears. Horrible things. Adults hurting a child. An aunt turning a blind eye?

'Jim Baker…' said Pamela. Reluctantly. 'I mustn't speak ill of the man, but it's known he's got a side to him.'

Nell knew about 'side'.

When she was still small her stepfather beat her, waiting

until no one was around, careful to make sure Nell wouldn't bruise.

It was his duty, he said. To cleanse her mind of bad thoughts.

She shivered. Pamela sent her a sharp look. 'Are you all right?'

'Just... just a memory,' Nell replied. 'I had... I have a stepfather who... but we must *do* something if Jim is maltreating Joey.' Her hand clenched. 'We must.'

Pamela glanced at her. 'Call Dr King again?' She got up, plugged in the kettle and made tea. 'I never had children. Maybe, maybe I've been blind where Joey's concerned, which makes me feel so bad. I was fond of Bess. It never occurred to me that he was being badly treated. *If* he is. For his last couple of years, your uncle and Joey were company for each other. Your uncle was so... so debilitated that he didn't have much of a life, but he loved the railway. I think he... loved Joey. Spent hours up there with him.'

'You're right,' said Nell. 'We should ring Dr King.'

For a second time, Dr King's green Ford Cortina was parked in the drive. 'We need to talk to Molly,' he told Nell. 'I'll drive you down there.'

On the way he outlined the situation. 'It's difficult for the Bakers at present. The baby's only a few weeks old. Molly's over forty and her arrival was a shock. They already have two boys. Plus Joey. It's a small cottage and space is tight.'

'How did Joey's mother die?'

'Bicycle accident. Joey was three. Bess used to take him up to the big house regularly. Bess told me that he got used to going up there and was no trouble while she worked.'

'You must have an idea about his father.'

Dr King concentrated on the road. 'Bess never said.'

Nell said, 'There can't be many things you don't know about, Dr King.'

He turned into Yew Green's main street. 'I'm a secular priest and this – ' he came to a halt by the church – 'is my parish.'

Molly and Jim Baker's cottage was close to the church.

'I'm sorry Joey's caused you so much trouble... We do our best with him,' said Molly, letting them in. 'He's a tricky one.'

The room into which she ushered Nell and Dr King was spartan but chaotic. Shoes were heaped in one corner. A nappy bucket made its presence felt in another.

'You'll have to excuse the mess,' said Molly. 'I haven't got a moment, what with the baby and everything.' Her pallor was marked and her eyes ringed with black. 'Can't keep on top of everything at the moment and I'm so tired I can't think. It's not like when I had Tom and Ollie.'

'Ollie is nine now, isn't he? And Tom is seven, if I remember right,' said Dr King. 'I trust they help you a bit.'

Dr King wished to know if the midwife had called. He and Molly discussed a visit to the surgery. Molly said she didn't have the time and Dr King said she had to make time.

A baby wailed above them.

Molly's head jerked up. 'I'll have to fetch our Daisy.' She returned with a furious baby wrapped in a shawl. 'If you don't mind, I'll have to feed her.'

Milky, snuffling baby. Engorged breast. A drained and exhausted mother. This was to be up close to maternity – and as close as Nell wished to be.

Dr King probed further. How did Joey get the bruises? How was he doing at school?

He went carefully and Nell admired how gently and skilfully the questions were slipped in.

The baby fed. Cried. Was patted. Fed again.

'Mrs Baker… Molly…' Nell went carefully. 'Would it be helpful if Joey was looked after for a few more days by Pamela and myself?'

Molly's relief was blindingly obvious – but she scrambled to cover it up. *She couldn't allow that. She was perfectly capable of looking after him, thank you very much. If the doctor was worried about Joey's bruises they could stop worrying. The bruises were perfectly normal. There was no need for anyone to interfere. Joey was needed at home.*

Nell glanced at Dr King who seemed to agree with her suggestion. 'I would be pleased to have Joey. He would keep me company. Perhaps he can tell me a bit about my uncle before I return to Switzerland. He can help me pack up the model railway.'

At Woodspring, Joey developed a temperature. Then Dr King said that, after all, he thought Joey's ankle should be X-rayed and he must stay off school. This entailed a full-scale expedition to the nearest hospital. Joey was inserted into the back of the car. Pamela clutched on to him and Nell drove them (nervously) with a road atlas beside her on the passenger seat.

Dr King was correct. A hairline fracture was revealed, and Joey was clapped into a plaster cast. His cries almost broke

Nell's heart. Back at the house, Pamela rustled up a boiled egg with bread-and-butter soldiers and with the promise that if he ate everything up he could have a jammie dodger.

Nell dipped a soldier into the egg and fed it to Joey. 'You've been a very brave boy.' She smiled at him.

He scrutinised the soldier before taking a bite. 'You're not cross with me?'

'No, no, Joey. Not cross at all.'

For the first time since she had met him there was a glimmer of a smile.

After he had eaten, she tucked him into bed. Leaning over it, she brushed his hair back from his forehead. 'How did you hurt your ankle, Joey?'

Joey seemed puzzled. 'I fell over,' he said.

'And why did you go to the wood?'

He sighed. A shuddery sound. 'Uncle Jim was cross with me. He shouted.'

'Did he hurt you, Joey?'

He moved his head from side to side.

'Joey?'

'Uncle Jim was cross.'

He whispered the words but that was all. He was exhausted and she knew to let him be. Nell reached over and cupped a hand around his cheek. 'It's all right, Joey. Go to sleep.'

His gaze caught hers, as if seeking permission. But for what? Then he sighed for the second time and closed his eyes.

By now, Pamela would have left for her quarters and silence encased the house. But it was not threatening. Or uneasy. Rather, it was the natural equilibrium at the end of a long day.

Dusk fell.

Hands in lap, she sat very still.

Joey muttered in his sleep.

As she watched him, the shade of the young, unhappy Nell materialised. The Nell who had searched for the one good thing in the day. Sun on her face. A biscuit. Solitude.

Then she had grown up and biscuits no longer did the trick.

George had given her a house plant. 'Something to think about when I'm not here.'

She hadn't wanted it, didn't like them in general and this one proved needy. It cried out for water, for pruning. Twice, a bud fattened on a stalk. She had watched its efforts to reach full bloom, a riff of petal, sepal and colour.

It died and George had been disappointed. 'You're not great at looking after things. You haven't the nurturing instinct.'

She thought about the wood and the fields belonging to Woodspring. If... if she planted up one of the fields with extra herbs and wildflowers as her father had done... it would be akin to putting down a taproot here. It would be to acknowledge there could be harmony in the coexistence of humans and nature in this place, and she wondered if that had been her father's thinking. Or had he merely wished to maximise the yields?

Joey cried out and Nell bent over him. 'Hush, Joey. Everything's fine.'

She looked up. Her life – white wine on the terrace, ragout and fondue, shaping coherence out of chaos and need – was far away.

Joey slept in for most of the following morning and Nell made a beeline for the study.

Repairs, bills, decisions.

There was no chance of settling down, however. Pamela stuck her nose round the door. 'Joey is trying to get up to the attic.'

Heart in mouth, Nell hightailed it up the stairs and caught Joey clinging to the rickety banister.

'What are you doing out of bed?'

She knew the answer. Joey wanted to see his friend.

At her approach, he shrank away.

'It's all right, Joey. I'm not cross.' Nell reached out her hand and captured his small one. 'But the stairs are tricky and I don't want you to fall.'

Joey's plaster cast clunked against the wooden treads. Nell held on tight to him as she helped him up to the attic and across to the railway.

The spring chill had given way to the upcoming summer and the attic was airless. Nell wrestled with the skylight above the railway and succeeded in prising it open an inch or two. A smell of moss and wet tile hit her. 'That's better.'

'Thomas…' Joey greeted the engine like the long-lost friend that he was. Nell helped him to sit down, and he was instantly absorbed by the railway's landscape.

'Mr Robert said Thomas always did what the Station Master asked.' His eyes sparked with appreciation of such goodness. Reaching over, he moved a pine tree beside the station buildings into a different position. 'Mr Robert said that tree should be there.'

Nell made herself comfortable beside him. A voice in her head muttered, *So, in for the long haul then.*

'Joey, tell me about Captain Robert. He was my uncle, but I never met him.'

'He liked Thomas and said Thomas had a friend called Gordon. He told me stories.'

Nell cast her mind back. Her childhood? Where were her stories? Of engines and giants and adventure. She had none. Lucy was not that sort of mother. Her stepfather was not that sort of stepfather.

His defences lowered, Joey engaged in conversational forays. 'Mr Robert said he dropped out of the sky and blew up a train.'

'Good Lord. When? Where?'

But that was as far as Joey could, or would, go on the practical details.

'Lots of noise,' he said.

She observed the fair head bent over the objects that gave him joy. Vulnerable and, she acknowledged with a twist of her heart, beautiful.

'What are you thinking about, Joey?'

The question seemed difficult for Joey to answer. 'Nothing,' he said. 'Nothing, miss.'

He seemed terrified that he would be punished for thoughts, and Nell was shocked. 'I'm thinking nothing, too,' she said.

'Am I going back, miss?'

He meant to Molly and Jim. 'Well, I wondered if you'd like to stay here for a little while. You can come up here and you can tell me about Captain, I mean, Mr Robert.'

Joey did not reply.

'Would you like to take Thomas back to bed with you?'

For the first time, Joey smiled properly.

It was late. Very late.

Nell was in the study, combing through papers in the recently recovered file. There were a couple of letters.

The first was written on rough lined paper which had been torn out of a notebook.

*Harry, my mind is like a bed today which I should be making for Mrs Turner. Frowsty and full of crumbs and the mattress needs a good shaking. I've been thinking so much about you. We don't know each other very well but, yet, we do. Isn't it odd?*

*But I needed to write to you, Harry. Providing I'm allowed, I shall drop it off at the big house.*

*Meeting you has made me conscious of, apart from the obvious things, that I should be doing something for my country. As soon as I am able, and that is not to wish Mrs Turner ill, I shall go down to London and see what I can do. Do I sound pompous? But I like the idea of being unselfish for once and it is all hands to the pump. Please don't tell me not to be silly. You are putting yourself in danger. Or will be.*

*Scrub that. I can't bear the thought of you being in danger…*

Written at the top of the page were the words, 'Her only letter'.

The second letter was headed, 'STC, The Big House, 10 July 1940'.

*I don't have much time to write this, darling, but I was determined that I would reply to yours. You will be busy with Mrs Turner and probably have as little time to read it. I am working out what equipment is needed to climb chalk cliffs. Confidential, by the way.*

*Your letter made me very happy and I want to tell you that since I've met you everything is different. Trees, rivers, food, making love. All is recast and fresh.*

*I've never felt this way before. If we survive and we are together, I hope we will have children. I struggle to explain how I feel about it but here goes. I haven't been a good father so far, deficient in all sorts of ways. But I think I know this much; to have a child is to understand what it is to live without artifice and it is to relive one's own life through theirs.*

The space had run out but there was no following page.

Written at the top in the same handwriting was, 'Never sent.'

Stapled to it was a typed-up page. *The flesh and blood of Faith might be dead which hurts the living who loved her… who knew her. We… I… must carry on. I don't know what happens after death. I don't think I care. But I have a duty to keep her alive in my mind. And she is there.*

Nell read and reread it. Harry was articulating his love: so big, so tumultuous, so life-changing. There was no doubt of what he felt and no doubt of his grief.

Fixing a spotlight on her father's emotions made her uneasy. Nell replaced the letters in the file and rested a hand on them before closing it.

*Dear Harry… Father… Be at peace.*

Before she went to bed, she crept into Joey's bedroom

and removed Thomas, who was clutched to his chest.

Next day, over a mid-morning glass of milk and several biscuits in the kitchen – a treat which was received in astonished silence – Nell endeavoured to find out a bit more about Robert. After some probing, Joey revealed that Mr Robert had a pain in his head and playing with the railway helped to make it go away.

Pamela hovered with a dishcloth. 'That's right,' she said. 'I sometimes took a sandwich up to him when he didn't want to come down for a meal.' She sounded troubled. 'I never understood what he was thinking. I should have done.'

Nell looked up from the biscuit tin. 'We never know what anyone is thinking.'

'I don't like to think your uncle was haunted.'

'Mr Robert said he blew up a railway but would never blow up this one. He said that I was to keep it safe.' Joey was eager to tell them of his role. 'Mr Robert said… He said that it was my railway. Mine.'

A satisfactory milk moustache was outlined on his top lip. Nell made to wipe it away. Joey flinched, which hurt Nell too. She leant over him.

'Listen, Joey, I'm not going to hurt you. I would never hurt you.' Joey's eyes flew to Nell's. *Is that true?* Nell nodded. Carefully, carefully, she wiped his mouth. 'There. You're now fit to guard the railway.'

For the second time, Joey smiled – with such sweetness that Nell almost cried.

Over his head, she encountered Pamela's gaze. In that second, Nell read speculation, questioning, apprehension before Pamela turned away.

Two days later, she drove Joey back to the Bakers'. She knocked on the door and Molly called out, 'Come in.'

She was feeding Daisy in a chair. Exhausted. Beaten-looking, with thinning hair and swollen ankles.

She greeted Joey with, 'Hello, you. I hope you're not going to cause any more trouble.'

There was no substance in the greeting. No kindness nor welcome. Nell was holding Joey's hand and it went rigid in hers.

He was old enough to understand that no one wanted him. Not even his aunt. *OK, Joey*, she thought. *I must try to make it different.*

'You're to thank Miss Dane for all she has done for you,' said Molly. She avoided Nell's gaze. Molly had her reasons to grudge any kindness given to Joey. Of course she did, and Nell was sympathetic. The Bakers did not want charity. Nor did Molly wish to have anyone probing into her family's history. *My stupid sister spreading her legs.*

Joey's breathing was audible.

'No such thing as hello, I suppose,' said Molly. 'Too much to ask for.'

A shudder went through Joey.

Nell bit her lip. Hard. So hard she nearly cried out. Her professional detachment in danger of dissolving, she said, 'Joey had a lot of bruises. Dr King wanted to talk to you about them.'

Finally, Molly looked at Nell. Her gaze narrowed. Neither woman liked what they saw. 'I'll have you know Joey's fine.'

'The bruises?'

She knew, she knew this was to overstep the mark. Propelled, though, by an intensity, a fear for Joey.

'Normal. Thank you for bringing him back.'

It was the order to leave.

'Say thank you, Joey.'

'Thank you,' Joey whispered.

'You must come and see Thomas,' Nell was shaken by the depth of her fear for Joey's future, 'if that's all right with your aunt.'

Molly winded Daisy. *Pat.* A sated, milky baby. *Pat, pat.* Done mechanically. Wearily. 'You mustn't worry yourself about us, Miss Dane, Joey has plenty of things here.'

'Call me Nell.'

Never had the invitation been so inept, the attempt to build a bridge so maladroit.

Molly pulled her jumper down over her chest and dabbed at the baby's face with a threadbare muslin. 'There's no need for Joey to bother you, Miss Dane. He's got plenty here.'

Nell understood.

Back in the car, she shook with anger that Joey might be denied his small, tender pleasure.

That night, she woke and was astonished to find that she was crying. The tears rolled over her cheeks and were blotted on the pillowcase.

Joey must be protected.

No, more than that. Loved.

# CHAPTER FIFTEEN

Ada was fascinated by Harry's romantic history.

They were in the Currant Bun enjoying what Ada called 'a necessary gossip'. Gossip is like a blood transfusion, she said. 'Life-giving.'

'And she was killed in the London bombings and he put up a memorial to her?'

'Yes.'

In the excitement, Ada abandoned her attack on the polenta cake. 'How *tragic*,' she said enviously. 'Truly so.' She paused. 'Do you think your mother minded?'

'I don't think she knew anything about it. Anyway, it was she who left my father so presumably she wouldn't have minded if she had known.'

'Ah,' said Ada. 'But feelings are never cut and shut. You think you've sorted out the best way, the adult way, to approach something lurking in the past, but,' her mouth turned a little tragic, 'feelings don't *behave*.'

Nell thought of George. 'Yes.'

Ada stabbed at the cake with a fork. 'I mean, if one had the choice whether to marry a kind and sensible man who would pay the bills or a wild broth of a boy who tore your heart out but was never quite sober, and you chose the former, it doesn't mean you don't think of the latter.'

'No,' said Nell.

'But wonderful to have a grand and doomed love affair.' Ada observed the grainy yellow heap on her plate. 'Which reminds me. I want to cast my net wider.' She lowered her voice. '*Hamlet* is on in Stratford. Not the main theatre but in a studio. I'm told it's a wicked production. Very surprising.' A pair of disingenuous eyes fixed on Nell. 'I don't suppose you'd like to come?'

'Why not?'

'An adventure,' said Ada.

'Yes, adventure,' echoed Nell.

Ada picked Nell up from Woodspring in a new car. 'A Chevette,' she said, wrestling with the gears. 'Only just launched. Fraser is very proud of getting in early on the waiting list. It's Britain's answer to the Fiat or the Renault but I say it's just another plonker.' She wrenched the gear stick. 'Fraser says if anything happens to it, he'll kill me. I say bring it on.'

Nell laughed.

To see this 'wicked' production required a night away. The drive took most of the morning and Nell spent much of it looking out of the window and acquainting herself with the country to which she belonged but of which she had no working knowledge.

The route took them through Swindon and up to Moreton-in-Marsh. Nell took over the map-reading, made unpredictable as the page in the atlas divided at a crucial juncture.

As they approached Stratford, Ada exuded excitement. 'I was reading up about Shakespeare. He knew everybody in the theatre. Jonson. Burbage. Fletcher. I imagine him having a great time with them all. Drinking and swaggering and writing.' She laughed. 'I know, I know, I sound mad. I'd better concentrate.'

Having negotiated the run into the town, she returned to her train of thought. 'Those friends must have loved him. Apparently, when he died they put together the First Folio and saved his work.' She plunged on. 'Do you know about Shakespeare in the States?'

'Of course,' said Nell. 'We weren't a backwater.'

Ada swung around a corner. 'Lordy, these streets are tricky. I didn't mean to be rude about America. But,' she propelled her husband's precious car down a testingly narrow street, 'you never know about other countries, do you? You're so madly busy living life in your own.'

Located off what Ada referred to as the 'historic spine' (once the main route from Stratford's centre to the parish church), their hotel was small and did not aspire to luxury. No matter, the bed looked fine and the sheets clean. Plus, thank the gods, the Chevette was safely parked.

They made for the High Street, the site of many of the Elizabethan buildings, and trawled up and down, with Ada pointing out features of interest. Nell enjoyed herself. Here she was. Shakespeare's heartbeat could be heard all over, the buildings were venerable *and* she didn't have to think about work and Woodspring.

'Look at *this*,' said Ada, planting herself before a lingerie shop whose window was occupied by a black satin nightdress.

But Nell's attention was fixed on the toy shop next door. Displayed on a pedestal in the window was a green train with brass wheels and GWR on its side. *Hornby Pannier engine*, read the label.

She pictured light stealing into a small face as she handed it over. She felt the surge of a child's joy at taking possession. It was witchery… and she couldn't explain it…

'We must go,' said Ada, presumably abandoning a vision of a passion-filled encounter in a black satin nightdress.

Her wistfulness struck Nell. 'Do you like being a wife?'

Ada frowned.

'I shouldn't have asked,' said Nell. 'My big mouth.'

'It's tricky,' said Ada eventually. 'There's such a strong notion of what a wife *is*.'

'Forgive me,' said Nell. 'Thelma, the therapist I used to see, advocated asking questions.'

'You had a *therapist*?' Ada was electrified.

'In Geneva.'

'Lordy. Never heard of anyone having one before.'

They continued down the street, leisurely and unhampered, a hugely impressed Ada chattering away.

'You know,' she said, 'being a wife is nice if you like the person who you married. I do like Fraser. He's sweet and kind. Bit old-fashioned, but tries to make me happy. But… but I can't help thinking that I was meant for bigger things. What exactly, I don't know.'

She halted and brought Nell to a stop. 'Before you ask. I don't want children and Fraser doesn't either.' She frowned. 'It just wouldn't be me.' She glanced at Nell. 'Am I a beast?'

'No… *no.*' On an impulse, she leant over and kissed Ada on the cheek. 'You're the new woman. Arranging your life as you wish. That's great.'

A converted tin shack, the Other Place was so small that the audience were almost on top of the actors. Nell and Ada were up close. Very close – and Nell loved it. As played by Ben Kingsley, Hamlet was a man having to make huge decisions in isolation from everyone else.

'Fascinating,' said Ada in the pub afterwards, drinking sherry. 'I liked the Japanese-y backdrop.' Her gaze slid from door to crowded, noisy bar. 'Keep an eye out. An actor might fancy a beer.'

Nell had ordered wine and was discovering this was a mistake. Good-quality burgundy it was not.

Ada raised an eyebrow. 'Is it filthy? Thought it would be. What did you think of the modern dress?'

They talked about the production and of Hamlet's treatment of Ophelia. 'So romantic,' said Ada. 'Going mad for the love of a man.'

'Is it?'

'Not in real life. Obviously. But it's allowable on stage. That's the point. And Shakespeare was writing at a time when women were chattels. I reckon she had more power going mad than retreating to a nunnery.'

'Why should she be either a nun or mad? Hamlet is cruel and a bully. You can argue that anger at his mother is the reason why he takes it out on Ophelia, but it's not wise or kind.'

Ada nipped in. 'But human nature.'

The noisy, smoky pub. The aromas of gin and beer. Here Nell was. Discussing Ophelia and her doomed love affair, and the intentions of the playwright. It was way, way away from the hurricanes and levees, the petrochemicals and Huey P. Long Bridge of Baton Rouge of her childhood.

'Ada, did you know your grandparents and where they came from?'

Ada shook her head. 'They were dead before I was born. Because they were dead, I wasn't interested.'

Nell thought back. The thing about being a child was you were only interested in the here and now. Past and future inserted themselves later.

'Have you fallen under the spell of the place yet?' Ada had finished her sherry and was eyeing the empty glass. 'You know how it goes. An old house, its ghosts, the fight to get it up and running.'

'Makes a good story. I'm not sure I've bought into it.'

'Sorry. Being nosy.' She shot Nell a look. 'You mustn't worry anything you say will get back to Fraser.'

They both knew that was only half true.

Conversation lapsed. After a bit, Ada returned to the subject of the First Folio which, she said, contained many sayings that we still use today.

'Like?' asked Nell.

'"The play's the thing".' Her eyes shone.

An actor, any actor, having failed to materialise, they cut their losses and took themselves back to the hotel.

As she lay in bed some of those phrases spooled through Nell's mind.

*Brave new world.*

*Sea-change.*

*Tomorrow, and tomorrow, and tomorrow.*

*

'What *do* you know about Uncle Robert?' she asked Lucy on the phone after returning to Woodspring.

'Robert…' As always, Lucy was reluctant to talk about the Danes. 'I've told you most of what I know. He was your grandmother's favourite. Not that your father minded. Handsome, a little wild. Always had a girl in tow.'

'I still can't work out why you never told me anything about the family.'

'No point,' said Lucy. 'You were here. Not there.'

'But didn't you owe it to me?'

'While you're busy being offended and righteous you might like to put yourself in my shoes. Divorce is painful. It's not just a signature on a piece of paper.'

Nell eyed Fraser Allen's file on the desk. 'Did you ever regret it?'

Lucy cleared her throat. 'More irritating questions, Nell. Why ever should I have done? Your stepfather is a good man and made good money.'

'Masses of money, actually,' said Nell.

'He would have done more for you if you hadn't insisted on going to Europe to university. I never knew why.'

Nell thought for a moment. 'If I said I wanted to escape.'

'You don't mean that.'

Nell did – and it was a letter from her father that made it happen, written before he died and forwarded on to her on her eighteenth birthday by Fraser Allen's predecessor.

*It's too early for you to be thinking of these things, Nell. But, for many reasons, I must, not least my health. When the time comes you should spend some of your education in Europe. I would urge Switzerland, a neutral country, where someone I loved once lived and found peace and beauty. I will fund this, not your stepfather. I have been an absent father but not an unloving one and I have thought of you often. Often.*

Reading it had quenched some of the indignation about her father. But not all.

Lucy had worked herself up. 'Your stepfather has been very generous to you, Nell. I'll thank you not to forget it.' There was a pause. 'I can't believe how ungrateful.'

The discretion that Nell maintained so scrupulously dissolved. The intensity, the fear for Joey had infected her. 'How well do you know your husband?'

'What kind of question is that?'

'He used to spy on me. Didn't you realise? Barging into the bedroom. Or the pool changing rooms. When I was little and you weren't around, he beat me. Very cleverly so it didn't leave a mark. But he did it. Punishment, he said, for being naughty. He said that you were too nice to bring me up properly.'

'You're making it up...' Lucy sounded almost hysterical. 'Making it up. How wicked of you.'

The phone went dead.

Nell stared at the desk, noting that her hands were trembling.

What had she done?

After all these years, it had been said. The bullying of a child had been dragged into the open. Never quite bad enough to damage her physically. But bad, bad, all the same.

Into the silence crept a scintilla of relief. The relief at the notion of a scummy pot scoured clean. A ditch drained of fetid water.

Later, Nell went up to the attic. There were a couple of boxes she thought might yield more information. She had had the forethought to bring up some cleaning cloths, rubbed away a coating of dead insects and dust, and opened the first one.

Inside was a photograph album. That was all.

From the second, she retrieved a compass, a map-case holster, what might be an ammunition pouch, and binoculars.

Back downstairs, Pamela snatched the cleaning cloths away from Nell ('I've just scrubbed the table'), and fetched a newspaper which she spread over it. She cast an eye over the objects Nell laid out. 'Probably Captain Robert's,' she said. 'His stuff from the war.'

'Such a waste.' Nell fiddled with the compass. It pointed south. South, where her life and work lay.

'Could have been worse,' said Pamela. 'Captain Robert was always calm… docile, perhaps. He had his routines and seemed content. He liked fish paste sandwiches for supper. He loved the model railway.'

Nell had an impression that Pamela was feeding her select information very carefully.

She was.

'He took a shine to Bess, as you know. A big relief. She soothed him. She knew how to manage him too when he seemed particularly lost. Awful, what happened to her.' Her voice dropped. 'Awful. Bess was a nice girl. No beauty, but had something special.'

'What happened?'

'She was bicycling into Hungerford and some fool in a car hit her. That was that. Terrible. Joey was so young.'

In those seconds, Nell was plunged into Joey's bewilderment, his sadness… and it was as if a nail was being driven into her hand.

'Poor Joey.'

'Are you all right?' asked Pamela.

'Never better.' Nell peered inside the map case. Astonishingly, a map still roosted inside.

Faded, blotched and creased, it was a detailed and well-used map of the west coast of Scotland and the islands of Rum, Eigg and Muck. The date '1940' and 'Home Office' were stamped in the margin.

Nell read out a list of unfamiliar places. Mallaig, Arisaig, Glenfinnan… names that had heft on the tongue. She unfolded the map to the full extent. In the top right-hand corner the word 'Inverailort' had been written in black ink.

She looked up at Pamela. 'That's my father's handwriting.'

'I think Captain Robert said that your father and he had trained in the Highlands. Now and then, he would let slip information and then forget he'd said anything. It was hard to make sense of it.' Pamela resumed her kitchen activities. Saucepans moved. The cutlery drawer shut. 'If you don't want these you could get rid of them. A jumble shop. Or, if…'

'If?'

Pamela began to say something and checked herself. 'Nothing. Just if you had children, they might like them.' She backtracked further. 'Or another member of the family.'

An uneasy silence. Finally, Nell said, 'I'm not likely to have children.'

She opened the photograph album. The spine was fragile and protested. Loosened from their moorings, a couple of photographs slid onto the table.

The first showed a statue of three massive bronze figures carrying rifles and dressed in cap comforters, webbing and boots, positioned in an empty landscape. An inscription on the base of the statue read, *United We Conquer*.

Pamela peered over her shoulder. 'I think that was something to do with your father as well as Captain Robert. I think I'm right in saying they both fought in the same outfit during the war. The Commandos.'

The second photograph was of two men on the terrace at Woodspring. The one closer to the camera obscured his face with a hand. 'That's your Uncle Robert,' said Pamela. Nell caught a hint of sadness. 'He never did like his photograph being taken. The other one, I think, is your father.'

The second man, lined and older-looking, was in a wheelchair. A gaunt figure in a tweed jacket who was familiar but not. He looked directly at the camera as if to say, *I wasn't always like this*. Between them was a table laid with a cloth, a silver tea service and cups and saucers. In the background a small figure – the gardener? – was bent over a flower bed.

The photograph was of damaged men. But there was more embedded into the scene. The substance of the setting – the silver, the tablecloth, the gardener, the formal tweed jacket – were so definitely from another era. Although she was not of that world, and would not wish to be, Nell would have given much to hear their voices, to touch her father's sleeve, to pour out the tea.

*

Pamela took the call in the hall and searched out Nell in the study. 'A Nigel Clifton for you. He says it's about the house.'

Nell was working through material that had been sent over from Geneva. 'Who is he?' She reached for the phone on the desk.

'Miss Dane,' said an unfamiliar voice.

It was a tone she knew from work. A touch entitled. Used to being listened to. Someone who knew they had money to hand which would be deployed to get their way.

'Miss Dane, this is Nigel Clifton here. I appreciate this is out of the blue and you must be busy.'

She said nothing.

'I head up the Perryfield building company, responsible for many new homes and renovations in the area. Our record for delivery is excellent and we are proud of the care we take to preserve the environment and to ensure the community supports us.'

He went on at some length.

Still Nell did not reply.

Silence often put someone off their stride.

Not Nigel Clifton.

'We have a mandate to convert a big house into a care home for the elderly and are on the lookout for suitable properties. If you were considering selling Woodspring...' Had Fraser Allen been talking? He ended by saying, 'I would be happy to put in an offer.'

Hackles up. Nell's intensely fierce reaction – protect Woodspring from the carpetbaggers – was unexpected.

'What makes you think Woodspring would be for sale?'

'Miss Dane, it's our business to know what's going on. The death of your uncle was a major local event.' Nigel Clifton knew a thing or two about flattery. 'And there's speculation about the fate of the house. You might not like it, and I suspect that you don't, but it's not unreasonable.'

'Not unreasonable, no,' she replied. 'But intrusive.'

There was a click on the line. Nell's lips twitched. Pamela had given in to the temptation to eavesdrop – uncharacteristically, Nell would bet – and was only now replacing the receiver of the phone in the hall.

The smooth delivery of information continued. 'House prices have risen 70 per cent since 1971, demand is high and supply limited.'

Nell supposed he knew what he was talking about.

'In my experience,' said Nigel Clifton, 'a telephone conversation is not the best way to put a case across. Would you be prepared to meet me?'

Nell shucked on her outdoor shoes and headed for the wood. It was a damp day and moisture from the previous night's rain was slicked over the stone wall, scattering diamond raindrops over the lichens and baby ferns.

She had taken to pausing in front of Faith's memorial. The woman whom her father had loved. A woman who wanted to serve her country.

The notion of fighting for your country seemed, in profound ways, old-fashioned. Wars were done and dusted. Other considerations fought for space in the national audit.

Making money – her stepfather knew how to do that with mail order and petrochemicals, and no doubt there were many like him over here. Development – Mr Clifton was on the case. Political – did the UK wish to stay in the Common Market? Aid – how much and how often should the richer nations give to the poorer?

Tied to a past where it had flourished and a present where it didn't, Woodspring sat uneasily among those national concerns.

# CHAPTER SIXTEEN

Nell was not going to allow Nigel Clifton anywhere near Woodspring. Instead, she agreed to a meeting at his office behind Marlborough's High Street.

She was ushered into a large office by a girl with glossy fair hair ('I'm Belle, by the way'), where Nigel Clifton was sitting behind a large modern desk, with nothing on it at all.

Smartly dressed, pleasant-featured, he rose to his feet. 'I've been looking forward to meeting you.' His handshake was neither too lengthy, nor too feeble. He indicated the sofa. 'Belle will get us some coffee.'

Belle clearly took this as an on-the-spot demotion, tossed back her waterfall of hair and disappeared. Mr Clifton turned his full attention onto Nell. 'You are very good to have come. I know it was against your better judgement.'

'It was,' she said.

His smile was attractive. 'But you felt there was something in what I said, and you had to give me a fair hearing?'

'Something like that.'

She had dressed carefully in a sleeveless shift dress, which she was regretting as the weather was cool.

They gave each other the once-over.

She didn't dislike what she saw but supposed they were antagonists.

Mr Clifton extracted coloured pamphlets from a drawer and spread them out in front of Nell. 'These are two of our previous developments around the town. We are proud of them.'

The colours were lurid. As for the houses? Row on row of them, with little space and minimal greenery. The kindest way to categorise them would be to say they were unimaginative.

'You don't approve?'

'I don't see any meaningful connection between your previous work and taking on a house such as Woodspring.'

Nigel was nothing if not a professional. It was also clear that he was protective of his projects.

'We have regulations, little land, not much money and a huge demand. I argue that we have done well in the circumstances. But…' His tone verged on the wistful. 'Woodspring is another matter. To work on such a beautiful house would be… a tonic.'

'You say you wish to develop it as a care home for the elderly.'

There was a slight hesitation. 'That's the intention.'

The door swung open, and Belle edged in sideways with a tray. She placed it between Nell and Mr Clifton and shot a speculative glance at Nell from under her lids. 'It's only instant,' she said sourly. Her exit was a triumph of flounce.

'Sorry about that,' said Mr Clifton. 'We must have run out of proper coffee.'

Nell left her cup half drunk. He glanced at it. 'I don't blame you,' he said, 'but if I don't drink mine Belle will think she has won.'

Nell raised an eyebrow. 'Is Belle not on board?'

'Oh yes, and very good she is too. But she baulks at making the tea or coffee.' He indicated the coffee pot, and poured himself a second cup. 'I know you were reluctant to come this morning so thank you for doing so.' He looked directly at Nell. 'You could make a lot of money.'

The latter statement could have been offensive, but Nigel Clifton uttered it with the almost charm of the realist: *It's a new commercial world. Are you part of the conversation?*

Being fluent in that language, her stepfather would understand Mr Clifton perfectly. He would recognise the logic and snatch at the chance. *Two seconds late is two seconds too late*, he said – frequently and tediously. Nell had done her best to ignore him.

There was a knock on the door. 'Come,' said Mr Clifton.

Except that they were younger, two identikit Nigel Cliftons, down to the copy-cat suits, filed into the room.

'This is Greg, our numbers man.' Mr Clifton indicated the curly-haired one with a marked jaw. 'And this is Dominic, who handles all matters legal. Ask them anything you wish.'

The three men formed a tribunal and loomed over Nell.

'How thoughtful,' she said, looking up at the serried rank. 'But I have no questions at the moment.'

The sidekicks registered disappointment.

'Would you at least consider our proposal?' Mr Clifton nodded at the hapless Greg and Dominic who each handed Nell papers. 'We took the liberty of making some preliminary calculations…'

'How kind.' Nell got to her feet. 'You could help me in one respect, Mr Clifton.' He sprang to attention like a guardsman.

'Could you tell me if there's a toy shop in Marlborough? One that would sell things for a model railway?'

His expression amused Nell for days.

Summer arrived, transforming the landscape and the grounds which had been shrouded in chill. The temperature rose and the mist and dew of the early mornings sifted up from wet grass and vanished. The land began to dry up, the leaves on the trees went from pure viridian green into a mixture of greens, ochre and Umbrian brown.

More than once, she stood by her bedroom window and thought of her father putting up the memorial in the wood to the woman he had loved.

She knew what Lucy might say: *They probably hadn't known each other long enough for the passion to wear off.* Lucy's worldliness had helped her negotiate what she considered a successful life. Money, matrimony, a settled existence. Yet... and yet. *There are more things in heaven and earth*, said Hamlet.

Too right.

Then there was Joey. Any thoughts of him caught her by the throat and hardened her determination to make things a little better for him.

She elicited Pamela's help.

Joey answered the door when Nell knocked at the cottage in Yew Green and, for a second, one glorious second, his face lit up.

Nell asked if she might come in and stepped into a room cluttered from adults living cheek-by-jowl with a baby and children.

Wedged between a nappy bucket and toys, Molly was sprawled in a chair, her eyes now shockingly black-ringed. She did not get up at Nell's entrance.

Nell wasted no time. 'Mrs Baker, would you consider… I would love to have Joey up at the house as he used to be with my uncle. Perhaps an afternoon every week during the school holidays? Until I return to Geneva.'

'I don't see why you should bother.' Molly eyed the Victoria sponge which Pamela had made. An excellent charm offensive. 'Has he been telling you tales? He's got a good home here.' She pulled down the sleeves of her cardigan. 'We do our best.'

'Mrs Baker… Molly, if I may, I'm not suggesting otherwise.'

Draped around the doorframe, a lick of hair flapping over his forehead, Joey was listening. Molly sent a sullen look in his direction. 'Go upstairs, Joey. *Now.*' Joey disappeared and Molly said, 'I'll have you know he could be in an orphanage.'

'Molly, Joey doesn't say anything to me about you. He doesn't say much at any time.'

'Is that my fault?'

Nell stepped warily. 'He wouldn't be a bother. He'd be company for me.' She lowered her voice. 'It would be nice for me.'

Molly did not see this as an advantage. 'He'll get used to you and then you'll vanish back from where you came.' Having located a salient point, she drove it home. 'What good would that do him?' There was silence. 'He was spoilt by my sister. And the Captain. Gave him ideas.'

This situation was light years away from the safe, clean, coffee-scented office in Geneva – from the obedient agendas and data on which she relied and with which she decided the future of many.

She summoned what skills she had which she could apply to the situation that was in danger of slipping the leash.

'Wouldn't an afternoon help you? You must be so busy. I could feed Joey,' she cast around, 'and bath him if you would like.'

Molly barely responded. 'We're not on the charity, you know.' Her voice dipped. 'We can cope.'

Reaching out (as Thelma would have it) to someone whose predicament was complicated required wit and dark skills. Plus the empathy which Thelma suggested needed hard work. 'Joey could help me clear out the attic,' she said.

Molly hauled herself to her feet, dark mussed hair hanging down. It was plain she resented Nell. But, it appeared, not enough. Her gesture registered defeat. 'Tuesdays would be good.'

Nell ignored the hostility. It seemed to her that, if she listened on another level, she would hear Molly silently screaming.

*Is that good enough, Thelma?*

Taking Joey's small hand in hers was a different order of experience to manipulating statistics and projections. Observing his reactions at close quarters tapped into a singing, stirring, rippling area of Nell's heart. Unfamiliar territory over which she was now groping.

Joey gulping down cake and milk. The skip he gave on seeing Nell. The anticipation as he and Nell climbed the attic stairs. The gasp followed by profound silence when Nell gave him the box containing the Hornby Pannier engine which she had tracked down in Marlborough.

He stood back from the box, hands clenched at his sides.

'It's for you, Joey.' Joey did not move – but Nell had the extraordinary idea that he was on tiptoe, alight, ready to fly. 'See what's inside.'

'Miss, you open it,' he said. She did, and deposited the engine into his arms. He held it tight. So tight she worried it might be damaged.

His possession of it was complete. Wholesale. Body and soul. So profound was it that a thank you (which she didn't get) was irrelevant.

Ada was dubious about the Tuesday afternoons. 'Why tie yourself up unnecessarily?' Her lips pursed in thought. 'Won't he miss you when you've gone?'

Was Ada right about this? Watching Joey positioning the new engine on the track, Nell asked of herself: *Was it OK for an adult to dip in and out of a child's life?*

'Are you pleased, Joey?'

He was poised over the engine, head turned, and she could again take note of the silky hair and the beauty of his vulnerable childish body.

'Are you going to give him a name?'

No reply. Joey was wrapped around his new engine, hands placed carefully, but his attention and focus were on a place Nell couldn't reach.

Eventually, Joey announced he would call the new engine Bess.

'That's a girl's name, Joey. Are you sure?'

Joey was sure. Of course he was and it was of a piece that he called his engine by the name of his mother. Bess, closely followed by Thomas, was sent on a journey through the pine trees and cardboard mountains to Father Christmas who inhabited a snowy, echoey place with reindeer (Joey was firm on this point). Nell found herself providing the commentary on the progress of the engines. 'They're by a river, Joey, which is frozen over. It is very cold. Oh, look at the pine cones on the trees.

'We are nearly there, Joey. Just a couple more puffs.'

Joey clung onto Nell's hand.

'What did you want to ask Father Christmas?'

'I want…' Joey stumbled over his words. 'I want…' His whisper was practically inaudible. Nell bent over to hear. 'Please make Mike at school my friend.'

The return journey from the Land of Magic and Father Christmas took time. Joey was reluctant to return. He wanted to remain there, among the snow-laden trees, making wishes come true. Nell fed him sandwiches as he described, slowly at first, but with increasing excitement, a cave in the mountains where Father Christmas kept his presents and Thomas and Bess lived in a shed with a red roof.

Nigel Clifton proved to be a doughty campaigner. A sizeable document arrived in the post, containing specifications and figures. Plus a map – which annoyed Nell because it suggested that the Clifton team had indeed snooped around Woodspring and its land.

It was a professional piece of work. *To provide affordable high-quality care in beautiful surroundings has to be our aim…*

In this spec, the coloured illustrations were subtler and showed groups of happy elders dining in elegant surroundings, walking in curated gardens and at ease in comfortable bedrooms.

'Certainly, the elderly must be looked after,' Ada rifled through the pages, 'but not necessarily in your house, I don't think.'

Yesterday, Tommy Fry had snared a rabbit which could not be allowed to go to waste and Pamela put it into the pot. Ada and Nell were now consuming it in the dining room – Nell knew better than to suggest the kitchen. Pamela was in charge, of course she was, and the ease and intimacy of eating at the wooden table surrounded by pots and pans was not on offer.

Nell had accepted that certain standards were expected of her. Of course she had. To do otherwise while she still hovered in that liminal space between one decision or the other would have been unkind,

Having brooded on the Clifton spec, Ada constructed a dramatic scenario. Nell was invited to imagine a hatch knocked through the kitchen wall into the dining room occupied by rows of tables, cutlery heaped in baskets and stacked glasses. 'It was like that when I visited Fraser's mother when she was in a home. Communal eating. It's an acquired taste.'

Nell observed the rabbit leg on her plate. 'Woodspring is a big house.'

'You might want to get married and have children. Then what?'

Nell speared a piece of rabbit and ate it.

'But you have your job and a *much* more interesting life to think about. If I was being honest,' Ada's gaze wandered to the window, '*sensationally* honest, I'd choose the interesting life. Something glamorous. Like you.' She refocussed on Nell. 'You went ahead with the Tuesday afternoons.'

'Yes. Joey and I play with the model railway. The one built by Uncle Robert.'

It had been painful to watch Joey cling on to Bess when it was time to return home. So much so, Nell agreed he could take Bess with him. 'He's a sad little boy. Although he's hard to read… but it reminds me of when I was told my father had died.'

'You poor thing,' cried Ada.

'I was older and living in the States and he was here, so we didn't see each other. But I think I know what Joey feels. A little, at any rate.'

What did Joey *feel*?

The wind whistle of loneliness? The drumbeat of unfairness? In a household that tolerated him, at best. Disparaged and hurt him, at worst. Did he accept unquestioningly that his presence was an awkward one? But then, he had never known different. She hoped against hope that Joey didn't know that he was sad.

'Nell…' Ada peered at her. 'Nell. Come back from wherever you are.'

After consuming Pamela's raspberry tart, Nell conducted Ada up to the attic to show her the railway. 'This is Joey's escape. His safe place.' She pointed to where Joey had parked Thomas in the station. 'When it's time to go home, he wraps up Bess, the engine I gave him, and takes it with him. It's… it's…' She failed to finish the sentence.

'Why Bess?'

'His mother's name.'

Ada paced around the circuit. 'I can see it. The valleys cutting through the mountains, the villages clinging to the sides, snow melting in the sun.' She halted. 'Is that how it is?'

Nell laughed. 'Something like.'

Ada hunkered down beside the station. 'One has to have an outlet,' she said. 'An escape from the church cake sale. Otherwise one goes mad. Even someone as young as Joey.'

It was warm and close in the attic.

'*Are* you going mad, Ada?'

After a moment, she replied: 'I could easily.'

Maybe change had triggered them… maybe it was a consequence of living at Woodspring… but Nell found herself rehashing the memories of her affair with George.

*There's no room in your head for anything else but work*, he accused her towards the end. *Because you don't want to face anything.*

At the time, she had shrugged it off. Now, as she walked over the Woodspring fields which were rapidly drying up in the heat, sweat licking her arms and upper lip, she conceded George had had a point.

Those years in Geneva when she could have run amok, sexually, businesswise, socially, could have been messy. But she was too self-contained. Too ungiving of herself. Too unwilling to lower barriers.

George had a point.

With Joey, it was different. Maybe in a weird reciprocity she wanted to give him a chance to discover that sorrow and bewilderment were not an inevitable punishment for being a child?

Maybe.

Close to Faith's memorial, her booted toe snagged against a lump of soil. She bent down and picked it up. It crumbled and a pale, jagged shard emerged out of the chocolatey earth. She held it up. It was curved and cup-shaped with a flower pattern.

Back at the house, she washed the layers of dirt off until it was clean. Retrieving the photograph of her father and uncle, she used a magnifying glass to examine the china laid on the table. The flower pattern on the shard matched.

She balanced it in the palm of her hand.

*Naturally*, Harry would talk to Faith. *Naturally*, he would take his cup of tea with him. He may have talked about Woodspring and what to do about the land. He may have talked about the loneliness of not having her to help him through. How he missed her pressed against him at night. All that. Then one day, he must have dropped the cup. There it must have remained.

She wrapped it in tissue paper and put it away in the desk in the study. A memorial to a strange dialogue, now safe in shuttered darkness.

'Can I have biscuits?' Joey asked each time Nell fetched him. 'And sausages?' Nell reassured him on all points. This teatime, flanked by Pamela and Nell, Joey perched at the kitchen table with Bess beside him, and scoffed as if his life depended on it.

On finishing, he slid down from the table and scampered upstairs to the attic.

Her expression unreadable, Pamela stared at the disappearing Joey.

'Do you know something?' Nell asked. 'About Joey?'

Pamela carried the tea things over to the basin. She was wearing black trousers and a forest-green cardigan which was just a shade too tight but, as ever, she looked comfortable in her skin.

'What sort of things?'

'You saw a lot of Bess, you said.'

'Bess was a good person.' Again the sadness. 'We were friends.'

'Did she consider adoption when she knew Joey was on the way?'

Pamela ran the hot tap into the washing-up bowl.

'Never. Dr King tried to arrange it. He wanted to help, but Bess wasn't having it. She said that no one else was having her baby. She was absolutely decided about that.' She turned off the tap. 'Bess was a funny one. I always said she could have worked in an office if she had put her mind to it. Could have made something of herself, but she preferred to work as a cleaner. That's why I suggested she came up here to help me out with the chores and the Captain. She ended up here most days. It was difficult when Joey came along. Obviously. The Captain was always asking for her.'

Nell snaffled a tea towel from the rack. 'Let me help.'

Pamela handed over a wet mug. 'Tommy sometimes had a pint with Jim. Jim never liked Bess but, after she was killed, Molly begged him to take on Joey. Jim wasn't happy about *that.*' She emptied the washing-up bowl. The gurgle of water sounded very loud. 'Tommy has a theory that Jim fancied Bess and she wouldn't have anything to do with him and he married the other sister.' She draped the dishcloth over the rim of the bowl. 'There was gossip, a lot of it cruel, when Joey was born. But Bess carried on regardless. I remember her once wheeling Joey down to the doctor's. She was thin, very thin, but she was singing to him, and he was looking up at her and laughing.'

Nell swallowed. She sat down on a kitchen chair. 'I've meddled. And I'm supposed to be a professional.'

Pamela wiped her hands on her apron and turned around to face Nell. 'Well, yes,' she said. 'Joey will mind terribly when you leave. But Tommy and I thought you knew what you were doing. He's a little boy who hasn't got parents and no hope of help in this world.'

Of course, of course Pamela would chew over Nell's business with Tommy. The to and fro of information. That was how it was.

'Did you ever want children, Pamela?'

'Yes and no,' she swished water around the bowl, 'but, like you, my work is important. Anyway, we couldn't afford children when it might have been possible.' She shrugged. 'We don't have power over these things and it's no use fretting.' She gave a final once-over to the already spotless sideboard. 'Word has it that you have been in contact with Nigel Clifton. You might like to know he was nosing around here before you arrived.'

What Pamela was really asking about was her and Tommy's future.

'I'm considering his proposal. One thing... if I sold Woodspring, I would ask the new owners that you be kept on. That is, if you wish it.'

Pamela shot her a sceptical look. As if, it said.

*

Nell set herself the mental exercise: *Imagine what it would be like to live in the house.*

Locked into its rooms was the music from the past, replaying the anguish of the father she never knew, the love affair cut short, the decline into incoherence and sickness of the unknown uncle.

And all the other Danes.

Could she live with them? What would it take to mask the sounds of those elegies?

# CHAPTER SEVENTEEN

Gabriel, her boss, rang from Geneva. Nell was to cut short her leave. A situation was brewing, and he wanted her on the case. There was a marked irritated undercurrent in his voice. (Gabriel was never a man to tolerate shirkers.)

Theirs was an organisation that could not often declare that situations were cut and shut. Paradoxically, Gabriel liked things to be just that and was unsympathetic to the more flexible attitudes creeping into the workplace.

'Get yourself over here and we can discuss.'

They agreed that Nell would fly over on the following Thursday night for a meeting on the Friday.

She slept uneasily. What to do? Go? Stay? Slough off an old skin?

And…?

When she woke up at 5 a.m., she waited for the answers that very often arrived when she was asleep. They failed to materialise.

She padded into the bathroom. The face reflected at her from the mirror looked puzzled and heavy-eyed. Also, Joey had wriggled into the heart of the conundrum. Abandoning Woodspring would leave him vulnerable. How would it be possible for her to offer help for his littlelife?

Easier by far to abandon the wood, the fields, the handsome house than him…

Nell telephoned Ada. 'How about a trip to Geneva?'

'Don't joke.' Ada sounded weary.

'If the church cake sale can spare you, I'm going next week. Come too.'

There was a millisecond of silence. Then: 'Bugger the cake sale.'

'You can stay in my flat. Go shopping. See the sights while I'm in the office. At the weekend, we'll do nice things. Take the train. Go up to the mountains.'

'If you're joking, I'll kill you.'

'There's a catch. I want to bring Joey with me… us. I can't look after him while I'm at work. Would you be prepared to do so?'

'That's quite a responsibility.' Ada was dubious. 'I mean… what does one do with a child?'

'I'm not sure,' said Nell. 'But I would like to give him a memory. Something he'll look back on often.'

'That means you are not planning to stay.'

Nell found it impossible to reply one way or the other.

Mid-morning she walked down to the Baker cottage in Yew Green and knocked on the door. It was a while before Molly peered through a crack. 'Yes.'

'May I come in?'

Molly had a deathly pallor and her hands shook while Nell explained what she would like to do. 'Jim,' she called. 'Come and listen to this.'

Jim obliged and then said, 'The school won't like it.'

However, he was quick to spot the advantages. No Joey for a week. His expenses paid.

Molly appeared beyond caring. 'We could allow it.' She sent her husband a look. 'Don't you think?'

Jim did think.

Joey needed a passport and Nell found herself, plus black-and-white photos and a letter from Dr King certifying that Miss Dane was *in loco parentis*, making a trip to the passport office in Little Venice in London. She coached Joey carefully as to what would happen, showing him a picture of the plane and an airport, and gave him the new passport to hold. 'You won't be sad coming with me and Mrs Allen, will you, Joey?'

He shook his head.

All the same, when, having arrived at her flat in Geneva, she put a frazzled, unwashed little boy to bed, he cried bitterly. For Molly? From bewilderment?

'It's all right, Joey,' she said, stroking his head. 'It's all a bit strange, that's all.'

On arrival, there had been no time to rejoice in the familiar scenery, in the re-entry into her immaculate flat, or breathing in sharp, exhilarating Swiss air. Ada and she had to cope with a little boy who complained his stomach ached and slumped down onto the floor of the airport arrivals lounge and announced he was too tired to walk.

Joey turned his head away and closed his eyes. The tears had wet his cheeks and he looked as alone as a child could be.

'Joey…' Nell propped herself up on the pillows, drew him close. 'It's all right. I'm here. Mrs Allen's here and you're going to the zoo.'

But it wasn't that simple or easy. Joey had no one, and no points of reference. All he knew was that he was in a strange place with strangers.

His head was on her shoulder. An imprint on her flesh.

His head grew heavy. The breathing slowed.

At work, a percentage of those in need always, always included children. Those theoretical children did not press against her arm until cramp threatened, nor leave a dribble patch on her blouse. They did not demand. They did not wrench bewildering visceral reactions out of Nell.

At work, the modus vivendi was to be controlled and intellectualised. Here…? Here, Joey's breath on her cheek shredded the safety curtain between a number on a list and the dampish, unwashed reality which demanded, saddened and puzzled all in the same pulse beat.

She squinted down at him and found herself absorbed by the childish cheek and the shape of his fair head. An outstretched hand with curled fingers. A breathing child. There was, she realised, no greater incursion into the serenity of an ordered emotional life.

Ada declared herself to be in seventh heaven and awed by the flat which Cecile, the cleaning lady, had as always left immaculate. The view from the window, the scented soap in the bathroom, the unfamiliar bedding called a duvet.

It was all heaven.

'Women can do so much better here,' she said, sweeping around the sitting area.

'Yes and no,' said Nell. 'Swings and roundabouts. They only got the vote in 1971.'

Ada peered out of the large plate-glass window to the

buildings and the lake beyond. 'It doesn't look antediluvian. It looks civilised. It looks everything that Berkshire ain't.'

The following morning, Nell took them out for breakfast – croissants, hot chocolate, coffee. Joey had recovered his spirits, ate his croissant and begged a second before Ada, armed with Nell's instructions, headed off to the zoo with him.

Nell took the tram to the office, where the familiar, slightly antiseptic smell enfolded her into the mainframe, and colleagues greeted her with teases. 'It's the woman with the house.'

In his office with the magnificent view, Gabriel waited to piece together a future.

They knew each other well. In another life, they might have been friends. She knew he suffered from indigestion which made him short-tempered. He knew that she disliked any reference to her stepfather.

He was sitting behind his desk with a tray of coffee at the ready. He pushed a cup over to her. 'You look as though you've been drinking too much tea.'

'Ha,' said Nell. 'Funny. Very.'

'It's time to come back, Nell. There's a famine brewing in Africa. I need to work through plans with you.'

'There's much still to sort and I would like more time, Gabriel. I'll put in a formal request.'

He poured himself more coffee but did not offer her a second cup. 'It's unlike you.' He looked down at the cup, presumably calculated it would not do his stomach any good and left it. It signalled a mood – she was used to reading them. He picked up a folder which she recognised as her employment file. 'We both know you have an excellent record, Nell. Promotions could come your way.'

'What am I meant to take from that? That I won't get promoted if I don't return to work immediately?'

'Your house is a first-world problem. Our business is dealing with third-world ones.'

'First-world problems don't deserve attention?'

Gabriel took a risk and drank the coffee. 'It should be simple to sort,' he said. 'Either you want the house, or you don't. Either you wish to work here, or you don't.'

Gabriel possessed the ability to reduce a conundrum to a simple proposition. Nell admired it. She pointed to the folder. 'My record is good. Won't that buy me time?'

'No,' Gabriel replied. 'This is an office. You're an employee. The dispossessed and suffering don't wait for people to decide their property portfolios.'

Nell went into battle. She talked about unforeseen events which he, Gabriel, knew all about, but she must deal with them. She outlined the legal processes in the UK. The problems of disposing of land and a house… (She could see his eyes beginning to roll back in his head.) How much better, she argued, for an employee's peace of mind to deal with them.

'That's what I intend to do.'

Both understood the art of negotiation.

In the end, he relented and ratified the leave that she had negotiated earlier. 'Only because I can't bear the thought of getting used to someone else.'

'You mean no one else would put up with you.'

Back in her flat, Joey wanted to tell Nell about the animals they had seen. In minute detail.

Nell listened to his descriptions of goats, ducks, pigs and ponies. Every so often she glanced over to Ada who was slumped exhausted in a chair.

Joey grabbed Nell's hand as he described how a pony tried to eat Ada's handbag, and she cradled the small fingers as if they were the most precious thing in her possession.

'Spot any handsome well-dressed men?' she asked Ada when Joey's microscopically detailed report came to an end. 'The ones you don't see in the UK?'

Ada said, 'I'm going to die of exhaustion.'

After Joey was in bed, Ada roused herself and enquired about Nell and the office.

Nell explained that Gabriel wanted her back as soon as possible and wasn't interested in her predicament.

'The house has got to you,' murmured Ada.

'The house?' Nell was startled. 'What do you base that on?'

'Wouldn't you have said you were coming back at once if it hadn't?'

Nell took a large mouthful of wine.

'People change, you know,' Ada continued. 'It's not a crime. You now have something else to think about.'

On the Saturday morning, they climbed onto a train with a heavy-gauge red engine and set off for Lausanne. Joey sat bolt upright by the window – but whether from awe, from pleasure, or from fright was impossible to deduce.

At Lausanne, they took themselves down to the marina and showed Joey the boats. Boats, it turned out, had nowhere near the pulling power of the train. Boats were second-class citizens.

The sun came out, hot and strong. Nell realised that Joey needed protection from it and bought him a peaked cap with a train motif which was a lot more successful in pleasing him.

They settled at a café for lunch which overlooked the marina. Nell ordered rösti and sausages for herself. Ada ate raclette and drank a glass of wine.

The rigging on the boats clacked and clicked with the breeze. Joey made short work of the ice cream. Nell ordered coffee and had an exchange with the waiter in French.

Ada listened in. 'You can't abandon here. You *can't* come and live in boring England. Even if we do have polenta cake in the Currant Bun.'

On their final day, Ada took herself off to look at the shops. Nell took Joey to the bird sanctuary near the Nant D'Avril walk. If Joey was up to it, she planned to show him the river and the waterfalls.

They didn't get far. Joey was tired and hot. He announced that his leg hurt and he wanted to go home. Nell found a bench and lifted him up onto it. She sat down beside him and put her arm around his thin shoulders.

'You'll be going home tomorrow, Joey. Don't worry.'

He sniffed. To her distress, tears rolled down his cheeks.

'You *do* want to go home to Aunt Molly?'

Joey stared straight ahead. 'I hid Bess from Uncle Jim.'

'Why did you do that?'

He shifted on the seat and took a long time to answer. 'He hates Bess.'

'Your Aunt Molly would never let anything happen to Bess.'

‘Aunt Molly cries all the time. She says that the baby is going to kill her.’ He looked up at Nell.

Nell tightened her grip around Joey’s shoulders. ‘No,’ she said urgently. ‘No. No, Joey. Your aunt didn’t mean it.’

For an answer, Joey leant against her, warm and a little damp. ‘I’m hungry,’ he said.

In the two days she had been with Joey, Nell had learnt to carry an emergency supply of biscuits in her bag. The small-boy education. ‘Here.’

Joey bit into it.

‘It’s coconut,’ she said.

Joey ate it and asked for a second. They sat peaceably together watching the waterfall before Nell said they must return. Joey held her hand as they walked back along the path. He was mostly silent except when he described being tripped up by Mike in the playground.

‘Why did he do that, Joey?’

‘He said because I was smelly and nobody wanted to be my mummy.’

Nell bit back anger. ‘You’re not smelly.’

‘I don’t have a mummy.’

‘I didn’t have a daddy while I was growing up.’

Joey looked up at Nell. ‘I don’t have a daddy.’

In the dark gaze lay bewilderment and unfathomable sadness and she bent over and kissed the top of his head.

Ada wrote in her thank-you letter that it had been the best holiday ever and she couldn’t thank Nell enough.

‘Some of the biddies on the rota were shocked that I had

gone on holiday without my husband. I say they belong to another century. A holiday without the husband is the way to go… let me know what you decide to do.'

Nell made an appointment to see Dr King at the surgery, which was shoehorned into a cramped house at the centre of the village. It smelt of disinfectant and floor polish and had a big stack of out-of-date magazines on the table in the waiting room.

'We're hoping to build a new surgery,' said Dr King. 'The plans are drawn up but we're having trouble with the funding even though the area is filling up.' He was resigned. 'When… if… we have more space, we'll have a proper reception and an office for a practice nurse. Even…' He looked past her. 'Even a second doctor.'

'I wanted to talk to you about Joey,' said Nell.

Dr King removed his glasses and put them down on his desk. 'That's difficult,' he said. 'Patient confidentiality.'

'I understand. Why don't I just say what I feel and we can leave it at that?'

Dr King considered. 'Should you be so involved?

'I've spent my professional life learning that to be involved in what happens to others is a good thing.' She tried to read his expression. 'I know, I know, it makes me sound very missionary in the field.'

He laughed. 'Helping others is never straightforward.'

She thought of her office, its plate-glass window and the lists behind which she retreated. 'Do-gooders are the stuff of jokes, but I'm pretty sure Joey is being badly treated at home and at school.' Dr King jotted something on his pad. 'I'm probably returning to my job in Geneva for good and I would like to know that someone will keep an eye on him.'

Dr King continued writing. 'I'm sure those who have Joey's interests at heart will be grateful. But, to be blunt, you'll be in Geneva, not here.' He was direct and matter-of-fact. 'It's a pity,' he added. 'I gather your family have lived at Woodspring since the Regency. Your father…'

'Did you know my father?'

'Not well. He was almost at the end when I arrived in the village as a young GP.'

She leant forward, ravenous for detail. 'What was he like?'

'He didn't fuss. He said to me he had to get on with the business of dying because it wasted everyone's time if he didn't. He was concerned about your uncle and I promised to do my best for him. I got the impression that your father was slightly maverick. In the best way.'

Nell looked down at her lap. 'Did he ever mention me?'

'Not to my knowledge.'

'Did he mention anyone?'

Dr King considered. She was beginning to understand that he was a man who chose his words carefully. 'He said he was going to meet Faith, and he was happy about that.'

There was a pause.

'I knew your uncle much better. Provided everything was organised for him, he was as content as it was possible to be in his circumstances. A combination of shell shock and a head wound. There was therapy for the shell shock… developed in the first world war… but his brain damage was irreversible.'

Nell now looked up.

'I always took consolation from your uncle. The fact that he was able to live contentedly. Towards the end, he became physically unstable. Had a lot of falls, one quite nasty. Ended up in hospital.'

'He had sufficient money and backup,' said Nell. 'That must have helped.'

'Yes. Others are not so fortunate.'

She thought for a moment. 'A developer's interested in turning Woodspring into a care home for the elderly.'

'Perryfield, I take it?' Dr King got to his feet, indicating that the session was over. 'I'd be surprised if there are enough elderly people in the area who would be able to afford it.' His next comment surprised Nell. 'If I was a developer keen on profit, I'd consider the demographics. I would demolish the house and build as many smaller houses as I could on the land. Commuters are crying out for family homes.'

'I wouldn't have put you down as a cynic, Dr King.'

'A realist.'

'Dr King… do you know who Joey's father was?'

There was a pause. A long one. 'You can't expect me to discuss that.' He smiled to take away the sting. Equally, there were boundaries over which she could not stray. 'But I'll help Joey in every way I can. It may be that social services should be involved and Joey should be fostered or go into a home.'

# CHAPTER EIGHTEEN

That Sunday, Nell attended matins in Yew Green's church.

*Not* something which she did normally. In fact, she couldn't remember when she had last been in a church other than as a tourist.

The church was originally medieval but with ugly Victorian additions, a whitewashed interior and a large painting of John the Baptist's head on a plate embellished with lashings of gore.

The congregation was modest. The vicar, the Reverend Stack, arrived in a rush having bicycled over from his second parish. Nell decided that he looked hungry and needed a rest. His sermon lingered on the perils of debauchery and self-indulgence, which, observing the spare, slightly tatty figure, Nell reckoned was a form of wistful thinking.

'Ah yes,' he said when Nell introduced herself to him at the end of the service. 'Miss Dane, I was hoping… I've been meaning to get in contact.' He sounded as though he had been guilty of the grossest dereliction of duty.

Nell was fascinated to spot a small gold stud in his left ear. 'I've been coming and going,' she said, to help him out.

A couple of elderly ladies from the congregation lingered at the entrance to the church where he was positioned. Reverend Stack's gaze swung between them and Nell. 'What I was going to ask was, would you consider holding the church fete in the grounds of Woodspring?'

Nell consulted Tommy Fry. 'Oh yes,' he said, 'the fete was always held here in the old days. Took a bit of preparation.'

'But could you get the grounds ready?'

He took off his cap and scratched at the thinning hair underneath. 'That's my job.'

Pamela informed Nell that Tommy was pleased. 'He likes a challenge,' she said. 'He likes to think it's the old days.'

Nell glanced out of the window at the garden. 'If he wants a challenge, he's going to get one.'

Much mowing, trimming and pruning ensued and the lawn at the back of the house was subjected to a ruthless manicure. Trestle tables and chairs were brought up from the village hall, a small tent arrived for 'sanitary' arrangements and Pamela set about an ambitious programme of cake- and biscuit-making.

The rain held off and the day dawned not exactly sunny but fair. A group of women from the village set up the hoopla and apple bobbing and arranged chutneys and jams on a table. Tommy constructed the barbecue and the unbeatable aroma of grilling sausages and bacon floated through the air.

Reverend Stack arrived on his bicycle and threw himself into the role of host, standing at the top of the steps down to the lawn to greet arrivals. As he explained to each, the entrance fee would go towards the roof repairs for the church.

'Excellent,' he said. 'Most of the village has turned out. They say it's for the roof, but we all know they want to look at you.'

'I feel an impostor,' said Nell.

His gold ear stud glinted. 'We all do, Nell.'

Ada strolled over carrying the garden gnome she had just won in the tombola. Having risen to the sartorial challenge in a long, floaty dress, she was attracting attention. 'A scene out of Jane Austen,' she said, gesturing to the crowd. She laughed a trifle grimly. 'Bit short on Mr Darcys though.'

Nell spotted Molly, her two boys, the baby and Joey heading for the hoopla. Jim homed in on the drinks stall where bottles of cider – called 'White Paradise' and apparently lethal – were ranged beside the Tizer and orangeade. He grabbed two of them.

Nell focussed on Joey. He was running about, absorbed in his private thoughts, stumbling a little on his not-quite-healed leg. Molly sat in a chair and fed the baby. One of the women brought her a plastic mug of tea and she murmured something but did not touch it.

'You not talking to Joey?' asked Ada.

'I didn't want to single him out.' Nell pointed to a posse of the other children who had their faces painted and were stuffing buns.

'But you've singled him out already,' said Ada.

Every so often, Joey looked up towards the house. He was too far away to read his expression but Nell was pretty sure he was sad.

By the end of the afternoon there had been fights between the children, knees had been scraped, the cider had been drunk, cake crumbs were scattered over the lawn and a dubiously coloured bottle of liquid soap was all that remained of the tombola. Ten-year-old Emily Swift had been crowned Queen of the Fete.

'That's nice,' said Pamela, who had been commissariat for the afternoon and had spent much of it ferrying in cakes. 'Emily's parents died within weeks of each other when she was a baby.'

'Sad,' said Nell.

'Dr King arranged for the Swifts to adopt her. They couldn't have children. So it all worked out.'

Molly called to her sons and winched herself to her feet with the baby clamped like a brooch to her chest. She picked up her basket and made her way towards the exit, with Ollie and Tom jabbing at her heels. She heaved herself up the steps and vanished.

Joey was standing by the barbecue, gazing after the vanishing figure of his aunt. Nell went over to him and said, 'Joey, I think you're going home.' She led him up the steps and caught up with Molly.

'You forgot Joey,' she said.

'Oh, Joey,' said Molly. 'I suppose I did.'

Fraser Allen required Nell's presence in the office. He wished to review the financial situation with her, he said, sounding pessimistic.

She agreed with him. The original endowment for the house had been generous but factors such as inflation and the increasing cost of repairs were eating into it. After discussing the figures with him, and some wrangling, Nell asked, 'If I sell Woodspring, what happens to the money?'

'It will revert to you on your fortieth birthday, with the proviso that 2 per cent of it is donated to a charity of your choice.'

'Quite an incentive.'

'Yes.' Fraser took off his glasses and placed them on the table between them. 'You've indicated you might return to your old life and dispose of Woodspring.' A pause. 'Your family have been here for a long time but things change.'

'You mean no more Lords of the Manor.'

'As I say, times are changing.'

'Just to be clear, you told me earlier the house couldn't be demolished for a housing development?'

'No. Not unless it burnt down or was destroyed by other means. The land isn't listed. That could be sold.'

Later that afternoon, Nell shut herself up in the study. She read and reread her father's and uncle's wills.

Her finger traced the lines of type, dense and lawyerly. Bequeathing… beneficiaries…

Turning to her uncle's much fatter file, she flipped through the papers at the top.

Bills for house repairs running over the years. A contract of employment for the Frys. Invoices for a specially adapted bed for her uncle, the installation of a range cooker in the kitchen and a couple of oil radiators.

A note had sneaked into the pile. *Bess*, was written in pencil in capital letters on lined paper, *miss you.*

The writing was uneven but the yearning expressed was not.

A large envelope contained details of the arrangements for his funeral. Plus a copy of the funeral eulogy given by Reverend Slack, published in the parish magazine.

*By the age of twenty-six, Robert Dane had been promoted to captain in 4 Commando, a new, specially trained and top-secret branch of unconventional warfare. He distinguished himself on D-Day when he and his men landed at Sword Beach on 6 June, 1944. He fought his way to the Pegasus Bridge and was instrumental in establishing a bridgehead against fierce German opposition. Unfortunately, when advancing further into France, he was wounded in the shoulder. He was at first given a clean bill by the medics but later wounded in the head. It was clear that his injuries required expert attention and he was invalided back to the UK. He always lamented leaving his comrades behind. He shared his family home with his elder brother, Major Harry Dane, who was also wounded and predeceased him in 1950.*

*From time to time, Captain Dane was able to recollect his war experiences in detail. He had nothing but admiration for the Commandos, always clear that he never regretted his part in the fight against Hitler. He maintained his training had been a privilege and, yes, they had been fearful at times but fear nurtured strength and dexterity. 'We had to learn to fend for ourselves, like the men of ancient Sparta.'*

This was a window into her uncle – and her father. Nell looked up D-Day, about which she knew only skimpy facts. An army (was that the word?) of battleships, cruisers, destroyers, tank landing-craft, assault landing-craft, motor launches, torpedo boats and minesweepers had been secretly amassed. An army (that *was* correct) of foot soldiers, commandos and the accompanying commissariat had boarded them and under the cover provided by thousands of aircraft, the war chariots of the air, had surged ashore onto the Normandy beaches, among them her father and her uncle.

She closed the file, shutting off a record of that violent, killing, momentous war that belonged to no one and yet affected everyone. Even now.

She lifted her head and listened to the rain battering the trees outside – and spotted a damp patch that had appeared below the window frame.

She noted it on her to-do list. *This* was the present.

Later in the day, she went out for a tramp and circled around the village. Taking a shortcut through the churchyard back to the house, she stopped to look at the gravestones.

It was a pleasant and tranquil enough space over which the yews mounted dark-green guardianship. Grass grew thickly around the older graves, many of whose inscriptions were indecipherable, but the more recent graves were better tended.

She discovered Bess under one of the yews, isolated from the main grouping, with her name and dates engraved on a flat stone.

If Bess had lived, she and Nell would have been the same age. Nell crouched down. 'Dear Bess,' she said. 'I think I love your son. Do you mind?'

'A graveyard is always educational,' said a voice.

Reverend Slack had come up behind Nell. 'It reminds one how lucky we are to be here. Poor Bess there did not reach her threescore years and ten.'

Again her eye was drawn to the small gold stud. 'Did you know her?'

'Yes, I saw quite a lot of her after Joey was born. I don't think it's giving any confidences away to say that she needed help from time to time. Being a single parent in Yew Green is not easy.'

'Is that why her grave is on its own? Isn't that very Victorian?'

'Perhaps.'

'Forgiveness is supposed to be all.'

'It is.'

'She didn't consider moving from the village and starting again?'

Reverend Slack took a moment. 'No. I believe that was not her way.'

They walked down the path together to the gate. 'Will I be seeing you again on Sunday, Nell?'

He was the first person to call her by her Christian name without being invited.

'Probably not,' she replied.

Reverend Slack's earring glinted. 'That's not a no, then,' he said.

# CHAPTER NINETEEN

Nell was enjoying her breakfast coffee when Pamela burst into the kitchen, her normally level expression replaced by one of extreme distress.

'There's trouble at the Baker cottage, Nell. Bad. Tommy's down there now.'

Nell leapt to her feet so fast that she knocked over the coffee, which streamed across the table and onto the floor. Neither woman paid any attention to it.

'How bad?'

'Molly had a haemorrhage and collapsed. She's been taken to hospital.'

'Joey?' cried Nell.

'He's disappeared.'

'I'll get the car.'

In her haste, she left the back door wide open.

That didn't matter.

The scene that met them at the cottage was awful. Ollie and Tom were in in the downstairs room. Both were sobbing with fright for their mother. Jim was slumped in a chair, flanked by Tommy Fry and Reverend Slack. There was blood on his hands and a streak of it on the wall.

'The baby?' asked Nell.

Reverend Slack explained that Daisy had been taken to Jim's mother, the other side of the village.

'This is none of your business.' Jim addressed Nell.

Nell faced him. 'What's happened to Joey? What have you done with him?'

'What do I care?' replied Jim. 'If it wasn't for him none of this would be happening.'

'That's a terrible thing to say,' said Nell after a shocked silence.

At the same moment, Dr King arrived and overheard Jim. 'Jim, that's not the case,' he said. 'What's happened to Molly is the result of childbirth.'

'Have you hurt him?' Nell was wild with worry. 'Where is he?'

Reverend Slack said, 'Nell, he'll be somewhere.'

'It wouldn't be for the first time. His life here has been… awful.'

The words left her mouth and could not be unsaid. Reverend Slack held up an admonishing finger. *Be careful.*

Jim heaved himself upright and dropped a hand on each of his sons' shoulders. 'He's a bloody cuckoo and not wanted here. I told him so.'

'When did you tell him?'

Jim shrugged. 'He's always known it.'

Pamela was comforting Ollie and Tom. 'Why don't you come with me up to the big house.' She glanced at Nell. 'There's biscuits and milk.'

'Is nobody thinking about Joey?' Nell rounded on the adults. 'We should be out looking for him.'

Without waiting for Pamela and the boys, she ran out of the cottage and into the car. Within minutes she was back at Woodspring and hurtling up the stairs.

'Joey... Joey...'

The attic was empty. No Joey crouched over the station. No Joey waving on Thomas around the lake. Or Bess into the station.

But Nell sensed he was here, somewhere, lost and bewildered. Terrified he had fallen on a joist, she carefully checked the attic space, searching behind boxes, dragging out the fire screen, the chairs, even a stack of pictures.

He wasn't safe. Of that, she was sure. She felt. She *knew*.

Where would he go?

What would he be trying to do?

The skylight. She glanced across to it, set into the slope of the roof. Since the heat had arrived, it had been left open and a stepladder positioned underneath it for easy access. It was a tight fit but, fear lending dexterity, she managed to pull herself up and onto the roof.

'Joey, Joey... are you there?'

The skylight was close to the intersection where the roofs sloped towards each other and met. A flat gully ran between them. Tiles had recently been replaced and Fraser Allen had made a point of telling her that whoever had done the repairs had left a bucket behind.

*'Joey...'*

There was no answer. Then she saw him.

He was standing at the end of the gully, gazing down over the wall of the house into the drop to the drive below.

He didn't look very steady.

Nell pulled together every scrap of wit and cunning she had ever possessed. 'Joey, darling, would you mind coming over here? I want to ask you something about Thomas.'

At the sound of her voice, he swivelled around and for one appalling second, his foot balanced on the edge.

'I want to talk to you, Joey. Can you come here?'

He didn't move. 'Uncle Jim told me to look over the edge. He said it would be fun.'

Nell froze. The space between her and Joey shimmered with danger. And with murderous fury at Jim.

'He said I must count to a hundred.'

He was poised, there on the edge. Golden and unloved.

In that instant Nell understood how profoundly she had changed. Annealed by a new and indelible emotion.

'Joey, you want to hear about Thomas, don't you? So come over here.'

Still he lingered.

Nell's life flashed through her mind.

The vague figure who was her father saying, 'Goodbye, Nell' in New York. Her mother weeping angrily after that New York visit. (Her mother *never* cried.) Her stepfather saying he wasn't sure that he liked little girls but if she took off her clothes he might change his mind. The bullying when she never did. The relief of being in Geneva after her flight to Europe. The determination to shake that life off her dusty feet.

'Sweetheart…' For he was her sweetheart. In that moment, she knew that for absolute certain. As never, ever before. Joey wasn't unloved after all. Nell loved him. 'Joey, come here.'

Joey didn't move. 'Uncle Jim doesn't like sissies.'

'Come here, Joey.'

He seemed frozen. 'Can't.'

The gully did not look safe. A section of the guttering had shattered along it and the smashed and discarded roof tile had been left. She dropped to her hands and knees. 'I'm coming to get you,' she said. 'Don't move.'

The debris bit into her knees and ripped at her hands. She barely noticed and didn't care.

Inch by crippling inch, she edged towards him.

'Stay absolutely still, Joey.'

She smelt his fear and distress before she got to him. She grasped his leg. 'I've got you, Joey.' She pulled him to her and held him tight in the embrace of a lifetime. Every nerve capable of feeling aflame. Every emotion – terror, rage, deep, deep love – taking charge. 'You're safe now.'

Joey clung to her.

'You had me worried. Did Uncle Jim really send you up here?'

His voice was muffled by Nell's chest. 'Uncle Jim said I should go up on the roof. He said you would like it if I did.'

'What did you think when you came up here?'

He stirred in her grip. 'Don't know. But I didn't want Uncle Jim to be cross.'

'Oh, Joey.' She kissed the top of his head and his cheek. 'No one's cross with you.'

She let him down through the skylight and followed. Hand in hand they went downstairs.

Pamela was in the kitchen with Ollie and Tom. The table was crowded with plates of biscuits and half-drunk glasses of milk.

Pamela's gaze met Nell's. 'You all right? You're very pale.'

Joey climbed up into a chair and Nell poured out a glass of milk and placed it in front of him.

Only then did she slump down and drop her head into her hands.

Pamela opened the store cupboard, produced a bottle of cooking brandy, poured out a glass and placed it in front of Nell.

'Drink.'

Tom and Ollie were taken back home by Tommy Fry.

Nell flatly refused to allow Joey to go with them. 'He's staying here,' she said.

She rang Dr King and explained that Jim had encouraged Joey to go up onto the roof and look down. 'He wanted him to jump,' she said. 'He wanted Joey dead.' She repeated what Joey had told her.

Dr King listened. 'You must be careful what you say. The facts are important.'

'Those are the facts.'

'According to Joey.'

She turned on Dr King. 'Come what may, I'll defend Joey. He must be taken away from Molly and Jim. Molly wasn't coping and now's she's ill and Jim will let him come to harm. I know it.'

'You don't *know* it,' said Dr King. 'What you've told me won't hold up in a court. Or with the social services. Nell, it isn't your place to decide what happens to Joey.'

'I'll take him,' said Nell. 'I'll look after him. Then it would be.'

Dr King countered. 'There are rules and regulations about taking in children. For good reasons.'

'He's staying here for the moment,' said Nell. 'No ifs, no buts.'

'For the moment,' echoed Dr King.

And so it was that Joey was given his favourite supper of sausages and mashed potato, which Nell managed to cook, and put to bed in the bedroom that had been her uncle's.

He lay flat on his back gazing at the ceiling while she read him a story. When she finished, she shut the book.

'Did you know my mum?'

'No, darling Joey, I didn't, but Mrs Fry did. We could ask her if you want to know anything.'

'I wish,' he said, his eyes closing. 'I want…'

Nell stayed up late to ring her mother in Baton Rouge. Since their previous, shattering conversation they had not spoken.

Lucy said, 'Before you begin, I demand an apology.'

Nell considered. 'I'm sorry if the truth was awful.'

'You said wicked things.' Lucy sounded hoarse. '*Lies.*'

'I had to tell you one day,' said Nell. 'But… but I've survived.'

'But what do I do?' asked Lucy. 'How do I deal with it?'

'I can't say, but I suppose you must talk to your husband.'

'He's a good man. He wouldn't have meant any harm. He just wanted you to grow up a good American.'

Her mother was never going to admit anything. *Think* anything other. Why would she when her existence depended on the millionaire she had bagged?

For this moment, enough had been said.

'What would you say if I kept Woodspring?'

The familiar Lucy took a few seconds to shake back into life. 'Sakes. Whatever next? You've gone on for ever about working with refugees, which prevents you from settling down. Now you tell me you've decided differently. I can't keep up.'

Nell rolled her eyes. 'Before you ask, I haven't been in touch with George.'

'George was nice.'

'So you've said. Many times.'

'Keep Woodspring.' Nell could hear Lucy thinking. 'I would like to come and visit. Your father always wanted me to live there. He said I would be adored. Like his mother.' Another pause. 'I never got on with her. Apart from anything else, she had terrible dress sense.'

'You've said that too.'

Lucy was warming to her theme. 'Your father talked about beehives in the fields and promised the honey would be liquid gold.'

So Harry, her father, *had* been a romantic.

'Is this definite, Nell? For real?'

'Things aren't sorted. Yet.'

'Let me know if they are. I'll book a ticket. Make the pilgrimage.'

Nell directed her gaze out of the study window towards the strip of woodland and the dry-stone wall with Faith's memorial. Wood and wall blended with the landscape. The sky was what she had come to see as a typical English one: stippled blues blending with cotton balls.

'Your stepfather's been ill, you know.'

'Then you won't wish to leave him.'

Having finished the call, Nell stood by the study window for a long time.

Molly had been referred to a special gynaecological care unit near Marlborough, where she had an emergency operation with a second one scheduled. Dr King said she would be there for some time and that the treatment for this kind of condition was complicated. He had seen it more times than he cared to remember and, he said, still it hadn't been properly studied by the medical profession. Molly would be out of action for quite a while.

Violence and famine and drought were devastating – and Nell had dealt with their fallout. Just as debilitating was a cramped cottage, a sick mother, an angry husband, little money, three children and a new baby.

She asked permission to visit Molly and was granted access for fifteen minutes. She set off in the car with the map beside her on the passenger seat.

The hospital was a pleasant-looking building outside the town and she found Molly in a side ward with two other new mothers, propped up in bed with Daisy in a basket beside her. She seemed dazed and shrunken and barely reacted when Nell explained she was looking after Joey.

A nurse arrived and took Daisy away. 'Time for baby's bottle.'

Nell embarked on one of the most important negotiations of her life.

'Molly, I think I heard Jim say that he didn't want Joey in the house. It was very generous to take him on after your sister died but it must be difficult.'

No reaction. Or not one Nell could fathom.

'Molly…' If Nell had imagined that a well-shaped argument could be presented as smoothly as giving a briefing, she was wrong. Of course she was. She was staring a woman's sickness and exhaustion in the face.

She fell back on a direct question. 'If having Joey is difficult, why don't I take him? For the time being?'

It was said.

Not much appeared to be getting through to Molly. 'Bess doesn't have to think about anything.' She wiped a finger with a bitten nail across a wet cheek. 'Bess always had the luck.'

Was the longing in Molly's voice for oblivion? To get out of the world? Whatever, it hinted of descent into darkness. Disturbed, Nell took a chance and reached for her hand. 'I'm sorry things have been so hard.'

Molly focussed a pair of dulled eyes on Nell and removed her hand.

'Molly, do you know who Joey's father is? Is he alive? Could he help?'

Molly sounded drugged – which she probably was. 'Never would say. Mum hated the talk about it. Sent her to her grave.' She stared at the empty cot beside the bed. 'Bess had that on her conscience.'

'Did Bess have a boyfriend?'

This was none of her business. But she asked the question all the same.

A baby cried. A phone rang on the ward desk.

Molly turned her head and stared at Nell. 'She was at the big house day and night. Don't you see?'

Nell looked down at her hands folded in her lap. They were shaking. What Molly was suggesting had an enormity that, in that moment, she couldn't process.

'Can I take Joey for the time being, then?'

'Do what you like,' said Molly.

Ollie and Tom were packed up and sent to stay with Jim's mother for the duration.

And…

Joey came to stay with Nell.

When he arrived with the entire tally of his clothes stuffed into a shoe-bag, plus a manky toothbrush, she hugged him tight. Breathing in his essence so that he became part of her. Silently swearing to make his life light and joyous.

It wasn't that easy. Not that simple. A child, she discovered, did not behave like a list. Or a column of figures.

Joey was fretful and jumpy. He wasn't sure where he was, or what had happened. He didn't like it much when Nell told him what to do. He frequently refused to cooperate. He hated the bath. Also refused to let go of Thomas or Bess. Fled up to the attic whenever he could. Hid in the garden.

Dr King laughed when Nell rang him after a couple of days of this behaviour. 'A child who is feeling better and safer is probably going to be naughtier.' Then he grew serious. 'You shouldn't have gone to see Molly,' he said. 'It was ill-advised. Please don't do it again.'

His reproof was surprisingly upsetting and she took it to heart.

Ada said she hadn't a clue about children. She placed a hand with freshly painted nails on Nell's arm. 'I so admire you taking on such a *burden*. Bold and brave.'

'I'm no help,' said Pamela when Nell asked her opinion. 'But I imagine that a good routine helps.'

Together, they hacked out a timetable of meals and bedtime (with a story) and pinned it onto the noticeboard.

The very hot spell had long gone but the evenings were fine and settled. Nell took to sitting out on the terrace and to listening to the night sounds while she made her plans.

## CHAPTER TWENTY

Days later Molly died.

'There were complications from the operation,' said Dr King. 'They took her back into theatre, but it was too late.'

He had driven to Woodspring to deliver the news very early in the morning and caught Nell in her dressing gown. 'Jim was at the hospital and he will have told the children. Daisy has been taken to her grandmother to join the boys.'

He was pale and stubbled and distressed. Nell clattered around the kitchen making tea and toast. She sat down opposite him and watched him drink and eat, relieved she was able to help on that small level at least.

'I'm so sorry,' she said. 'So very sorry.' Then, 'I'm grateful you came in person.'

'I thought we needed to tell Joey together.'

'Of course.' Nell groped through the shock. 'What will it do to the children? What will Jim do?'

'For the time being, the children can stay with Jim's mother.' He looked up at Nell. 'We will organise extra help. That's one of the things I wanted to talk about. I don't think she'd have Joey.'

'I'll have him,' Nell said, without a second's hesitation.

'I know you will.'

She felt the weight of this new commitment, the terror of accepting it, the enormity of it being thwarted. 'I mean permanently.'

She said goodbye in that moment. To the mountains, to speaking French, to the life she had created. To the glory that was Europe.

Dr King said, 'May I point out that whatever happens to Joey will need careful consideration and it's early to make decisions.'

*But he's mine*, she thought. *He is.*

She poured him out more tea. 'Does this… can this happen after having a baby?'

'Obviously,' he said. 'More often than is supposed.' Dr King was tired and her question was ill-timed. 'Not enough is known about what happens to a new mum's mind and body post-partum. Molly's deliveries were all difficult. She was exhausted. The operation took its toll and her body gave out.'

'You must brief me on how to cope with Joey's questions…'

Dr King sent her a look which was as much as to say: *Be careful, you are in this deep. Yes, yes, I am,* she almost responded.

Instead, she said, 'I'll fetch him.'

Joey did not react very much to the news his aunt had gone to heaven. Nor did he seem to mind when he learnt that Ollie, Tom and Daisy would be living somewhere else.

'Where can I stay?' he asked.

Nell knelt beside him and put her arms around him. 'Here,' she said. 'You're staying here with me. I think it's the best thing and,' she glanced over her shoulder, 'Dr King agrees.'

She drew Joey closer and kissed his fair head. 'Mrs Fry is going to make you a special cake.'

Molly's funeral took place at the church.

It had been decided that it was best that none of the children attended. Dr King's wife had kindly agreed to look after Joey and had taken him off for the morning to Hungerford with the promise of a ride in a canal boat.

The mourners filed in, the pews filled up and Mary Blatchford ground out sombre music at the organ that had seen better days and needed an overhaul.

'Both sisters now gone,' said Mr Morgan, the sidesman. 'Bad business.'

Jim sat in the front pew. He had lost weight and was flanked by men in suits that strained over the shoulders and women in black crepe dresses. These Nell presumed were relatives and friends.

The coffin, with a small posy of ox-eye daisies and hogweed on top, was carried in and placed in front of the altar. The congregation rose, and Jim stared rigidly at the east window above the altar.

Reverend Slack, subdued and measured, took the service. He opened his sermon with the words, 'We will give thanks for our sister Molly who died in the supreme service of giving life which is the privilege given to women. There is no better sacrifice.'

*Such nonsense. Such utter nonsense*, thought Nell, and wondered how many of the women sitting there would agree.

After the service, the congregation filed into the church hall, which smelt musty and needed redecoration. A couple of trestle tables had been set up and laid with cups and plates of digestive biscuits – bought, she heard someone say, with Green Shield stamps. Helpers poured out the tea.

A queue formed. As she waited for the tea, Nell was tapped on the shoulder by an elderly woman in a tweed coat that looked too thick for the weather.

'You've been looking after young Joey at the big house,' said the woman. She was not friendly. 'Has he no kith and kin?'

'I'm very happy to step in. He's a lovely child.'

'Very nice, I'm sure,' said the woman. 'But he should be handed over to the authorities.'

Nell's rage swelled hotly, savagely even. She mastered it. 'He's safe and as happy as he can be given everything that's happened to him.'

The woman in the tweed coat turned away and muttered to her companion.

That night, Nell read Joey several stories. She was attempting to branch out from tales of shovelling coal into engine tenders and was trying out *The Magic Faraway Tree*. Explaining the Land of Dreams to him definitely tested her powers.

'I want a Thomas story,' said Joey. All the same, he listened to Nell reading and his eyes grew heavy. At the last moment, they flicked open. 'When will I see Aunt Molly?'

She thought fast. 'I'm going to read you a bit more then I'll answer your question.'

By the time she had finished it, Joey, as she had hoped, was asleep. She resisted the temptation to kiss his cheek in case she woke him and went downstairs to phone Dr King for advice.

She waited until teatime the next day. Pamela had made yet another cake and she cut him a slice and watched him devour it. When he had done, she took a deep breath.

'Joey, do you remember what Dr King and I told you, that Aunt Molly has died?'

Joey stared at her.

'It means that her body is no longer working like yours and mine do. Aunt Molly is now very quiet and still and she won't be coming back.'

Still no observable reaction.

'But, Joey, we love you and will look after you. You won't be on your own.' She slid her arm around his thin shoulders and felt them stiffen and shake and held him tight while he cried. 'It's all right to be sad, Joey.'

He turned his face up to hers and she wasn't sure what to read into it.

A week later, Jim Baker turned up at Woodspring, accompanied by a man he said was Mr Gildchrist, who introduced himself as from the local council.

Mr Gildchrist looked overworked and indicated he was in a hurry. He informed Nell that he had arranged for Joey to be rehomed in the orphanage which was the other side of Hungerford. Would Nell be kind enough to pack up his things?

'No,' said Nell, feeling flames licking through her. 'I'm willing to keep him here. He's happy and beginning to settle.'

Mr Gildchrist turned bureaucrat. 'Don't get me wrong, Miss Dane, you've been very kind in looking after the young chap, but we have to sort out his future and have a duty of care to see he is provided for.'

'I'm looking after him,' said Nell.

'Miss Dane, correct me if I'm wrong but you are not a relation. Or a designated guardian.'

Jim sent Nell a look as if to say, *Go back to your other life.*

Clearly, Mr Gildchrist was not unkind, but he had things to do. He sounded regretful. 'I'm afraid I must ask you to fetch the little boy and to pack up his things.'

Nell found a happily occupied Joey helping Tommy to sweep the yard, conducting a conversation mostly in grunts.

When Joey saw Jim, he flinched and pressed against Nell. She laid a hand on his head. 'It's all right, Joey.'

Mr Gildchrist observed Joey's reaction and frowned.

Nell retained her hold on Joey. 'Mr Gildchrist, is there no way I can keep Joey?'

'No,' said Jim.

She swallowed her pride. 'Can't he be with his cousins? He'll have no one.'

'No,' repeated Jim. 'My mother can't cope.'

Nell knelt beside Joey. 'Joey, darling Joey… this very nice man is going to take you to a new home where there will be lots of other children and you will have a lovely time.'

Joey began to cry, each sob a knife slash through Nell's heart. He looked up at her as if to say, *You are betraying me.*

His few things packed by Pamela, who was as shocked as she was, Nell helped Joey into the back of Mr Gildchrist's car. Leaning in, she gathered him to her. The small body collapsed against her.

She thought of the lines of the dispossessed that had, metaphorically, wound through the Geneva office. She thought of how she had fought with wits and legal knowledge and with professional detachment.

This deal was not the same. This parting was spilling her life blood. 'Joey, this is not the end. I promise.'

Mr Gildchrist hovered. 'Miss Dane, please don't make promises that cannot be kept.' He motioned for Nell to step away from the car. 'We have to be on our way.'

Burnt into Nell's memory was Joey's ashen face looking out of the car window as it drove away.

Joey was gone.

She went to find Pamela who had taken herself up to the linen cupboard.

'So, he's away then,' she said, folding a towel into a neat rectangle. 'Had to do something.'

Nell removed the towel from her grasp and put it down. 'Pamela, I want to ask you a question.'

Pamela already knew what the question would be. Of course she did.

'Was my uncle Joey's father?'

Pamela inhaled audibly. She began to say something, stopped, began again. '*I* believe so. I've always believed so.'

Her answer was wrung from her, but it could never be unsaid.

That night, Nell woke up and sat upright. Her pyjamas were damp with sweat and her cheeks were wet.

It was that black witching moment before dawn when problems seemed insuperable, losses most profound and decisions hardest to face.

The truth was… the truth was… she loved Joey in a way that she had never loved anyone before. It was oh-so deep-rooted, fierce, and, perhaps, shared some of the instincts of the tiger protecting its young. It was unexpected, inconvenient, disruptive. And… indelible.

*The child who is inadequately parented*, said Thelma, *can be hyper-independent. It's a survival strategy and becomes habitual. You care for others but interpret your own needs as a sign of weakness.*

She got out of bed, reached for a jersey and made her way up the stairs to the attic, where she stood vigil by the model railway. The emptiness and silence had never been so marked.

Thelma had also explained about trauma. How it was buried. How it returned. How it should be recognised.

Perhaps at this moment a wakeful Joey would be thinking he had been abandoned – and she could not bear it.

She thought of what it had taken to be where she was now – a series of decisions concertinaed into each other.

Removing herself from her stepfather.

Obeying her father's request to go to Europe.

The charity work.

Declining to marry George.

Feet cramping on the makeshift floor, arms and legs a mass of gooseflesh, she bent down and touched the track with a finger.

Decision.

'You must be off your head,' said Ada when Nell confided what she was doing. 'This is serious. You can't play around.'

‘It’s not playing around. I have an appointment on Thursday up in London.’

Ada was as solemn as Nell had ever seen her. ‘You’ll ruin your life.’

They had met in Hungerford, where they decided they needed a dose of polenta cake and were heading for the Currant Bun. Ada tugged at Nell’s arm, which forced her to stop. ‘Did you hear me, Nell? Mad.’

‘Haven’t you ever done anything mad?’

‘Well, no,’ replied Ada in a tone heavy with regret. ‘No.’

‘Will you help me, Ada?’

A canal boat was making its way under the bridge, accompanied by a flotilla of ducks, and Ada concentrated on its disappearing stern. ‘I don’t think I should. I don’t think I can. As your friend, I must tell you it’s a bad idea.’

Abandoning Ada on the bridge, she returned to the car. They had not known each other long but Nell was more hurt and troubled by her lack of support than she cared to admit.

At Woodspring, she holed up in the study and, for the *nth* time, combed through the financial records. Every so often, her eye was caught by the framed photograph of her father and uncle which now stood on the desk.

*Her father with his suitcase beside him in New York. Her mother wrapped in a fur. ‘Say goodbye to your father, Nell.’*

Even then, she must have sensed that he was gone.

Thursday morning. Nell drove to Hungerford, parked at the railway station and caught the early-morning London train.

She had settled into her book when a voice said, ‘Nell?’

Ada.

High-gloss lipstick, hair artfully flicked into waves, large handbag over her arm, balanced precariously on platform shoes as the train jolted forward.

'You need a companion.' It wasn't a question.

Nell laughed. 'I'm very particular about who.'

That was that.

Ada looked down at the handbag now colonizing her lap. 'I think I understand,' she said. 'You were a child from a broken home. It never leaves you.'

'No,' replied Nell. 'I don't think it ever does.'

In London, they took a taxi to St Catherine's House in Kingsway. There Nell was to collect Joey's birth certificate, which she had requested.

Ushered into the waiting area, they sat for over an hour on hard chairs. Eventually, Nell was summoned to the counter and a copy of Joey's birth certificate was handed over in brown government stationery.

She held it in her hand unopened as they walked back through Covent Garden, past the Actors' Church. The old fruit market had moved to Nine Elms but, in places, they were hit by a lingering suggestion of vegetable decay. Only when they were ensconced in a café in the Strand did Nell permit herself to open the envelope.

Her eye homed in on the space for the father's name. It was blank. She pushed it away and covered her eyes with her hand.

Ada retrieved it. 'His name is Joseph and he was born on 1st May 1970,' she said, 'Joseph Arthur.' She looked up. 'I feel I should have Joey's permission to do this. Mother, Elizabeth Malloy. Father…'

'But no father,' said Nell, desolate.

The solicitor's wife through and through, Ada explained, 'Bess was unmarried. She would not be permitted to give the father's name unless she had applied to court for an affiliation order. It's unlikely Bess would have done that. More than likely, she had no idea.'

Nell sent Ada a sharp look.

'Men don't have to put their names on a birth certificate?' she said. 'They get away with it?'

'Many do.' Ada's reply was as dry as desert sand.

'I'm not giving up,' said Nell. 'Just so you know.'

Ada reached across the table and took Nell's hand. 'With you,' she said.

They took themselves off to Leicester Square and a showing of *Picnic at Hanging Rock*, and emerged chastened and intrigued.

Nell drove over to Hodgkin House, a large Victorian pile near Reading.

The house was surrounded by trees and Nell fretted that it would be damp and dark. A notice under the bell read, *By Appointment Only.*

Where were the children? There was no suggestion of them anywhere in the paved area in front of the house where the cars were parked.

She was shown into a waiting room. There was no sign of children in here either. The chairs were hard and the hush marked. Only her elevated heartbeat thudding in her ears broke the silence.

'Miss Dane…' A man in a blazer and cravat advanced into the room and held out his hand. 'How do you do? I'm Eric Plume, director of Hodgkin House. You have requested to see Joey Malloy.'

'Correct. I phoned and made an appointment.'

'I'm very sorry but you've had a wasted journey. I'm afraid that won't be possible.'

'Of course it's *possible*,' said Nell.

He looked at her. 'Quite right. As an ex-headmaster, I should know better than to be imprecise. It *is* possible but not desirable. Or, permissible. Joey is settling in and it would upset him to see you.' He took a step back. 'I'm sure you wouldn't wish that.'

Was that right? The memory of meeting with her father in New York… much longed for and a disappointment. Leaving in its wake an ache, a grief. Disturbance.

Yes.

'The experts agree,' Eric Plume continued, 'that until a child has settled with the new surroundings and adults, it's best not to disrupt the familiarisation process.'

But Joey had to know that she was there for him.

'Mr Plume, I would like to see him. I demand to see him.'

Too late. She sounded unbalanced. So very unlike the professional she was. Had been.

He frowned. 'You mean well, Miss Dane. I mean well. All of us mean well and try to do our best. Sometimes our emotions get in the way, but we must take the advice of the experts.'

'Perhaps you don't realise that Joey has lived with me for several weeks. We know one another. He was very, very upset to be taken away. He has no one else and it's a crucial time for him.' She spun the roulette wheel. 'I have reason to believe that we are related and, therefore, I could adopt him.'

He looked at her and she read, *desperate spinster.*

'Mr Plume, I suspect you might think a single woman is incapable of looking after a child. But this is 1975.'

'Indeed yes,' he replied. 'We have moved on from Victorian times.'

Every line in his posture suggested he thought the observation irrelevant.

'Miss Dane, I applaud your kindness. But more than kindness is required. Evidence is what is needed.'

'I'll get it,' said Nell.

Eric Plume was skilled at handling situations such as this one. 'Let us compromise, Miss Dane. I suggest you take a look at Joey through the window to see for yourself that he's fine. Then I must ask you to leave and not to return.'

The five minutes or so that she was allotted were anguished. Looking through the window to a group of children playing outside in a sandpit, she spotted Joey instantly. Standing alone. Bewildered. Uncertain. Thinner. Seemingly less sure on his feet. Pulling at his forefinger because he was sad.

The ever-present knife slashed away at her heart, drawing arterial blood.

'Miss Dane, it's time to go,' said Eric Plume. 'I'll show you out.'

'I'll be back,' she said, so angry she was almost speechless.

He smiled politely.

# CHAPTER TWENTY-ONE

Dr King had recruited a new appointments secretary. 'It's a sign of the times,' he said. 'People aren't any sicker. Just less prepared to put up with illness.'

Muriel Chester now acted as gatekeeper for the surgery. She was not to everyone's taste. The words 'bully' and 'Rottweiler' had been uttered. This was not entirely unfair. Muriel Chester regarded patients as an inconvenience and acted as an efficient deterrent to keep Dr King's workload to a reasonable level.

Very grudgingly, Nell was granted an appointment.

Dr King was writing out a prescription as she came into the consulting room. 'Nell.' He took off his glasses and laid them on top of the pad. 'How very nice,' he said. 'I hope you're not ill.'

The nights were chillier now, but the days were still warm and the consulting room was stuffy.

Nell sat down and began a negotiation. 'I gather that in the UK if a doctor or a vicar or a lawyer agrees to an adoption, they can arrange it. Pamela Fry tells me that you have done so in the past. The Swifts adopted a little girl.'

'It doesn't happen very often.' Dr King got up from his chair and opened a window. Fresher air swept in. 'It's a big responsibility and I'm happy to say the adoption agencies are agitating to regularise the process.'

She extracted a file from her bag. 'I'm here to ask if you will help me.'

'You wish to adopt Joey.'

'Yes.'

Dr King retreated behind his professional manner. 'You're a single woman, which means the odds are against you. Nor do I know you very well.'

'You know something of me.' She played her opening move. 'Forgive me, but did you know Mr and Mrs Swift who took in Emily?'

'The Swifts are married and the family has lived in Yew Green for a long time.' A slight reproof? 'You would have to persuade me that you're able to take on such a responsibility.'

She looked Dr King straight in the eye. 'I suspect I'm in a better position to look after Joey than Bess was.' *Maladroit.* 'I mean financially and *no* disrespect to Bess. Nothing replaces being the parent.'

*Bess singing to Joey in the pram.*

His tone was neutral. 'Bess's parents were deeply upset and urged her to give up Joey for adoption. Bess was ill after the birth and they almost succeeded. But she kept him.'

Intimacies of pregnancy and childbirth were alien to Nell. The firestorm of physical and mental changes. She could only envisage a Bess weakened by childbirth and by her terror for the future. Harried, too, by the acrimony surrounding her.

What she did have in common with Bess was her resolution to hold on to Joey.

'Can you tell me anything?'

'It is common knowledge that Bess fought tooth and nail to keep her baby.' Dr King was prepared to let a few details drop on which Nell feasted. 'She was good with your uncle. Patient and non-judgemental. She was anxious when she became pregnant that your uncle wouldn't employ her any more, but he loved Joey too. And didn't see him as a problem. He insisted that Joey continue to come up to the house after Bess was killed.' Dr King fiddled with his glasses. 'Why are you doing this?'

'Simple. I love Joey. He needs a family.' She spoke passionately. Urgently.

'A lot of people love a child. But they don't adopt them.'

She looked down at her hands in her lap. 'Dr King, you know about desire?'

Dr King looked startled.

'I don't mean physical desire between a man and a woman. I'm talking about the deep feelings for a child. The desire to love and nurture them. I've seen how complicated they are. Wise and angry. Sad and mean. And defensive.' Nell summoned every strand of reason and rationality, the tools she was so used to working with. 'To usher them into adult life, safe and well in mind and body, is the prime duty of adults.'

And yet, and yet, as she now knew, reason and rationality were not the whole story.

Dr King remained silent and Nell added, 'I'm connected to Joey. I can't explain it, but it's there. I want to give him a home. I want to protect him.'

Dr King said, 'If you make a formal application, you'll need to be assessed and I would need to assemble a case.'

She was anxious that tears were edging closer to the surface. Took a deep breath, brought herself under control. 'Dr King, I think Joey is my uncle's son and therefore my cousin. Is that not a solid enough reason?'

Dr King didn't pretend to be surprised.

'You knew who his father was?'

Tactical error.

Dr King frowned. 'You can't expect me to answer that.'

'I'm going to give up my job and live at Woodspring. That's proof of how serious I am.'

Silence.

'Is there anything else I can do to persuade you?'

Dr King levelled his gaze at Nell. 'You don't intend to coerce me?'

'God, no.'

'Then you must accept that it is a judgement that must be objective.'

Nell picked up her bag. At the door she turned. '*Please*, Dr King. Joey's in a bad place.'

Nell flew to Geneva and emerged from the airport into strong autumn sunshine. On the way to her office, she stopped for the coffee for which she had longed – and drank two cups.

Gabriel was waiting for her in the office. 'I can't say I'm surprised,' he said when Nell gave in her notice. 'But isn't it high-risk to do this before you know if you can adopt the little boy?' There was a touch of condescension in his bearing which was not unusual.

She looked out of the plate-glass window to the city comfortably settled around the lake. 'It is.'

'Is there any way I can persuade you to stay here? It won't be easy to replace your cool head. It's been your life's work. Your job. Your identity.'

'It's a gamble,' said Nell.

'You're not a gambler,' replied Gabriel. 'You stick to the straight and narrow.'

Gabriel knew how to wound.

That night, his questions tormented her. How *would* she cope with no longer being a professional woman? Not to mention coping with Woodspring?

She thought of the hot, blood-dotted cycles of being female. She thought of a foetus in the womb, sucking greedily at the manna offered by its mother. She hadn't appreciated before that it was a process that locks a woman into profound altruism. Giving endlessly of her body to her own detriment. So mundane, so ordinary a thing that it is rarely noticed.

Bess had done that. Given and nurtured. The gods being willing… the gods being willing… Nell could take it further.

She packed up her possessions, thanking providence (or whichever quirk of inherited behaviour was responsible) for her dislike of accruing stuff. Thus it was only clothes, a chair and a lamp which she arranged to be shipped back.

Two weeks later, she stepped out of the flat for the last time. On the flight back, she was engulfed in gloom and regret. Taking this gamble was alien to the creed she had lived by – all that she had made of herself.

Ada and Pamela were waiting at Woodspring to welcome her back, and her spirits lifted. Pamela served tea in the drawing room and… polenta cake. 'Mrs Allen persuaded me to have a go. It was a nightmare getting hold of the flour.'

'There's a new delicatessen opening,' said Ada. '*Italian.* We won't know ourselves.'

The idea of a new delicatessen was extraordinarily cheering and she and Ada hatched plans to buy tomato puree, Parmesan and Parma ham. Pamela said that, personally and not to get her wrong, but she preferred a good pot of Branstons.

Nell waited.

Long walks up to the downs where the horses exercised were one diversion. What was Dr King thinking? Concluding? Her stomach ached. Her mind was fogged. She walked for miles. Back at Woodspring, when the sun dipped in the late afternoons and the birds quietened, Nell worked through the remaining house documents.

She thought of Joey alone and seemingly abandoned – and that was excruciating. *That* did made her weep.

Her father's and uncle's papers were sorted into separate folders. Rifling through Harry's, she found the bill for his funeral and a handwritten invoice for Faith's plaque, plus a stack of invoices for medical expenses. These she threw away. Robert's file also contained medical invoices, plus a couple of reports on his condition. Saddened by the decline of the two brothers, she threw these away too.

Replacing the folders in the bureau drawer, she dislodged a smaller pile of papers at the back. They turned out to be documents and bank statements, dating from five years back. She was on the point of transferring them into her uncle's file when one of the documents caught her eye. In 1973 her uncle had signed a request, via Fraser Allen, to transfer £20,000 out of the family trust to Elizabeth Malloy.

The numbers blurred. Coalesced. With the renewed focus came clarity.

She reached for the telephone and dialled the bank.

After the call was finished, she sought out Pamela who was in the stable flat. Tommy was out at the pub.

'I'm sorry to intrude,' said Nell as Pamela led her upstairs to the sitting area.

The flat was neat and very clean. Astonishing really, considering how much work Pamela did in the main house.

'Pamela, there must have been periods when my uncle was lucid. I mean, could he, did he, have had a say-so over his financial affairs?'

'Yes and no. But once he had an idea in his head, he was very stubborn.'

Nell swallowed. 'You think Joey is my uncle's son? Why? Can you say?'

'Not for sure.' Pamela frowned. Shifted in her chair. Looked away. 'But Bess was such a loving person.' Her eyes filled. 'She was always hugging people. Your uncle depended on her visits. I wouldn't be surprised if she comforted him in that way. He was handsome, you know, until the end. I did ask her about it once after Joey was born and she wouldn't answer, but the look on her face said it all. She was glowing. "It will be all right, Pammy," that's what she called me. "I'll have money. Captain Robert will see us all right." She was killed not long afterwards. Captain Robert took a downward turn after she had gone.'

It wasn't exactly a conspiracy, but it was a silence. A silence that had enfolded Bess, Robert and Joey.

No one had wished to break it for reasons of loyalty. Nell got it – but also raged that discretion and silence had cost Joey.

The following morning she was waiting outside Dr King's surgery before it opened. The minute Muriel Chester folded back the door, she was inside. 'I *have* to speak to him,' she said.

'He's having breakfast with his family,' she said. 'His son is visiting.' She lowered a censorious gaze. 'He's allowed some private time, you know.'

Nell said she would wait.

Other patients filed in, some of whom she recognised. Mrs Herbert who had run the jam and cake stall at the fete, and Harold Peters who had organised the hoopla. Each acknowledged the other but conversation was not on offer. Not that she wished it.

Her world narrowed to one sharp focus point. Nell sat in the hard chair and watched them pass one by one into the consulting room. Eventually, Dr King poked his head around the door and beckoned her in.

She settled in the chair. 'Can we establish something, please?' He frowned, wary and more than a little watchful. 'I know you can't divulge confidential information about others.'

She was calm.

He took out a handkerchief, polished his glasses and gestured for her to continue.

‘My uncle wanted to pay Bess Malloy £20,000 from the family trust. A lot of money, but she died before the payment was made. I’ve checked with the bank manager and there’s a letter written by my uncle’s lawyer instructing the transfer.’ She looked up into the face which had witnessed much during his tenure at Yew Green. ‘Why would he do that if he wasn’t Joey’s father?’

‘Many reasons, Nell, and you should consider that Bess might have had another lover. Even if your uncle was Joey’s father, it’s debatable he had the capacity to understand it.’

Nell squeezed her hands together, so tight they hurt, but kept her voice level. ‘What colour were my uncle’s eyes?’

‘Brown.’

‘And Joey’s are brown. What colour were Bess’s?

‘Not brown.’

‘Brown is the dominant eye colour, isn’t it?’

‘It is.’

‘I rest my case.’

‘It’s not proven,’ said Dr King.

Nell looked away. The strength of her despair took even her by surprise. ‘Dr King, we have to think of Joey. I could make up for some of his losses. Not all, of course. There must be some way of convincing you.’

To her distress, her eyes filled.

Dr King got to his feet. He shut the window. He looked down at the prescription pad on his desk.

‘You’re serious, Nell.’

‘You know I am.’

He returned to his desk. In those seconds, something had changed in his demeanour.

'I must trust you, it seems,' he said.

'Yes.'

'There's one thing. But it's difficult and expensive. It's a new technique.'

'I'll pay,' she cried. 'Whatever it takes.'

'It would involve Joey having a blood test.'

Nell grimaced at the thought of a needle in the little arm.

'Towards the end of his life, your uncle had a fall and sustained a serious cut. He was hospitalised and had a transfusion. We have a record of his blood type in the surgery files. This new development is called HLA typing, which could compare the genetic material of Joey's white blood cells with your uncle's. If there's an 80 per cent match, it would be considered proof.'

Incandescent with hope, she said, 'Arrange it please, Dr King.'

Sick and sleepless, Nell waited.

The house reached out to wrap her in the spirits of her dead family. *This is your place.*

The backlash arrived. *What was she doing?*

Deep down, she was living with a continual astonishment that she, cool Nell, was in this pitiful, vulnerable state.

How precarious outcomes were. How little control anyone had over life. Of all people, she should have known. But she hadn't *known.* Which is why, she supposed, people went on crazy pilgrimages, married disastrously or took to drink.

When would Dr King contact her?

Six weeks later, early in the morning, the phone rang.

Nell now faced Eric Plume in the waiting room of Hodgkin House. He did not hide his disapproval. 'I feel this is tenuous,' he said, 'but if Dr King has put his stamp on it then…'

'I'm sure you're a man of science…' Nell interrupted, grateful that the relevant documents had been duplicated, deposited in the bank and copies sent ahead to Hodgkin House. 'The science shows that Joey and I are related. Cousins.'

'Science does not solve everything. Joey was beginning to settle and I hope this does not disturb him. I hope this is not more about you, Miss Dane, than about Joey.'

'Possibly some of it is,' she replied. 'None of us act without some kind of selfish impulse. But it's mostly about Joey.'

Anger at regulations and lack of imagination. Anger at Joey's needless distress and at Eric Plume's insinuations.

'Let us hope so,' he said.

Yet, watching Joey being led into the waiting room and his face lighting up when he saw who was waiting, her anger burnt into nothing. It was irrelevant.

He ran towards her. She bent over him, wrapped her arms around him, inhaled a grubby little boy smell, felt the soft curve of his cheek and said, 'Darling Joey, you're coming home with me.'

He looked this way and that. 'To the big house?'

'Yes. You and I will live there together. I will look after you. We're family.'

There was silence.

Then… 'Can I see Thomas?'

# MIA
# 2005

# CHAPTER TWENTY-TWO

MI5 surveillance officers are considered the best.

(Give or take.)

They're there to protect.

Training takes months, plus the year on probation.

You learn the skills in your specialist area – security, counterterrorism, money laundering anyone? – swear the Official Secrets Act a thousand times and, presto, you are bound hand and foot to your country.

She, Mia Greene, bought into the idea of protection, for it was lazy to imagine there were no bad actors. The world was full of them. *That* she learnt early on with the dismembering of Albert. (For information, Albert was, had been, a duck.) Even lazier not to prepare to act against them. The UK had its faults and enough operational kleptocrats, narcissistic politicians and feral youth to people an army, but it was *decent* at heart and worth guarding. Cities, towns, villages, fields, rivers.

Seven years in, even she was astonished at the number of those bad actors. It was non-stop. They kept on coming… terrorists, ideologues, religious fanatics. Only one thing united them. They tended to be young men.

What was it with testosterone?

'Guys, you'll get to push the boundaries,' said their instructor. 'A lot. You'll be tempted to overdo it.' He rolled his eyes. 'With reason. Oh yes, with reason. Talk to us if you feel that way.'

Mia avoided the talking. It was a point of pride. She was in the business and that was that. She knew the rules. Sometimes – no, increasingly – she felt a flutter of discontent. Was there a new way of living maybe that she could get her head around? At those moments she visualised the pale spring sunshine filtering through the window of the bedroom she had shared with her brother on the Yorkshire housing estate. 'No dissing this house,' said her mother. 'We're lucky to have it so.' She remembered then her escapes to the river which ran alongside the estate. The *best* place for a child. A treacherous riverbank. Bulrushes. Mud, masses of it. The branches overhanging the water. Clumps of marsh marigolds and cuckoo flower. The tree – the Tree of Secrets – in which she had confided because she knew it would never tell.

She thought, too, about Albert. First seen as a ball of duckling. Enchanting and noisy. Then the grown mallard, all glossy and iridescent. Still noisy – testosterone again. Then his bloodied corpse on the riverbank. Kicked to death and decapitated by local boys who worked always as a pack because they couldn't face what they were on their own. Avenging Albert had taken ingenuity, but she had managed to throw lit fireworks into their paths which made one of them pee in his pants. He was never allowed to forget it. Albert had come to her in a dream. 'Thank you,' he said.

These days, her milieu was the city streets, walkways smelling of urine and littered with rubbish. She moved through a soundscape of traffic, humans and machinery – interestingly, the city duck had a louder quack than his country cousins. No mouthing of confidences now to a tree or to anyone else for that matter. She had to be as silent and as closed as the clam.

She first encountered Joey Dane on a warm May morning – when anyone who possessed a heart, however flattened, could not fail to feel recharged.

She had boarded the 7.46 from Letchworth to King's Cross, on the tail of a self-radicalised suspect. Intel chatter had alerted the team that he had launched himself on a one-man killing spree and they had moved into place.

It was the kind of operation at which she was adept, possessing the ability to disappear into the crowd. 'It takes skill not to be noticed,' said Team Leader. 'You have it.'

The younger Mia, mousy, a bit chunky, awkward, would not have known whether to laugh or cry. Nowadays, slim and super fit, she accepted it as a big, big compliment.

Clutching a coffee cup and dressed for the part in a dark jacket and trousers, plus trainers, her hair pulled back, she walked down the platform.

Last thing the previous night the team lost the suspect, who had holed up in a hiding place. That was always cause for worry. Hiding places indicated a helper somewhere in the equation. The situation was not unusual, but it was at the end of a hard day and frustration and fatigue gripped the guys by the scruff of their weary necks. But luck held (yay) and Zero Six picked the suspect up early in the morning leaving a block of flats on the outskirts of the city.

The team threw their radio net over him. 'Target approaching station. Black rucksack, green combat trousers, brown hair, red baseball cap. Approx five foot eleven.'

Zero Five chipped in. 'Entering station. Used pass. Approaching Platform 2.'

The ops room would be coordinating updates and orders.

The suspect boarded the train and sat down close to the door. Mia found a seat further down the carriage, raised the coffee cup to her mouth and muttered into it. 'Carriage 3, seat 16. Facing engine.'

She leant back against the tacky plush and permitted her eyes to close for a couple of seconds. Operations such as this one were invariably tedious and tricky.

Adopting a persona was a process. She left her hair unwashed and pulled it back tightly. No make-up except for a smudge of unflattering lipstick. Modest and unassuming was written all over her.

She opened her eyes and clashed with the gaze of the man sitting opposite her.

Her first thought was: *I know him.* Her second was to tell herself to shut up. Thinking that you knew someone was a result of heightened sensitivities encouraged by the training. Developing extra-sensory response to an expression, a gait, posture was part and parcel of the mind enjoying introducing red herrings and false assumptions.

The suspect was sitting with his rucksack on his knee. Mia got to her feet, took off her jacket and slotted it into the luggage rack, which gave her a chance to check out the target and the shapes inside the rucksack from another angle. There were too many passengers to continue to use her body radio undetected.

There was nothing for it but to sit it out and to pray he didn't try anything on the train. What could happen did not bear thinking about. So she didn't.

That, too, was part of the training.

The man opposite continued to observe Mia intermittently.

Half an hour later, the train drew into King's Cross.

*Brace. Brace.*

The suspect queued to get off the train. Bending over, Mia fiddled with the lace on her trainer and muttered, 'Suspect disembarking. Carriage 3. Repeat 3.'

Straightening up, she encountered the gaze of the man who had been opposite her. Dark eyebrows raised in astonishment above a pair of brown eyes.

No time to worry about him.

Mia's gaze slid past his shoulder. The train doors opened. The suspect moved towards them. She grabbed her jacket and headed for the door at the other end of the carriage.

The station reception team should be in place – but you could never be sure, and she stepped down from the train with care.

'Zero Five has sight,' a voice said in her ear.

Mia walked fast towards the ticket barrier. The tannoy blared incomprehensible information. Passengers eddied. An aroma of overcooked coffee percolated through the concourse.

The suspect kept pace with the drift of passengers, his thumbs tucked into his rucksack strap. Ensuring the weight was evenly distributed?

'Suspect heading for left-hand barrier,' she said.

A shout sounded through the hubbub, spooking their prey. In the seconds that followed he understood he'd been blown, took off across the concourse and jumped over the barrier.

Could the team get on him fast enough? In a split second she decided not, sprinted towards the barrier and vaulted over. The suspect was up ahead, making for one of the smaller exits from the station. She raced towards him.

In that moment, a bewildered member of station staff obviously assumed that Mia was the problem and stuck out a leg. The last thing she remembered with clarity was the ground coming up to meet her.

When she next opened her eyes, she was lying in the recovery position and pain was shooting through her left hand and up her arm.

'Can you speak?' asked a voice.

She did her best to focus on the face from which it had issued. He seemed familiar but she had no idea why. 'Yes.'

'We're waiting for an ambulance. Broken finger I think and concussion.' He touched the side of her head and she flinched. 'That needs looking at.' He leant over. 'Your wallet dropped out of your pocket so I came after you. You could say the day has got off to a flying start.'

Passengers and trolleys flowed around this oasis where she was marooned with a stranger.

Mia tried to shift position and hissed with pain.

'Best not to move,' he said. 'If you're wondering what happened to the guy with the rucksack…' He glanced up. 'Looks like he was arrested by two men in tracksuits.' The breath sighed from her. He checked the pulse on her uninjured wrist. 'Great disguise. Tracksuits.'

Dozens of pairs of feet crossed her vision. 'Don't assume

anything,' she said haltingly and tried to move her injured hand. Her reward was an extraordinary bolt of pain. 'God...' she said through gritted teeth.

She must have fainted, for the next thing she knew she was in the ambulance and her rescuer was there too, talking to a member of the crew.

Did she have clean underwear on – of the sort, of course, that her persona would wear? Yes, yes. Thank the gods, for the plain white pants and workhorse bra she had put on that morning.

Turning her head cautiously, for any movement did not agree with her, she looked towards the frosted ambulance window. Her mother would be pleased. She rated sensible underwear.

'My name is Joey Dane...' The voice of her rescuer dragged Mia back to the present. 'You're probably concussed.'

'Joey Dane. Sounds like a film star.'

'You're definitely concussed.'

He had good features and a nice chin. The brown eyes, she decided in her mental fug, were both watchful and expressive. 'Where am I going?'

'A & E,' said the crew member. 'And you're going there in the latest model of ambulance, which means all your vital signs are being monitored and transmitted to the hospital ahead of us.'

'Brilliant,' said Mia and closed her eyes.

No surgery was required but two fingers of her left hand were splinted together. That was a bummer. The concussion was diagnosed as slight, but she was to be kept in hospital overnight. Which, she was informed, was lucky as beds were gold dust. The decision was just as well. Each time she tried to sit up, a wrecking ball knocked her back onto the pillows. The radiographer supervising the X-ray had been very, very gentle. The nurses lovely… Some people were good… her thoughts flew around on airy painkiller wings. It was bracing to be reminded about decency.

*Take the week off.* The message from her current handler also instructed her not to make contact until then.

No clue in the message as to whether the mission had been successful or not. No doubt a punishment for being caught out by the oldest trick in the book. Grabbing at her thoughts and tethering them, she reckoned the suspect had been hauled off for questioning at the police station used to hold high-profile terror suspects.

My God, it was noisy in the ward. Trolleys rattled. Patients called out. Even so, it was wonderful… yes, wonderful… to be lying there. Switching off rarely happened in her profession.

Her profession. Her profession?

The propulsive energies and desires and ambitions of her early twenties were softening in her thirties. Odd? Or to be expected?

Growing older… growing older.

The downswing from the shock and painkillers now kicked in.

Inactivity was not a positive state. Her mood deep-dived. You arrived on this earth, did a few things. Died. Did it matter if the latter took place before the threescore years and ten?

The bad actors, the ones she mulled over, and of whom she was reminded most days, they were not the whole story. She must believe that. Vigilance was good. Surveillance was all. But she couldn't deny that much of her working life was dealing with rubbish people and it was rubbing off on her.

Twenty-four hours later, Mia took a taxi back to her own flat – permissible since she was off the deployment. If she had been working, then she would have been directed to a safe house.

The block of flats had been crammed into a space created by bombs during the war in a road estate agents called Battersea but which was really Clapham Junction. Its developers hadn't concerned themselves with elegance, only profit, but Mia wasn't bothered about the aesthetics. Provided she could afford the rent, it did her fine.

She stepped out on the second floor and opened her front door. The sitting area fronted onto a street which had a deal of traffic and was always parked up, and her bedroom was at the back.

She entered cautiously. It smelt unoccupied but, sticking to procedure, she made the security check before opening the windows and shaking up cushions. She yearned to make up her bed with fresh sheets, but she was already exhausted.

Should she be worried? It had taken only a bang on the head and a broken finger to knock her right back.

Cradling her injured hand, she stood irresolute, out of line of sight of the window.

She rang base using the safe line to get her position sorted.

'Who's a bloody fool?' said Team Leader. 'I've put you on sick leave for two weeks, then it will be a desk job until you get the medical OK.'

'Was the job done?' Mia knew she shouldn't ask.

There was a hesitation. 'Job done.'

So… whoever it was had been thwarted from committing an appalling act in a public space and big thanks should go the way of the team. Plus the listeners and intelligence analysts, of course. The whole enchilada.

She sat quite still, questioning her fragility, sorting her priorities.

Her mobile rang.

'This is Joey Dane. Is that Mia?'

She would never be able to describe what took place but, at the sound of Joey's voice, something woke up.

'I wanted to check you were OK. I hope you don't mind, I got this number from your wallet.'

Fuck. In her dopey state, she hadn't been protective. That meant confession time in the office, a reprimand and a new number.

'Oh.'

'Are you OK?'

'I don't know,' she said truthfully. 'I've never felt like this before.'

'Like what?'

'Brittle.'

'Poor you.' There was a sweetness in his inflection. Kindness too, which brought a lump lumbering into her throat.

'I owe you many thanks.'

'All in a day's work. Are you too fragile to go out? Coffee perhaps? Lunch?'

Twenty-four hours later they met for lunch in a café close to Battersea Park. He helped her off with her jacket. 'Day Three is always the stiff and battered one.'

Mia allowed him to seat her in a chair by the window where a weak sun warmed the panes. He reached over the table and touched her hand, which had gone all shades of a fetching yellow-green spectrum with a hint of plum thrown in. 'How's the sensation in the fingertips?'

'It comes and goes.'

He smiled at her. 'I won't ask what you were doing.'

Deflection was second nature. 'Why were you on the train?'

'Visiting a friend and her latest baby. Her fourth.'

'Goodness. Heroes. Or masochists?'

Joey picked up the menu. 'Both, but to have a large family must be something.'

She reckoned he was, as she was, in his mid-thirties. A clue lay in the lines radiating from the corners of his eyes, matching the ones on her own face. Smile nice. Hands well shaped with trimmed nails. Professional expertise noted the small cut under his chin, the jeans and trainers… She halted mid observation. The assessment was not professional.

He put down the menu. 'My turn to scrutinise you.'

To her consternation, Mia blushed. 'Sorry.'

'Don't apologise. I enjoyed it.'

Over their salads, Joey told her that he was a vet working at a practice near Clapham Common and Mia told Joey that she worked in a security firm. He raised his eyebrows but made no comment. Over coffee – his an Americano, hers a double espresso – he told her that he was brought up in the country. And she reciprocated and told him about the river and the Tree of Secrets, which made him laugh. She didn't tell him which county, though.

They shared the bill and, when they left the café, he took her arm and steered her across the road into Battersea Park and settled her on a bench.

'Sit,' he said with a hint of sternness. 'You can't overdo it.' For once, she did as she was told. 'Thank you,' he said. 'Relapses are forbidden.'

The sun had grown warmer and stronger. Joey shrugged off his jacket and rolled up his sleeves. 'Vitamin D.'

In the distance the traffic circulating around the park sounded lazily. Closer to them were the cries of children and dog owners calling their dogs.

'Did you always want to be a vet?'

'Once I had moved on from desperately wishing to be a train driver, yes.'

Mia peered at an elderly dog walker. 'How lucky to be so certain.'

'Yes.' He turned to look at Mia and a key in a complicated lock turned.

*Oh my Lord*, she thought.

'I suspect I can't ask anything about your job.'

She answered indirectly. 'I was a buyer for sports equipment once. Didn't work out.' Sticking to the truth wherever possible was how it worked. 'Now, I manage a team that checks out companies' security systems. We work all over the place.'

'And run after suspicious men in railway stations.'

'There's a lot of industrial espionage,' she said. 'You've no idea.'

They were silent.

'I used to work in Hungerford,' said Joey eventually, 'but

came up to London after Nell, my cousin, died.' He responded to her unvoiced question. 'She adopted me when I was little and brought me up. Long story. After her death, I needed to get away.'

So, he had loved her.

'It was just her and me.'

*Just her and me.* Families worked in strange ways. She was fond of her family and they of her, but she got from Joey's tone that a deep connection had run between him and his cousin.

He added, 'Nell saved me.'

Mia thought of her parents. Still living in the house on the estate, increasingly cluttered with walking sticks and medication. Still hanging on to every word of her infrequent phone calls.

The sun hit Mia's cheek. 'This is great,' she said. It had been a long time since she had relaxed in this way. Even when off-duty she remained wired for danger but here, in a London park and in the sun, torpor claimed her.

'You can doze if you want,' he said. 'Use my shoulder.'

To her surprise, as soon as her head touched his shoulder she fell into a darkness smelling of flowers and hay and alive with the chatter of children. Dimly, she felt Joey put an arm around her. When she woke, it was still there.

Embarrassed, she disengaged herself. 'Have I been asleep long?'

'Twenty minutes or so.' He eased his shoulder. 'Did you know you're lovely when you're asleep?'

It seemed too upfront to say that no one had ever said that to her before. 'That's nice of you.'

His eyes glinted with… what? She wasn't sure. 'Shall I take you home? You should get some rest. It's important.'

'Why are you taking so much trouble?'

'I don't know,' he said. 'Friendship?' There was a question mark in his voice.

Friendship?

'I'll send you my new phone number,' she said.

The next day she went out and bought herself a second phone, which depleted her savings.

Before she returned to work at the end of her sick leave, he messaged, 'Are you up to a film?'

Yes… yes she was.

She dressed with care in a black jersey skirt – it was a challenge to wear one for a change – an electric-blue cardigan and hoop earrings. Sitting in the back row of the playhouse, breathing the smell of popcorn, with the adverts punching in, she relived the time when adverts were fun. Sitting beside Joey, she almost enjoyed the spectacle of a car being driven down a glacier and the admonition to dive off a coral reef in a skimpy bikini.

The main feature drew them into an alternate dream world of the golden eagles that lived with the Kazakhs in Mongolia. A cool, beautifully shot piece of reportage, underlaid with reverence for the wild and made with devotion, about the eagles that lived and hunted in the ochre-coloured landscape and their interaction with humans.

Taken as fledglings from their nests, the eagles stayed with their human keepers for five years or so. An intense, almost loving relationship. Certainly one of respect. They are only borrowed, said the Kazakhs, and released them back into the wild to breed after their time together was up.

The camera fastened on feather, claw and beak. It focussed on the eagle eye, the shape of the hooded head, it eavesdropped on the cries of the hunter swooping down towards the unsuspecting fox or desert rat.

Mia was mesmerised.

*Centuries of tradition were under attack,* said the voice-over. *The pylons being erected between growing cities were deathtraps for the eagles, who were frequently electrocuted on their wires. Ever more cattle on the plains invaded their hunting grounds. The need... the duty... to preserve the birds and a way of life was growing.*

She sat very still at the finish while the (meagre) audience filed out, aware that something had turned over in her mind.

'Awesome,' said Joey.

Because of who she was and what she did, the next stage in the evening was never easy. Sometimes it was fine. An encounter. Nice. Brief. Pleasant for both. Moments to be relished and then forgotten. Sometimes, it led to tears and complications – and had done so once or twice in the past.

They taxied back to her flat. At the door, Joey said, 'I'd like to come in.'

There was silence. Then, she nodded.

The stairs under her feet were just as per normal. So, too, was the flaking paint on the walls and the uninviting lighting, but she perceived them from a distance.

At her front door, she inserted the key and stepped inside. Joey bent over and kissed her and she thought, *I haven't checked him. I should have checked him out.*

It was too late. They were in the bedroom, and he was undressing her, taking care not to knock her hand.

She lay and waited but Joey seemed in no hurry. He propped himself up on his elbow and said, 'You're especially lovely with nothing on.'

'Is this friendship?' she asked.

He traced a line up from her thigh, over her abdomen, running lightly over a breast, and came to rest in the hollow between her neck and collarbone – an exquisitely responsive spot.

'You can be friends as well as lovers.'

Mia shivered and encountered the brown eyes. Containing a question mark, yes, but also tender.

The moment held, extended, and a promise was there. Already, this encounter was different. Usually, any man in her bed went about it with dispatch and urgency.

He brushed her cheek with his mouth, and she melted into the bedclothes. 'Keep still,' he said. He must have seen her frown and grinned. 'I'm only making love to you with care for your arm, not taking over your life.'

When he kissed her properly, Mia forgot objections.

Much later, she surfaced. Drowsy and quiescent. For once, work did not come pressing down. Beside her, Joey slept, one hand flung up over the pillow, his face turned away.

He looked so boyish that she smiled. After a moment, she turned over to look at the clock and to check her phone.

There was a message: *contact pronto.*

Making every effort not to wake him, she slid out of bed, grabbed her dressing gown and the phone and padded into the sitting room.

'We want you here at seven a.m. for briefing,' said Team Leader. He was icy calm, which meant something had come up. 'You'll be in the car.'

She checked the time: 11.10 p.m. 'Understood.'

She woke Joey with a cup of tea. 'Not so romantic, I'm afraid, but I thought it would go down better than gin, which is all I have.'

He accepted the mug. 'Nice.' He pointed to the poster on the wall. It was of a meadow dotted with flowers. Chocolate-boxy but cheering. 'Reminds me of a wildflower meadow,' he said. 'The one Nell created back home.'

There was sadness. Obvious sadness. *Nell. Back home.*

She scrutinised her bare feet. 'I'm going to have to ask you to leave, Joey.'

'Ah.' He placed the undrunk tea on the bedside table and swung his legs out of bed. 'Of course. Is there any particular reason?' He was cool. Very cool.

'The office has just called. I must be in very early.'

He sat on the edge of the bed. 'Your work is important. Right?'

She nodded.

Within two minutes, Joey was dressed and snapping on his watch. 'That was awesome,' he said from the doorway. 'I'll let myself out. If you have trouble with the hand, see the doctor.'

## CHAPTER TWENTY-THREE

Mia made no move to contact Joey. This did not mean she wasn't preoccupied by him.

Her unconscious was misbehaving. Which she didn't like. Or rather, mistrusted.

Her mind threw up cinematic shorts of running into him, of being enmeshed in conversation, of lying in bed together. He had a trick of narrowing his eyes when making a point – that had been in the cinema waiting for the eagles to begin. He had a scar down by his ankle – she spotted that in bed. His seeming liking for blue – he'd worn something blue each time they had met.

Falling for a scar, brown eyes and a colour was odd. Of course, behind all that lay the notion of the gentle vet who dealt with sick and suffering creatures… but it was odd for her, all the same.

Although she had always enjoyed her affairs (as opposed to flings), none of them had shredded her soul, even if the finish had been a mess. Except for Lucas, that is, whom she had loved, but her caginess had driven him crazy. A year in, he had swapped her for a fuller-breasted, chattier model.

She thought, too, about the eagles. Feather, beak and claw.

Perching on the arms of their temporary owners. Hooded heads bent.

Would anybody come to their aid and cry 'stop'?

She returned to work. Left arm and hand aching from time to time, and dexterity impaired, but she kept her mouth shut. There was no mercy to be had from her colleagues. *Only fuckwits trip over.*

As indicated, her injury meant she was placed on light surveillance duties. It had its advantages. Instead of working the streets, she operated from a car with a driver. The team went in for the kill. 'Well, stone me,' said Brian (not his real name). 'That's how you get a chauffeur.' Jane (not her real name) stuck out a leg. 'Anyone like to trip over me? We'll split the sick pay fifty-fifty.'

In the car, she was reminded how linear and unyielding were the streets. How the trees ranked second place to street architecture. How the colour green was an infrequent interloper between the greys and red brick of the buildings. How the dos and don'ts of city life – speed limits, one-way streets, parking restrictions – restricted freedoms.

But that was the city. Her territory.

On the Saturday, a big peace rally walked along Piccadilly and into Hyde Park. 'Par for the course,' Team Leader briefed, 'but the intel suggests a group of extremists are agitating.' Ringleaders had been given the code names of 'Green Fleece' and 'Mud Slide'.

In the best traditions of protest, the crowd snaked slowly and almost without incident along the route. From her vantage point close to the car, Mia observed a minor kerfuffle at its edge and a couple of the police acting aggressively.

She returned to the car. Her driver, who had been in the business more years than he could count, started up the engine. 'Things getting brisk.'

Base came in on the car radio. 'Did you locate Mud Slide?'

'Negative,' she replied.

'Move to next street and wait.'

The driver was already nosing out of the parking slot. They headed for the next location.

It was a long day and, in the end, non-productive. The team ended up having to scatter and head back to HQ as Mud Slide cottoned on that he was being tailed and melted away.

Base, a woman of sharp tongue, did not mince words. 'Let that happen again, you lot, and you're jobless.'

They had been on the case for hours without food or rest, not even a bathroom stop, and the jibe went down like lemon on the tongue. Muttering rebellion, the team dispersed to their homes.

Mia picked up her bag and made for the cloakroom, ran a basin of hot water, splashed her face and plunged her hands into it. In her post-op routine, hot water soothed after fieldwork. It had also been recommended by the medics for the broken finger. Did she mind that this op had failed? She raised an eyebrow. Less than she might have done.

It was normal for confidence in what she was doing to go down the pan from time to time. Totally. Being good at the job did not offer a mental safety blanket.

The trouble was she was used to being A1 fit. She relished always that she was strong and physically capable and not being so made her feel unbalanced. Not in control. She gave herself a straight look in the mirror. Dilution of intention was a downer. Don't let it happen, Mia. Stick to your business of working in the shadows for… not to be too smug or hotshot priggish… the greater good.

Waiting to check out, she bumped into Team Leader who was obviously smarting from the unproductive day. Conversation was not on the cards, and she touched him lightly on the shoulder. His job was lonelier than most and he was better at it than most.

She wanted exercise and walked back home through Battersea Park, varying the route as per normal, eyes flicking here and there. OK, she was officially off-duty but, as all the operatives concurred, that meant nothing. She was on duty. All the time. What was that car doing parked so close to the tree? Did the man with the rucksack seem uneasy? Hypervigilance was a consequence of the trade. There was no point to it and there was every point to it.

She noted how the summer sun was already drying patches of grass, speckling it with yellows and bleached greens. She registered the screech, harsh and attention-seeking, of a parakeet and the shaggy odour of damp dog.

Post-op fatigue, and being stuck in a car, had knocked her systems awry. At this moment, despite the warmth, she was cold.

Cold reminded her of school. A place of boredom and unease – apart from Miss Mendes and her classroom. With her swirling skirts and glossy hair piled up in a knot, Miss Mendes had been stylish and invited adoration which Mia offered in spadefuls.

Years later, she heard Miss Mendes had descended into

alcoholism and died young and derelict. The knowledge still bothered her.

A dog tore across her path.

'Come here,' ordered a voice and she swung around.

Joey.

'Thought it might be you,' he said.

Both recognised mendacity when they fell over it. He had known it was her. She had wished it to be him. Still, every caveat pushed its way to the top of the list. How had Joey known she would be in the park? Had he been following her? If so, why?

'That look tells me you think I'm stalking you.'

'Are you?'

'Yes, but I'm not great at stalking. I went to your flat, almost rang the bell and then came away thinking it made me look a loser. Came here instead.'

'You could have called.'

'Far too easy.'

Mia looked away first. 'Didn't know you had a dog,' she said.

'I don't. He belongs to a friend who's away for a week. He reckoned, top vet that I am, I should look after him. All I can say is, never again.' He raised his voice. 'Come here, Hannay.'

'What sort of name is that?

'The gods know but I don't. Not my choice.' Joey collared Hannay and attached the lead. 'How are you?' He touched the arm, which she instinctively cradled against her body. 'Does it ache?'

'Yes.' She shrugged it off. 'But as long as I can go climbing again.'

Hannay was interested in the base of a nearby tree and Joey paid out the lead. 'Where do you climb?'

'Haven't done it for some time, but Switzerland or the French Alps. Mostly on the lower slopes. Sometimes up high. I'm far from professional but I love it.'

*Rough unspoken translation*: she had trained on the mountains. They all had.

Hannay lifted his leg and deposited a quantity of urine at the base of the tree. Joey turned to Mia. 'I'm going back home now. Want to come?'

The seconds she took to answer elongated. She knew what she wanted. She knew the risks.

'Where's home?'

The answer was a flat in a road close to the park. 'My uncle Harry bought this house after the war. He was sentimentally attached to it for some reason. It had been badly damaged in the Blitz, but he rebuilt it and turned it into flats. Rather badly.'

Joey wasn't joking. The flat, which had had two rooms carved out of what must have been a large, graceful one, was a clumsy conversion – not that she was in any way expert in the cheesy perfect interiors seen in lifestyle magazines. 'Life was hard after the war,' said Joey, observing her expression. 'My uncle had been wounded and wasn't up to much and it was difficult to get building materials. Or so Nell told me.'

'It's great to have a place,' she said. 'Most people don't.'

'One day I'll do it up properly. Restore it.'

Joey made tea and ferried the mugs into the larger of the rooms where there was a sofa covered in black-and-white ticking material.

She sat and drank the tea. It tasted of… bergamot?… whatever, it was nice.

'I take it your not getting in touch was deliberate.' He was standing by the window.

'Yes.'

A look flashed over his face, but she couldn't work out what it signified. 'Is that set in iron?'

'Nothing's ever set in iron.'

He shrugged and set down his mug. 'But you're reluctant for some reason. You don't have to tell me why. I'm fine with that.' He raised an eyebrow. 'Whatever.'

She looked away. This was no hook-up and more difficult than she had anticipated. Much more so than was convenient.

'You look tired,' said Joey.

Unsure whether to be affronted, she pushed back her hair. Under her fingers, it felt dry and untended. Like a lot of things. She walked across to the mirror hanging over a vintage-looking gas fireplace and peered at her face. She was also scanning the room for clues, for traces, for things that would tell her to get out. 'I'm OK.' She pushed away a strand from her cheek. 'After not stalking me at the flat, you took a chance on the park?'

'Calculated,' he admitted. 'It's a great evening and I had a dog that needed exercise… keep reminding me never to do a friend a favour again. You like to walk. I took a punt.'

Rule number… she couldn't remember the number. There were so many. *Never take anything at face value.*

'You might have been there for hours.'

'Yup.' Joey put his hands on her shoulders. 'And no. I would have given up after a bit. I have the oddest notion I should be looking after you,' he said. 'Don't ask me why.'

That went against the grain. Against scruple and the need for scepticism. Joey, it seemed, was one of the decent people in whom she believed. Wanted to believe. She blinked back tears of post-accident weakness. 'That's ridiculous.'

'I know.' He turned her around to face him and kissed her and it didn't feel ridiculous at all.

Later, Mia lay with her head on Joey's chest. She had forgotten how good flesh felt on flesh. Warm with just a hint of sweat.

Her eye wandered over the framed photograph on the wall opposite. It showed a teenage boy and a woman with her arms wrapped around him.

'Is that you? And your cousin?'

'Yup. That's Nell. At Woodspring, where I grew up. Before the money ran out.'

She focussed on Nell. 'She looks happy.'

'She had me.' He squinted down at her. 'Joke.' He removed his arm from around Mia. 'Taken before the real worries began.'

'Money worries?'

She felt him distance himself. 'It was a big house, with land. Plus a bit of woodland. Not forgetting the deer and the bats.' He paused. 'And the rabbits. And hares.'

Her empathy muscles were often out of practice, but she got how much it mattered.

'What happened?'

There was a silence.

'Long story,' he said, finally. 'I must go, the animals overnighting in the surgery need checking. But you can stay here if you like.'

She struggled to a sitting position. 'I've things to do.'

Joey got out of bed. 'It would be nice to think of you being here when I return. Mad, I know.'

'Yes, mad.'

'It's just, with you I feel I can cut the preliminaries.'

She swallowed. 'Do you take Hannay with you?'

'I do. I was warned he won't be left. Equally, he hates going into the surgery. But it won't be for long.'

As if to concur, Hannay clicked down the passage outside the bedroom.

'It must get to you dealing with sick animals.'

Joey buckled up his belt. 'I like to think I can help.'

They said goodbye outside the front entrance. Joey touched Mia on the arm. 'That was nice. More than nice. See you around?'

'Yes.'

He did not move but put his hand on the small of her back and pressed Mia to him. A kiss brushed across her forehead and every defence was disarmed.

Later, as she ran up the stairs to her own flat, her phone pinged with the message, *Hope you got back all right?*

Inside the door, she paused. The traffic streamed outside. The sun was sliding away from the day.

Seven years ago she had read about the Service in a discarded newspaper on a bus. *Come and join us. Train.* An imp hissed in her ear, *Be different.* It also said, *Escape.* And, *Purpose.*

The last seduced her. Purpose was good. She craved it.

She applied.

A new life unrolled in A Branch. *The most effective surveillance operators in existence.* That was the self-administered pat on the back from an instructor. *The best.* Pat, pat.

Plenty of purpose then.

It was a hard apprenticeship. Learning how to operate.

*What was that vehicle reg. number? The A–H of the woman in the street (age, build, ethnicity, distinguishing features)? Names of the last eight streets you've walked down?*

Understanding how the work fitted in. Whereas the police liked quick results and arrests for any potential atrocity, the service operated with different objectives. It wanted the whole picture – organisation, funding, the helpers. It was more patient. More devious.

It demanded silence from its operatives. A lifelong commitment to that silence.

Halfway through the night, she woke. She had been dreaming of Joey and felt his warmth and solidity and the response of her own body.

*Hope you got back all right.*

Sex and love were balancing acts. Always.

Could that text be the equivalent of a hand reaching out in the night to soothe and reassure? Or was it a hard-nosed, calculating data scrape?

She reread the message on the phone. After a moment, she thumbed a reply. 'Are you checking up on me?'

'Yes.' The answer pinged back within seconds.

She flopped back on the pillows undecided whether she was pleased or annoyed.

She decided she was both.

## CHAPTER TWENTY-FOUR

When training, Mia had been warned that the service driving instructors had their own sweet ways. 'No use having a mind of your own,' her first one offered. 'And, just so you know, I'll push you to the limit.'

He was not a man for a joke.

One tactic had been to tape a drawing pin, pin side up, onto the gear stick. No automatic cars at this stage. If she rested a hand too long on it, the instructor banged down onto her fingers. 'Hands on wheel.'

Parking in front of Joey's flat, the early-morning sun hitting the windscreen, she recollected the harshness verging on brutality that had made her into a good driver. A cruel-to-be-kind technique mixed in with actual sadism. Great recipe.

She messaged Joey. A few minutes later he emerged with Hannay on a lead. Opening the rear door, he spread a rug over the seat and ordered the dog to jump in.

He got into the passenger seat. 'Good morning.' He smelt of aftershave and soap, undercut by sleepy male. 'I would kiss you on the cheek, but you don't look the sort.'

'There's always a first time.'

Joey leant over and kissed her on the cheek. After a moment, she said, 'Shall we go?'

Joey remained quiet as he observed Mia manoeuvring fast through the streets. Then he said, 'Should you slow down?'

She took her foot off the accelerator. 'Sorry. Habit. I like speed.'

'You love speeding fines too?'

They headed out of the city and south towards Birling Gap where they planned to walk along the coastal path and hoped to tackle at least a couple of the Seven Sisters.

As they went, Joey talked. A lot. About being a vet. About Woodspring. What he thought about hare-coursing, nuclear power and the upcoming winter Olympics and many other things.

He wanted Mia to understand who and what he was – opening a door to intimacy, inviting her to step through it.

They parked up. It was one of those rare days when the combination of sun and bright blue sky took the breath away. Hannay loped on ahead. The sea was calm, almost glassy. It was warm. There was chalk and grass under their feet, the cry of birds above and, because there were not many others around, a rare solitude.

Impelled to spread her hand over the turf, she knelt and did so. Dried earth filtered between her fingers.

Joey watched. She looked up. 'Grounding myself.'

They covered the distances with ease. Her fitness was coming back. A couple of miles along the path, they stopped to look out across the water towards France. 'Fancy a trip?' Joey put his arm around Mia.

Of course, there were periods when the creep of dissatisfaction was obvious – that post-op, broken-fingered moment being one. Usually, when she was beaten wordless by fatigue after a big, tense operation, or when either the target or an operative (bad) had got killed. But not always. Then she had to remind of herself why she did what she did.

Other days were fine. Just fine.

But this one? This one was different. She felt she was wading, not into the sea, but into the elemental. Enveloped by colour and warmth.

'Paris?'

Yes. One day… one day… they would go to Paris.

Joey said, 'I don't know the sea… who does?... but I am drawn to it. When I'm old and decrepit, I'll retire to a bungalow and watch the waves. When I'm not at Woodspring, that is.'

'I fancy a chalet on a Swiss mountain.'

'Chocolate and snow. Plus, cuckoo clock.'

'That's it.'

He shot a look at Mia and smiled.

She glanced down. A solitary bee foraged among the pink rooms offered by the sea thrift. If you owned bees… Scrub that. She had read somewhere that you don't, and can't, own bees. If you offered, and they accepted, a living space, then the convention was to tell them your news.

You must do so religiously. That was the deal.

The news today would be that something new had entered her life.

They dropped in at a pub which had oak beams and casement windows. They sat on a bench outside, ate cheese and cucumber sandwiches and Joey told her stories from the life of a vet. 'A market trader brought in a pigeon which had fallen onto the pavement from a roof. It was so injured that it was a relief to put it down. Then I had to help break up a puppy factory in a high-rise. Little things were starving. Reported the buggers responsible.'

Mia picked up her cider. Over its rim, she interrogated him. 'I've been puzzling over your accent. You've a slight American one. Not entirely, but a word here and there.'

'Nell had an American accent. She was brought up in the States. She was my mother in many ways. My real mother was killed when I was three. Nell stepped in.' He smiled. 'I had a model railway. We lived at Woodspring, and she roped off a bit of the garden which was mine. I dug a pond for frogs and grew nettles for the caterpillar colonies. My triumph was a hedgehog highway.'

'She died quite young?'

He regarded the remainder of his sandwich. 'She did.'

'Tell me?'

Joey considered. Did *he* trust *her*?

She settled to listen to his history. His and Nell's. Brought together by love, and a powerful instinct. Joey told of his mother's death, his aunt's death... and of being saved from Hodgkin House...

'Terrible,' Mia said.

'Nell wanted to rescue me before she knew that we were cousins.' He gestured to take in sun, sea, sandwiches. 'She was willing to gamble on me. When I was younger, I didn't understand the leap of faith. Now, I do.'

Hannay crawled under the bench.

Joey nudged Hannay's rear end sticking out from under the bench. 'If it was now, she would have had to have gone through many more hoops to adopt. It was easier then.'

'You had a lot of death,' she said. 'For a small boy.'

He touched her arm. 'OK?'

'It's ridiculous. I seem to cry a lot these days.' She smiled. 'Post-broken-finger shock.'

'Nothing wrong with that.' He accepted her explanation. 'There are times in one's life.'

Mia disliked revealing weakness. 'Inconvenient though.'

His hand rested on her arm. '*Are* you OK?'

She focussed on the sea, which had developed a few white crests. 'It's you,' she conceded reluctantly. 'You're making me feel things.'

Joey pulled Mia to her feet. 'That's the best news I've heard for a long time. But I'm alarmed you're sad about it. I was hoping for happy or excited.' He kidnapped one of Mia's hands and kissed it. She looked up at him. After a moment, he pulled her close.

When they drew apart, both were smiling. There had been an exchange during that kiss. What it was exactly Mia would think about later.

Joey wrestled his Nokia out of his pocket. 'I'd like a photo.'

'No,' she said quickly. 'I'd rather you didn't.'

He said nothing for long seconds. 'OK, we'd better get going.'

They retraced their steps, the sun now on their backs.

'Where's Hannay?' she asked.

Joey whistled. Mia shouted but no Hannay presented himself. A couple of walkers headed towards them along the path and Joey jogged over to them to ask them if they had seen him. He beckoned frantically. 'They saw him on the cliff edge barking at a bird.'

Both broke into a run.

Mia outstripped Joey and dropped to her stomach and worked her way to the edge of the cliff by the time he caught up.

Hannay had fallen onto a chalk outcrop in the cliff about four feet from the top. The ledge was reasonably wide but looked unstable. Below was a sheer drop to rocks and a churning, hissing sea. Hannay looked up at Mia, shifted and sent a cascade of chalk pebbles downwards.

'Sit, Hannay,' she said. 'Sit.'

Joey wriggled up beside her. 'Sit, Hannay,' he repeated calmly enough but with an edge of fear. Hannay's ears slotted back.

Mia was already sloughing off the jacket tied around her waist. 'It's too dangerous to leave him and get help. Give me your jacket.' A pale Joey obeyed.

Remaining flat on her stomach, she tied the sleeves of both jackets together in a tight reef knot, making a rope of six feet or so. Rolling onto her back, she unbuckled her leather belt, a good strong one and nicely supple. 'The ledge is big enough to take me.'

'No,' said Joey. 'Hannay is my responsibility.' He edged his way to the cliff edge.

Down below a distressed Hannay whined. Mia held on to one end of the makeshift rope ready to anchor it – but Joey froze, and it struck her that he might be afraid of heights.

Mia wasn't. It was one of her things.

'I'm going,' she said. 'Take this end.' She shoved a sleeve at him. 'Wrap round your arm and hold.' Inch by inch she edged backwards over the cliff. Hannay whined but remained still.

The toe of Mia's boot made contact with the ledge and she eased herself down. Crouching as low as she dared, she ran over the options. Stay here with the dog until the rescue services arrived? Possible: but the ledge was dangerous and the wind was rising.

'I'm sending Hannay up,' she shouted. Gently, oh-so gently and carefully, she slid one end of the belt under his collar, fastened it, attached it to the sleeve end and gave it a tug. 'Pull.'

The improvised rope tightened. Mia put her hand under Hannay's hindquarters and eased him up. 'Go on, boy.' She raised her voice. 'Call him.'

'Hannay.'

Hannay scrabbled and choked. She pushed harder upwards at his rear quarters. For one moment, she thought they were both going over the edge of the ledge and cursed her weakened left hand. 'Up, Hannay. Up.'

Joey called again. Hannay pricked up his ears.

There was the danger that the belt would slip off. Or throttle Hannay. Or Joey would lose his grip on the makeshift rope. Then Hannay got it and, with Joey pulling frantically, scrambled up the remaining couple of feet.

Now for her.

She turned her head to the sea. If she was going to die, and there was a chance, she had an urgent desire to look at it one last time.

Joey lowered the improvised rope back down.

Moving with extreme caution, Mia extracted the penknife that was always in her pocket and selected the largest blade. Reaching up as far as possible, she drove it into the cliff face. 'OK,' she called, and Joey pulled. Winding her arm into the rope, she grasped the penknife as a makeshift marlin spike and eased her way up.

The hard work at the gym paid off. Left arm was not so brilliant. Right arm did the work for both. Inch by inch, Joey hauled her up. Muscle and sinew were in danger of snapping. This was the type of situation for which she was trained. Note to self: it didn't make it any easier.

*White knights are fantasy*, went the training. *The only person to get you out of a tricky corner is you.*

Seconds later, Joey eased Mia back over the top onto springy turf that had never been so green or so inviting. Or so safe.

They fell back into a heap.

'Thank God,' said Joey. 'Let me check you over.'

'No.' Mia rolled away. 'I'm fine.'

They lay a few feet away from each other, stretched out. Both panting, Mia's heart racing. Joey covered his eyes with a forearm and, with the other, held Hannay's lead.

Mia stared so hard up into the sky that her eyes watered, and willed her heartbeat to return to normal.

Her vision adjusted to a new set of senses. Being alive had been recast.

She turned her head towards Joey. 'OK?'

Joey removed the sheltering arm from his face. 'It should have been me who went over.' He got to his feet and, holding tight to the lead, dusted himself down. He held out his hand to help her up. 'I'm not much of a hero. No head for heights.'

'Some can take heights, some can't. Don't apologise.'

He rolled his eyes. 'Let's pray that if I'd been on my own, I could have forced myself to do something.'

He had kept hold of Mia and she looked down at their dirt-encrusted, grass-stained hands and the sun was hot on her neck. 'You mustn't mind, Joey. Not important.'

'You could have been injured or killed.'

'But I wasn't.' She sought to reassure. 'I wouldn't have done it if I hadn't thought it was possible.' His fingers tightened. 'We've reached the age when we know ourselves. Right?'

Soberer than on the walk there, they retraced their steps with Hannay on the leash.

But it was still glorious. The air warm and winey. The sun steadfast. The sound of the sea soft on the ears.

'Joey, you mustn't beat yourself up. Promise?'

'It's a deal. And I won't.'

They began the descent to the parked car, and Joey swivelled to face her.

'Mia… I'm serious about you.'

Hannay strained at the lead.

It was if she had been waiting without knowing it for these words for a long time. Except it had only been a short time since she'd met him. 'Are you?'

'I wouldn't have said it otherwise.'

*Now what?*

'I'm hoping you feel the same.'

They held each other's gaze. Hannay whined. A couple of walkers headed in their direction.

'Don't worry,' he said, reeling in Hannay and instructing him to heel. 'You don't have to say anything.'

In bed that evening, after consuming Joey's meal of steak and red pepper confit, she snaked her arm around his midriff and held him close and tight.

'Hey,' he said. 'I'm not going anywhere.'

'That's good.'

Joey was silent. 'You believe in fate?'

'Nope.' She was drifting towards sleep. 'But it would be nice to believe in God. Any God. The one who loves you unconditionally. All that. Someone to look out for you after a lifetime of sinning and, hopefully, forgive you.'

'You sound almost religious.' Joey was amused. 'I'm cheered to think I'm making love to a moral woman.' He was murmuring into the back of her neck. Sleepy. Intimate.

'Is that important?' she asked.

Their breathing slotted into the same rhythm. 'Probably.' Another pause. 'Nah.'

There she was being rocked by peace and the pleasure of being with Joey.

After a few minutes, she said, 'You know what I really mind about?'

'What?'

'Leaving my penknife behind.'

## CHAPTER TWENTY-FIVE

On their next outing, it was Joey who drove them out of London to Woodspring.

It was a moment, this… a pilgrimage to the house.

Not, she reckoned, to be undertaken lightly.

It was a fine, hot Saturday. No Hannay this time. He had been returned to his owner. 'They miss him in the surgery,' said Joey. 'Even I'd got used to him.'

Mia was surprised to feel an affinity with Hannay. They had been through a lot together. 'At least there'll be no cliffs to fall down.'

Joey stiffened and Mia would have bitten down hard to shovel the words back into her mouth. Joey's fear of heights would be a sensitive subject.

It was her work, she almost confessed. It coarsened empathy, tore away subtlety and nuance. It was work where toughness was the most useful tool.

Then, 'I'm missing the hero gene,' he said, easily enough. 'I own it.' He didn't seem fazed.

She looked down at her hands clasped in her lap. To confess to a shortfall was a strength and she must practise it.

She had a stab. 'Try and get me underwater,' she said. 'No can do.'

Joey laughed – which informed her that he had understood the transaction within that exchange. A weakness for a weakness.

Two hours later, Joey turned into a drive at the end of which a handsome, largish house came into view. He ignored the front and drove around the back to a stable yard. A couple of people carriers were parked up there with 'Woodspring Hospice' inscribed on their sides.

'Your home is a hospice?' Mia was astonished. 'You never said.'

'In its glory days it wasn't. Now it is. The story of big houses everywhere.'

He ushered her through a door beside an empty stall in the stable block. 'But this is my kingdom. Let me show you.'

Inside smelt unlived-in, but underlying that was a not unpleasant suggestion of hay and horse. It was small, almost cramped. Downstairs, there was a sitting area into which was squeezed a table and a couple of armchairs. Containing an odd pot and pan, a kitchen area was curtained off. Upstairs, there was a beamed bedroom, plus a bathroom with an old-fashioned bath.

'No shower?' Mia was only half teasing.

'No shower. Never got round to doing it up,' Joey said. 'The flat was lived in for years by Pamela and Tommy Fry who helped Nell run the place, and they weren't keen on showers.'

Downstairs, he said, 'Make a cup of tea and I'll air the place.'

Many teas colonised the cupboard above the toaster. Ginger, mint, lime… an entire herbarium. She chose mint.

Waiting for the kettle to boil, she checked out a second cupboard. Marmite, jam, nut spread. Honey. She picked up the jar. Its contents were golden and still liquid – hers always crystallised after a time. *Made by our bees*, ran the legend. *Nurtured and encouraged and free from pesticides and nicotinoids.* Underneath in smaller type, it said, *No bee on our land dies unnecessarily.*

Holding the gold of it between her hands, she entertained a vision of fields thick with clover and Queen Anne's Lace and insects. A humming paradise with bees – drunken, stumbling, sated. Contrast that with the city buildings and schools where no bee ventured, and children wore out their knees pounding across tarmac.

After tea, Joey said he would show her around. Mia fetched her boots from the car and laced them up. Soft, supple boots which had taken her many places. Now, she would walk in them across Joey's territory.

He glanced at them. 'You've great outdoor kit.'

'Good boots are the key to happiness.'

He led her around the house, across the lawn towards a strip of woodland which was flanked by a wall.

On the wall there was a tablet with an inscription. 'Faith Yorke…' she read.

Joey pointed to a similar one beside it. 'Harry Dane, 1910–1951. Robert Dane, 1915–1975. "United we Conquer".' Mia raised an enquiring eyebrow. 'Uncle Harry and my father. Commandos in the war. Both wounded in Normandy. I put this up as neither have a place in the memorial garden at Glenfinnan.'

'Glenfinnan?'

'The commando memorial is at Glenfinnan.'

'And Faith?'

'Uncle Harry fell in love with Faith during the war, I think, but I'm hazy on the details. He scattered her ashes here.'

'And what about Nell?'

They had progressed into the wood, where the trees threw their shade over them.

'Nell... Nell... died five years ago. Cancer. She was Uncle Harry's daughter.'

'I'm getting muddled. Who was who?'

Joey went through a history of family, children and war damage. Of Nell being brought up in the American South by her mother and stepfather, and her uncle and father living at Woodspring.

'So Nell... gave up her job in Switzerland to look after you?'

'Yup.'

'And your mother?'

Joey bent down and picked up last year's acorn and offered it to Mia on a spread hand. 'I don't remember her. Only flashes of what she looked like. I wish I did. My father's head wound was serious and affected his mind and I don't know if he knew I was his son or not. *I* didn't know he was my father. It was Nell who found everything out.' Mia gave him back the acorn and he heeled it in carefully between two trees. 'He liked to spend time with me on the model railway.'

Mia ached for the small Joey – which, as likely as not, he would not appreciate.

'When Nell became ill, we sold the house and most of the land to a developer, but we kept the wood and two of the fields. The wildflower meadow and one which was used as a herbal ley. They were Nell's cherished projects, and I refused to allow her to let them go.'

'Ah…' She watched him covertly. Any fool, and she wasn't a fool, could see he loved this place. It was part of his blood and bone.

'Before coming here expressly to save me,' he sounded wry, 'and having given up Switzerland, she yearned for Alpine meadows. I owed it to her.'

She thought back to her own childhood and its tricky patches. 'What's it like to be saved?'

He turned his head away. 'I didn't understand at the time. Now, it's everything.'

She was trespassing. Possibly stepping roughshod over tricky feelings. 'The… herbal ley? What on earth is that?'

'An agricultural project begun by Nell's father. She wanted to continue the tradition.'

'Sounds like a drink.' Bad joke. How out of practice she had become at being… normal. Or even emotionally intelligent. 'Sorry.'

He touched her arm – and his acceptance of her, of what she was, dispatched her embarrassment. 'Things change. The farmer sold up and there's no cattle to graze any more. It's a quirky project and I haven't decided how to deal with it yet.'

'Management crisis?'

'Yup.'

The path through the wood led into a field enclosed by hedgerow. Joey shaded his eyes. 'This is the South Field. The herbal ley.'

She peered sceptically at what to her eyes appeared to be ordinary scrubby grass and a carpet of thistles.

'The theory is… Technically, it should be sown with clovers, trefoil, wild carrot and other herby things which strengthen the soil and fix nitrates. If plentiful, it can be cut for hay. Mainly though, it has to be scented which lures the insects to it and they create colonies. The bees and butterflies come in too. Like the common blue butterfly, which is in danger of not being common any more.' He shrugged. 'But there's no time. No manpower. And no happy insects.'

She breathed in deep. No concrete here, either. No harsh lines of buildings. No human subversion.

Not yet.

A thought occurred to her. 'What happened to the land sold for development?'

'Nothing. I'm told the planning permissions are stuck in the pipeline.'

He led the way up the field, through a gap in the hedge into a second, smaller field.

'This should be, is, the wildflower meadow, but it's having a struggle. It takes time and effort. I'm short on both. I've planned it to be a perennial one and I did a bit of replanting earlier in the year. Cornflowers and field poppies to mix with the ox-eye daisies and field scabious. The trick is to keep the grass in check, otherwise it takes over. I'm hoping it will shape up.'

'But hope isn't enough?' she said.

He sent her a look. 'What do you think?'

They skirted the field. In places the grasses were knee-high, others shorter, and where they brushed over Mia's legs, they released a faint, sweetish scent. Except for the rustles and, distantly, the fading sound of a car, all was quiet.

Fresh.

Fragrant.

She felt a tug. Of what, exactly? Of loyalties shifting? Of recognition?

'You can look it up,' Joey said. 'It's an old tradition.'

'Old and new,' she said. 'Old ways, new plants. Nice.' Projects and visions like these surely required a plan? 'There must be grants to help out with this sort of thing.'

'Probably. I'll investigate them when I come back full time.'

'You're going to live here?'

Her disappointment was sharp.

'One day. Quite soon… maybe.'

'Oh.'

'One or other of the family have always tended to return. They gravitate instinctively to the place.'

'Oh,' she repeated. 'I'll show you what I can of the house.' Joey led her up the front steps and into a hall. 'Obviously, the patient area is off-limits.'

In Reception a desk was positioned by the window, flanked by computer screens and a vase of white roses tipped at the edges with pink.

'Hi Joey…' The girl at the reception desk was pleased to see him.

'Hello, Sarah. Wedding arrangements going well?'

Sarah frowned and smiled at the same time. 'Shall we say the groom is not into them.'

Mia spun slowly around, appreciating the sweep of the

staircase and the light spilling from the windows. Less enjoyable was the dull paintwork, a faint smell of cooking and a stack of plastic chairs. An old grace married with contemporary utility. And yet, and yet, the atmosphere was of calm and orderliness and, despite the dull paint and what was happening to the patients, an openness – death comes here – and a cheerfulness. A contrast to the games of hide-and-seek with which she engaged.

'The family had lived in the house since it was built.' Joey placed a hand on the banister, an affectionate gesture. 'There was a trust set up for its upkeep but it got eaten into. Nell was determined that I would inherit what was feasible to manage.'

It was a shame. Of course. But not the end of the world. Was sympathy warranted here? Or acceptance that it was life? Just life. 'I'm sorry about the house.'

He looked up the stairs. 'TLC and money. Lashings of it was going to be required. Still is. I got the flat and the hospice got the house. Fair deal. The hospice was needed. I can make my own way.'

'You think of yourself as a Dane?'

'I do. It took a bit of time. I was an outlier without legitimacy, but hey. Nell insisted I took the surname.'

'A Great Dane.'

'Do you know how many times I've heard that joke?'

They exchanged grins.

It was lovely here. They were enjoying themselves. There was an understanding between them.

'So, Nell lived here with you and died… here?'

Joey didn't reply immediately. 'Yes. She always said the

house would be the death of her.' He ushered her towards the door. 'Sorry. Still a bit raw.'

She looked up at him. 'Because she found you and loved you, she changed her life?'

'Nell meant everything. Mind you, I gave her hell when I was a teenager. Did I just. "Joey darling," she'd say. "I'm not going away, I'm not leaving you, so why don't you let up. It'll be easier on you."'

In life, in death, Nell was powerful. Very. Jealousy crept though Mia. Novel and unwelcome.

At that moment, she discovered that she loved Joey too.

So… love had been unleashed. With no rationale for its arrival, as she did not *know* Joey that well. Plus, it was inconvenient.

Three things were clear, however. Joey was dedicated to his work… as she was to hers. It was his vocation, he explained over a shared bottle of Australian red after they returned to London, adding, 'I know that's pompous.'

'Yup.'

Secondly, Joey was tidy. (So was she.)

Thirdly, he would be returning to live at Woodspring, surrounded by herbs and grasses. Providing he got them under control, providing (she prodded him silently) he planned how to run his land.

Joey was about continuity of plant, animal and place. She was about the so-called defence of the realm, the concrete jungle, the threat of the moment, wherever that might be. North, south, east, west…

She was about the bollocks brought about by bad actors. Queen and country and all that. He was about (but hadn't quite got there) small insects crawling towards a place of safety. A Garden of Eden whose blueprint, if she remembered correctly from the crap school lessons, never quite made it into the world.

For the next week or so, she was on duty a fair amount. Watching a suspect in Brixton. Endeavouring to work out the scope of a network in Holloway.

Same old same old.

'What's up?' asked 'Jane' over a coffee. 'Forgotten the happy pills? Going off Team Leader?'

'Nah,' Mia replied. 'The usual bellyache.'

She was operating on different levels. *One*, she went to work and walked the streets wherever she was put: in London, out of it. *Two*, she looked up from her phone, or across a room, to be assaulted by thoughts of Joey. *Three*, the strange, mad notion that she was turning her face away from *One* and asking a question: *Is this my life? Is it truly my life?*

Joey had educated her in pleasure, in the deepest and most satisfying manifestations of it. Of skin on skin. Of damp English air and good wine. Of being part of… well, what? Love for a place which was herb-strewn and humming with bees?

To feel joy made her vulnerable. It had consequences. Surveillance officers did not need, should not entertain, that brand of turbulence.

Yet when they next met in Joey's London flat, they clung together so tightly she thought her bones would break. Pressing her face into his chest, she inhaled deeply. 'I'm so glad to see you.'

'Where've you been?'

'Away. North-ish.'

'Are you ever going to stop being mysterious?'

'Probably not.'

'Too bad.'

'I've been reading.'

'Extraordinary,' he said.

'About fungi, moulds, dormice, newts. Those should be in your wood.'

'Should they?' He backed Mia up against the wall, pulled her T-shirt up over her head, dropped it onto the floor and unhooked her bra. 'That's better.'

Light-headed, she laughed. 'What's sauce for the goose…'

'Point taken.' He kept her pinned to the wall with one hand and, with the other, made a stab at unbuttoning his shirt.

She glanced at the window, and her second nature kicked in. 'People can see in.'

He reached over and pulled down the blind.

They remained on the uncomfortable floor for a long time but were too drowsy and satiated to move. Eventually, Joey propped himself up on his elbow. 'I suppose this is because we don't see each other very often.'

She smiled but didn't bother to open her eyes.

'Well, it hasn't worn off.' He traced a circle on her bare stomach. 'Somehow, I think it's going to take a bit of time to do so.'

Mia's nerve ends were taking their time to return to normal. 'Is that your considered opinion?' A finger traced her nose down to her chin. 'Novelty is good. Very good,' she murmured.

They dragged themselves up on the sofa. Joey reached across and threw a rug over them. 'Drink?'

'Yes.'

Joey didn't move.

'Did you say "drink"?'

'I did.'

Neither of them moved.

'I want to know the detail,' he said.

'Detail?'

'What you do?'

She was jerked fully alert. 'Very boring. I think I told you. I manage a team that checks out companies' security systems.'

He was silent. 'You're not telling me the truth,' he said. 'But I'll assume there's a good reason.'

Long silence.

'How do you feel about snakes?' Joey asked.

'Wary.'

'They have such bad press.' He shifted. 'It's a throwback to when snakes were a real problem to humans. It's more logical to be afraid of electricity. Or flying.'

She let her head droop against his shoulder. 'Why are we talking about snakes?'

'Because we're going to check up on a garter snake at the surgery. His name is Sampson.'

'When?'

'Now.'

Neither moved.

*A sick snake. What am I doing?* An hour later, Mia followed Joey into the surgery at the clinic.

The smell of disinfectant hit her. So did the noise of the caged animals. An assistant with a blonde ponytail looked up as Joey entered and smiled entrancingly. Mia disliked her on sight.

Joey introduced them. 'Mandy, this is Mia. Mandy is training and, lucky her, she's taking the weekend shift.'

Mandy shifted closer to Joey. 'No problem. I want to learn.' Mia noted the coffee cup beside a substantial textbook on the table. 'But do you mind if I pop out to get a couple of things from the Co-op?'

'Pop away.' Joey checked the notes before approaching a glass-fronted cage at the back of the room.

'How can you tell when a snake's ill?'

Joey glanced at Mia. 'Observation. Instinct. How do you know when anyone is ill? Samson has cloudy eyes and discharge from his nose. The poor old boy must be feeling manky.'

The snake was slumped in his cage. 'Will he make it?'

'Probably not. He's eight years old.' He opened the cage and gently, oh-so gently, wiped Samson's mouth and nose with a cotton bud. 'There, Samson. Hope that makes you feel better.' He closed the cage, dropped the cotton bud in the bin and washed his hands. 'His body is collapsing.'

'Can you put him down?'

'Not yet. Unless he's in such pain that his life is unbearable. Euthanasia is the last resort.'

An unobtrusive steel door had opened onto Joey's convictions. No animal to be put down unless the provisos – carefully considered ones – had been observed.

Considerations and provisos. Ethics. They, too, applied to her work but issued from a different stable. This made Mia uneasy. Keeping the peace sometimes involved violence. It was the joke… the not-so-funny one, but a running one.

The Labrador in the furthest pen barked. Joey let himself in and hunkered down. 'Easy, boy.' He ran a hand along the dog's flank, deploying his capable fingers to check and to analyse what was going on. 'Easy now.'

They emerged into pale sunshine. Mia found herself taking in gulps of (comparatively) fresh air. 'I had never thought you could smell animal distress. But you can.'

'You're right.' Joey laced his fingers into hers. 'And very, very perceptive for a girl.'

'Chauvinist pig.'

'Why bring pigs into it?'

She was too happy to argue. Anyway, he was teasing. Happiness took away the desire to pick up on things, she found, and it was strange. Walking back across the park, Joey held her hand in the loose warm grip that was becoming familiar.

And loved.

The word, so novel and so little used by Mia, slid across her mind and she gave a small gasp. Joey squeezed her hand. 'OK?'

'Fine. Just a twinge.'

'Where?'

'Base of the spine.'

His fingers pressed hard into the base of her spine. 'I can take remedial action.'

'So you can.' She smiled up at him and he smiled back, his eyes pooled with feeling.

# CHAPTER TWENTY-SIX

It was a hot summer and people talked in increasingly loud and doomy voices about climate change and the world tipping into danger because of pollution.

It added a new dimension to her thought processes – even a pinch of spice. Yes, the world was not yet terminal but the abyss over which it might slide was in sight.

She and Joey discussed the problem. As thirty-somethings, it was their future, and they ought to look after it. 'You're lucky,' said Mia. 'You've got a chance to make a contribution to a greener world.'

'Very small,' said Joey.

She was almost irritated by the lack of ambition. 'Small is good,' she said.

Then… then on 7 July London was shaken by bombs detonated on the underground. All hell broke loose over the city and Mia was slipstreamed into the security backlash. The team was run ragged. Considerations of pollution and climate change were sent packing.

Her first weekend off, she rang Joey. 'Come to Wood-spring,' said Joey. 'It's going to be hot.'

She packed a T-shirt, a pair of shorts and her walking boots

– of course – and slung her bag into the boot of his car. They opened the windows. Air streamed through the car interior and she pulled back her hair with a scrunchie and slumped back.

They talked about the bombing. Who? Why, and where next? He asked her about her childhood. Deep breath, and she told him about the house on the estate, her brother, about Albert and how the casual cruelty and senselessness of his death haunted her.

'Ah, the Tree of Secrets,' he said. 'It got to know about Albert.'

And now she loved him for understanding.

She told him about the time she absconded from home and took to the streets. 'I wanted to make my parents sorry. We had been shouting at each other for months.'

'And?'

'I went to the railway arches to hang out with the street sleepers.'

Even in summer the space under the railway arches was a place of darkness and chill. A place of overflowing rubbish bins which stank of siphoned-off petrol and the smell of dope, sifting stealthily from lockups and sheds.

'I hated who I was,' she said. 'It made sense to head for a place that was rock-bottom. I could have been killed or worse. You know what, though, the men there were nice to me. Shocked that I was there. They looked after me as far as they could. I've never forgotten that.'

'Christ,' said Joey. 'Could have been bad. Really bad.'

'I returned home. What made me think I could survive more than a day on my own? My parents were incandescent. Thought they were going to kill me.'

'Of course. And then?'

*Warning*, said her training. *Careful.*

He persisted. 'You've got over the mean streets. What about university? The first job?'

Releasing just sufficient information to sound plausible had been soldered into them. No one in their right mind went through the training, its rigours and sacrifices, only to be disarmed and dismantled by lust.

'Manchester Uni. Degree nothing much. Geography, actually. First job assistant in a sportswear shop. Then buyer. Cosmically boring.' She grinned. 'What I don't know about walking boots is not worth knowing.'

Joey looked straight ahead. 'Big leap between sports clothing and systems security.'

'I know. Obviously, I had promise. They trained me well.'

Maintaining a fiction required a stout construct of lies. By now, she should be ace at it. Was ace at it. Although you could never be too careful.

He eased the car onto the motorway. 'I'm getting there. I have some idea now.'

'Of what?' she managed to ask.

'Of you. Of how you were formed. Your pedigree, if you like.'

'A vet speaks.'

'You obviously gave yourself a bit of tough time. That kind of experience, or trauma, in childhood can make for the deceptive adult.'

'A psychologist speaks.'

'A wounded, vulnerable child resolves, *I will never feel like this again* and devises all sorts of shields. Such as "I don't care" or "I'm very tough".'

'Joey, I wasn't that wounded or traumatised.'

He was silent.

'You're talking about yourself.'

'You're right,' he admitted.

He grasped the wheel tightly. Looking at him, Mia felt boneless with love but also wary that psychology was too easy a refuge. Yet his tone indicated real feeling and an honesty, and she knew that her instincts about him were correct.

'I was fine,' she said. 'Only a tad misunderstood.'

He took his gaze off the road to look at Mia, as if to say, *That's not the whole story of you, is it?*

An increasing problem – his scepticism, her commitment to silence. Maybe, maybe it was the crossroads moment. If he wished to know about her, if she wanted to stop arsing around the truth, he must be prepared to be vetted.

The process should be triggered. Yes? Yes. She must trigger it.

Later that evening, they carried chairs and table out of the stifling flat into the stable yard and ate tomato salad, oatcakes and cream cheese outside. That was fun and they talked of nothing. Which was fun too and she didn't want to break the mood. Afterwards, stowing the chairs away at the back of the room, she managed to overturn a cardboard box. Papers cascaded onto the floor.

'The Woodspring papers.' Joey hunkered down and gathered them up. 'The solicitor no longer had room for the complete archive. Want to see?'

There was a map of the Woodspring boundary. Foxed and fingerprinted. She traced it with her finger. 'Not a rabbit hutch, then.'

Joey's finger stabbed down. 'That's where I used to walk. There's where I made a den. There's where the bourn rises. Those are the fields we sold off. These are the two I kept.'

The original deeds were folded and cracked. Written on them was: 'Property of Richard Dane, Esquire.' Underneath, an architect's drawing of the house was dated 1805.

'It hasn't changed at all.' Mia squinted down at it. 'Built as is.'

'Do you want to see a copy of a census?'

She held out her hand. The census was dated 1841 and written in black ink. The location was Woodspring House, Yew Green. The head of the household was James Percy Dane. His wife was Amelia and ten years younger. He had two sons, Rupert (12) and Charles (10) and a daughter, Theodora (7). Under the column labelled *Profession* James was listed as a gentleman, his sons as scholars.

Mia grappled with the writing. Its spidery explorations filled up most of the allocated spaces.

'Listen to this.' She shook with laughter. 'The daughter, Theodora, is listed as, *She does what she pleases.*'

She gestured at the box. 'These papers need sorting. Would you like me to do it for you? It might be of help.'

He looked at her. She looked at him.

'If you like,' he said.

'We'll set a date,' she said.

As they lay in bed that night – as far apart as possible because of the heat – she thought about James and his family, including the wilful Theodora. James Percy Dane had been landed and comfortable and she had an idea that he lived with certainty and, perhaps, a touch of humour.

How odd to be speculating on the past. It was not her sort of thing.

Think about the papers which required sorting.

Think about the animals. Not Joey's household pets but the deer and the bats. Hares and rabbits. The water voles down by the bourn? Frogs? The clues they left would not be tidy – spore, nests, damaged fencing, trampled grasses.

Their domain *was* shrinking. Their energies would be taken up in fighting the laying-down of concrete and avoiding the humans who thought it was their right to do so.

She slept.

Joey dropped her off at her flat. He got out of the car and put his arms around her. 'How about we move in together? You could give up paying rent.'

In any situation, she took note of possible exits – the open windows, the side entrance, etc.

In this situation, her planning and decision-making disintegrated. *Nada* presented itself. Sliding her arms around his torso, she held him close. He was very warm and smelt of the smoky aftershave he favoured. 'Oh, Joey.'

'Hey.' He pulled her even closer. 'What's with the drama? I'm not asking you to surrender your identity.' He touched her cheek. 'Any kind of answer spring to mind?'

'Can I think about it?'

'Sure.' He looked at his watch. 'We'll talk about it some other time.'

'Joey…'

'I've got to go,' he said. 'See you.'

Back to work.

The team was put onto Operation Fir Tree whose target was Game Hunter. Game Hunter was clever. Worse, he was trained in counter-surveillance tactics. The objective was to head off his attempt to deal in damaging industrial espionage.

Nothing much to look at – a key advantage – Game Hunter never stepped out of line, never overdid it. A grey suit, a beige mac. Black lace-up shoes. His hair was mouse-ish and there wasn't too much of it. No one would ever suspect that he was out to steal British industry's cyber secrets on an epic scale.

He was good, though. After several weeks of intense scrutiny, no intelligence of real use had emerged, and the team had been ordered back to base to confer. The intelligence analysts had chomped through the available data and had decided they were running along the wrong highway.

'Trained by the experienced,' said Team Leader and everyone immediately thought, *Russians.* She fiddled with a biro. 'We're switching track. Can't pin him down. But another string indicates that Game Hunter has recruited a stooge, code name Haggis. Haggis is good-looking and a known womaniser. Game Hunter has tasked him to seduce a Syygote female employee, code name Dragonfly. This conveniently distances Game Hunter from direct action, which is what he's looking for. The grooming is under way. Haggis has told

Dragonfly that he's a doctor working for an NGO in the Middle East and currently on leave. He's given her the sob story about needing rest and recuperation. It's likely Game Hunter will order him in to get the information in the next few days.'

'What's Game Hunter got on Haggis?' asked Mia.

'Debt.' Team Leader was impassive. 'The old story. Haggis is a gambler.' The clapped-out coffee machine rumbled. 'Sure as sure, he's been promised his debts paid, a job out of the country and a new identity if necessary.' He stood up. 'Haggis and Dragonfly are meeting at Bistro Charlie this evening. This will be their sixth meeting and things are hotting up. Half of you will be there. The other half will keep watch while the bugging boys do over their respective flats.' He sent the first smile of the session over their heads. 'Stand by for some bed activity.'

Normally, Mia would have been on the case. Thinking. Examining the task from top to toe. Inside out. Ready for all eventualities. This time, not.

It was, she concluded, a case of transferred empathy which was never, ever a good thing. What would she feel knowing she and Joey were being watched? Their pleasure in each other rolled out over the radio net?

The team filed out of the room. Team Leader accosted Mia. 'Not at your best today?'

'I'm fine.'

'Any probs, you need to discuss them with me. No ifs.'

The team leader had a duty to make sure they were in good shape physically, but more importantly, mentally. Doubt, or revulsion, at their tactics at an inopportune moment could jeopardise an operation.

Yes? No? Mia decided. 'I'd like to have a word, but not today. OK?'

'OK.' Team Leader stepped back. 'Don't overdo it. Rest up a bit if necessary.'

'No need.' No weak flanks exposed. No misgivings must be chalked up.

Whatever. Even so, studying Dragonfly's dark hair and huge eyes in the photographs on the data file, she felt pity. Dragonfly was being wooed into behaviour that could ruin her life and Game Hunter was engineering it with cool, professional skill.

It would be good to confide in Joey. A relief. She could tell him how unease had struck up a companionship with her. How a layer of her professional skin had thinned, how her nerves cried out at this exposure. For the first time she could remember, she had a nightmare from which she awoke damp with sweat. The bedding was on the floor, tangled as if she had fought it to a standstill.

She and Zero Five now sat at a table at the back of Bistro Charlie. It was a nice place, not too flashy, and comfortable, which the surveillance teams had learnt to prize. He nursed a half-pint, and she sipped a fruit juice.

They watched dark-eyed Dragonfly fall further under the spell of good-looking Haggis. Mia could document the beats. Captivation by the set of a head, the line of a chin. Netted in by a joke. The laser look that set the pulses going.

She knew… she knew.

'Targets drinking white wine,' reported Zero Five into his

body radio. 'Haggis has his arm around Dragonfly.' It took an hour of not finishing their drinks until he muttered, 'Suspects on the move.'

The rest of the team would take over now.

Zero Five leant back in his chair. 'That's us done, then. Shall we have a proper drink?'

Back in the flat. Mia slept OK but the filaments of her dreams recollected the following morning featured Joey.

*You don't know me*, she told him in the dream.

He was bending over her, smiling. *Yes. I do.*

She rolled onto her stomach. Her throat was dryer than toast. To long for someone was hard. Harder, when questions and uncertainties lodged in the operational mindset.

Here she was moving through the world. A free woman. Unencumbered.

What she did was worth it and had been her choice all the way along. The malign wished to destroy the peace of the national status quo and she and her team were parts in the machine constructed to prevent that happening.

Maybe there were other ways? A rusty mindset was finally acknowledging there was a larger universe. Acknowledging that she had been missing out. Acknowledging that adrenaline and cortisol were not the only fuels in life.

Her phone lit up. *Lovebirds leaving flat.*

Haggis had had his way, and was almost certainly seducing Syygote's secrets out of Dragonfly. Next up, Game Hunter would begin siphoning off information obtained from her. The upshot? Theft of valuable industrial intel and, blissfully unaware of how her every word and action was up for scrutiny, a compromised Dragonfly.

Intel told them that Haggis had arranged to meet Game Hunter two days later at the airport. Best not to enquire how the team obtained the information. Probably physical snooping. Almost certainly, Game Hunter would have instructed Haggis not to use electronic equipment. Messages could be intercepted. This was to assume Game Hunter had been expertly trained by… well, take your pick.

Zeros Five and Six reported from Gatwick's South Terminal where they were tailing Haggis. The rest of the team infiltrated in at intervals. Dressed in a smart grey flannel suit, Mia was first into the check-in area.

'Target heading for Costa Coffee outlet,' dribbled into her ear. Glancing at her watch, she made for the queue.

'Stand by. Haggis approaching. No briefcase.'

This meant that, if Haggis was carrying documents, he had hidden them on his body. Probably he had pushed them into the waistband of his trousers at the back. Or they were slotted into a pocket in the lining of his mackintosh.

Yup. Haggis had been well trained by Game Hunter.

'Haggis behind you in queue.'

She didn't turn her head. When her turn came, she ordered a flat white and took it over to a space on a standing table overlooking the runway. A vantage point where it was possible to get a partial reflection in the plate-glass window.

'Haggis at table under Flight Status. Has produced file and placed mobile phone on it.'

She drank a mouthful of the coffee.

'Attention, Game Hunter approaching.'

Zeros Five and Six appeared. They had taken off the jackets they had worn on the airport train and replaced them with jumpers. It was a given that Game Hunter's handlers would be watching *him*.

'Game Hunter buying coffee. Joining Haggis at table. No acknowledgement of each other.'

Mia searched her handbag. Out of the corner of her eye, she observed Haggis pick up his mobile phone and turn away from Game Hunter to make a call. Game Hunter flicked open the file and glanced at the papers.

Ten seconds later, he got up and walked off.

'Fuck it,' said a voice in Mia's ear. 'They're on to us.'

By leaving the folder with Haggis, Game Hunter could deny accountability, plus – technically – he hadn't stolen anything from anyone if caught.

'Don't think so,' countered Zero Eight.

More likely, Game Hunter was layering up his security. He had checked out the document and was planning to pick it up at an alternative drop.

'Game Hunter heading for exit,' said the voice in Mia's ear. 'Keep tabs on Haggis.'

Mia dabbed her mouth with a paper napkin. Brushed down her skirt and took her disposable cup over to the bin. At his table, Haggis gulped down the rest of his coffee, binned his cup and headed for the exit.

'Game Hunter picked up by black taxi in pick-up area,' reported Team Leader. 'Heading out of terminal to motorway.'

'Haggis exiting building. Also making for pick-up area,' said Mia into her mouthpiece.

'Zero Five, you're on it. Stand down, Zero Four.'

That was it. The bikers standing by would take over and follow the taxis to the drop.

She pictured the two taxis drawing in at a motorway service station which was the obvious meet place. The bikers throttling back. A car team drawing in behind them. None of them acknowledging the other. They would wait for the document exchange to happen and… then… pounce.

Mia would probably never know the outcome. If anyone got away. If they didn't.

Hey, she didn't mind. She really didn't mind.

'Zero Four extracting,' she reported.

It was warm outside, the sky was blue fretted with cotton-white clouds. Check. She caught a gorgeous, expensive whiff of perfume from a duty-free store. Check. She had lost weight and the waistband of her suit was pleasingly loose. Check.

It didn't last long. The habit of vigilance was ingrained.

Young male standing in train corridor, guarding bulging rucksack.

White van with tinted windows parked up alongside tube station.

Number 10 in her street has top window open.

So it went on.

She rang Joey on her return.

He was at Woodspring. 'I'm here for a few days,' he said. He didn't offer for her to come down. 'You're right, I need to sort stuff out. So… I'm tackling Nell's papers. She worked for the Red Cross and never lost touch, Didn't let go and kept the papers. They must go but I couldn't bring myself to do it before.'

The dead were powerful, and her gut instinct had been correct. Nell's ghost would stick around.

Nell was in danger of becoming a plaster saint.

Nell – she constructed Nell from the fragments Joey had let slip – had lorded it in a glossy office in the clean and sparkling Geneva. Nell had inherited a big house. Nell had been adored by Joey.

Nell had never been snotty with sobs, run ragged, blown, shaking, all the states which had overtaken Mia at one time or another.

What did Nell know of the dirty business of defending a country?

'Nell could do no wrong,' she said, as lightly as she could muster.

'I don't know why you're angry,' said Joey, divining her irritation correctly. 'But it's wasted on me.'

There was a silence.

'See you around,' he said.

She sat quite still, taken aback to discover how capable she was of small-mindedness.

Her anger dissolved and mean, unwarranted jealousy was replaced by embarrassment.

She poured herself a glass of wine and picked up *The Secret Lives of Animals.* A cheap, highly illustrated children's book which had caught her eye at the station bookstore.

She turned the pages. Mice, lions, monkeys and… a duck rippled through her fingers. 'Hello, Albert,' she said.

On the final page there was a list of animals at risk. Leatherback turtles, pangolins, mountain gorillas…

The Kazakh eagle soared through that rusty mind of hers.

What was she stumbling towards? That there was more to living than was to be found in the mental and physical enclosure of her current work? Much more than being an unsung cog in keeping the peace for the British government? It was the world that required saviours. The overcrowded, overused world.

A summer rain lashed at the window and she shut it tight.

# CHAPTER TWENTY-SEVEN

Mia was sent north to Manchester for a job which might, or might not, take several weeks.

It was a complicated, potentially horrifying assignment. An intelligence string had uncovered a plot to slaughter shoppers in a mall.

The murmurs were vague. Insubstantial. But there, and had to be taken seriously.

They didn't know which Manchester mall. The Great Northern? The Arndale? Or further out at Cheetham Hill? Where, and to a lesser extent, why, kept the team sleepless and on edge.

Day One, they reconnoitred. 'For Christ's sake,' said Brian. 'Where to begin?'

Day Two the intel sharpened up: it was the Arndale.

Next problem: how to decode when it was planned.

They had one advantage; the parameters of that 'when' were dictated by the shopping hours.

A huge operation. Short tempers. Questions that could not be answered. 'Professionals don't get nervy,' said Jane, who was distinctly so.

Did the would-be assassin, or assassins, have financial

backing? Was it a singleton or a team? If the former, where was he in the hierarchy? Would he have backup when he became operational?

Brian had made the rare mistake of reconnoitring an aisle on the lower mall – which he reckoned was especially vulnerable – in too obvious a fashion. 'Do *that* again and your head's on a spike.' Team Leader enjoyed giving Brian an earful. 'Not fucking on.'

'Nor is slaughter,' spat Brian, who was angry with himself as much as the situation.

'May I remind you all that you are not here to indulge your paper-thin hero fantasies. You're here to do the job.'

A string of curses issued in an undertone from Brian. Mia poked him in the thigh to shut him up before he said anything stupid and landed himself in the real shit.

It was hard, exhausting work with barely time for meals during the day or to have a wash in the cloakrooms. For obvious reasons, the Centre's administration had to be kept in the dark, which layered on an extra worry, and they had to be meticulous in their fieldcraft so as not to attract attention.

Mia was detailed to monitor the Centre's security procedures. Not great, for their purposes. To make things even trickier, the lower and upper aisles did not have clear sightlines.

The demand on all their concentration was brutal, and the deal was three days on, then three days off to rest at home. After her first shift, Mia slept on the train and arrived at Euston thick-headed and tousled. Back at the flat, she threw her clothes into the laundry basket and took the longest, hottest shower her hot-water system could muster.

Dried and dressed, she inspected herself in the mirror. Joey hadn't rung. Nor had she rung him. Listen up, she instructed her reflection. *This is who you are.*

Back in the day, Lucas (the love that never made it) had been withering about how little Mia was prepared to let go. 'Do you get a kick out of being stupidly mysterious?'

She supposed that she did. Then.

Today – any day actually – the mirror failed to flatter. She stared at the reflection with fatigued dulled eyes. Beyond that image were ghostly reminders of the journey to this point.

University had been a dull interlude, and impoverished. Even duller was working in the sports shop (which had taught her a thing or two about entitlement, petulance and shoplifting). She had been lucky. The secrecy and discretion into which she had segued suited her so much better. She derived a status from living and moving in the shadows.

Good? Yup, good.

Intriguingly, other things turned out to be secret, too. *If* she liked secret. Which she did. There was another world which was a law unto itself. That teeming wildlife universe contained in a couple of fields, Joey's fields. They also required protection.

She thought of the fungi strung along a branch, the push through the earth of the speckled mushroom.

The fox slipping through the grass at dusk.

An insect alighting on a rush at the bourn's edge.

The-not-so-secret, high-pitched cackle of the male frog mating with the softer-voiced female. (Or so Joey had described it.) Its thick slick of spawn. Its noisy, rough sex.

*The Secret Lives of Animals* had much to answer for.

She was rueful. She was sad. She was learning... she was learning that, after all, she hadn't known herself. Then or now. Street warrior? Lover?

Wildlife warrior?

She licked a fingertip and smoothed her eyebrows.

Did she deserve Joey?

In the end she called him, as she knew she would.

They lay in bed in Joey's flat, where they tended to end up. It was more comfortable than hers. He folded his arms behind his head and closed his eyes.

She sneaked a glance at him. His profile was beautiful, clean and sharp-boned. When he closed his eyes, he looked tranquil. When he opened them, life flowed into his face.

She wanted to run her finger down his cheek, but hesitated to intrude on his peace. There was so little of it. Instead, she looked towards the window and a darkening sky.

Casing the streets… threats to national security… the stealing of military intelligence… the sleep-deprived aches of watching and vigilance.

She could hear him asking silently, *Are we going to live together?*

She rolled over to him and buried her face in his shoulder. *I don't know.*

After a minute, she got up and padded into the kitchen and consulted the London herbarium of teas. 'What would you like?' she called. 'I'm having Builders'.'

His voice sifted through the door. 'Your taste in tea is almost a deal-breaker.'

She padded into the bedroom with the tea, got back into bed and leant against the pillows. Their legs lay parallel. His longer but hers no less firm.

'What's been happening at the surgery?'

'Two cats in for spaying and a dog with an infected foot.'

'And Sampson.'

Joey was silent.

'He didn't make it?'

He answered by wrapping his arms around Mia and rested his chin on the top of her head. 'No.'

'RIP Sampson. So sorry about that. So sorry about his runny eyes and his discomfort.'

'Nice that you mind.'

An exquisite sensation broke in her chest and travelled through her. Aware that sensations such as this choking happiness had only moments to exist, she closed her eyes and concentrated.

How mysterious things were. How mysterious the engines that drove her. How they suddenly roared into life and bore her in a direction of which she had had no idea.

Above her head, Joey was saying something. 'You make me happy, Mia. I don't know why, because I don't know you. I don't know your politics. Or if you like children.' A pause. 'I do know you're handy with a penknife.' In the same quiet voice, he continued. 'But you make me happy.'

'Oh, Joey.' She sat upright to look at him.

'Just "Oh, Joey"?' His mouth twisted into the half-smile which so intrigued and enchanted her.

The confession was torn from her.

'I love you, Joey. That's what it means.'

*

He took her back to Woodspring. He wanted to touch base, he said. He needed to do that from time to time, otherwise he felt his spirit drain, his heart ache. He always returned, he said. Anyway, he had something he wished to do and he needed her help.

'What?'

'Wait and see. I don't think you'll object.'

It was colder than the summer visit. The lawn had erupted with worm-casts and the leaves on the trees in the wood were shading into a palette of golds and browns. As they drove up the drive, an ambulance eased back down to the road.

They dipped into Reception to say hello to Sarah who was back from honeymoon. 'What do you think?' he asked as they climbed back into the car.

'She's got a mega tan and her hair is several shades lighter.'

'You didn't notice the sad expression?'

Mia hadn't, and maybe she should have done.

'Early days,' said Joey. 'I don't think the honeymoon turned out perfect. They often aren't.'

Mia laughed. 'How do you know? You've never been married.'

'Well spotted.'

They parked up in the stable yard. 'Boots on,' ordered Joey.

It was drizzling as they walked across grass damp and slick from previous autumn downpours, Joey hefting a large cardboard box, a hammer and nails.

'Are you going to tell me what we're doing? Or is the fun never to know?'

'I want help putting up dormouse nesting boxes. Think I'm just about in time before they hibernate.'

'As a matter of interest, do you know you have dormice?'

'I don't *know*,' he said. 'I hope.'

'Then why?'

They had reached the edge of the wood, and he set the cardboard box down. 'Because I like to think there's a chance.' He poked a finger into her chest. 'Hope is good.'

A slick of rain touched her cheek. 'Ace thinking,' she said, and couldn't dampen the wistful note in her voice.

He looked at her. 'It only takes one, Mia, and he'll tell his mates about the real estate.'

He set the box down, opened it and produced the first nesting box. 'Same design as the ones used for birds, only the entrance will be up against the tree. They won't use it if their doorway is exposed.' He lifted the lid which acted as a roof and checked out the interior. 'Great, no nails. Made from cedar, Douglas fir and larch. Approved forestry from a place in North Yorkshire. Feel it.'

She ran a finger around it. Smooth and solid under her fingertips. Safety for a small animal.

There were four and Joey took his time to decide which trees were the best. Mia was ordered to hold them in place against the trunks. *Up. No, down. Sideways. Keep still.* Joey hammered and she observed.

In the quiet of the wood the rustle of their feet in the undergrowth, the hammering, the commands, seemed thunderously loud. Were woods always this quiet? They were light years removed from street turmoil and terror. These were the places where an animal could seek out a habitation and safety.

Except nothing was truly safe. Not the animals, who were chased and predated upon, depending on their size and status in the chain, nor the humans who were predated upon by those in the grip of manias and politics.

Joey knocked the nail into the trunk of a mature beech and, together, they finessed the final box into place.

They were to spend the night in his stable flat, squashed into the inadequate double bed, but first took themselves off to Hungerford for a meal, returning to the flat in the dark.

Joey switched on the lights. The interior, with its wood, its flagged floor, the basic stove and the row of blue-and-white china (Nell's, she reckoned) strung out along a shelf, swam into focus.

'Was it always just you and Nell at Woodspring?' she asked over a mug of rosehip tea. 'Nell didn't have a partner, or husband?'

'I remember one or two hanging around. Nell liked them but not enough to change anything.'

'So you were her world.'

Joey glanced at the china. The tender blue-and-whiteness of it. 'I was lucky.'

Joey slept but she lay in bed and thought. She was beginning to piece together what Woodspring was. How it was shaped. The house, the fields, its emotional territory. How they now functioned. She thought over what could be done with it. Half-formed ideas which would require fleshed-out detail to achieve traction, but possible. Very possible.

At 6.00 the following morning, she was woken by Joey sitting upright. Punishingly early starts were nothing new for Mia, but this seemed over the top.

'I can't remember where we put the third box,' he said. 'I'll have to go and check.'

'Ten paces from the centre. The tree with a log beneath it. It has a white fungus growing along it,' she murmured. 'A broken branch beside it.' She grinned into the pillow. 'If you like, I'll take you there.'

'Witch.' Joey leant over her. '*Witch…*'

They lingered in bed. Then, because it was a nice day, pulled on boots and went out for a walk.

The heyday of the wildflower meadow was over, and its colours wouldn't return until the following year, and honestly – yup, honestly – the herbal ley was nondescript. But, she instructed herself, as damp and bland as the surface appeared, underneath there was a whirlwind of the aerobically dynamic. A reconstruction of cellular structures, a refurbishment, a replenishment.

Joey led her into another, larger field. 'This field was sold off. The other is over there.'

'Sold to who?'

'A property development company. They had got in touch with Nell when she first arrived. They had plans to build a small estate here. She held them off for a time, but she had to let it go in the end.' He smiled. 'Nell was practical and Woodspring needed repairs.'

'Are the plans to build still on ice?' Mia squinted across the field, which stretched into the distance before dipping down at one end.

'The planning permission was hell to get. It was rumoured Perryfield's funds were running out. Building costs soared. They've ended up land-banking, at a guess. We didn't mind.

We got the money and the field remained intact.' His phone buzzed in his pocket. He killed the call. 'It'll happen eventually. I don't want it to, but it will. People have to live somewhere.'

She thought about the city high-rises with which she was familiar. 'Probably sooner than you think.' She stopped in her tracks. 'Joey, the dormice will need protection. And all the other animals. The land, the trees. Have you… have you thought about that?'

'Yup. I have.'

'I'm thinking too,' she said.

He smiled. 'That's good. Very good.'

They walked around the edge of the field and slithered down the sloping and muddy path towards a line of bulrushes where water flowed sluggishly along the ditch.

'The winterbourne has risen.' Joey held out his arms – an apostle welcoming a returning member of the flock. Mia laughed and he did too. 'The water. It disappears in summer. Returns in autumn.' He slipped an arm around her shoulders. 'By next week it should be roaring. Come and see it.'

'I can't,' she said. 'I'm sorry.'

He glanced sideways. 'Can't or won't?'

'Can't.'

After a minute or so, they made their way back to the flat and packed up their bags.

Driving back to London, Joey didn't say much. Eventually, he asked, 'Anything happening this week?'

'This and that,' she replied. 'I have to take a trip.'

'Security systems and all that?'

'Yes,' she said. 'They're always defaulting.'

He lapsed into total silence until the outer reaches of the city were in sight. 'You must think I'm a complete fool, Mia.'

She had known this was coming. She knew, she knew, that the exhaustion and tender exhilaration of loving Joey presented an obstacle until she acted. Which she had failed to do. 'Not a fool, Joey. Never that.'

'How can we deal with each other if I don't *know* you?'

She didn't have to ask what he meant. The well-rehearsed caveats slid through her mind.

*Don't trust. They may be the enemy.*

Holding down a job, *this* job, was important. The work defined her, had made her. Joey might not accept that.

Joey kept his eyes on the road ahead. 'I thought we were going somewhere, Mia. I had hoped.'

As always, he was direct.

'Joey, do we have to at this moment?'

'I think we do. Otherwise it's a waste of time.' The traffic had formed a queue for the lights at the Robin Hood Roundabout and the car came to a halt. 'I want to offer you… things. Us.'

It would soon be dusk. A light appeared in a house across the roundabout. Then another.

He flicked a look at Mia. Angry and a little hostile. 'You don't want to talk about important issues. That's your choice. I think it's the wrong one, which leaves me to speculate as to why.'

'Don't.'

'Saying "don't" doesn't get us anywhere.' He eased the car onwards.

She saw his point. Yet the warnings that were in place were heavy duty ones.

*Do not trust.*

'Joey…'

'Let me see, you might tell me it's complicated. Or classified. Or…' He braked. 'You are very skilled at eluding me, very clever in turning questions around.'

An SUV edged past.

'There's nothing to tell.'

'You might tell me I wouldn't understand.'

'Security systems are more boring than paint drying.'

Mia's insides shredded in a way that was new. She sensed what was coming.

He smiled grimly. 'Give me credit. That's not you. Not in a million years, and I need, would very much like, to know who you are.'

*Always plan your escape route.*

The entrance to Richmond Park was a hundred yards away.

'We've spent time together,' he said. 'We've talked. We appear to share a lot without thinking about it too hard. But you must see… must understand that we need honesty between us.'

'Joey…' She was panicking, which was so not her.

'But that's not the main thing. It's the… skin-to-skin of us. In every possible meaning of the words. I merely have to look at you and… I know. I *know*.'

The car was still stationary in the queue. Fatalism, déjà vu, slid their cold fingers around her.

'I've tried,' he said.

The panic took control.

'Joey, please. No more.' She opened her door, stepped out, retrieved her rucksack from the back seat and leapt onto the verge.

Ignoring his expletive, she headed for the park and dodged inside the gates. It was a mile or so to the next entrance. It wouldn't take her long to jog over to it. There she would take stock.

She was fit. She was used to this kind of exercise. Her body was back in peak condition. Her mind focussed.

Evasion, escape, avoidance… those were what she had trained for. The pounding of her feet, the raised heartbeat; the distance was nothing.

Yet, it was everything.

## CHAPTER TWENTY-EIGHT

On the train going north, Mia watched the suburbs whip past. As always, it was a greyish, sometimes brutalist, panorama.

Whoever decreed that effing ugly buildings were acceptable? Given a chance, she'd line up architects and... well, do something unpleasant to them in return for the evils they inflicted with their high-rises, dangerous corridors (where many of their targets lurked), cramped interiors and their contempt for what gave humans pleasure and optimism.

Mia bit her lip.

Joey's text had been sharp. *We are done. You have your reasons for not being open with me. I will move on.*

Yes, they were done.

The carriage was full. A hen party, decked out in glittery headbands and matching T-shirts, sat opposite necking prosecco and perry cider. It was eleven o'clock in the morning.

The bride fiddled with her headband, which trailed a veil. Drank long and deep from her bottle while her entourage watched with awe.

*We are done.*

They were. Her fault.

So be it.

Electing to work as a dark asset had a price. She had known the deal and had only twice taken issue with it. Lucas and, now, Joey.

The bride was singing. Or what passed as singing.

You were born, you paid taxes. Then you died. What she did in between birth and death mattered. It had to have meaning, pleasure, tenderness. As from now, she appeared to have dropped them down the pan.

*We are done.*

She should have taken the risk of explaining who she was to Joey. She should have also added, *I realise now that protecting the streets isn't the only way to be a protector. There are other ways, and I would like to show you what I mean.*

The bride had fallen silent which was a mercy.

Up north, the intel string had gone quiet. This was not necessarily disastrous, as murmurs were often picked up on alternative strings. In this kind of work, silence could be eloquent, and they had the skills to interpret it. They knew about watching and waiting. Nevertheless, because the target, and what might happen, was so unthinkable, Base and the analysts were atypically worried. Not something they normally displayed.

They called in two other teams.

Instinct told them the assailants – and it looked as if there were two of them – were readied to strike. What they didn't know was who was backing them. *If* they had backers and weren't just a group of politicised youths who had worked themselves up via the new medium of texting. Or, was there linkage to the London bombers or a terrorist group?

The team was briefed and debriefed. Briefed and debriefed.

Where would they enter? Their weapons no doubt hidden, how could they be picked out from the hundreds of people streaming in and out of the centre?

Mia argued the attackers would come in from Market Street.

'Too obvious?' said Brian. Persuasive and experienced, he argued the would-be assassins would make their way into the crowded Lower Mall via a smaller entrance.

'Market Street is more accessible.' Jane agreed with Mia. '*They* don't know we're on to them.'

Brian, Jane, Mia and Tom, who had joined them, went over and over the pros and cons of their allocated area. With the other teams, they pored over the street maps of the city. Each junction. Each bus stop and the traffic flow. Tensed and primed, they checked over their equipment and weapons.

The listening and observing continued round the clock.

These were the preliminaries to any operation. Normally, she would be galvanised by its purpose, prey even to an excitement that was not laudable but useful. Telling herself that this was the job at which she excelled.

Not this time.

'Sharpen up,' said Jane. 'You look terrible.'

In the basic hotel room to which she was allocated, sleep was, at worst, elusive. At best, fractured. That long-ago, glamorous alcoholic teacher had once quoted to the class a line of poetry: *Mine eye had taken a shine.*

None of them had paid much attention, certainly not Mia.

Now, she did.

The first time she had seen Joey, her eye had taken a shine.

Her heart had taken a delight.

Her body equally so.

And this too: her eye had taken a shine to the place from where he came. Its colours, its solitude, its hidden life.

No doubt Joey was back in his flat in the house which had been bombed, and bought by his uncle Harry. Perhaps his ghost and Faith's were there too.

She pictured him getting ready for work. A blue shirt. Damp hair swept back. As it dried, it would become less Gordon Gekko. She pictured him at the surgery, with Mandy brightly popping up here and there, handling the first animal of the day. Quietening the dog or the cat. Or the parrot.

In the mornings, Mia got up gritty-eyed and hungry, with a mind emptied.

Strange… but she had grown to be protective of the shopping centre with its frenzy of consumerism. On the duty days, she traced behaviour patterns. Harassed mothers of toddlers holding it together. Just. Teenagers eyeing up trainers and T-shirts. Pensioners clutching overlarge plastic wallets and purses.

On this morning, one little boy trailing behind his mother caught her eye. Five? Six? Tousled-haired and dark-eyed. Almost… almost… the child that she imagined Joey might have been. He wore round, thick-lensed Harry Potter glasses which marked him out. She recognised his anxiety, his dislocation – once experienced, they were never forgotten.

She named him Timmy and it helped her to think about his life, of which she knew bugger all…

Interesting, though, how she was changing. To search beneath the skin, to match thoughts was, she reckoned, to grow the empathy that she felt she lacked.

Joey… Timmy… Timmy… Joey.

She checked out the positioning of the team. Zeros Two and Three (Brian and Jane) were ensconced at one end of the mall. Zero One (Tom) lurked by the central coffee shop.

In a black jumper with her hair tied back and a neck scarf concealing her mike, carrying a canvas shopping bag, Mia strolled up to the bench close to the coffee shop and sat down.

The aroma of coffee mingled with the cosmetics smell from the shop selling soaps and lotions. At this time of the morning, it cloyed big-time.

Then her antennae went up.

'Zero Four to Base,' she muttered. 'Lone male in green hoodie with bag by H&M.'

'Roger.'

'Zero Four to Base. Green hoodie with rucksack heading for ice-cream booth.'

Out of the corner of her eye, Mia caught a movement. A second male in a grey hoodie was also heading for the ice-cream booth, which had a queue with approximately ten children in it.

The training whacked in. No tension. No fear.

'Zero Four to Base. Second lone male. Grey tracksuit with hood up. White trainers with green laces. Rucksack. Eye contact made with green hoodie.'

'Team, did you hear?' Base replied into Mia's earpiece. 'Zeros Three and Four follow behind them. Will send additional backup.'

'Zero Two to Base. Going in closer.'

That was Brian.

Green hoodie and grey hoodie swung their rucksacks to the ground. They had a brief exchange. Innocent students?

As always, there was a balance. And split-second timing and decision-making. If they rounded up a couple of innocent bystanders, the real assassins would vanish.

Mia focussed. Grey hoodie had a sheen of sweat on his upper lip. Green hoodie's hands were shaking. This would suggest they were the correct suspects. 'Zero Four to Base. Grey hoodie sweating.'

'Target them,' said Base.

Big question. Were they trained? The shaking hands and sweat suggested not. This gave Brian, who was approaching the ice-cream booth at speed, an advantage.

Accomplices? She raked the faces of the shoppers.

She bent over and fiddled with her bag of shopping. 'No helpers visible,' she said.

The noise in the mall swelled.

'Base to Zero Four. Updates?'

Her gaze swivelled.

'Need to clear mall. Need to clear.'

'Go,' said Base.

Mia leapt to her feet. 'Turn round, turn round…' she shouted at surprised shoppers. 'Now.' The queue for ice cream fractured. 'Go. Danger.'

Simultaneously, the hoodies reached into their rucksacks.

They were all rehearsed.

'Drop everything. Go,' shouted Mia at the bewildered shoppers. 'Run.'

Some obeyed, grabbing their children and running. Others were frozen to the spot. The hoodies pulled guns – she couldn't see the type – out of their rucksacks and raked the ice-cream queue with bullets. A man crumpled to the floor. A red pool seeped from under him.

Shouts and screams. Terror and incomprehension.

A firestorm crackled through Mia. She was incandescent with rage and, at the same instant, icy cold.

A mother running past with her toddler sobbed. An elderly lady dropped her shopping bag and scrabbled to retrieve it. The crush intensified.

Again the two hoodies raised their guns.

'Zero Four to Base,' she said. 'They're firing. Going in.'

More shots rang out.

'Zero Four,' Base spat out in her ear. 'Stay put and get shoppers out. Reinforcements going in.'

Another shot. This time from their lot. Zero Five or Six.

Grey hoodie dropped to his knees and slumped over, blood welling over his back. Green hoodie swung around in the direction of the shot. This gave Brian his chance. He came up fast and jumped on him from behind. In a microsecond, Jane joined him and they neutralised him with practised manoeuvres.

The floor near the ice-cream booth was slippery with jettisoned ices and coffees and obstructed with dropped shopping bags. Adults shrieked. Children cried.

Grey hoodie had remained quite still. A woman shouted 'You punk,' and he raised his head. The hood fell back revealing his face and hair, a young face distorted by pain and hatred. Wounded, hampered, he scrabbled at the floor.

He was going for his weapon.

'Back, go back...' Zeros Six and Five were now marshalling the shoppers down the mall towards the exits.

Base was asking in her ear, 'Give us a steer.'

Before she could answer, grey hoodie raised his arm and took aim at the backs of two children being pulled along by an adult.

She launched herself at him.

A bullet cracked into Mia's shoulder.

Then nothing.

Dreaming, she decided, was the best. Dreaming, she could mix past and present, ghosts and the future. She could be the shape-shifter, both wild and tamed. She could be a hero. She could explore her confusion, her doubts. She could range over herbal leys and walk through wildflower meadows and weep for joy and laugh with despair. She could shed the practical, tough-talking, hard-trained Mia, delve deep, follow a new romantic consciousness as it searched for resolution.

Dreaming was intense. Mysterious. Brimming with poetic passion.

It was a shock to wake up. Shoulder shrieking and head aching, with a bruise like a breastplate smudged over her torso. Tubes snaked in and out of her arm and a machine blipped alongside her ear.

Team Leader was beside the bed. 'Debrief, I'm afraid.'

She did her best. Frowning with the effort to remember.

'Fine,' said Team Leader. 'I'll collate the reports.'

'Many dead?'

There was a hesitation. 'None. A couple wounded, one badly. Many traumatised but OK. You collapsed onto the gunman and it took him out. They are both in custody.'

Mia thought about this. 'So, we did it.'

'We did it.'

There was a pause. 'I'm told you took a bullet in the shoulder and they've operated. Might need another op, but it should be fine.'

'Others OK?'

Team Leader nodded, then said, 'I'll piss off. I don't want to overdo it. The team sends its best but is there anyone you want me to contact?'

Again she thought. 'No.'

She didn't know how long she had been in hospital or whether it was morning or evening because a fog had carefully wrapped itself around her mind. Thinking coherently was a lost cause, particularly as pain lurked with malign intent. At this moment she did not care what was happening to her or what lay ahead, which, in a way, was liberating.

*I know…* well, what? That she was exhausted by the way her life was conducted, by the nature of the work, by the diminution of belief in what they were doing. Or to be precise, her part in it. None of those conundrums could be solved from the hospital bed, and she slept and slept. The following day, she was taken down to theatre for her second operation. On return, she was very sick and unable to sit up. More days elapsed, floating by in semi-consciousness.

The nurses pushed and pulled her. Slapped drugs into her veins. Settled her onto pillows. Pulled the sheet tight across her abdomen.

Her eyelids closed and she dreamt of blue cornflowers, the feel of the sun on her hands, of grasses brushing against her legs. She remembered the chalky texture of the cliffs under her feet on the day she and Joey had rescued Hannay.

All her working life she had taken risks. Risks for which she had been trained, bolstered by colleagues and teamwork.

This risk would be different.

For this one, she would be, was, alone.

Once you're out of the business, you're out. She knew that, having watched other colleagues during her time. It was hard but necessary. The enemy changes, methods change, equipment and training change.

They were good to her when she signed off. Partly because the operative who keeps getting injured was an increasing liability. Thanked her and, in the same breath, demanded back her radio kit, the Security Service ID badge and the office pass. Because of the injury to her shoulder, she was told she would be awarded a compensatory pension and she was warned there were certain countries which she could never, ever visit.

Fair enough.

Doing this was to hack through the root that fed her professional being, her sense of self. The secret Mia.

Recovery was stop-go. One day she felt fine, the following day not. She spent a lot of time in her flat – not her idea of fun

– and contemplated the amputation of the profession that had kept her in the shadows.

Regrets were for the piss-poor feeble. *Think, girl*: she was free to contemplate a future where she could walk around without looking over her shoulder.

Rule number one: establishing normality was important. She contacted her brother and gave him the heads-up (an edited version), and rang her parents. She told them she'd had an accident in the gym and broken her arm, but she was fine and would come up and visit them very soon.

Rule number two: work on the blueprint for the new Mia Greene life. This would take resolve, fine-tuning and a big leap.

By the second week, she decided she was strong enough and sent a text to Joey. *I will be on the park bench at 2 p.m.*

There was no reply.

On the bus there, she logged the landmarks. The traffic lights. The fish-and-chippie takeaway. A tree at the corner of the road which was shedding its leaves.

She was shaking. *It isn't nerves*, she told herself. *You're still weak. Your muscles don't yet function correctly. You've left the Service and you're in shock because you've nothing to replace it.*

It took her a bit of time to get to the bench, which was slicked with moisture from a recent shower. Nauseated and hollow-legged, she sat down. The old habits shot in. Weak sun, a scattering of fallen leaves, dog messes that should have been picked up, a woman loitering by the adjacent bench…

She shut them down. *Finished.* Her business now was to function in a world without those reflexes. No testing for exit.

No hard surveillance. No calculation of potential harm and violence. *The End.*

She extracted a bottle of water and her painkillers from her bag. Necked a couple. Waited for them to kick in. Still battling the nausea, she inhaled deeply and closed her eyes.

She must have dozed. Sleep was merciful. It so helped. As she slipped between dozing and waking, she firmed up the plans made in the hospital bed. Made on painkillers, it had to be said. All the same, they were plans. Yes, they would have to be slapped into a business shape. But that was fine. She could do it.

Feeling a presence, she woke, opened her eyes, looked up – and the equivalent of a burst of golden fire erupted in her chest.

'You came.'

'I did. I reckoned you were in trouble.'

Joey bent down to kiss her damp forehead. It was a friend's kiss, not a lover's, and a chill settled over her.

She was aware she still smelt of hospital, and of illness, which he must have got.

He drew back. 'Have you been ill?'

'Shot, actually.'

'Jesus wept.'

'I'll explain.'

He sat down beside her. 'I thought I'd lost the capacity to be shocked.'

'It was my work… the work I couldn't tell you about. Still can't, properly. But I'm free of it now.'

He looked away. Then back at her. He was making up his mind. 'I'm listening,' he said eventually.

The afternoon rolled on and grew cooler. She told him that she had been a small cog in a big machine. What it involved. How sometimes it went wrong. Cue to wince nobly as she moved her shoulder. How it placed its operatives in a glass box which muffled contact and sealed them off. How relationships, unless with other operatives, were compromised.

He turned his head away. 'What made you jump out of the glass box? Being shot?'

She thought about it. There was so much to say. So much that was important. Much that was funny and frivolous – and yet, was just as important.

'The dormice. They need saving. You can't remember where they are. I do.'

Joey shouted with laughter.

'I've thought about it. If you turn the wood and the fields into a wildlife haven, I could run it. Get grants. Open it to the public. Use it as an educational tool.'

He didn't react and she thought, *I've lost.*

Not without a fight. 'This is the moment to say sorry, mega sorry, for… the silence, Joey, and to try to repair the damage. I would like… want… very much… to start over.'

It wasn't often she tore her heart out, pitted herself against her own pride and the habit of self-containment.

Joey took his time. He was owed that. 'If you promise never to be silent again.'

Tears of weakness rolled down her cheeks.

She stretched out her good hand and he took it.

Her hand rested in his.

'Come to Woodspring then, Mia. We can live there with the dormice.'

She did a mental sweep of the subdued wildflower meadow. 'And the cornflowers?'

'Those too.'

# EPILOGUE

## 2025

Not long after Joey and Mia got married, the construction of the housing estate by Perryfield Associates began.

The formalities were done, planning permission unblocked, the documents signed, the earth paced and measured. The lorries rolled in (luckily out of earshot of the hospice), the earth was churned, trees and hedgerows were felled. Dragonflies, toads, rabbits were uprooted and she mourned for them.

They remained in London while it was taking place, and Mia took courses in land management, ecology and wilding. It wasn't easy going. She was not, *no never*, a natural scholar but, shaken by the despoliation of Woodspring territory, she drove herself hard.

'I have one advantage,' she informed Joey.

She sure did.

The habit of surveillance. She had been trained to look deep and close at objects, people and plants, and now directed that laser beam at the small beings that crawled through grasses, woodland and undergrowth.

When the building and the churning had concluded they went to live in one of the new-builds on the road named after the bourn. The stable flat was taken over by a couple of the hospice care workers who were keen on DIY and were always throwing up another bookshelf or cupboard.

In its literature, Perryfield Associates portrayed the houses as more gracious than they were in the flesh. The 'three-bedroomed family dwellings' were a little sterile, a little boxy. Too bad, they told each other. The world was crowded. If the house was pokier than it could have been, it left more space for the animals and uprooted plants to regenerate.

In spring and winter they caught glimpses of the big house from their bedroom, filtered through bare trees. Once, she caught Joey gazing at it, distress written on his face. By that time, they had been married ten years.

She wrapped her arms around him. 'You still miss the house.'

'I'll always miss it.'

At first their immediate neighbours, Stan and Carole, regarded them with suspicion – Joey being seen as lord of the manor (sort of), but they got over it. Both couples were childless, which made a bond. Mia turned vegetarian and Stan liked to help out at the allotment where she and Joey grew their vegetables. (Their tomatoes were famous.)

Joey's practice was outside Hungerford and Mia occasionally drove in with him to see a friend or catch the train up to London to meet ex-colleagues. Less and less frequently, she had to admit. The contacts dwindled into silence.

In their place was what had become her vocation. Wilding, wildlife, education.

There were now bees and hives producing honey on Joey's land. It was hard work, keeping them healthy and balanced, but worth it, oh-so worth it. She was working on data for a bee foundation that was engaged in developing power bars for bee nutrition to help the endangered urban bee.

The dormouse colony was thriving, and deer could be seen sometimes flitting along the ride in the wood. When the bourn rose in winter, retaining its waters into spring, the migration of frogs and toads was a joyous thing. Visitor numbers were up. They came to hear the birds, to walk through the wood, to watch the butterflies and, in the season, the moths at night, and paid well to do so.

No animal was ever killed here. None uprooted.

All this she observed and noted with obsessive attention to report back to the organisations trying to preserve natural England.

There had been bad years, very bad ones (Covid, anyone?), good years and magical ones.

She had three employees and a thriving enterprise. 'You should be running the world,' said Joey.

A third plaque had joined the other two on the wall by the wood. It read, *Nell Dane 1939–2000, greatly loved.* Joey had wept when it had been put up and Mia had held his hand very tightly.

Sometimes, when they lay together in bed, he would ask again about the moment when she was reborn. It was not too strong a word.

In that instant between the bullet being fired and its plunging into the flesh and sinew of her shoulder, she understood.

She would never sacrifice work for Joey. But then she couldn't, and wouldn't, sacrifice Joey for work. Before the pain flooded through her, she knew that love for him now possessed her, body and spirit. His dragonflies and frogs. His dispiriting-looking herbal ley and less-than-flourishing wildflower meadow. House. Land. Joey. She loved that he, and they, needed protection.

There was more.

With the shattering of bone and muscle arrived the realisation that she had failed on a profound level to understand what it was to be alive. Which was what, exactly? Grass, sun, warm skin, wine. Joey. Many, many things.

A privilege, in fact.

That's all.

That was everything.

**1998**

Nell was up in the attic.

She and Joey agreed that it was time to dismantle the model railway. Joey said he would do it, but she had looked into his eyes and seen the sadness that had once been a constant in his expression.

She knew him so well.

She resolved to wait until he was out with his friend Zeb and the rest of his mates from veterinary school and then to act.

Here she was, then, with a duster and screwdriver and a stack of tissue paper.

The attic hadn't changed since she had first discovered it and the adventure of life with Joey had begun. When she had decided – no… no…that was to be imprecise. It hadn't been a *decision*. It had been a *propulsion* so profound and primitive to save a small boy that it bypassed anything as rational and cool as logic and decision-making.

That hadn't prevented her bringing much of herself to Woodspring or from taking a vow to run it efficiently. Tidy habits and orderly methods kept her sane during the years she weeded out unnecessary expenses and established orderly systems.

Joey was in his twenties, newly qualified, and his focus would be, must be, on his own life and work. The time had come to ask him if he wished to take on the house, whose costs were beginning to run wild. She had no idea what his answer would be. And, of course, what he felt now might be different from what he felt in the future.

One by one, she lifted the segments of rail and dusted them before wrapping them up and layering them into the wooden chest, followed by the station buildings. The pine trees were stowed on top.

Now for the engines.

Thomas and Bess were silent and shrouded by dust, exuding resentment, she felt, for being abandoned. Had they not given of their best? Had they not comforted a small boy?

They had.

First up, Thomas. Now battered and in need of the equivalent of a model-train MOT. If Joey ever had children, she would make sure it was done. She wrapped him up and placed him at the top of the box. Bess was next and slotted in beside him. She closed the chest, inserted the key into the lock and turned it.

That part of Joey's... her... life was over, its echoes and fragments still drifting in Woodspring's rooms.

They had been happy years. Fraught at times and, at others, there had been estrangement. It never lasted. Nothing unusual for a growing child, said Dr King. 'Call yourself lucky.'

Nell bit her lip. She had been diagnosed with cancer which didn't care about love and tight-knit bonds. It was self-centred and greedy and bent on domination.

The diagnosis still felt unreal. *We're so sorry, Miss Dane, but ovarian cancer is difficult...* It was as if she was floating above herself, looking down at the body which had been informed it had an error in its functioning.

How she was going to tell Joey she hadn't yet worked out.

It mattered how he would feel. Greatly.

It was the last thing, perhaps, she would do for him. Showing him that dying was part of it.

She eased to her feet.

To have custody of this child, she had plucked the feathers from her breast. She had spread protective wings over him and flown with him into maturity, his and her own. She had offered shelter and her deepest feelings. In return, Joey had ushered her into the land of colour and delight of a small boy's love and trust.

She had dug deep to give him nourishment, spilling her blood and opportunities for him and never once – never by one heartbeat, one tear of frustration – had she ever regretted it.

All was well.

# 1944

On 6 June, Harry awoke before dawn on board HMS *Amazon*. In his dream, he had combed through the names, addresses and next of kin of each of the men. 'Don't worry, you won't be unknown soldiers,' was the joke. 'Survivors will write your epitaphs.'

That was all right, then.

Wills had been written and deposited in the appropriate War Office department.

He shaved, showered and washed his hair. There was no telling when next he would do so. Fighting his way down France was going to be a long slog.

His identity disc was a hard leather hexagon, stamped with the regimental number, name and rank. As he bent over to do up his boots, it dangled outside his shirt. Tucking it back in, he had a flashback to Faith placing a hand on his chest.

Yet again, he checked over his Bergen and the contents of his pockets. Field dressings in groin pocket? Vital. The rule was: no one shared their dressings and never count on medical aid being close at hand.

The ship's engines throbbed under his feet. His orderly knocked on the door.

'Come.'

He edged in. 'Brought your tommy gun, sir. Checked, cleaned and one filled magazine. If you want grub, sir, it's being served.'

The idea of a hot breakfast was more than appealing. The condemned man ate a hearty meal. For the first time, Harry had a real understanding of the point. He made his way along to the wardroom where bacon and eggs was served up and jokes about the 'Last Supper' were flying thick and fast.

Naval officers as well as the stewards served the food. The jokes widened to ones about the navy being very happy to look after wives and sweethearts until the men's return. 'You can rely on a sailor.'

Back in the cabin, the orderly helped Harry on with the Bergen and waited while he went through the drill. Check magazine of the Colt .45 and check safety catch. Reload tommy gun and check safety catch.

Harry thanked him – he looked as though he could do with a good meal himself – and made his way to the deck. Similarly burdened, Peter and Trelawney joined him. It was closing in to 5.30 and lights on board ship were doused. Slowly the D-Day armada coalesced in the grey light.

Peter clapped his hand on Harry's shoulder. Neither man said anything.

Without warning, the engines quietened and the ship lost momentum. A tannoy leapt into life. 'This is your captain. Crew to action stations, units to assault craft.' There was a pause. 'And the best of luck, gentlemen.'

The green light flicked on. The sergeant major shouted, 'Get moving, you lot.'

Aided by their rubber-soled shoes, Harry and the men scaled the companionways to the upper deck. The salt air hit him in the face.

The landing craft had been readied at the davits. Some wit joked, 'Can I have water wings, sergeant?'

Their positions on the LCA had been allocated and rehearsed many times. Harry edged forward to his allotted slot at the bow – he would be the first out when the ramp went down. Within a minute, the craft was tightly packed with thirty-five men and bristling with Bren guns, rifles, tommy guns and Bangalore torpedoes.

The advice had been to wear the tin helmet. 'Lots of metal will be flying about, old boy.' But when Harry looked around at the men, it was clear that all of them had opted for their green beret. *Green for go. Green for Commandos.*

Earlier, up on deck, Harry had observed the old hands pack their cigarettes and matches into Elastoplast tins, seal them with a precious length of Sellotape and stick tougher adhesive tape over the muzzle of their weapons. He had copied them.

'Steady.'

The pulleys went into action and the LCA swung up and out, hitting the water with a smack. A naval lieutenant and his coxswain went to work on righting the craft and it veered away from the steep side of the mother ship and went to join the flotilla ready for the off.

They waited in silence with only the sound of the sea to break it. One or two of the men found that silence worrying. Harry did not. In that grey, silent dawn, he was being held in the balance between life and possible death, and his mind was tranquil.

*Strange, isn't it?* said Faith in his ear. *I always thought the boundary between life on earth and death was so tough and impermeable. But it isn't, you know.*

Every sense in him quivered with longing. 'Where are you?'

His serenity vanished and he was consumed by longing to hold her once more.

Looming out of the darkness were the shapes of the other craft, bobbing lazily on the swell. There was a cough, a sneeze, a murmured 'Shut up.'

Dawn's pink light crawled over the waiting seaborne army of invaders.

'Go… go.'

The Allied guns blazed out, their missiles hitting the shore with great gouts of sand and rock plummeting skywards.

The LCA leapt forward, hitting the wave with a crash. His stomach lurched. A couple of men instantly vomited.

Ahead of them, the 3rd Infantry Division was taking the brunt. The beach was already littered with the dead and the dying. Everywhere the eye could see, LCAs were disgorging men and weapons. Out to sea, the Allies were firing hell and damnation at the German positions high up on the cliffs. Salvo after salvo stretched red and yellow death. By now, the Germans had got their wits up and running and were returning fire. More than one craft was hit by their fire or a tidal wave.

Men were dying at sea and they were dying on the beach.

A landscape where the spirits from the battlefield were already roaming. When the men would vanish into its earth, leaving behind a deposit of bones and flesh and the spirits drifting back towards the land from which they had come, to be captured in memories and by memorials.

The bottom of the LCA dragged along the sand, the navy bod pulled at the lever and the ramp clanged open.

Harry took a deep breath. And went.

Faith.

Ahead of him lay unimaginable death and destruction and danger and to survive would take all that he had.

'Where are you, Faith?'

*With you,* she answered. *Where else would I be?*

# ACKNOWLEDGEMENTS

Huge thanks as always are owed to my editor Sarah Hodgson and the superb Corvus team: Felice McKeown, Dave Woodhouse, Laura O'Donnell. Also my agent Judith Murray and her team at Greene & Heaton: Kate Rizzo and Mia Deakin. Without them the novel would not have made it to publication. An especial thank you to Rachel Wright for her skilled and sensitive copy editing.

My debt to the following books is enormous. *Don't Cry for Me – The Commandos: D-Day and After* by Donald Gilchrist (Robert Hale, 1982), *Commando Country* by Stuart Allan (National Museums of Scotland, 2007) and *Soldier Spy* by Tom Marcus (Michael Joseph, 2016). I have taken facts and scenarios from these inspiring books and acknowledge my debt to them. Any mistakes are mine.

Family and friends have stood by me and my gratitude to them goes beyond words. I would also like to thank my readers, some of whom make contact, which I always love. It goes without saying that they make a life in writing possible. What more could I ask?

If you enjoyed this book, why not join

# Elizabeth Buchan's Mailing List

Members are the first to hear all the latest **book news**, have the chance to win in regular **competitions,** and get **exclusive** writing from Elizabeth Buchan delivered straight to their inbox.

**Plus you'll receive a FREE short story by Elizabeth Buchan as soon as you join.**

To join, simply scan the QR code or visit

**www.elizabethbuchan.com**

for more information